Book 3 Shawna!
Del, what to say about
Mr Tall, Dark, and handsome?
Hope you enjoy!

UNCIVILIZED

LAURA STAPLETON

Laura Stapleton

DEDICATION

Dedicated for all the readers who have read the series so far.
You are exactly why I do this.

CONTENTS

ACKNOWLEDGMENTS

So many people to thank with this one! First off my family for tolerating my computer time and going to every museum. Their patience while I read all the historical markers helped, too. If your last name is or has been Kelley, Rowland, Stapleton, Baker, or Foutz, I'm talking to you.

I'd like to thank Julie Mason, Wayne Keeler, Nancy Rodman, Donna Rogers, Philip Lacasse, Miranda Nading, Jane Jobson, Kelly Abel, and Cassandra Janey. This group encourages my good and helps fix my bad. I love them.

Finally, the original pioneers. Without them, I'd have no facts to check and this would be science fiction or fantasy.

CHAPTER 1

Ellen Winslow stared at the tall savage talking to her friends before going back to the shoes for trade. She tried not to frown, not wanting the native girl in her buckskin dress to think she disapproved of the moccasins. The outdoor market, dignified in being called a trading post, closed in around her. Had she not seen enough of the smelly brutes today? She glanced back at her trail leader, Samuel Granville, as he chatted and laughed with the man as if they were old acquaintances.

The darker man stood there like any other human being wearing a white man's plaid cotton shirt. She squinted to focus better on him. The buckskin britches he wore and his long braid of black hair suited his cinnamon skin. This sudden approval startled her. She wondered where such a silly thought had come from. Who cared about how this *thing* looked in clothes? Ellen snorted when seeing him nod at a passing lady. He'd learned to mimic whites well, she thought. If her father saw this almost animal in their camp, he'd throw a wall-eyed fit.

She and everyone in her family had heard her father, Jack Winslow, say he considered Samuel far too forgiving when it came to the natives they had encountered. Her father railed about how the newspaper back home reported new massacres every day. Women and children slaughtered like cattle, he'd reported, and yet, Mr. Granville treated this beast like any other citizen they'd encountered. She watched as the male held Marie Warren's hand, hers dwarfed in his. Sam surprised Ellen by taking her elbow. She'd not seen him walk over to her, too focused on the interloper.

Sam led her closer to the others. "I have a friend I'd like you to meet. I think you'll find him endlessly fascinating. Ellen, this is Adelard Du Boise. Del, this is Miss Ellen Winslow."

"Mademoiselle, is it?" He took her hand and kissed it with a European flourish. "I'm very charmed and pleased there's no Mr. Winslow."

Ellen struggled to keep her expression blank despite the disgust filling her. Maybe women of his own kind found him appealing but true ladies? She suspected not them. Ignoring the man she'd just met, she turned to Sam. "Mr. Granville, I'm sure this, um, gentleman will find me far too fussy for his tastes."

"*Qu'est que c'est?*" Del stared at her for a few seconds. "Fussy?" She gave him a tight grin. Of course he wouldn't understand and she'd need to explain the simple word to him. "Hmm, maybe picky is more the word I should use." Ellen withdrew her hand from his, ashamed at how long he'd touched her and she'd not noticed. How her light skin had appeared porcelain when next to his warm brown must have distracted her. "So are you from this area?"

Adelard's eyes sparkled when he grinned. "Yes. I live with my mother's people, as you can see, but still appreciate my father's society very much. I've had adventures in both cultures."

She glanced at Sam, wondering how much nearer Adelard could venture before the other man intervened. Mr. Du Boise's personal space seemed smaller than hers. He didn't smell bad, but she averted her head as if he did, unable to step back without being obviously rude. Aware of him waiting for her answer, she said, "How interesting."

"It is, actually," said Sam. "However, I've heard this story before and need to get supplies."

"So do I, Mr. Granville," Ellen interjected. "I'll accompany you while Marie might keep your friend company."

The creature held out his arm for the other woman to take while walking. "Excellent idea! I'll escort Madame Warren while you work."

Marie took his offered support. "I wouldn't want you to be troubled."

"Bah! It's no trouble for you. If Samuel is agreeable, I'll bring today's hunt to tonight's dinner at your camp and share. Maybe then he can tell me how he let his Anne get away."

Sam's affection for Marie shone in his eyes as he led Ellen away. "Dinner tonight will be good. There are plenty of other ladies for you there. Be aware, his tales can be taller than he is."

"Shh, Samuel, let me tell the lady my secrets myself." Adelard put his arm around the woman, leaning in to tell her, "Monsieur Granville exaggerates my faults instead of my charms. He's misguided."

Ellen watched and waited until Del and Marie strolled out of earshot. A tug of worry nagged at her. Keeping sight of them until the last possible moment, she sighed when the crowds swallowed them from her view. She turned to Sam. "Do you think he will be back this evening early or very late?"

"I'm counting on early, since he's bringing us dinner."

She searched his face for any hint of joking. "Him? Bringing us dinner? Should we have him taste it first to see if it's safe to eat?" She clenched her teeth to keep from blurting out the savage more likely was stealing the main course.

A long silence stretched between them as Sam stared in the couple's direction. He at last said, "Du Boise is one of the finest men I've ever met. One of the most brave and trustworthy friends I've known."

Ellen crossed her arms, unwilling to believe anything positive about such a brute. "He's a brave, certainly." She glanced at Sam, his mouth set in a thin line and his eyes glittering with anger. Fury radiated from him like heat from the sun, and she knew she'd crossed a line with him.

He examined the moccasins and leather boots laid out in front of them. "I don't doubt there are some Indians who have earned your harsh judgment of them. This particular one does not. Your opinion of Del couldn't be more wrong." Sam smiled at the Indian woman seated behind the selection.

Chagrined at his stern tone, she acknowledged, "You're probably right. He's rather fair-complected and speaks French."

"His father is French."

Small wonder his skin seemed paler, and weren't his eyes lighter than the others too? No matter. She grabbed at the slight straw of an excuse to redeem the man and regain Sam's good humor. "Oh! So he's not all bad."

"No, just half, and I already disagree with you on which half that is."

His statement gave her butterflies in her stomach. No, more like moths, the kind like when she'd angered Papa. Sam had somehow known Ellen didn't believe her own words. Not wanting to continue on in angry silence, she tried another tactic. "You must admit, newspapers and other first-hand accounts haven't painted savag-, um, natives, in the best of light. I might be forgiven for thinking they're a deplorable race of people."

"Have you ever considered a legal career? You're persistent in debate." He exhaled, his face and shoulders relaxing just a bit.

The change in his demeanor reassured her. "I've been told that by those who know me." Ellen followed his line of sight. Watching Marie walk with Du Boise had him distracted. Everyone knew Sam and Marie had a close friendship. People out here seemed to grow together or apart. She glanced at him, seeing how much he cared for the woman as if it'd been inked on his face. Were they intimate? Searching her recent memory, she didn't remember a single instance where Sam and Marie's relationship seemed inappropriate.

The other Warrens, though, Marie's husband Charles and his own sister, Hester? Ellen shuddered at the revolting memory of seeing them disheveled and together in the cedars near Fort Laramie. Her friend deserved a husband better than that old coot. Before she could change her mind, Ellen nudged Sam. "Mrs. Warren is a lovely person, isn't she?"

"What? I suppose so." He added, "She's kind to others."

Ellen gazed at various goods without really seeing them as they strolled. She'd startled him out of his daydreams and tried not to gloat. "She is. Her husband is very charming. Marie has a huge blind spot where he is concerned." Giving him a sideways glance, she added, "Most do, I've seen."

"What do you mean by blind spot?"

She shrugged, intent on staying casual. "A lot of people think he's a wonderful man."

"I see."

The lilt at the end of his sentence made it sound like more of a question than a statement. His failed attempt to glean more information amused her. "You don't right now, but keep your eyes open and you will."

"Is there something you need to tell me? As captain of the wagon party, I need to know when it affects the group."

"That's a good question," she said, stalling for time. Ellen couldn't just say outright what she'd witnessed between the Warren twins. Who would believe her? She'd not believe her, either. "It's not my place to tell you and if I did, it wouldn't affect everyone in our group. Keep your eyes open and you'll see soon enough."

He stepped aside to let a family pass by him, his eyes still staring her down for answers. "I'd prefer it if you just told me flat out."

"So would I, trust me, but it's not for me to tell you." She sighed, frustrated with her urge to be honest fighting with her need to not meddle. "When you learn for yourself, remember that I did want to tell you but…."

"It's not for you to say."

"Exactly! Please believe that, all right?" She linked arms with him, nodding in Marie's direction as Du Boise led the woman back to camp. "Come on, let's catch up with the others. You'll find out soon enough, and it'll most likely end up well for you."

As she and Sam walked back to camp, Ellen worked to keep her mind on their conversation. She fretted over whether or not she'd told him too much about the Warrens and what she'd seen. Their actions weren't her business, and yet she felt compelled to help Marie.

Once in the Granville camp, she smiled when Sam tipped his hat farewell. He'd been talking about his friend and Ellen now regretted not listening to every word. The Indian's refined manner had led her into trusting he wouldn't slit their throats as they slept. She shuddered, imagining her little brothers harmed in such a bloody way. He might merely need to kidnap one of them as a slave. Their mother continued her slow recovery from an earlier illness, but she'd not survive being captured. Her father? Ellen didn't even want to admit to him she'd talked to the beast, never mind that she'd accepted a kiss on the hand. Mr. Winslow's explosive temper could cause a war.

Keeping quiet about her fears, she helped her stepmother lead their two milk cows to good grass. All during chores her mind was unable to let go of Du Boise. No matter how it offended Sam, she couldn't help but think of the man as a half crazed savage. Even if he'd spoken his barbaric native language, Ellen knew how well he'd behave in regular society. Anyone could see the intelligent light in his handsome brown eyes. She paused while thinking of what she could learn from Adelard if he were as civilized as Sam had said.

"Ellie?" Lucy Winslow drew near with the baby on her hip. "Are you doing well? You've been quieter than usual."

"Yes." She hoped omitting her thoughts wasn't the same as lying. "Just dwelling on all the people at the trading village."

"Oh?" Lucy licked her fingertips and wiped Buster's dirty face. As the child squirmed, she continued, "I was concerned about you three girls going until I saw Mr. Granville with you."

Glad to find something to agree with, Ellen said, "So was I."

Her stepmother gave a tsk-tsk sound while setting the baby on their wagon's tailgate. "Such a shame he's so fickle with the ladies. Your father and I had hopes you'd catch his eye."

Ellen repressed a sigh. This was an old refrain sung by her parents. She did like Sam, even loved him like one of her brothers, but had never thought of him as a romantic interest.

Lucy changed Buster's diaper, giving him fresh pants as well. "You do know Mr. Granville invited us to dinner tonight, specially."

The news surprised her. "Oh? Did he mention why us?"

"No. I think he's just being neighborly." She sighed. "All his crew will be there. Maybe you'll take a liking to one of them."

Ellen tried to agree. "It's possible, I suppose."

"You jest but another man in our family would make life easier on your father." With Buster back on her hip, she faced her stepdaughter. "You're very close to spinsterhood. Not that it's important out in the middle of nowhere, but still."

Ellen felt sure she already helped out as much if not more than any son or son-in-law. "I'll see what I can do to find a husband to help Pa." She almost wanted to marry the first male who'd have her, if only to appease her father.

"Good. Your pa is already with Mr. Granville and his company. Would you please bring our dishes? Thank you, dear."

Skeeter ran up to her. "Sis! Did you hear? We're going to a dinner with Mr. Sam and his new friend!" He grabbed her free hand. "Did you see him? He's a real live Indian!"

"I did see him. He's a very nice...person." She grinned at him, putting the last fork in the bucket.

The boy bobbed up and down like a yoyo. "Did you talk to him? Did he talk back?"

They walked toward Sam's camp, and she chuckled at his amazed expression. "We did, both of us to each other. Imagine that." As soon as the words left her mouth she wanted to grab them back. Now she'd need to think of a good, calming excuse to tell Pa as to why she had to speak to Adelard.

"Gosh! He knows our language?"

She had to admit the truth to Skeeter despite her prejudices. "He does and a couple of others besides."

He shook his head. "A real Indian who can speak to anyone?"

6

The boy looked up at his sister. "I want to be like him when I grow up."

Ellen gasped. That wasn't something their father needed to hear. "Anyone can learn another language. You already know English. German is similar and would make Pa happy, while Mr. Granville and Mrs. Warren could speak French to you. I know they would be willing to teach you a few words." They reached the main wagon, cutting off any further conversation.

Their parents waited for them while seated on a blanket. She stumbled a little when seeing her father's furious expression. Had she been so long in bringing their dishes? She glanced at her little brother. It couldn't be either of their faults. She scanned the group seated and trembled at the sight of Del. The stone-faced fury Ellen saw on his dark face terrified her. While her father scared her, his temper was a known danger. Adelard was just danger. She stood transfixed, not noticing until Jack bumped into her that he'd stood and was leaving.

Jack barked, "Family, follow."

His wife jumped up, obeying without hesitation. Lucy held their youngest son and gave him no chance to argue. Before minding out of habit, Ellen paused. Her family hadn't eaten this well in a while, and the heavenly smell of food tempted her sorely to stay.

"Ellie, I don't want to go," Skeeter whispered as he clung to her arm.

Winking at her, Del said, "I did say distressed, didn't I?"

She didn't know what to say, not understanding his sentence. Ellen looked back to see the rest of her family walking away. No matter what his status in society, Del had brought them fresh meat. Every breeze carrying the aroma to her nose kept her rooted there.

If Pa was mad when they returned to the wagon later, she would take the punishment alone, and under the circumstances, it would be worth it. Skeeter's cheeks looked gaunt and under his eyes dark. The boy needed a decent meal with real meat, fresh meat, and with it roasting so nearby it made her own stomach lurch, she couldn't deny him. She'd pay the price for it if she had to.

Sam tapped his fork against his tin plate. "I'm thinking it's the insincerity of your tone, my friend. What counts is that the remaining Winlows are in for a treat."

Ellen knew her father hated when she excused his rude displays. However, he never had to live with the social consequences afterward. "My father has a bit of a temper." No one reacted, so she tried to smooth any ruffled feathers by adding, "I'm sure he's already regretting his actions, and I'd like to apologize on his behalf."

Del looked up from preparing the food and smiled. "Apology accepted, miss. *Monsieur* is entitled to his opinion. This is a free country, after all." He glanced behind her. "*Bonjour,* ladies. Did you bring your appetites this evening?"

She turned to see her friends Marie and Jenny. Sam stood to greet them, as did all his men around the campfire.

"We did, Mr. Du Boise." Marie gave him her hand.

Jenny held back, turning his greeting from a kiss to a more formal handshake. "Mr. Du Boise. I have to admit, the smell led us here."

The group settled in around the fire. Lucky sat next to Jenny, giving Del her plate. Del filled hers and then motioned for Skeeter's plate. The boy looked to her for permission. Ellen wasn't sure. She searched for Pa first then listened for his yelling. Lucy had been keeping him calm lately. Maybe she'd convinced him to let Ellen and Skeeter stay for dinner. That must be why he hadn't dragged them back to their camp.

She nodded at her little brother, giving him permission to stay. Del gave a couple spoonfuls of dinner to the youngster before gesturing for Ellen's plate. She let him serve her too and glanced at her brother. The boy's stomach ruled him, too, it seemed. He took huge bites until he saw her stern expression. Smiling, he shrugged and the next forkful was lighter. Ellen grinned back as she sat and nodded her approval. He ate, all the while staring at Del.

Del sat next to Ellen and Sam when he was done distributing the food. She envied his easy grace. Glancing up, she saw him wink at her and frowned at his familiarity until she noticed his amused expression. She returned his smile, not wanting even a half white Indian to think he had better manners than she did.

The entire group remained silent for most of the meal. Ellen ignored Charles and Hester, disgusted at how the two had behaved earlier in the week when they'd thought they were alone. Their business wasn't hers, she reminded herself, quelling the need to end the charade. She pushed the Warrens from her mind. She kept busy with chewing instead of talking and covertly examined the man sitting next to her. Tonight's journal entry might be her best so far. She'd never been so close to a native for so much time and wanted to examine him. Whenever she glanced at him, she noticed he looked back at her if only for a second or so. She'd have to use a little more stealth if she wanted to glean clues about his life and about him living as a person in two worlds.

What was maddening to her was how he spoke French with Marie when they did speak. Who knew what they were saying? Sam might, since he spoke it too. Ellen decided she needed a plan to question Sam about his friend without him being suspicious of her curiosity.

Soon finished with her meal, Ellen patted her little brother on the back. She felt his backbone and was compelled to put a little meat on him. She wanted to encourage him to eat more and asked, "Did you get enough, Skeeter?"

"Yeah, and it was good." He whispered, "Do you think we should bring some back for everyone else?"

Having heard the question, Del interjected, "Yes, but of course you should. It will waste if you don't."

Sam added, "It's a moral imperative. I'll find a bowl."

"Miss Winslow could take the cook pot, yes?" The native stood, taking the container by its handle, and set the dish in front of them. "Since this is my friend's, please keep it as long as you like."

Glaring at him, Sam retorted, "Which, I hope isn't too long a time. Otherwise, I'll be dining with the Winslows."

She wanted to reassure him. "You're always welcome to join us, but I'll make sure you're able to cook in this first thing tomorrow morning."

Sam smiled his thanks, and not for the first time did Ellen need to ignore a pang of loneliness. She felt he was the big brother she never had, and Marie her very best friend. Mr. Lucky seemed more like a younger sibling, and she loved Jenny as a sister. All her friends appeared to be matched with one another. Recalling Lucy's earlier insistence she find a man, the couples left her feeling more alone.

He continued, saying, "I'm certain of that, Miss Ellen. Skeeter? Can you help your sister take the food back to your family?"

"Sure, Mr. Granville." The young boy picked up the pan and stood tall. "I'd be glad to."

He didn't seem to adopt the same serious tone. "Which chore is everyone willing to do? I can stake out the animals tonight."

"I'll help you," said Joe.

Lucky shrugged. "I can help Lefty wash dishes."

"That leaves me to set up bedding," Arnold volunteered.

"With my help," Del added.

Everyone got to their feet, and the various men set off to get their work finished. Ellen suppressed a sigh and looked at Del from under her lashes as he spoke with the others. She paid more attention to how he appeared than to what he was saying. If she were honest in her feelings, she'd admit he did cut a formidable and handsome figure. Just her luck, the only man anywhere near attractive to her was a redskin. Skeeter leaned against Ellen, his eyelids drooping and the quarter full cook pot shaky in his arms. She smoothed down his cowlick, asking, "Do you want to go back?"

"Not yet. I like Mr. Do Bose."

She put her arm around him. "Very well, we can stay for a moment or two longer but not much more."

"Yeah." He yawned. "We don't want to give the others a cold dinner."

"No, we don't." She took the food from him as he yawned, not wanting to think of the towering anger her father might have after all this. He wouldn't understand how she'd stayed for little Skeeter's sake as well as her other family members. Two mouths eating elsewhere even for one dinner helped their wagon's stores. Maybe this food would mollify him.

Ellen didn't feel right just leaving without thanking the men for including them. She waited, using Del's distraction in chatting with Sam to stare at him from the corner of her glasses. She liked the calm air the darker man had about him and his deep voice. His English held a strong French accent mixed with the staccato pattern of the few Indians she'd heard in town and on the trail. She almost liked listening to Del even when he seemed to speak gibberish. He made a fascinating subject to study.

He seemed so calm for a man half modern, half primitive. If not for their animal hide tents, she just knew the natives would be living in caves like prehistoric peoples. Ellen squinted her eyes. In the firelight, Del seemed much more savage than civilized. His high cheekbones and piercing eyes fit any nobleman she'd seen in her hometown. If he cut his hair and wore pants to match his shirt instead of those horrible buckskins, he'd almost pass for a proper gentleman. She frowned, knowing if his skin were a few shades paler her father would do anything to call Adelard Du Boise his son in law. The very idea of marrying him sent a shiver through her.

Her little brother stirred and she glanced down at him. He was almost asleep as their family's food dried into jerky. Analyzing her feelings about Mr. Du Boise would have to wait until later. Ellen hugged Skeeter before she felt a rustle to her left.

"Mademoiselle Winslow?"

She looked up into his eyes to catch the full force of Del's attention on her. "Yes?"

"I suspect you must go?" His nod indicated her near sleeping brother.

"You suspect correctly." She patted Skeeter on the shoulder and he woke with a protesting groan. "Thank you so much for the dinner, and my family thanks you as well."

"My pleasure. Would you like an escort back to your home? Or is it wagon?"

She shook her head, not wanting to let her father see them together. "There's no need. We'll be fine. I doubt much could happen to us between here and there."

"I agree. My friend hired the best men for your journey. He'll ensure you and yours sleep well."

Ellen stayed silent, at a loss for words yet not wanting to say goodbye. "They've been doing perfectly so far."

The boy rubbed his eyes. "You're a good cook, Mr. Do Bose. You can fix supper for us anytime you like."

"Skeeter! Such rudeness! You know better than to invite yourself for dinner!" She gave him a warning look and took his hand. "It's bedtime for you."

Del ruffled the boy's hair. "*Merci, monsieur.* I'll remember next time the buffalo is too big for me to eat all at once." He shrugged. "It occasionally happens." Turning his attention to Ellen, he said, "From one coast of this country to the other and after visiting two continents, to think I'd find a treasure such as you here. Goodnight, *ma coeur.*"

When he held out his hand, she took it without thinking. Del bent to kiss her hand, his lips warm in contrast to the cool night air. The tingle raced along her nerves where they touched, at last settling in her heart. This is how Cupid's arrow must feel, she supposed but stopped just short of returning his smile. The reminder that arrows must be Del's weapon of choice sobered her as Ellen's hand slid from his. No matter his refined language and impeccable manners, he wasn't a true man but an animal. "Thank you, I appreciate the sentiment."

"I look forward to our next encounter."

His grin and warm eyes caused her heart to skip several beats. She glanced around, seeing the other couples saying their goodbyes. They lingered while all she wanted to do was escape. "Oh, well, thank you." Ellen needed to examine the odd feelings Del caused when talking to or touching her. She addressed the others as they carried out their evening tasks, "Goodnight, everyone."

They all responded as a mob, each distracted by another. Her brother tugged at her arm. "Sis, can I carry the food to Ma and Pa?"

"Yes, you may. Again, thank you, Mr. Du Boise." She smiled at their host and handed the pail to Skeeter. At Del's acknowledgement, they left the group.

The boy carried the pail until it grew too heavy. Ellen took it from him and held his hand as they walked. Now lighter, he hopped over tufts of grass. "Ain't that indun amazin', sis?"

"Isn't he amazing?"

"He sure is."

Ellen suppressed her amusement at how her subtle grammar lesson went unnoticed. He'd learn soon enough in school. Until then, she'd keep trying to be a good example.

"Wonder how long he'll camp with us. Likely he has lots of warpaths to go on, don'tcha think?" Stumbling over a jump, he grabbed onto Ellen with both hands. "Mr. Do Bose prolly has a lot of scalps. He looks and acts nice, but I'm bettin' he's gone all over, massacrin' right and left."

This drew Ellen up short and she almost stopped in her tracks. Had he been on a true warpath, collected scalps, and killed women and children? "Probably so." She shuddered at the thought. Del seemed so calm, kind, and handsome. He cut a different figure than the begging or hostile types of his people. Somehow, he'd been educated and she wanted to know where. How else had he learned such charm and grace? Tall, certainly dark, and yes, attractive, he might appeal to a woman wanting a man less ordinary.

She also noticed how he'd caught her looking at him every time. Ellen's face grew warm as she realized Del had been examining her just as much as she had him. Maybe he'd not met many tall women wearing spectacles. Most Indian women she'd seen until now had had neither attributes. With an unconscious nod she decided that must be the reason for his understandable curiosity. At least they both had that trait in common.

Once at their wagon, Skeeter ran up to their father. "Pa! Pa! We ate dinner with a real indun, and he didn't kill us or nothin'! He was real nice and all!"

"Well, I'll be." Mr. Winslow ruffled the boy's hair, grinning at him. "Go on and help your ma with little Buster."

Ellen took a deep breath for bravery's sake and stepped up to her father. "Pa, the others wanted us to bring you what was left."

His face in stone, he took the pail and threw it with all his strength. The meal went several yards into the dark outside the campfire light.

"Pa! That was your—"

Before she could react, he backhanded her. The force threw her to the ground. She landed on her left elbow and knee hard, while her right hand took a lot of her upper body weight. Ellen closed her eyes, waiting for more. Sure enough, he kicked her lower back once, then again. Much to her dismay, she whimpered from the sudden shock of pain and gritted her teeth. Ellen didn't want to give him the satisfaction of crying.

He grabbed her arm and jerked her off the ground. His anger gave him added strength as he shook her. "You were told to have nothing to do with that animal. You were told to leave with us. Are you some kind of Indian lover? You want to run off with the tribe?"

His fingers dug into her arms and she winced at the pain. "No, I don't. I'm sorry, Pa." He squeezed harder. "Please, Pa, I really am."

Lucy patted his back, distracting him. "Now, Jack, she apologized. Let's forget all this before someone sees."

He shrugged off his wife's hand. "Stay the hell away from that man. I don't like Granville associating with him and others like him, and I won't have you doing it too." He shoved Ellen backward.

Taking his arm and not letting him pull away, Lucy led him toward their bedrolls. "Mr. Granville is most likely placating them while we pass through. I can't imagine him having anything to do with such people after reaching Oregon Territory."

Now distracted, Jack agreed with her. "I expect you're right. No decent man would, and Granville's that at least."

They disappeared around the wagon, and Ellen heard their voices but not the words. She glanced around to see if there were witnesses. Sometimes Pa could curse loud enough to make the earth shake. Even as noisy as he'd been, her father's outburst had attracted no attention. She wiped tears and dust from her eyes. The bridge of her nose stung, and still a little dazed, she knelt down, searching for her glasses. She could take anything but hits to the face. Those hurt when smashing into, or worse, breaking her glasses. No blurred people stood around gaping, so that was positive. She disliked the prospect of finishing the trip while nearly blind and sighed in relief at finding her glasses, although she was reluctant to put them back on until her nose stopped throbbing.

"You're all right, dear?"

"Yes, Ma." Ellen appreciated how her stepmother had been there to distract her father. "Thank you."

"You know he doesn't mean to hurt you. He just has a terrible temper, and you knew staying with that man insulted him and hurt his pride. He thought you'd chosen an enemy over your own father."

Did Lucy know she babbled when making excuses for her husband? "It's fine, Ma. I did know what I was doing." She brushed the dirt off her skirt. "Skeeter got a good meal, and Pa was spared two mouths to feed tonight." She waved at the bucket a few yards away. "He only harmed himself, you, and Buster with that display."

Anger flashed in her eyes. "I don't agree, but let's talk about all that later. Are you injured anywhere?" Her stepmother took Ellen's right hand, waving it to see if it had been broken, then lifted her arm to check her elbow. "No more than usual it seems. The bleeding will stop soon, I'm sure. Rub a little dirt into it and—"

"I know the routine, Ma." The words came out sharper than Ellen intended. Her right wrist shot pain through her arm with each heartbeat. She smiled at the woman in reassurance. "Don't worry, I'll be fine. Everything will be back to normal tomorrow, you'll see."

Nodding, Ma replied, "Yes, normal, mostly. Your father was very angry at your betrayal, don't forget. Maybe you could be on your best behavior tomorrow."

"I will, I promise. Meanwhile, I'll care for this and get ready for bed." As soon as her Ma's back turned, Ellen stopped smiling. Taking a deep breath hurt but nothing poked. She knew how a broken rib felt. She extracted any little splinters from the ground-in dirt in her palm. Her wrist would never heal at this rate. She'd fractured it in a wagon accident weeks ago and wanted to wrap the aching joint with a stiff strip of cloth after this fresh injury. Doing so would attract unwelcome attention, so she decided to ignore the pain. She tried moving her hand normally and winced from the sudden stinging. Ellen blinked back the tears as she went to retrieve Sam's food bucket. Being a baby solved nothing.

She picked up Sam's cookpot from the darkness, a step landing in squishy food. At least her Pa's temper hadn't included someone else in her family. Better her than anyone else, especially Skeeter. Buster was still safe for a few years, like Skeeter had been. She'd seen the boy earn Pa's wrath once and had put herself between the two ever since. Exhaustion hit Ellen like a gust front, and she longed to write in her journal. After cleaning up, of course, and only after getting breakfast set out for cooking tomorrow. She went to the water bucket not surprised to see it dry. She suppressed an irritated sigh, scooped it up, and carried pail and pot to the Green River.

No full moon lit her way as she walked past the night guard. She hated this. Hated how every evening before it grew so inky dark, no one else could manage to get water for the morning. She wasn't the only adult in her family. Too exhausted to stay angry, she forced her thoughts into a positive direction, like how she'd soon have a fresh drink of water. Ellen took her time in going to the river's edge, allowing her eyes to adjust to starlight. Prior travelers had worn a trail in the grass and she followed the faint path, careful with each step. A stumble and fall might mean hurting her wrist again or worse, a dented or torn up pail. Glancing up, stars filled the night just like campfires dotted the land. She wondered at how the sky seemed hazy in between the brilliant pinpoints. It seemed even light could be dusty out here. Various insects hummed to the faint tune the river gave them. If she listened close, Ellen could hear voices carried from where others sat around their little worlds of brightness.

She closed her eyes, breathing in deep the cool night air with its scent of sage and broken weeds. Others had said earlier today that the Oregon Territory promised more than this camp. Yet, Ellen couldn't see how. Before she could take another breath, a sweaty hand clamped over her mouth and pulled her to the ground. Essential seconds ticked by before she recovered from surprise. Only then did she start to struggle.

He rolled her over, pinning her under him. "*Mon coeur*, promise you won't scream."

"Mm hmm," she tried to say against his palm. How dare he? Trust a dirty brute such as Adelard to attack her when least expected. If he'd been even a little less gentle, she'd have tried to bite his hand. She put her hands on his shoulders. He wasn't wearing a shirt! She gasped and moved away from him. Ellen tried to remember if he'd worn one at dinner. Of course he had or she wouldn't have let little Skeeter sit there all evening with him. An Indian at dinner was one thing, a near naked Indian intolerable.

He whispered in her ear. "You won't cry out for help?"

Ellen paused, unwilling to sentence them to either fate, but also unwilling to be kidnapped. No matter which she chose, she deduced having her mouth covered stalled any convincing Del to get off of her. Nodding again, she asserted, "Mm hmm."

"Very well." He slid his hand from her mouth to behind her head and kissed Ellen's forehead.

She kept her voice low, hissing to him, "You might have whispered a hello or bonjour."

"Maybe so, but my way is more enjoyable." He eased up off of her, pulling her into a sitting position then closer into a tight embrace. "I think the punishment might be worth this."

"Please, let me go. My wrist is injured." She held up her arm for him to see in the very dim light then regretted doing so when he took her hand.

"*Mon petite coeur*," he whispered. "*Ou est*, ah, where are all the places you hurt? I would kiss them all." His thumb rubbed the palm of her injured hand before he let his fingertips slide to her elbow, cupping it gently. "I saw you with your family, saw what happened. I am the cause, yes?"

"Yes," she murmured before catching herself. "Um, well, yes, a little." Ellen didn't want to admit it, but confessed, "If not you then something else might have set off his temper. Usually, I'm better at avoiding a slap or two, never mind a shove." She felt the man's emotions change without him moving a muscle. In fact, he scared her. He moved so little, Ellen wasn't sure he still breathed.

"You did not fall, but were pushed onto the ground?" He stood, pulling her onto her feet at the same time.

"Oh! I'd assumed you saw everything." She reached out for his shoulder to steady her. "Forget what I told you. It's family business and nothing that concerns you."

Del took her good arm, turning Ellen to face him. "Is it your father who hit you?"

She guessed he must have only seen what happened after Pa pulled her off the ground. Del's fingers dug into the same bruises Jack had pressed into her skin. "Please, you're hurting me."

Shocked, he let her go and whispered, "*Mon Dieu*! I barely...I would never...."

"Oh, no, don't worry." She didn't want to tell him the truth. "My arms were sore already from chores. You didn't know."

He ran the back of his fingers down a painful spot on her upper arm. "This is warm. Tomorrow, it will be purple." Del paused for a moment. "Even in the dark and behind the glass, your eyes tell me you're a terrible liar."

She crossed her arms in front as if to block him learning anything new. "Pa didn't mean to hurt me. Most people never understand a person with a quick temper. They either ignore what they see and try to pretend everything's ok, or put their nose in and try to fix a situation that isn't broken."

"Then I must be in the fix category because I want to help."

"Oh." Ellen shook her head with impatience. "No, there is no fix. My father doesn't need it. I knew better than to stay with you at dinner tonight, but did anyway."

"You made the meal a pleasure." He leaned in toward her. "I merely sought a private conversation with you, not to cause harm." He retrieved Ellen's buckets for her. "You'll need to return before you're missed." When she took them, he said, "*Au revoir* until tomorrow."

A little tremor of something ran through her. Excitement or disgust, she didn't know but filed away the feeling to examine later. "Goodnight." She ignored the urge to watch him walk away and focused on filling the water pail before washing Sam's cook pot. The earlier anger from Pa, her hot and cold skin, the violent outburst, and at last Adelard's attack all churned her stomach. She paused in her washing and bowed her head. A couple of tears fell onto her lenses before Ellen sniffed and sat up. She shook off the nausea and sadness while cleaning her spectacles. Neither feeling could ever help anything.

When finished and back at their camp, Ellen checked on her brothers. They slept soundly as did her parents. She hoped to take a page out of Del's book of stealthy movement and worked at placing the water near the wagon and getting into her bedroll without a sound. Once her body was settled in for the night, her mind couldn't keep away from him. Plenty of men lived in Oregon Territory. Most of them had to be white and thus acceptable to her father. She gazed at the coals. Tomorrow always crept in too early. Ellen closed her eyes, forcing out her questions and feelings. No sense in mulling over a man most likely riding away tomorrow to his next warpath.

From habit, Ellen woke a little before daybreak. She stretched her sore muscles and put on her glasses. She glanced around at her sleeping family while rubbing her hands together for heat. Little Buster and Skeeter slept between their parents, all huddled for warmth. The low fire jogged her memory. She'd forgotten to scout out firewood for this morning's breakfast. If not fixed soon, her father would be furious. She stood. Every muscle ached and what didn't hurt was too cold to feel. She chewed on a chapped part of her lip. The pain served her right for being curious about forbidden fruit in male form during supper last night.

Her father stirred, redirecting her attention. She stoked the fire a little. The flames stopped just short of flaring. She crept away from camp towards a far off grove. The more she walked, the further the trees seemed. She'd be late fixing breakfast at this pace. Unease, like bile, began to rise in her throat. Now breathless, Ellen forced herself to be calm. She had long legs and that meant big steps. She ignored the knot in her stomach, certain she'd get there and back before breakfast. Worry made everything seem worse and she tried to calm her heart. Ellen counted one, two, with each step to keep her mind focused.

She reached the small stand of trees to find the firewood already scavenged. Nothing remained but kindling sized twigs and she needed more than that. Ellen wanted to sit and cry in frustration but couldn't afford the luxury. Battling the fear growing in her chest, she tried to think and looked up for any sort of dead branches hanging from the trees. Nothing. She glanced to the east. The sun still hovered below the horizon. Plenty of time to find something and be back soon. Ellen kicked away tufts of long grass under the young trees only to find damp earth instead of hidden sticks. A shock of panic gripped her stomach. There was nothing here to use.

"Mademoiselle? Why are you so far from camp?"

She turned and saw Del leading his horse. Ellen didn't want polite conversation and used a clipped tone so he'd ride on down the road. "Good morning. I'm having no luck finding firewood for this morning's breakfast. I'm also in a hurry, so, if you don't mind, I need to get back to searching."

"You found nothing?"

"No, and I need to get back. Please excuse me." She stopped just short of yelling at him as her father would her.

"One moment, I can help."

"I don't see how, unless your saddlebags are full of dry firewood." Urgency harshened her tone and she already regretted her rudeness. She watched as he scooped a long tuft of prairie grass. He wound the blades around, twisting them. Though interested in what he was doing, Ellen continued, "I apologize to be so curt, but I'm in such a hurry this morning, so please excuse me." When the twist looped in on itself, he let it bend and held the top and the bottom together. In a quick motion, he drew his knife and cut off the bottom from the clump from which it grew.

Del tucked in the ends like Ellen would have a skein of wool and handed the results to her. "*Voila.* It's not wood but will be good for heating a meal. I'll cut a couple for later if needed." He worked up one more, then another. Handing both to her, he added, "Close your mouth, *s'il vous plait.* The mosquitoes are bad here and not tasty from what I've heard."

"Oh!" She laughed a little too loud. "Yes, of course." Ellen inhaled and realized she'd been too scared to breathe. "Thank you so much. This will help me so much this morning." She hugged the fuel he'd made for her. "I need to run I'm afraid, but again, thank you."

"Would you like me to take you back?" He patted his horse. "Pomme doesn't mind."

"Ha! No!" She caught an odd expression on his face, as if she'd hurt his feelings with her refusal. "I can't let you." Ellen wanted to explain her answer but took a few steps toward camp. "I'm in enough trouble for dinner last night, and now breakfast will be late no matter how fast this burns."

"I'll walk with you." He kept pace with her, leading his horse.

She wanted to beg him to leave her alone, but her innate courtesy proved too strong. "All right." Nervous, she chewed on her chapped lip until tasting blood. If she were quiet, if the sun stayed low, if everyone still slept, the smell of their own coffee and bacon cooking would wake them. They'd sleep through Del escorting her back.

"Were we on a casual walk, I would ask what or who waits at the end of this travail." He shrugged. "Alas, you are almost home and so I must wait until later."

Ellen stopped a few yards short of where her family lay. "Thank you for this, Monsieur Du Boise." She indicated the improvised sticks.

"You're welcome, mademoiselle." Del continued on, skirting her campsite.

She glanced at him as he walked. He wore a shirt again, the same one as yesterday evening. He still had on those buckskins. She almost tsked aloud at him being such a wild man. One of the boys stirred, reminding her of chores. The sun just now peeked over the horizon. She placed one of the grass sticks on the embers. It flared and settled into a slower burn. Ellen sighed in relief at how he'd been right. Now to start cooking and let the aromas wake everyone. She worked as fast and as quiet as possible to gather the coffee, bacon, and biscuit fixings.

Her father and mother woke when the meat began sizzling. The boys still slept. By now, the entire camp buzzed with the activity of a new day. Ellen sprinkled a pinch of sugar into her coffee. She justified the luxury by allowing it lightened their oxen's load.

Pa commented while watching her, "You know I always have my coffee black. That way, I'm not wasting sugar or cream. You never know if you'll always have enough out here. Better to do without, I say."

Ellen nodded, having heard this every morning before now. One day she'd learn to add sugar without him seeing and lecturing. Checking the food and finding it ready, she fixed her Pa's plate as her Ma fixed Buster's. Today, as every day, Ma waited until Pa had a couple of bites and nodded at her to make her own plate. This left Ellen to fix Skeeter's and hers out of the leftovers.

Her dad pointed his fork at her. "Don't be hanging around that damned Indian today."

"Yes, sir."

"He'll be back if you keep encouraging him." Winslow took a couple of bites. "Next thing you know, he'll be dragging you and Lucy here off by your hair to the others to be used as slaves. When he's done with ya, you'll wish you'd not given him the time of day. By then, it'll be too late. You'll be ruined, scalped, and left for dead like his other victims."

"Jack, please!" Lucy covered Little Buster's ears.

"I've seen it before now." He scraped the bacon grease with his biscuit. "They're called savages for a reason. They act like men but live and fight like animals. Remember that."

"I will." Ellen felt ill. If her father knew what happened last night and this morning, he'd be enraged. She wanted to reassure him. "I'll not talk to the man."

In a sudden fit of rage, he threw his plate into the fire "You sure as hell won't!" The dish knocked over the coffee, putting out the fire and soaking the remaining food. "What have I been telling you? Leave him the hell alone! You'll get us all killed or worse. Now shut up about that damned Indian and clean up this mess." He stomped off, cursing as he went.

"Isn't that nice?" Lucy remarked. "You've ruined lunch for us. I hope you think of something for us to eat by noon, or he's going to be angry then too." She stood, scooping up Little Buster and leaving the plates and a wide-eyed Skeeter behind.

"He sure is mad."

Ellen gathered the dirty plates. "He is, but he'll get over it after a few miles of walking. That'll cool him some."

"Hope so. He scares me when he's mad."

She reassured the little boy, "Me too, but he's the same as a thunderstorm: all flash and dash that doesn't last long at all." Ellen steadied her hands so her brother couldn't see the shaking. Like a storm, Mr. Winslow often struck like lightning, fast and hard. She never got used to his tantrums.

Breakfast dishes washed, Ellen hurried to put them away. Her father would need help with the oxen. This far into the journey, she knew exactly what to do. Unless an ox misbehaved, she could expect a peaceful departure. Mr. Winslow already had the younger animal ready to go. She wiped damp hands on her skirt and hurried over to lift the yoke. As she'd hoped, the oxen behaved and she sought out Skeeter before their wagon started rolling. He played at a distance with others his age.

Lucy carried Little Buster and walked up to Ellen. "Other ladies say the ferry costs at least five dollars. Your father isn't going to pay that, I'm sure."

Fear raced through her at the implication of them going across on their own. "Does he have a choice? The river is rather swift."

"He always has a choice and will do what he reckons is best."

She didn't want to argue with her. "Of course he will." Ellen tried not to say anything else but couldn't help herself. "It's just that the water could—"

"Shush up. Your daddy's right; you need to talk less and think more." Lucy walked away.

Ellen stomped her foot. She hated how Pa and Lucy left during a discussion. So maddening and yet what could she do about it other than stand there in mid-sentence, mouth agape? She put a hand to her forehead and took a deep breath. If her father didn't take a ferry across, she needed to prepare for a possible sinking. The very idea scared her. Her father and Lucy knew the consequences of their actions, but if the worst happened, Buster and Skeeter shouldn't have to pay for their parents' bad judgment. Ellen gritted her teeth in determination. She'd helped them across rivers many times before now without incident. She could do it this time too.

Rushing, she secured all their dishes and easy to reach food. The prior experiences readied her for this one. Ellen had cut ropes in exact lengths to tie down the trunks and everything else. She checked the oxen and loosened their yokes just enough to allow them escape if necessary. They could still pull the wagon but might not drown if it overturned.

She went to the water's edge where others waited for the ferry. Trees grew on the opposite bank but too far for her to throw a hook and rope she'd made. She paced. Maybe it'd been a bad idea anyway. The ferry carried over a wagon from another group. But still, she mused, there had to be a way for them to cross and somehow guarantee safety. She went a little distance up the river hoping to find anywhere shallow. As she walked, Ellen thought of the futility of her attempt. If a way to cross existed, there'd be no ferry right now. She sighed, wishing the day was already done and they were already safe at a new camp. Wishing wasn't doing, so she searched for a plan.

Jenny came within earshot, almost needing to shout above the noisy people behind her. "You have to tell me! What do you think of...? Goodness, I hesitate to call him mister, but what do you think of Mr. Du Boise?"

Her friend's enthusiasm pleased Ellen. She admitted, "I think he's a very interesting person."

"Ooo, do tell!"

"He's a bit of a puzzle." She fell in line with Jenny as they walked back to the others. "Mr. Du Boise seems very civilized, despite the fringed trousers."

"I know! He's so mannerly, and yet you don't know when he'll turn savage or anything." The girl picked a wildflower and plucked off the petals. "I wonder if he fights with himself, being both kinds of people and all."

Ellen laughed, imagining what that might look like. "I'd think he'd have conflicting emotions, for sure."

"Most likely. So do you think he's an Indian spy? Maybe he's really all white and only pretending to be half."

The women paused. Any closer to the melee and she wouldn't be able to hear Jenny. Ellen divided her attention between her friend and looking for the Winslow's wagon in line. "What would pretending to be a half breed gain him? He'd only be marginally acceptable in society."

"I heard at the last trading post how a white man dressed up like a brave and tried to steal a horse." Jenny tossed down the denuded flower, or what was left of it. "He wanted to blame them so he'd get away with the crime."

She frowned. "They're horrible as a whole, but to steal and blame someone else is wrong. Don't they do enough considered criminal as it is without framing them when innocent?"

"They are a rather sorry group of people. Mr. Du Boise is the first I've properly met. The others only stare at us as cattle do."

Somehow Jenny's strong opinions put Ellen in a defensive frame of mind. She didn't have time for a true rebuttal but had to disagree. "I don't know if I could compare him to a cow or even a bull. It seems Mr. Du Boise is rather intelligent."

"Yes, he does. That's why I'm not sure he is Indian. Maybe he was kidnapped or finds buckskin comfortable." She shook her head. "Even so, his hair is very long. You'd think a man wouldn't have just one long braid down the back, although, I think it's much better than one on each side. I mean, that's how little girls wear their hair. That can't be too manly."

Smiling at her friend's deductions, Ellen interjected, "It can't be and he strikes me as very much a man."

"My goodness! You must have learned more about him last night than Marie and I expected you would. Half the party argues Mr. Du Boise will steal everything we own while the other is sure he'll be our salvation. What do you think?"

She paused. This far away from her family, she knew her father couldn't overhear her now. If she answered with an innocent comment about how she enjoyed spending time with Mr. Du Boise, Pa would be in a rage if word ever got back to him. Ellen needed to give the most neutral and acceptable answer. Her family edged closer to the ferry, distracting her a little. "I'm not sure what to think. I've not had time to form an opinion."

"What? He's an Indian. What more is there to consider?" Jenny began strolling toward her family and Ellen went along.

"I've not had a chance to really talk with someone so primitive. My father forbids it which is why I don't think anything about him." She nodded at Arnold, one of Granville's men, as he rode by them.

"If Mr. Winslow forbids you talking with him, you shouldn't."

"Of course I won't," she reassured Jenny. "I'm not foolish enough to court trouble."

The other girl nodded. "I'm glad you are so smart. A more besotted woman would get herself kidnapped by him even if only by accident. I've heard horrible stories about such things."

"I have too and would never be so enamored of him." As she said the words, doubts began to sound in her mind about such rumors. Even the most honest man she knew, her father, had stories that became more incredible each time she heard them. Maybe what had begun as a simple argument between two groups of people had become a massacre with each retelling. If she weighed the evidence, none of the natives she'd encountered so far had been violent. In fact, having met Del now led her to believe his people must be quite charming.

"You're thinking about that man, aren't you?" asked Jenny.

The girl's question startled Ellen. "Oh, well, a little." She shrugged. "My interest in him is purely cultural and scientific."

"I'm not sure how to be interested in a man scientifically, but if you say so. At least it's not romantic."

"Romantic is not possible. We're halfway to Oregon and there are plenty of men there for me to choose." She watched as a family boarded the ferry. Sam and the others herded the livestock across before coming back for the next load. She couldn't see Del among them and it was just as well. "The last thing I need is a man like Mr. Du Boise chasing after me." An odd thought occurred to her. Ellen frowned and blurted, "Why is it men can have Indian wives? We can't have Indian husbands?"

"Dear me! No! Civilized men are wild enough as it is. I can't imagine how a lesser man might be to his wife. How terrible!" Jenny frowned. "Don't even think of it. Let him be an experiment but never a husband."

Ellen laughed at the notion. She glanced down the line of wagons waiting for the ferry and saw her father. His reaction to such intentions would shake the Earth like a natural disaster. "I'd sooner die than marry Du Boise."

"Mademoiselles," Del nodded in greeting as he rode past them and on up the queue.

Jenny waited until he was well out of hearing. "Do you think he heard?"

Certain she insulted him, Ellen responded, "I think he still does hear us."

"My goodness." She looked as uncomfortable as Ellen felt. "No matter what he is, we weren't kind, were we?"

"I don't think so." She glanced back, seeing Del speaking with

Sam and facing away from her. "As much as I'd prefer not to, I'll have to talk with him if only to apologize."

"I agree. You have no other choice. He might misunderstand and think you wish to die."

Ellen chuckled a little. "I hope he'd not think such a thing." A good excuse came to mind and she patted Jenny on the arm. "However, it is a good reason to chat with him, don't you think?"

"And to see if he's as interesting as you suspect. Maybe he's just a boring ole native better left alone. I think so anyway."

She looked for her family's wagon in line. They were third now. Ellen calculated how long the ferry might take based on past performances. Then, she needed to figure how long her father would argue before throwing a temper tantrum, stomping off, and ordering her to help him cross the river on their own. If he preoccupied himself otherwise, she might have a chance to really talk with Del, explain her conversation with Jenny, and apologize for being so thoughtless. And after all that? She still needed to find a shallow crossing for them as soon as possible. She looked back where Sam and Del stood. Their body language indicated a casual conversation, easily interrupted. She could give a quick explanation before beginning an even quicker search along the riverbank for a better way to cross.

She turned to Jenny. "Pardon me while I eat crow."

"All right. Let me know how you do with him."

"I will." Ellen gave her a little wave and started toward the two men. As she approached, her confidence ebbed. How could she apologize for the truth? She couldn't marry anyone her father hadn't chosen for her initially. Death would be easier than living with Mr. Winslow's infinite rage. She reached the men, standing there until being acknowledged.

"Miss Winslow," Sam said first. "How are you today?"

"I'm fine."

"Your wrist? Arms?" Del asked, reaching for her right hand.

"All fine." She grimaced when he eased her wrist into a slight bend.

He released her. "Again, you are a poor liar. Do not try for a senate seat. You might be able, but not effective."

Sam glanced from one to the other. "I feel I'm missing something important."

"You are not," Del replied, crossing his arms in front of his chest. "Mademoiselle Winslow is likely here to talk with you, Sam, not with me."

Ellen glanced at Del. "Oh, actually, I do need to talk to Mr. Du Boise at the moment."

Sam's eyebrows rose. "Alone?"

She did need to speak to him in private. She didn't want him embarrassed or humiliated with a backhanded apology.

Del answered for her. "*Non*. Not alone. She is a young single woman, after all, and I am a brutal savage."

Sam laughed until seeing his friend's stony expression. "Excuse me, I thought you were joking. Very well, I'll stay until the lady has her say."

Both men looked at her. Ellen fidgeted while gathering her thoughts. "Mr. Du Boise, Adelard, I'm afraid you overheard me make a rude statement about you, one that I'm rather ashamed of saying aloud."

"Which one might that be?"

His candor took her by surprise and she gasped. Taking a bolstering breath, she clenched her fists to avoid wringing her hands. "It was when I said I'd rather die than marry you."

"I certainly did miss something!" said Sam.

"No, you didn't," Del retorted. He continued to Ellen, "And you're afraid of saying this how? Did you lie to Miss Jenny?"

She wrung her hands. "No, I didn't lie at all."

"Death is more preferable to you than being my wife. It is an honest statement. Why would you be ashamed of this?"

"Because…." She first looked around to see if her family was nearby before answering. "I don't know how to explain other than by being direct." Ellen took a deep breath and began. "I think you're an interesting subject and would like to know more about you. However, my father will make life miserable for me if we even talk as much as we are now." She paused, waiting for him to respond. When he didn't, she continued, "Jenny and I were discussing this very fact when somehow the conversation led to romance, marriage, and, um, you." She paused, expecting a laugh from the two men. Sam seemed entertained while Del glared at her. "I couldn't let anything of the sort happen. Considering my father's opinion of native peoples and all." She held open her hands in an appeal. "So you see? My comments were more general than specific. My father disapproves of all natives, not just you."

He looked at her from toes to eyes. "What makes you think I'm interested in marrying?"

"Oh!" She felt sad and even a little ill from the embarrassment. Like her father always reminded her, Ellen had placed too much importance on herself. Her face grew hot and she wanted to disappear. Best to push through this shame, she decided and clasped her hands. "Nothing, I suppose. We can be distant friends with no harm done."

"I suppose so."

"Good, good." She paused. "I'll need to get back to our wagon. My father is probably deciding to cross the river on his own and I'll need to help." Ellen saw the look pass between the men. "Yes, it's not wise, but I've prepared our belongings as much as possible and will need to help him with everything else." She smiled. "I hope to see you on the opposite bank later today." Ellen hurried away before either could respond.

She rushed to their wagon to find Buster inside, crying with a soiled diaper. Skeeter sat on the tailgate in the shade, his hands over his ears. Tapping her brother, she said, "Come on down from there and let me change him." The boy nodded, stepping out of the way as Buster ran into her arms. "There, there," she managed to say after his smell reached her. While she cleaned him and put on a fresh diaper, Ellen warmed up to life spent as a spinster. No man was worth a brood of children, not when they all smelled like Buster most times.

Her father's raised voice caught her attention. She tilted her head to hear if he was just being loud or truly angry. Picking up the baby, she knew Skeeter had also heard by the way he clung to her skirt. She dreaded going over and seeing what the fuss was about, but avoiding Pa did no good. She took her little brother by the hand, settled the baby on her hip, and followed the shouting.

Jack stood face to face with the ferryman. "I don't give a God damn what you want! I'm not paying no thirteen dollars for this."

Skeeter slipped behind Ellen. Her glance skipped around the small crowd. She'd hoped no one saw the spectacle until catching sight of Adelard. He stood there, passively watching. She frowned at how he almost seemed amused at the rude display. Her face burned with the idea of him thinking how uncivilized her father behaved at the moment.

Lucy tugged at his sleeve. "Jack, please!"

"I'm sorry, sir, but that is the rate everyone pays." The ferryman's obstinate expression matched Winslow's.

"It's robbery and I won't stand for it!"

Sam stepped up. "Mr. Winslow, is there something I can do?"

"No, there ain't a God—" he paused, catching himself. "No, I don't suppose so. This man here is determined to rob everyone blind." Jack gave the ferryman a glare. "Taking advantage of decent folks. He should be shot."

"I'm sure he's just trying to make a fair wage," said Sam.

"Fair, my ass!" Giving Del a second glance, Jack asked, "What the hell is he still doing here? You ready to pick our bones too?" He turned to Sam. "This here man speaks English?"

Del glanced at Ellen and forced an easy smile before replying, "Not if I can help it. *Qui n'est pas clair n'est pas Fraincais. Et, votre anglais est merde.*" Sam laughed and changed his guffaws to coughs. Del smacked him on the back as he went on. "My father preferred French around the house; my mother, her language, of course."

Jack gave him a blank stare. "I don't care about all that. If I give you a simple order to go away, would you understand? Or do I need to draw a picture?"

He swallowed. "No need." Del turned on his heel toward his horse.

"Del!" Sam hollered.

"*Que?*" he said without stopping.

"*Aval avant le trempage?*"

"*D'accord. Je suis un imbécile pour amour.*"

Ellen shifted Little Buster to her sore hip, wincing at the pain. Out of her father's line of sight, she watched as Del strolled away from them. She'd give anything at the moment to know what Sam had asked and Du Boise had answered. Winslow's wagon pulled out of the queue, led by Jack. When Sam walked over and stood next to her, she took the chance to learn more about what the two men had said in French. "I've heard Marie say *merde* when frustrated."

He grinned at her. "Is that so?"

"Would I be embarrassed knowing the meaning?"

"Yes, and you'd be mortified at having said it just now." He winked, motioning for her to come along with him. "Don't step in the cow *merde* is a good example of the meaning." Sam laughed at her gasp. "Let's go. I have Del waiting downstream in case the worst happens and your family will need our help finding a shallow spot to cross."

Ellen shook her head. "I've already searched. There are none or others would be there already. We need to stop him. You know what happened to Biscuit the last time Pa tried to bypass the ferry."

"Yes, I remember. Putting down a horse is something I strive to avoid." He scanned the river. "You're right about the river's depth, of course." A scream captured both their attentions.

She watched as her father drove their wagon into the water. It rolled alongside as the ferry left the shore. Ellen stifled a curse when realizing he'd done so to prove a point to everyone. The oxen worked to pull the heavy load. They dipped below the water once before resurfacing. The animals brayed and struggled for shore. The wagon began swaying in the strong currents. She searched their surroundings and panicked when she couldn't find Skeeter anywhere. Ellen heard Lucy's cry and her heart stopped, certain her stepmother was drowning. While holding Little Buster snug against her, she ran toward the accident.

Jack stood on the seat, urging the animals onward despite their fear. They lurched forward as if stumbling over something on the riverbed and toppled him. He fell onto their backs, carried through the water as he held on to the yoke. The wagon followed behind, still attached to the oxen. The current lifted and pushed over the vehicle with all the belongings still strapped down inside. Sam's men rushed to the scene on horseback while he ran for his own horse. Their animals struggled to stay upright as the men strung a rope from one side of the river to the other.

Skeeter ran past her to the bank. "Pa! Pa!" She caught hold of him just as he leaped into the water. Ellen and Little Buster weren't enough to counteract both her younger brother's weight and force. All three tumbled in.

Ellen held the baby tight and pulled Skeeter close as well. The cold water shocked him motionless for a moment. She yelled, "Hang on and I'll get you out of here!" She kicked hard against the flow toward shore, relieved when he grabbed around her waist, then neck. She could let go of him, her arm free to grab any branch or tough grass hanging out over the water. She pushed her glasses up on her nose so she could see well but drops obscured her vision.

The current carried them down, close to where Del pulled

Lucy onto the bank. The baby cried in her ear, and Lucy stirred at the sound as the trio flowed past. Ellen's gaze met Del's, his face pale. As they went downstream, he ran along the bank, keeping up and at times passing them.

She grabbed onto Skeeter's wrists locked around her neck. He was cutting off her air with his grip, and she wedged her hand between him and her throat. With every swirl and eddy, Ellen allowed her head to sink below the water instead of theirs. As her gasps for air became more difficult, both children grew heavier in her arms. She tried and failed to stand every time her toes brushed a surface. Both boys clung to her so hard, Ellen took the chance to take off her glasses. She folded and slid them down the front of her bodice.

"Ellen!"

Del stood in the water further downstream and held out a bent tree branch. She struggled to swim toward him. Her skirt caught a snag, almost forcing the boys out of her arms. "I'm stuck!"

At her cry, he leaped onto the bank and ran up to where they were. Del leaned out as far as he could. "Grab my hand!"

She pulled Buster from her and held him out for Del. "Take the boys, I can swim. Please, Del! Save them!"

His mouth set in a hard line, he reached for Buster but the little hand swung out of his reach. The river pulled at them, drawing them to the center of the stream. Her dress still caught by the dead roots, she was afraid to struggle and pull them free. Del eased into the water, bracing himself while reaching for anyone he could reach.

Sam rode up and shouted, "Don't you dare get in there!" He threw a coil of rope to Del and wrapped the other end around the horn of his saddle. "Here, tie up so I can drag you both out."

Ellen sunk below the surface, afraid to kick and dislodge them from help. She stayed at the surface just enough to watch as he double knotted the rope around his waist. With some slack pulled, Del dove into the water. She held the boys above her. The water in her ears muddled his shout to her. An ebb of the river's current allowed her to surface and gasp for air. She saw him struggling as he swam toward them.

Sam held onto the rope, the end tied around the pommel of his saddle. He slid off his horse. Not letting go of his friend's lifeline, he went closer to the water.

Del reached them and grabbed Buster by his little outstretched hand. Ellen felt the tug and kicked hard to surface. Seeing him there, she let go of the baby while breathing in deep and as fast as possible in case the current pulled her under again. Both hands free now, she lifted up her younger brother. After swinging the toddler onshore and into Sam's arms, Del came back for them. She struggled to pry Skeeter from her. The boy whimpered, scared and clinging to her.

Del stretched a hand out, nearly touching Ellen. "Skeeter, come here! Buster needs you!"

The boy's grip around her throat eased, allowing her to take a deep breath as they bobbed. He climbed up to Del's reach. Skeeter grabbed onto the man's hand, planted his foot in the middle of Ellen's chest, and pushed her away in his efforts to get to shore. She relaxed; relieved the men had both boys. Her skirt tore from the branch as she fought to tread water and she went under. Surfacing several yards downstream, she grabbed at anything growing near the water. She swam hard, working her way closer to the bank. Each time she grew tired and eased her struggles, the currents drew her to the center. "Adelard!" she screamed before being pulled below again.

CHAPTER 2

Del ran along the shore, ignoring the sharp grasses cutting his arms. He stopped staring only long enough to jump over the small gullies lining the bank. Looking back at the water, he couldn't find her anywhere. She was gone. He halted to take in a deep breath and yell her name. She resurfaced for a moment but bobbed under again. She'd hit a snag. He hurried to the riverbank, knowing if he didn't get her now while he had the chance Ellen would tire and drown. He eased down the slippery ledge.

He searched for her but only saw water. The metallic taste of fear hit the back of his throat and his mouth watered. She bobbed above again, coughing. He knew from the raspy sound that she'd breathed in liquid. She'd been snagged again. Keeping his eyes steady, Del slid into the river and swam with every ounce of strength he had. The current too much, he struggled to avoid being swept downstream from her. The rope tugged at his waist, and he looked up to see Sam pulling him upstream. Now Del could focus on just getting to Ellen.

Just before she went under again, he reached her and grabbed her arms. He held her close, her head at his shoulder and above the water. "*J'ai tu, ma petite*, I have you." She coughed on his chest and he laughed, relieved she still breathed. "*Bien!*" He didn't have to swim, but merely held her as Sam pulled them toward the shore. Del scrambled to his feet as they left the water, still holding her. He patted her back when she couldn't stop coughing long enough to say anything.

"You're good?" Sam said as he recoiled his rope.

"*Oui. Merci, mon ami.*"

"I'll check the others." Sam rode away to the other Warrens.

Ellen leaned against him and shivered, the shock and cold catching up with her. "Thank you so much." She pulled away from him. "My brothers?"

His skin began cooling at the lack of her warmth. Del fought the urge to grab and hold her close again. "Safe."

"They're alive, thanks to you." She coughed again and looked over at the ferry crossing. "I owe you a debt I can never repay."

He cupped her face in his hand. "No, no debt. It was my duty to save them, my honor to save you." Del searched Ellen's eyes. Could it be affection he saw there? He lifted a hand to caress her cheek then reconsidered such a public display. She covered her mouth for a slight cough and he pulled back. "I am selfish, taking your air." She shivered and he added, "But how can I not hold you when you're so cold?"

"I think the bigger question is how are you not chilled?" she asked while untying the bow on the back of her dress. Her glasses fell from the dress's bodice to the ground and she picked them up, shaking off the water and dirt.

Watching her try to clean her glasses on her damp skirt, Del replied, "I'm from further north." She glanced up, her eyes focused on him without the glasses between them. He forgot to breathe for a moment. He stared into Ellen's face, his heart feeling too big for his chest. She shivered, breaking the spell and he gave her a wicked grin. "Cold is no bother to me. At home, I must chip through a foot of ice to the river underneath."

Her teeth chattered until she clenched her jaw. Ellen frowned and put her glasses back on. "You bathe in ice water?" She chuckled after glancing at him and said, "Oh no, not really?"

"Yes, I bathe in the dead of winter, but I heat water for a tub."

She laughed, coughing afterward. "I'd prefer warm water any day."

"So would I." He indicated the camp with a nod. "Let's go. You need care and must be curious about your brothers."

"I'm more concerned about the wagon and my father. I know Lucy and my brothers are well thanks to your bravery. I'm not so sure about Pa, the oxen, and our wagon."

"They must have reached shore. Otherwise, they'd have floated past us by now." He took her hand as they walked. "You have not reinjured yourself?" They paused and he turned her palm up, making small circles on her wrist with his index finger. "It hurts here, no?"

"It does, a little." Ellen squeaked when he brought her palm up and kissed her open hand.

She shivered under his lips and his interest turned to need. Looking up at her, he straightened and said, "I can kiss until you feel better."

"I'm better now, thank you." She tugged away from his hold. "You wouldn't want to continue this farce and thus start a fight neither of us want."

"Farce? *Non*, but correct. I'd prefer to avoid war for now." He turned toward the others, but paused. Thinking of her wet heavy skirts, he took her elbow in case she stumbled. "You have intelligence as well as beauty. No man's heart is safe. Shall we?" At her nod, they walked to the ferry and as they drew closer, his urge to escape with Ellen grew. He shook his head as he watched her father stomping around the Winslow's belongings on the opposite shore.

"Oh! It seems everyone is waiting for us." She lagged in her pace as the two of them approached her family. Several other people huddled together with the Winslows still a dozen yards ahead.

Del paused when she did. "*Ma coeur*? What is it?"

"I'm not sure I want to return—" Squeals of delight from Marie and Jenny kept her from continuing.

Jenny hugged Ellen while jumping up and down. "You're safe! We were so scared! You disappeared, then Mr. Du Boise, then Mr. Granville. After seeing the wagon, we just knew the worst had happened."

Marie went to Del. "I'll hug you for saving our friend's life after you're dry."

He laughed, not blaming her one bit. "I'll take you up on that, *ma coupin*." He leaned over to Ellen. "We should both find other clothes soon."

Marie spoke before her friend could respond. "Everything in your wagon is probably drenched. You can help me search our things for something dry. Your hems will be a little high due to our height difference."

"I'll be happy with whatever you find. Anything is better than this cold feeling for the rest of the day."

"Good." Marie turned to the youngest girl. "Jenny, your mother and Mrs. Winslow are similar. She and the boys might be able to borrow some clothes from your family too."

Jenny nodded. "I'll take them to Ma and see what she can find them." The girl hurried off to escort the rest of the family to the Allen's wagon.

Marie took Ellen's hand. "Mercy! You're near frozen. Let's go get started."

At his limit for listening to women talk about clothes, Del tapped Marie on the shoulder. "Madame, please excuse me while I'm finding other clothes. I prefer trousers to dresses."

With her nod, Del walked to his horse and the dry set of clothes in his saddlebags. Ellen's voice caught his attention and while he didn't stop, he did slow his pace a little. He heard her say, "... is a very good man for an Indian."

He continued to the Granville wagon, and once certain no one saw him, leaned against it. His horse, Pomme, ambled over to nudge at him. *"Allo."* Del petted the animal's neck. Now alone, he could rest for a moment and just be glad Ellen was safe. He closed his eyes to shut out the rest of the world. When had she become so important to him that he still tasted the fear over losing her to drowning? And when she'd stared into his eyes? He'd forever carry the memory in his heart.

"Napping already?"

Sam's smart remark amused Del and he opened his eyes. *"Oui,* or trying to do so."

"The Winslows owe you a debt they might not ever acknowledge."

He shrugged. "There is no need. I did what I must."

"They might not but I can." Sam put a hand on his friend's shoulder. "Thank you, Adelard."

He grinned at how his friend wiped a wet palm on his pants. "You're welcome."

"Let me get you something dry to wear."

Del motioned toward his horse. "I have clothes in my saddlebags."

"Save them for later. I brought extra and can part with a pair of pants and a shirt. No arguing and you can change in the wagon. Be quick because we're next across."

Del climbed in and took Sam's advice. His wet buckskins made changing difficult. Peeling them off took far longer than he'd planned and the wagon began rolling.

"Sorry," Sam hollered back at him. "We're the last ones across. I stalled as long as I could. You and Pomme can ride with us."

"Merci." He removed the tie keeping his braid together and

unraveled his hair to dry. He shrugged into a shirt and began buttoning it as they rolled to a stop. Hearing his friend talk to the ferryman, Del folded his wet clothes, making a mental note to get them later. He left the wagon and went to his horse, leading Pomme as they boarded the ferry with the wagon. Little waves splashed against the sides. Del squatted at the conveyance's edge to search for the riverbed, but summer thaw churned up too much silt. The water gave off a slight, fresh smell. It told him that the emigrants had fished out this part of the river. He straightened as they neared the bank. Animals, fish, wild fruit, and berries had all decreased in the past couple of years due to the influx of settlers. They all seemed to understand how to take far better than how to give.

Mr. Winslow's voice carried to him on the eastward wind. Del went to the front of the Granville wagon to see why the man fussed. Winslow stood on the bank, his arms around Mrs. Winslow and the boys. The ferryman tied them up and once secure, Del stepped down and onto the dock. He led Pomme out of the way as Sam and a couple of his men disembarked. He stopped and watched the little family. They seemed oddly placed until he realized how they all stood facing the disembarking people as if giving a stage play. He scanned the crowd for Ellen, wondering what her part was in all this.

Jack cried out to a gathering crowd as the wagons rolled past him. "The ferryman has taught me a valuable lesson: The man with the biggest pile of money gets to have his family. Otherwise," he broke off as if overcome with emotion. "Otherwise, he watches them die in a watery grave." Women around them dabbed at tears while the men shuffled and sniffed.

Winslow looked around him as if to see how much of an audience he had. He hugged his family closer. "Does he or the company handing out his pay care about us, the common people? Do they care about helping us reach a better land and life? Or do they only care about bleeding us dry to better fill their pockets?" When a frugal man in the group yelled his support, Winslow turned toward the shout. He nodded in approval much like a king would to a loyal subject.

Even at a distance, he could tell how something had caught Winslow's eye. Del followed the man's gaze to find Ellen. She'd changed into something of Marie's he supposed; her dress only reached her ankles.

"Daughter! You're alive!" he shouted. Her face reddened and she shook her head without breaking the stare she and her father shared. "Come to us, your family!" Winslow insisted, waving her over to them. She obeyed, and upon reaching them, her father looked her up and down. Still loud for the crowd to hear he asked, "Where have you been?" He held up a hand before pulling her into an oversized hug. "It doesn't matter; you're here now. It's a miracle!"

Del's eyes narrowed as Jack searched the crowd as if to make sure everyone saw his demonstration. Hate for the man increased in the pit of his stomach. Winslow's obstinacy had nearly cost him his family, and now the man used the occasion for showboating. And for what? Money, attention, perhaps sympathy? He didn't know her father well enough to more than guess at a motive. Leading Pomme past the family then, he lowered his gaze to the ground to shield his eyes a bit. He heard Ellen's voice and glanced up to keep her in sight. Even then, Del stalled and used checking the straps on his English saddle as an excuse to eavesdrop.

"Oh, Ellen!" Lucy hurried to her. "I'm so glad you're here." Still in her wet dress, she clung to her stepdaughter. Del winced before he caught himself. So much for the young woman finding dry clothes. The gray dress darkened wherever her stepmother hugged her. Mrs. Winslow picked up the wailing where her husband had left off. "It was all so horrible. Thank goodness you're here to help me dry our things and watch the boys. I'm so tired."

Jack stumbled over to her as if too weak to properly walk. "My dearest daughter, come give me another hug before you help your Ma. We were afraid you were gone forever."

"I was helping Mrs. Warren with her things, Pa." She hugged her father before stepping back. "I'm so glad we're all on this side and safe now. Are you hungry? It's past noon, so you must be. Let me fix you something, maybe tea and jelly biscuits?"

"Yes," he sighed. "Yes, I am hungry." After seeing the people go about their own business and not paying him any more attention, he walked with her to their wagon. "Let me get our rig out of the way and you can start all that."

"I'll be glad to," Ellen said as he walked away from her.

Lucy followed him a few steps but then staggered a little as if unable to continue. "You go ahead with him, dear. I'll be there as I can." She groaned before saying, "You're so much stronger than me."

"Very well. I'll begin unpacking everything."

"Thank you." She slumped a little then shifted Buster to one hip. "Thank you so much." Lucy put the back of her free hand to her forehead. "The day grows late. I shall be glad to see sleep tonight."

Del choked down a chuckle at the woman's melodrama. She and her husband were well matched. They both had a flair for the theatrical. Ellen turned toward him and their gaze met. Caught mid snicker, he schooled his features into something less mocking toward her family's act. She blushed, her face a lovely pink. Remorse kicked him and he stepped toward her. *"Mademoiselle?"*

Skeeter poked his head from behind Ellen's skirt. "Hey! Mr. Do Bose! You look dandy!"

He grinned at the young man. "Thank you, Mr. Winslow. You look fine too." He nodded at Ellen, checking to see Mrs. Winslow walking away from them, probably searching for her husband. Del hadn't wanted to cause problems for Ellen. "Miss—"

Sam rode over to them. "Everyone is across now. Go with your family, Miss Ellen, and we'll begin moving again." He slid down and held out a hand to Skeeter. "Come on, son. Let's follow your mother."

"All right, Mr. Sam." He waved to Del. "Mr. Do Bose, thank you for saving my family. You are good people and clean up real nice."

"Thank you and you're welcome." He watched as they left in the same direction as the Winslows. Del turned to find Ellen smiling at him.

"I should go with them." She crossed her arms, adding, "White is really your color."

He chuckled, liking the compliment. "Is it? You are white. Are you my color too?" Del took a step toward her family as if to walk her back to them. His tricked work when she joined him, keeping up to his pace.

"Oh, I'm not sure about that."

Del glanced over at her, enjoying how rosy her cheeks glowed. "Your dress matches the storms in your eyes." He took a sideways step closer to her. "The shade has become my favorite color since meeting you."

"They're just slate gray." Ellen shook her head before looking back at a trailing Pomme. "Nothing special, like blue or green, or yours even."

"Mine?" Had she meant to flatter him? Her intention didn't matter. He'd use the chance to get a compliment from her. "They're nothing special as well, the color of dirt or of the plainest pony in the herd."

She wrung more water from the end of her braid. "Yours are the warmest brown imaginable. I rather like looking into them and seeing the gold flashes."

He peeked over at her. Her hair, the strands loosened from their ordeal, dried in chestnut hued tendrils around her face. He'd seen a lot of women in his travels, but none tugged at his heart like her. "So I have the lightning in mine to the storm clouds in yours? The thought appeals to me."

"Me too." She gave him a sideways glance. "I also like your hair loose like that. Though I suppose if you let it flow naturally, I'm sure it'd be tangled in no time."

Grinning, he agreed. "One gust of wind and yes. Tangles."

Ellen slipped off the tie holding her braid intact. "Mine as well. I should let it down to let it dry faster too." Fluffing the damp strands, she added, "It's longer than yours, meaning many more tangles at the end of the day."

Del stepped closer to her. A dried, thin strand of her hair floated to him on the wind. He took the stray lock, entranced at how her hair cascaded to the small of her back. "Every evening before you slept, I would comb each inch of such beauty if necessary." He rubbed the strands between his fingertips. "*Mon Dieu*, this is too soft to feel."

"Oh?" She gave a quick look ahead before saying, "Let's see yours as well." She did as he had, touching his hair. "Very silky too. Is it so all along the strand?" Ellen let the pinch of his hair slide through her fingertips to where it ended just below his shoulders. "It is. I'd expected this to feel much like a horse's mane. A lot of women would love to have hair this fine. You're a very lucky man."

His eyes narrowed. She had expected him to feel like an animal? A horse was a noble beast, but still an animal. Del's affection for her closed in on itself like a morning glory in the afternoon. The next step he took was a few inches away from her as they walked. "Lucky, yes, but I'm not considered a man, remember."

Before he could add to his comment, she put a hand on his arm. "But you obviously are. Anyone can see you're very manly." Ellen held on to him, pulling Del to a full stop. "Listen, the length of your hair doesn't matter. I've seen many gentlemen with far longer manes and messier besides."

He glanced at where she touched his shirt, entranced by her closeness. A slight breeze carried her scent to him. He wanted to help her by cleaning the dusty smudge on her glasses. When they stood together like this, he barely remembered why he'd been irritated. The memory flashed in his mind and he frowned. "When you hold me as you do now, I'm the animal you have called me." Her shiver amused him as she let go. Maybe he should give her a solid reason to think of him as a true brute. Del leaned in to whisper, "If you ever let me maul you like the beast I am, you won't regret it."

She stared at him a couple of seconds, her mouth open until she closed it and shook her head. "No. I don't suspect I would regret anything from you."

"Ellen!"

Jack's voice from ahead startled her and she jumped a little. "Yes, Pa! I'm on my way. Good day, Mr. Du Boise."

Before he could reply, Mr. Winslow hollered, "You've spent enough time with the strays around here. Let's get moving."

Del turned to look at the retreating man. He refused to feel the little ache in his heart. Instead, he embraced the anger seeping through his body. Winslow might consider him the stray, but Del considered him to be the cur dog.

"Um, I'm sorry," said Ellen as she slowed her pace away from him. "He's just outspoken and doesn't think about his words most times. Excuse me, please."

He didn't want to hear any more excuses for the rudeness. "Good day, Mademoiselle Winslow." When she nodded before hurrying off, he gritted his teeth and swung onto his horse.

After riding a few miles further down the trail, Del's head ached. Never before now had he let small minded people and their prejudices bother him. A few sometimes worked their way under his skin, irritating him, but none had left him so angry and helpless. He wanted to pester her until she admitted she disagreed with her father's opinions. He discarded the idea. Pushing Ellen against her family served to only drive her away from him. He didn't want that so soon, not until he'd found a reason to fall out of love with her.

He heard Sam ride up, recognizing Scamp's hooves from the sound they made on the rocky ground. Del didn't look at him when Sam said, "Have you thought about a trim? You've not cut that mess since university, I'll bet."

He ran his fingers through his hair, separating the strands so they'd dry faster. "It is not a mess. I keep myself neat."

"You do. I'll give you that." They rode on for a while before Sam continued, "Do you want to talk about it?"

"There is nothing to say. *Monsieur* has a small world. Too small to allow my humanity." Each word hurt his heart to say as much as it had hurt his mind to think.

"His opinion is not the truth."

"I know *et merci* for saying so." He glanced over at Sam. "Practicality says I need to move on, not loiter around here with such meanness in people."

Laughing, Sam asked, "What is telling you to loiter near Ellen?"

"My heart." Del waited for a while but his friend had nothing to add. So much hovered unsaid between them. Silence never bothered him. In fact, he usually relished the quiet, but this time, he felt the words pulled from him as if some other being controlled his tongue. "She is both unremarkable and unforgettable. I wondered last night if she was merely the forbidden, if I wanted her only because Monsieur said no." He shrugged. "But when I saw how she and the children fell into the water, I feared losing her to the river. Is it that she's an enigma or my true love?"

"Miss Winslow? We are talking about her, correct?"

Del frowned, not liking the amusement he heard in his friend's voice. "Of course. Who else?"

"No offence. She's a sweet lady, one of the finest in our group. She's so studious, so mannerly, and very much against the natives. Ellen has made it very clear her disdain for your people."

More to himself than his friend, Del asked, "This woman, is she worth my convincing? Can she unlearn old habits?"

"Spending your time on wooing her is yours to decide. As for her low opinion of your kind, I suppose anyone could change their mind." He paused while Scamp scrambled up an incline. "We're going to need a guide along the Snake River. You could stay and see if Ellen's affection is worth the effort."

Grinning, Del retorted, "You've never needed a guide before, but when I think of her, I'm persuaded. Do you think the others will allow me to lead when necessary?" He drew up equal to Sam on the ridge, the dry creek bed below. "Not all are accepting."

Looking back at the group following them, Sam squinted his eyes. "What they want at this point doesn't matter as much as their safety."

His eyebrows rose at his friend's confidence. Del kept his own counsel. Sam must have been satisfied at the number of wagons because he clicked at Scamp to walk faster. With an accompanying nudge to Pomme, they kept up.

The sun cast a shadow to the east. Del unbuttoned his cuffs and rolled up the sleeves. The cool breeze refreshed enough from the midday heat to cause little chill bumps on his skin. They scouted so far ahead that Del heard the loose gravel crunch under their horses' hooves instead of the wagons' wheels. Topping a hill, he saw how the low, sage green hills hid a spring fed pond. He knew without asking they'd be stopping there for the noon meal.

They paused on the high ground. The low mountains loomed blue in the distance. The pond shimmered in the valley below, reflecting the sky while giving them a place to rest for lunch. The creek they'd been beside all day emptied into the larger pool of water. Their group rolled along the flat, wide creek bed. Sam and Del eased down the decline, steering their horses around the sage and clumps of yellow wildflowers. He spotted Marie alone and thought of a plan. Maybe Mrs. Warren could help him in courting Ellen.

Del stopped, surprised at the idea. Court? All of a sudden, his feelings for the girl seemed too much too soon. *"Non,"* he said to himself. He just wanted her to have a better opinion of him as a person. And possibly steal a few kisses too. Del stopped just short of laughing. "Sam, excuse me for *un moment, s'il vous plaît.*"

"Of course," said Sam over his shoulder.

He eased Pomme closer to the wagons, catching up with the lagging Marie. *"Bonjour,* madam." He dismounted a few feet away from her. *"Comment allez-vous?"*

"Très bien, merci. Et vous?"

"Bien, d'accord." Hearing her speak his language was such a relief. He knew he grinned like a fool. English was such work no

matter how high his skill in it. Its difficulty must be why he felt tongue tied around Ellen. He glanced over to see Marie looking at him.

She grinned. "Penny for your thoughts, Adelard, as if I didn't already know."

Del shook his head. "I can't admit to thinking of a certain woman."

"Good, because I'd hate to see my friend hurt."

Her statement took him by surprise. He knew some of what Ellen had said about him, but was there more? He had to know. "Hurt? How could I do that?"

"Probably in the same way she could hurt you."

"Not possible." The words that were so difficult to say to Sam still hurt when repeated. "I don't regard her as a savage and sub-human."

"It is possible. She's beginning to care a lot for you." Marie smiled at him. "She said a lot of complimentary things about you after the rescue. I'm not sure if she wanted me to tell you anything. She might want to give her opinion to you herself."

His practical side warred with his romantic side. He had a chance? Del wanted to believe so but didn't quite trust his new friend. He needed more information. "This discussion is somewhat futile. Her father has forbidden us to talk."

"Do you think she'll abide by his decision?"

He shrugged, wanting to be casual. "As much as she can, despite my tempting her."

"Are you sure doing so is a good idea? I'd hate to see her punished for your actions."

"As would I." He held his hand out for her to hold, steadying her as she inched down a steep decline. "She's in no danger, I can promise."

She waited until he led his horse down as well. "Thank you for the reassurance."

Lucky rode up to them and Del asked her, "We can continue this later?"

"Oui. I'd like that."

Lucky spoke first. "Ma'am, Mr. Du Boise, we're stopping at Emigrant Springs up ahead. Mr. Granville wants to make camp there this afternoon and tonight. He thinks it might be the last good water until Smith's Fork."

Del welcomed the chance to hunt and turned to Marie. "Madame, I see your family up ahead." He swung up onto his horse and nodded. *"Au revoir."* After turning north he spotted Sam and waved. When his friend returned the signal, Del knew he understood and nudged Pomme into a gallop. He'd need to get some distance between the emigrants and any possible game. A couple of miles later he spotted a valley with more water than most. He grinned at the thought. Out here more water could mean as little as a handful. Wind from the north helped him decide to dismount and leave Pomme to graze what little grass there was. Del crept forward into the breeze, not wanting to startle any animals nearby. He hoped for a deer but would settle for anything. Step by step, Del inched closer to the muddy water. A clump of shrubbery grew on the east side. He watched the leaves to see if a hiding animal moved within them. Pausing, he slid an arrow from the quiver and detached his bow from where it rested. He loaded the arrow, ready. Del held the pose, moving only his legs to ease forward without a sound. A gust blew the smell of water to him. He breathed in deep, enjoying the aroma, and kept his eyes sharp for any sort of movement.

A rustle he saw more than heard moved the grass beyond the wind's usual motion. The twitching nose of a rabbit poked out from the blades. Del held his breath, willing his heartbeat to slow. A minute later, the animal's head stretched out to test for predators. Seemingly satisfied, the rabbit hopped forward to the muddy pond's edge and bent to drink. Del quickly double-checked his aim.

The arrow shot through the animal's head. Birds hidden among the branches flew away with a rush. After a few twitches, the body lay still. Del straightened from the slight crouch he'd instinctively adopted, certain a place like this would never have just one rabbit. Taking out an arrow, he loaded the bow and took a step forward. Another nose stopped him cold. He held his pose. As the second animal sniffed around the dead animal's body, he secured his aim and fired. Both animals lay together. Del put up his bow, satisfied with the amount of meat. Overhunting made finding game difficult already. No need in him killing more than necessary and upsetting nature's balance.

He picked up the animals, leaving in the arrows. Later he'd remove and wash them. Now, they made a handy way to carry the hunt. He sat astride Pomme and rode back to the camp. He kept a subtle watch for her but didn't see Ellen at the pond or near the Granville wagons. Later, he hoped, knowing he needed to find a plausible reason to talk with her. He glanced around the camp. Sam wasn't there, but his men were. Lefty sat against a wagon wheel while reading. Lucky and Arnold sat on the other wagon's tailgate and played cards.

Uncle Joe knelt by the campfire, stoking it into a good flame. Catching sight of Del as he approached, the older man stood. "Looks like you have something for me to cook tonight. It's early enough for a stew. We can each flay one and I can butcher them while you rinse the skin."

Del held out one of the animals. "They're so fresh, I haven't had the chance to drain them."

Taking the offering, Joe led him over to the lowered tailgate. "I figure some rice and dried peppers I've been saving might go good with the meat." He hung up one of the rabbits by the back feet and began skinning the animal.

Spying a similar loop on the other side of the tailgate, Del did the same. After a few strategic cuts, both pulled off the pelt like a man pulled off his socks. A few minutes passed before he realized how quiet they were. He exchanged a rabbit for a pelt with Uncle Joe and put them in an empty pail. "I'll wash these and return to help butcher."

"Better hurry, these won't take long," Joe said, continuing his work.

He nodded, going to the pond with the two skins. Del rinsed out the blood since any left behind would stain the leather. He'd not thought to ask if Joe wanted the fur or just the skin. Either way, he wanted to return a perfect product since the man was doing the brunt of the work tonight. Once satisfied the flesh was clean, Del shook the excess water from the pelts. He placed them on grass high enough to keep them off the ground. Scrubbing the dried blood from the pail took little time, and soon he headed back to camp with fresh water and the furs.

After giving the work a quick examination, Joe said, "Good job, young man. I suspect you've done this a time or two."

Del chuckled. "Yes, two, maybe more. Do you have the soak for them?"

"Not yet, but I have a plan." He hopped in the wagon, careful to not upset the pot of rabbit meat. After some rustling around, he emerged with a large jar in hand. "This'll do until I get the solution mixed." Joe hopped to the ground. He packed the skins in the jar, filling the remaining space with the fresh water Del had brought. "There. I can start these soaking proper after dinner. I have some skins ready for pulling, so that'll free up my good jar." Del watched as Joe poured the rest of the fresh water into the stew pot. Dried peas and a few rice grains floated on top. "That little container is good, but my pickle jar keeps hides agitated enough I don't have to check until time's up." Joe set the cook pot on the fire. "Boss told us you'd be along for at least a week, so they'll be ready for you by then."

"Thank you, but I have plenty. Keep them for yourself, *s'il vous plaît*." Seeing Joe's frown, Del laughed. "I insist unless you have too many."

"Naw, I could always use new fur for winter." He put the jar back into the wagon properly. "Just wanted to be fair about it, since you shot them and all."

"I appreciate your concern but know you are a connoisseur of fine pelts." Del nodded toward his horse. "Excuse me, I must settle in Pomme for the night." At Uncle Joe's nod, he went to the animal, loosening and removing the saddle. He led Pomme to the pond for a drink then let him graze with the rest of the herd. Del kept watch for Ellen or one of her family members while on his errand but saw no sign of them. He returned to camp when done with his horse's care, and spying Sam there, he said, "The work is finished, dinner smells cooked, and you're here. Your timing is impeccable as usual."

Sam grinned at the jibe, setting aside his guidebook. "I did the difficult work of herding people."

Uncle Joe laughed. "Sometimes, skinning rabbits sounds a lot better." He stirred the food. "Eating time, boys."

Lefty hopped up and distributed the dishes and cutlery to everyone. Each man held out his plate for Joe and then settled in to eat. The first bite made him glad he shared with the others. Del would have roasted the meat over an open fire. He glanced around, enjoying how they all focused on their own food.

Finished first, Lucky leaned forward. "Is there more?"

Joe nodded. "Another half round for everyone, I'd guess." He dished up more for Lucky and the men as they held out their plates. Serving himself last, he set aside the pot to cool.

Arnold nudged Lucky and asked, "Reckon we get to wash up?"

"Probably," the other man replied and began rounding up the plates and forks.

Lefty stood, using his good arm to give Arnold the dishes. "I'll make sure the stock is secure for the night."

As the three younger men departed, Joe eased to his feet. "I have some mending to do. No sense in putting it off until tomorrow."

Del glanced up at the sky as the man rummaged around in the wagon. High clouds reflected the setting sun's orange light, giving everything a bright glow. The fire's warmth in front of him and Sam kept the cool night air at bay. He stared into the flames, hoping Marie stopped by for a visit this evening. She was a lovely woman. He hoped to talk about Ellen, his infatuation leading him to ask everything Marie might know about her. Maybe learning more details, unsavory ones in particular, would cure him of this interest he had. "Will we have evening guests?"

"Not formally." Sam paused, then grinned. "I've spoke to a few who might stop by to see what ground we're covering tomorrow."

Lucky and Arnold returned, distracting them both. Arnold hung up the pail and retrieved his journal. Lucky put away the dishes then reappeared from the tail end of the wagon with an instrument case and polish rag. Soon, both were busy, one writing, the other buffing fingerprints from his bugle.

Sam leaned back with his book upside down on his lap, open to keep his place. "Lefty should have returned by now. Wonder what's keeping him?"

Del offered, "Perhaps some young woman needed his care as well?" His friend snickered then looked past him as if something caught his attention. Del turned to see Marie approach and waved for her to join them. At last he had another chance to discuss Ellen with her.

"Good evening, gentlemen." She stepped into the firelight. "Is there room for me?"

Del scooted further away from Sam and patted the ground beside him. "Always, *ma coupin*. Have a seat between us."

Once Marie settled in, Sam leaned over to her. "Lefty is

checking on the animals, Jenny is staying at her family's camp this evening, and Ellen said she'd try to be here later in the evening."

"Thank you for answering my question before I asked." She cleared her throat and turned to Del. "Do you plan on staying here if Ellen joins us tonight?"

He saw her smirk. Wanting something to do with his hands, Del scooped up a handful of pebbles from behind him. He tossed them one by one into the fire. "I try to stay away, yet always find a reason to see her." As he threw the last two, the futility of winning over Ellen and defying her father overwhelmed Del. "Why do I do this when there are more important matters in my life?"

"Such as?" Marie asked.

Del leaned back, resting his hands behind him, and crossed his legs at the ankles. He watched the flames flickering beyond his feet. "Such as anything else except convincing Mr. Winslow I don't have designs on his daughter."

"Ah," Sam said. "But don't you?"

He paused before answering, unsure if they needed to know everything in his heart. Seeing the other men preoccupied with their tasks and hobbies, he shrugged. "I might or might not."

"More like you do and you do." Sam laughed at Del's scornful look. "Or are you interested in her as more than a temporary lady friend?"

After a quick search of his heart, he stopped just short of nodding. He grinned at Marie. "Every woman interests me more than as a temporary friend. Including you, *ma coupin*."

She laughed and shook her head. "Are you sure I'm yours? Or has the meaning of *coupin* changed in Canada to mean something less than a girlfriend?"

"Girlfriend?" Sam's eyebrows rose. "But you call every woman that. Which isn't a surprise now that I think about it."

Despite Marie's teasing tone, Del felt somewhat chastised. Maybe he had been rudely familiar in his address of her. He glanced at and ignored Sam's smug grin. "Forgive me, I've been too familiar with you. I'm not so much Canadian but French."

She patted his knee as if reassuring him. A movement behind Del seemed to catch her eye and she waved. "Ellen! Hello! Please join us! Mr. Du Boise was just explaining his citizenship in our two countries."

"Canada and the United States are the two countries?" She

carried a little journal and pencil. Still in Marie's dress, Ellen settled in at a discreet distance from the couple.

"More as in France and the United States," said Sam

"You're truly a French citizen?" Settled in, Ellen gave him her full attention.

"Yes, I am." He strained to concentrate on issues; difficult to do when she stared at him. He cleared his throat and continued. "The United States won't grant automatic citizenship to native people. Being born on its soil doesn't matter. Only if a person is lighter than my buckskins are they granted such an honor."

Her brow furrowed, she said, "I should think the native peoples would automatically be citizens, if they chose."

"*Non.*" He shook his head. "Not of the US. France is more inclusive, so, I claim its citizenship and it claims me."

Ellen smiled at him. "Have you ever been to France, or is it a distant thought and land?"

Del usually had plenty to say, but now, the firelight shining in her eyes held him captive. He liked how she looked at him. Did she know her face expressed her feelings? "I have been and lived, *ma coeur.*" He glanced at Sam to quell any remarks. "Then came back home."

"Did you like it there?" asked Marie. "I've never been, though my father was born there and came here soon after. He didn't remember anything, so you must tell me everything."

Sam laughed. "If he tells you everything, we'll be here all night. He's not had as many conquests here in the Territories. Unlike overseas, he's a face in the crowd instead of a face to crowd."

Del took the ribbing with a good nature he didn't feel. Deciding to give Sam a taste of what he dished out, Del used an even tone and said, "You are forgetting your own escapades with the fairer gender." Addressing Marie, he went on, "Our Samuel snuck out of many, many windows in the predawn when we were in France." The other man stopped smiling. "There were even a few he did not have to pay to enter."

"My goodness, Sam! You told me when we first met you'd never had need of...." Marie glanced at Ellen. "Need of a saloon."

He smirked at her polite way of saying brothel. Not liking Ellen's confused expression, he reassured her, "It is all in jest. The girls liked the idea of Sam being an uncouth American and found his accent appealing. Our friend here was the novelty all the ladies liked."

"I see. Well, I suppose we've established the women there are very friendly." She batted her lashes at him. "What was the countryside like, or did you see any while lurking around at night?"

Sam laughed. "She has you there, Del."

He chuckled at her retort while ignoring his friend. "The country is beautiful in a tame way. The mountains seem to hold up the sky, while every city's street follows the curve of its river. Row after row of grapes hang from fence-like structures." He looked at Sam. "What are they called?" Back to Ellen, he added, "No matter, the fruit hangs from the vine, begging to be picked, but you don't take a single one."

"You did," Sam chided.

Del laughed. "Yes, and an angry grower's pellet gun is why now I don't."

"How long were you there?" Ellen asked.

He liked her curiosity and her interest thrilled him. Noticing how Sam and Marie's voices lowered, Del took advantage of the chance to talk with Ellen while the others were preoccupied. "Two years for university. Sam and I met studying law. I wanted to learn how to navigate in both worlds of my parents."

"Oh, good! You answered two questions in one. So then you came back?" asked Ellen.

"I did. While I love my father's country, I understood why he called Canada home." He shrugged. "The land has a wildness that speaks to me and is where I belong." He indicated her journal. "May I ask you questions now, or must I read this to learn your secrets?"

"You can ask anything and I'll answer what I can." She held up her diary. "This has nothing secretive in it. My father thinks he's sneaking when he takes and reads it. I've had to tell him that he can have my journal any time he likes. I have no secrets."

The breach of her privacy bothered him. "Ah, so you write nothing from your heart?"

"Not at all. So, what's in my heart and mind isn't in here. I learned early anything I write might be used against me." She opened her little book and began doodling little squares on a page already full. "Instead of writing frustrations, I scribble like this." She stopped, smiling at him. "It's a little wasteful of a good pencil,

I admit."

He saw it for the emotional outlet it was and asked, "So you have no confidant?"

"Not really, but then do I need someone?" Ellen put her pencil in her book as if a placeholder. "I don't think so. I'm pretty self-sufficient that way." She hugged the journal to her chest. "Marie and Jenny are good friends and I can talk to them so that helps."

"The two ladies have romantic interests. Do you as well or does he wait for you in Oregon Territory?"

She glanced at Marie and Sam then down at her journal. "I don't. If someone waited for me, what you and I, well…I'd be very ashamed."

His blood seemed carbonated with happiness. "*Je,* I understand. No one has claimed your hand." Del held out his own hand. "Speaking of which, how has it been today?"

"Not bad." She placed her wrist in his palm. "It's healing too slow for my tastes."

He grinned, making little massaging circles on the injury. Del examined her face, looking for traces of tension from pain. Her relaxed expression reassured him. "An injury to a limb is always such. If it healed before it was harmed only that would be fast enough for me."

Ellen laughed. "I agree. Thank you for this. It makes my wrist feel better."

"My pleasure." He spoke in a quiet voice intended for her only. "I am glad there's no man other than family in your life." Del looked deep into her eyes, hoping she understood. "Very glad. I also would like to know when you need a friend." He felt the pulse in her wrist beat faster.

"If not for my father's decree, I'd already count you as one of my dearest friends." She looked at his hands cradling hers as he caressed. "You've saved my brothers' lives. You are already a good man, and nothing Pa says can change that fact."

Sam broke them out of their reverie. "Miss Winslow, I hate to break up what seems to be an intense chat. It's getting late, however, and I think your father would be happiest if you camped with them tonight."

She got to her feet. "I know he would. And after today's events, I'm exhausted."

Marie took Sam's arm. "If you'll see me back to my wagon, Adelard can walk Ellen to her camp."

Ellen looked from Marie to Del. "Maybe only halfway."

"Halfway, then." He'd take whatever time he could with her. Trouble was, halfway gave him little time to convince her the stars shone at night just for her. He'd not even get the chance to convince her how suitable he was as a friend. She began walking toward her family and he followed.

She stopped and looked around them. With a nod, Ellen took his arm and pulled him out of the protective wagon circle. "I've been thinking about you lately, Mr. Du Boise, and feel the need to apologize."

Her actions surprised him. "There's no need, *ma coeur.*"

"I do, and that begs another question. What does macoor mean? I hope nothing too familiar."

He grinned. "Sadly, it's very familiar. I'm calling you my heart."

"Oh. Yes, that is far too intimate. We can be friends, not sweethearts."

"I'll remember to call you *mon amie,* my friend, instead."

"Very well. Thank you. Keeping to such proprieties will keep us both healthy." She walked past him back into the circle's security. "You'll be an interesting person to know. I look forward to hearing more about life among the natives."

"I do as well." When she gave him a wry look, he realized his gaffe. "I mean I'll enjoy telling you more about life among my mother's people."

"This is where we should stop, Mr. Du Boise."

Del kept quiet, unwilling to ask for anything more than friendship and have her answer spoil his mood. He enjoyed having caught her attention too much. "Goodnight, *mon amie.*"

"Good night." She paused. "Maybe we'll talk tomorrow?"

"I hope so." He turned only after seeing her disappear around the Winslow wagon's corner. Grinning, he strolled to Sam's camp. Little nagging fears of Mr. Winslow's reaction to him chatting with Ellen kept his happiness minimal. He shrugged off the feeling. He reached his friends and saw how the men had prepared bedrolls for everyone, including him. The three younger men slept like exhausted puppies. Joe read a well-worn book while a reclining Sam stared up at the stars. Without a sound, Del slipped into his bedroll.

"Hey," Sam sat up onto one elbow. "Causing mischief among my people tonight?"

Del squelched a chuckle. "Yes, per usual, I scalped women, killed babies, and tied elderly to trees before setting them on fire."

"Good. I'd hate to think of you going against your natural tendencies."

He glanced over at his friend, giving him a death glare. Sam's smile was contagious and Del grinned too. "*Merde.*"

"*Merci.*" Sam put his hands behind his head. "I'm happy just as long as everyone isn't trying to kill everyone else."

He wondered how much his friend knew of Winslow's meanness. "I suspect her father has a temper."

"I know for certain he does. Hell, everyone knows he does after the Green River crossing and his temper tantrum."

"It's more than once. Last night, she angered him by staying to dinner with us, me."

Sam shook his head. "I've seen him angered, but never violent."

"Such men hide their tendencies well. Do we pretend not to see until something serious happens?"

"I can't keep you from Miss Winslow, can I?"

The question was more a statement of fact, and Del grinned at his friend. "I try, but no, I can't resist." He heard Sam's disgusted sigh and shifted to a more comfortable position. Remembering Ellen's flinching where he had touched her sore spots hurt his heart. He frowned, itching to give Jack a taste of his own medicine. The man deserved to feel what he inflicted on his daughter. Somewhere in imagining the war his defending her would cause, he fell asleep.

He woke to the air hanging heavy, dark, and cold. If the embers glowed any brighter, he'd be able to see his breath. As it was, the stubborn sun seemed to hug the eastern horizon. Del sat up, listening for anything awry. Nothing seemed out of place. His warm bedroll lured him back in, the soft fabric a siren song against his skin. He eased back down and snuggled deep under the blanket.

Lying there, he smelled the distinct perfume of rain. Wind from the northwest confirmed his prediction. Del made a mental note to put his oilcloth poncho at the top of the saddlebag. He flipped over onto his stomach and rested his chin on his folded hands. Staring at nothing, he wondered what the day might bring other than a drenching.

"Psst. Psst."

Del lifted his head and looked in his feet's direction for where the sound came from. He recognized a child's voice, just not the exact child speaking. "Yes?"

"Are you awake, Mr. Do Bose?"

Skeeter Winslow? He might have known the boy would find an excuse to talk. Del rolled over and turned his back to him. "No."

After a little rustle and a grunt, Skeeter tapped his shoulder and whispered, "When you wake up, can you take me back to my ma and pa?"

"Why aren't you there now?"

"I went to potty and got lost."

Del gritted his teeth to not laugh at the obvious fib. "Lost? Are you sure?"

"Yeah."

"Skeeter?"

"I wasn't lost. I wanted to see you."

He took a deep breath to keep from chuckling loud enough to wake up the others. Del turned to face the boy. "Thank you for being honest with me, but you need to go back to your family now."

"Can I ask questions when you walk me back to them?"

Del almost laughed at the boy's assumption of an escort. Maybe the child knew him too well. "Certainly. Let's go." He slid out of his bedroll without moving the covers, wanting to preserve as much warmth as possible for when he came back. Skeeter held out his hand for him to take. With a sigh, he held hands with the child. "What is your first question?"

"Have you ever scalped someone?"

"No. I haven't and don't plan to do so."

"Do you need to paint your face soon? It's been bare for a long time now."

He chuckled at how Skeeter's long time equaled his two days. "Not soon. I wear paint for ceremonies like weddings and funerals. I've not worn true war paint."

"I suppose that's good. War seems bad."

"I agree, and it is bad for everyone." He paused. "Here is your family's wagon. Get some rest. Tomorrow starts soon."

"Sure, Mr. Do Bose."

Del waited for a moment to make sure the boy got into bed. He fought the urge to search among the bundles for Ellen. But then, didn't he have to examine each one to make sure everyone was secure? Pleased with his excuse, he looked over each person and lingered a little longer at Ellen's sweet face. He shook his head at the absurdity of his thoughts and moved on to Skeeter. Satisfied he was tucked in, Del went back to his own bedroll. As soon as he was comfortable, he heard Sam stir.

"Did I hear something?"

"*Oui.* Skeeter Winslow needed help."

"This time of night?"

"Seems so."

Sam rubbed his eyes. "It's freezing."

Seeing his friend's breath in the frosty air, Del looked up at the sky to see the dawn. "And it's morning."

"I seem to remember waking up with you at University in worse condition but feeling better than this."

Del chuckled. "You are too young to be such an old man."

"On a morning this cold, everyone is an old man."

"It's no use sleeping while the day draws so near." He sat up, fighting his own unwillingness to begin so early and in such frigid conditions.

"I reckon not." Sam sighed. "How about you check our stock while I build up the fire?"

"*D'accord*, and I'll bring back water for coffee."

"Good man."

Del paused by the wagon only long enough to grab the water bucket. He saw Lucky still on guard and nodded. He knew their animals were all sound with him at the helm. Del continued on to the pond's edge while keeping an eye open for Ellen. He loitered but didn't catch sight of her before filling the pail. At camp, the fire roared and the sleepy men looked up at him as he approached. "Everything is well." He gave the water to Sam who filled the coffee pot before placing it on the fire grate.

Arnold added what was left of the water to the flour and stirred batter. While Lefty and Joe put away most of the bedding, Sam added thin sliced bacon to a hot pan. The meat sizzled, its smell making Del's stomach growl.

Lucky walked up to them. "Is breakfast ready yet? 'Cause I'm ready for it."

"Not quite," Arnold replied.

"Should I play some music?"

Del laughed before catching himself and Sam glared at him. "Do we have time?" he asked Sam.

"Doesn't look like it. Have a seat Lucky and leave the music for later to get us moving." The boss dished up everyone's plates.

Arnold added the biscuits, which looked suspiciously like pancakes to Del. He stifled a shrug and ate the flat bread. Everything tasted better thanks to hunger. One by one, each man finished, putting his dishes into the empty water pail. When Del saw Lefty begin to pick up the washing, he intervened. "Monsieur, let me clean them."

After a look to Sam who nodded, Lefty straightened. "Sure, sir. I reckon there are plenty of other chores to do before we go."

Del grinned, scooping up the wash, and headed toward the pond for another chance to see Ellen. He knew Sam had suspected his motives and appreciated his friend allowing him to do this task. Plenty of other people met him on their way to and from the water. Most looked at him as if he were a loaded weapon, while others in their group knew him well enough by now. Him wearing Sam's shirt helped give him an air of civility, he suspected. Never mind, he dismissed his usual irritation. He merely wanted to see Ellen, make sure her wrist healed, and maybe see her smile at him.

"Good morning."

He enjoyed the sound of her voice. "Good morning, *ma coeur*. How are you?" Pausing for only a moment, he glanced over at her. "You're looking well, as usual." A slight pink stole over her face. Her shyness warmed his heart.

"Thank you, Monsieur, as do you." She focused on her dishwashing. "It's lovely now, but I'm sure we'll catch rain later. We might want to hurry and get moving."

With a start, he realized his own task sat ignored. "I agree." Del began cleaning, trying to think of something else to say. He hurried after seeing her finished stack of dishes. Being done at the same time meant he might walk her back to the camp. "Your brothers, they are good too? Your mother and father?"

"We're all fine, thank you." She placed the last dish back in her bucket. "I suppose you are fine. You look so anyway. I mean, no dark circles under your eyes, so you slept well."

"I did, *merci*, thank you for noticing." Did she wait for him? He snuck a peek over at her. Ellen sat there, staring out across the water. His heart did a little flip. She might be reluctant to return to her family, he chided his hopeful thoughts, not eager to walk back with him. The girl disliked his heritage, he reminded his burgeoning optimism. Checking the last fork for cleanliness and satisfied, Del put it in the bucket. "May I walk with you back to the camp?"

"Yes, I'd like that."

"Only as far as the first wagon?"

"I'm sorry, but yes. That would be best."

Halfway between the pond and their group, Lucky's bugle gave the signal to start. "We ended in time, no?"

"We did indeed." She walked a little faster as they neared the others. "Thank you for the company."

"My pleasure." He slowed to let her go on ahead. Her cheerfulness brightened his day, and Del didn't want her father's anger to dim Ellen's face one bit. Once she disappeared around a wagon's corner and out of his sight, he hurried to put away the dishes.

Sam already sat on his horse. "About time, lazy."

Del shrugged, knowing the truth and certain his friend did too. He rushed to get Pomme ready, putting on the light saddle. As soon as his foot hit the opposite stirrup, his horse trotted to catch Sam and Scamp. Like yesterday, they scouted in front.

The men settled into an easy walk once ahead of the group a ways. The calm morning grew overcast as they rode over the rolling hills. A short stubbly grass covered the ground, spotted with sagebrush. When it began to rain, both men ignored the wet until the drizzle turned into huge drops. As they both shrugged into their individual oilcloth ponchos, Sam said, "I'd like to keep going while the ground is firm." He raised an arm and made a stirring circle. "Lucky will signal if the wheels start sticking for anyone."

The covering kept him warm and mostly dry despite how wet and cold his head became. He'd be glad when the sun appeared. Not until late morning did the rain stop. Even then, the sky stayed cloudy. Mud sucked at the horses' hooves, adding a squish sound to their every step.

Their group trailed behind them as he and Sam rode to the

spiny hill ahead. The sharp stone ridges rising vertically from the ground reminded Del of feathers along an irritated bird's back. A native trading village was usually underneath the rocky outcrop. The grass grew longer here than where they'd been so far, and stubby trees grew in clumps along the river's edge. He knew when his friend stopped what Sam had in mind. Their group rolled to them while they waited.

The wagons drew up in a semi circle along the river's bank. Both men dismounted and staked out their horses to eat and drink. When most of the people had a family member there, Sam said, "Everyone going to the village to trade can head over with me and Del. Otherwise, we'll spend noon here before heading up the fork for the best camping."

Del scanned the crowd and found Ellen. She stood with her father, who scowled and walked away from the group. When he left, she followed. Others hurried and shuffled to gather items to possibly trade. He waited with Sam, not intending to barter for anything himself. The sour faced older Warren woman stood with them. Miss Jenny came up, chatting with Lucky. Del couldn't catch what they said to each other and didn't try to listen. He'd been around enough love struck youngsters to have a guess. Hearing a rustle next to him, Del anticipated Sam's speech. Before his friend could say anything, Ellen walked up to them holding a cloth bag. He winked at her, delighted by the flush in her cheeks.

"Please excuse my delay."

"It's no matter, Miss Winslow. I'm not as familiar with this tribe, so it'd be best if we all stayed together. Shall we go?" Sam said and led the way forward.

Del kept up with his friend and resisted the urge to lag behind with Ellen. He glanced back to see her chatting with Jenny and Lucky. When he turned forward, Del caught Sam's smirk. "*Non, mon ami*, I've seen you stare at Mrs. Warren when you think no one is looking."

"Have I been too obvious?"

"Just to those who know you." They entered the trading area, Shoshone tipis in a row on the east side and the river along the west. Various people sat in front of their homes. Items for sale sat out on blankets. Children kicked up dust as they played. Their parents scolded them in their own language before going back to a simple English for the whites.

Sam paused at an array of moccasins. He knelt, asking Del, "How much Shoshone do you speak again?"

"Very little. My English is better."

"That bad, huh?"

The latter half of their group arrived and he said to Ellen, "I'm much better at French and its romance." Marie and Lucky rewarded him with a laugh while Ellen and Jenny just frowned. They walked on, engrossed in all the available goods.

Calling to him from his crouched position, Sam held up two pairs of shoes. "Del, which do you think Marie would like more?"

He glanced down at the two before continuing his watch of Ellen as she neared the center of the small town. When she and the others stood in front of the chief's home, he and several of the men with him stood. "Either are beautiful and would suit." He nodded at the young woman kneeling behind the display. "Who is your chief?"

She blushed before looking down and answering, "Running Cloud."

Sam decided on a pair of shoes, holding out a silver dollar piece as if asking if she'd take it as payment. The girl nodded, accepting the trade. "How do I say 'thank you'?" he asked Del in English.

"You are welcome," the young lady said.

Grinning, Sam got to his feet, tucking the moccasins in his waistband for safekeeping. "The pleasure is mine. Good day."

They walked on, wanting to catch up to the others and Del had to tease him. "Buying a gift for one woman and flirting with another? Who is the romantic here?" His jovial mood faded when they neared the others. Tension clouded the air like a late fall fog. A solid line formed by Running Cloud and what looked to be his best warriors looked ready to attack or defend.

"You say this is the man I speak to?" At Lucky's nod, Running Cloud addressed Sam. "Your woman, the tall one. What will you barter for her?"

Sam narrowed his eyes. "She's not for trade."

A younger man came up from behind Running Cloud and said, "I am Pointed Nose, future chief of the Shoshone! Everything is for sale. How many horses do you want?"

Del stepped up. "None. Don't ask again."

A flash of fury crossed the young man's face and he charged

at Del. Before he could step back, the chief's son pushed him backwards a couple of steps, yelling, "I want the woman! I'll take her myself if there's no trade."

Del grabbed the man by the wrists. "You'll do no such thing. Leave her alone."

"Let go of me! Who are you to speak to me this way? Nothing! You're nothing!" Struggling, he tried pulling out of Del's grip first one way then the next.

While stronger than the chief's son, Del still worked to keep a grasp of him. "Yet, I'm more than you."

"Stop this right now!" Sam stepped up, pushing both of them away by their shoulders. "There's no need for this! Adelard, tell him you two are fighting over my wife."

His breath caught in his throat at first. "*Vous? Non! Je—*" he began to protest.

"Yes, mine! Tell him!"

Sam's voice cut through Del's anger and stopped him cold. Instead of arguing with his friend, he glared at Pointed Nose "The woman is this man's wife. Your attempts are useless. Our fighting is useless." He nodded over at Sam as he held Ellen in his arms. With everyone's attention on them, he kissed Ellen on the forehead and hugged her closer. Del also caught sight of Lucky holding Jenny's hand and wanted to stop another fight before it started. "The two young women are spoken for, no trade for either of them for anything you own."

With a snort, Pointed Nose stomped off back to the center of the village. The chief frowned at both Sam and Del. "You needed to state this claim at the beginning. Now was almost too late. It may still be too late to stop war." He turned without waiting for a reply and followed his son.

The glare he received when Pointed Nose looked back at them over his shoulder unnerved Del. He turned to the whites with him. "I'm sorry everyone, but they are angry. We will need to continue on very soon."

Sam took a deep breath. "I agree. Let's go."

Ellen began, "Sam, I'm sorr—"

"No, don't be. The young man pressed the issue. I know how you feel." His arm still around her, he glanced down at her. "I should have stepped in sooner."

Del had to disagree with his friend's assessment. He cleared his throat, the adrenalin keeping him a little shaky. "*Non*. I should have imagined your solution sooner." He guessed that everyone else felt shaken as well, judging by their silence as they walked back to safety. As soon as they were alone, he would need to warn Sam further. Pointed Nose didn't seem to be the forgiving type, and Del wanted them all to be on guard until out of the area. No one dawdled on his or her way to the wagons. Once there, everyone scattered to their own family.

Del and Sam got on their horses with Sam saying, "Let's bring up the rear in case we're followed. You know more Shoshone than I do. I'll need your expertise if we have guests. Go on back if you want and I'll be there soon. I need to let the other men know what we're doing."

He nodded, steering Pomme to the back of the wagon train. Del went to the end, reaching the Warren's wagon. From the opposite side he heard Ellen and her friends talking. He continued on to the back of the line, not wanting to listen in despite his urge to do so.

Before he cleared the end of the wagon, he heard Ellen say, "I'm not going to be the slave of some animal."

Del gritted his teeth. He'd not made any progress with her in changing the woman's opinion of Native Americans. She'd been grateful and friendly, but because of his actions, not because of him. An uneasy ache settled in his chest. Later, when alone, he'd tell himself how one person's opinion of him didn't mean anything. Even if that person was Ellen. He didn't pay attention to his horse's motion and turned the corner into full view of them.

"Ellen!" Marie exclaimed. At his movement, she looked at him and swallowed before saying, "I know you don't think that."

"You don't know what I think. No one does," the young woman snapped.

Del wanted to stay and argue with her attitude but couldn't, especially since he agreed with her. Pointed Nose had acted like a brute expecting to buy and sell a wife. He'd been a decent enough looking young man. Pointed might have had a chance if he'd behaved with a little more charm. Del sighed, staring up at the sky at his own foolishness. Such a good idea to use good manners with Ellen, he thought to himself, because of all the supreme success he'd had in doing so.

He shook his head, knowing he needed to snap out of this

sarcastic and blue mood before Sam reached him. His mountainous amount of jealousy over Pointed Nose's interest also needed an examination. Del had wanted to snap the young man's neck when he'd threatened to kidnap her.

As Sam rode up, Del faked a grin, silently resolving to sort out his feelings, keep Ellen safe, and convince her he was civilized.

CHAPTER 3

They rolled along the valley and away from the natives' settlement. Ellen trembled when remembering the vicious look in Pointed Nose's eyes. Between his threats and Del's own anger, she fretted as the three women walked. Jenny talked the most with Marie adding in a word or two when necessary. Ellen tried to keep up with the conversation and only listened to every other word. Lost in her thoughts, Lucky's bugle noise startled her. She didn't laugh with the other ladies at how they all jumped at the sound.

"How are we surprised at something that happens every day?" Marie asked.

"His bugle always surprises me," Ellen confessed. "I'm not scared so much as I can't ever remember when he's going to use it."

Jenny sighed. "I love when he plays at night. He's such a talented musician."

Her gaze met Marie's and they both grinned. The girl certainly was partial. The older woman said, "I'll agree. His playing has been a pleasant part of all this." They paused while waiting for the wagons to move into their usual circle for the evening. Several trees grew near camp, some with dead branches under them for tonight's fuel. With plenty of grass, the cattle and other stock had already begun to graze. Marie stepped away from her friends. "Until tonight?"

Ellen nodded, hoping she'd have the chance to meet up after dinner chores. "Until then," she said to Jenny.

"Bye!" The girl waved and headed for her own wagon.

Ellen scanned the horizon, wanting to delay returning to her family and their fussing. A small grove of trees to the west promised additional wood. She'd have to scout a shallow place to cross later when time permitted.

Lucky walked up to her, leading his horse. "Howdy, Miss Winslow. I saw your folks near the tail end, just ahead of the Warrens."

"Thank you, Mr. Lucky."

"Let me walk you over there."

The young man's face glowed, and Ellen knew she wasn't the cause. "Why do I suspect you have an ulterior motive for this?"

His cheeks deepened in color. "I reckon I do."

"Jenny likes you too, in case that's what you wanted to know." Ellen laughed when he blushed even more. "I thought as much! Are we done talking, or would you like to continue?"

"I don't mind seeing you to your wagon, miss. You're a pleasant lady too."

"Thank you. You're a pleasant man as well." She glanced over to see her father staring at them. "Have a good evening."

He tipped his hat at first to her then to Jack Winslow. "Miss, sir."

Ellen gave a quick look around their camp. They'd not been stopped in one place long enough to start chores. Skeeter was most likely off playing, and she'd heard Lucy with Buster in the wagon. The oxen were still yoked, so she stepped toward them.

Before she could do anything, Jack said, "That Mr. Lucky is a fine young man."

She paused, turning to face him with a smile. "He seems to be. My friend Jenny thinks he's hung the moon. Mr. Lucky thinks the same about her." Ellen bit her tongue to stop her babbling.

He shook his head and walked over to her. "Now, if you'd talked to him more in the beginning, he might be your fella. Instead, you have that half-breed lurking around here. I wish he'd just steal what he wants and leave already."

Not censoring her thoughts, Ellen asked, "What makes you think he's here to steal anything?" His furious expression chilled her blood, and she wanted to grab the words back. She tried to placate him. "Mr. Du Boise has been helpful so far. We'd not be here now if he'd not saved us. He's only half Indian, so that's something, right?"

Jack stared at her with evident scorn. "No matter who his daddy was, no matter what good deeds he's done to win over Granville, he's still a filthy Indian who needs killing."

The injustice of such an idea infuriated her. Del being different from them didn't mean he deserved to die. Ellen studied her shoes to avoid his knowing gaze. "I see."

He walked past her to the front of the wagon. "No, you don't. If you did, I'd not have to hear about you cavorting with him every chance you get."

Ellen followed him. She had to convince Pa she'd not been doing anything to encourage Del. "Cavorting? I don't think we—"

"Don't give me that. You know what I mean, trying to talk to him every chance you get, hanging around, hoping he sees you." Jack paused and pointed his finger at her. "Mark my word: One day, you're going to get more of that man than you bargained for. When he slits your throat, none of us will be around to help you."

His words caught her off guard. Alarmed at the idea of Del killing her, Ellen stared at her father. He glared at her and she shuddered at the hate burning there. Maybe it was his feelings for the native showing in his eyes, she rationalized. "I do try to avoid him, Pa, and only speak to him when spoken to." She stared at her feet so he wouldn't guess her true feelings. "I do talk with him only so he won't be angry and start a warpath or something with us."

Jack snorted. "Well, I suppose as long as you weren't too friendly, making him want to carry you off like that other animal wanted to do back there." He smirked and spit on the ground. "Yeah, I heard about that. You need to stop being so whorish with them." He paused before tossing the milk cows' lead ropes to her. "Although, that would make one less mouth to feed around here. Let you be someone else's problem for a change." He laughed and then stopped when he saw her face. "Just joshing. You help out enough. It's no trouble having you around. Lucy needs the help with the boys, so it's good having you with us."

"Thank you, Pa. I appreciate you saying so." She tilted down her chin. Hoping she struck a demure pose, Ellen wished she were a man. A man would get on his horse, maybe make a rude gesture to Pa, and ride off into the mountains.

"You're welcome. Just keep up on the chores and stop jaw jacking with that animal and you'll do fine."

She nodded, and using chores as a reason to escape, began backing away from him. "Yes, sir, if you'll excuse me."

His attention caught by Sam at another family's nearby wagon, Jack waved her away and headed in the trail leader's direction. "See you at dinner," he called over his shoulder.

Ellen let their cows get a drink at the water's edge before staking them out for the night. Returning to unhitch the oxen, she then let them drink before being staked out with the others. She petted each animal. The poor creatures looked as tired as she felt.

She saw a lot of other people caring for their livestock too. Ellen searched for but didn't see Del nearby. She almost enjoyed the certain danger in talking to a man her father detested.

Did Pa know how much more appealing his order made Del? She chuckled. Probably not, or he'd burst a blood vessel. Pa had been nagging Ellen about what a bother she'd been since the boys were born. A person would think he'd be encouraging any man with two legs to take her off his hands. Even a damned dirty Indian, as he liked to call them.

The cows needed milking and she'd need to get fresh cooking water for the beans and rice. She hurried back to the wagon for a jar and a pail for milking. A quick scoop of water half filled the jar, and she kneeled with a pail by one of the cows. Milking gave her quiet time to think, so she took the chance. Her Pa's words about Del pushed their way to the front of her mind.

Yes, heaven forbid she like a man so beneficial to her family. Maybe she'd encourage Del to cart her off to be his slave. Then her father wouldn't have anything to complain about concerning her. He'd have no reason make snide comments like "You're eating our food; you're taking up too much space in our wagon; or when will you pay your own way?" Even better? She'd not have to feel guilty for breathing every day of her life.

A smart, dutiful daughter who wanted to help her family would set her cap for Uncle Joe, even if he were older than her Pa. She'd marry him and forget all about the dangerous and attractive French-Indian with the kind eyes. The same one who'd saved their lives and seemed awfully protective of the entire group.

When done with the milking cow, she headed for the wagon to start dinner. A fire burned hot while Ellen fixed their usual beans and rice mix. The soup cooked as she mixed flour and water with some salt. She stirred the biscuit dough with sharp, hard beats, still irritated at her father's order to ignore Del. She floured her hands and mashed the balls of dough into flat shapes a little too hard. Her palms ached afterward. Rolling the last bit of mix into a ball, she poked two eyeholes with the tip of her finger and made a frowning mouth with her fingernail. She wrinkled her nose at the little face and punched it. Childish, Ellen acknowledged as she turned the mangled face into a regular biscuit, but fun nonetheless.

"Ellen? Oh, there you are! You've started supper? Good girl! Your father will be so pleased."

She straightened at her stepmother's appearance. The woman had a freshly bathed little Buster on her hip. Ellen rubbed the doughy flour from her hands and tickled him under the chin, smiling at his giggle. She replied to Lucy, "I'm glad. It needs to cook a while longer, so I hope he's not in any hurry."

"I saw him with Mr. Norman earlier. Looked like they'll be visiting for a while, solving all the country's problems."

Ellen grinned at her stepmother. "Then we may be a while." Both ladies knew how much Jack liked to debate.

"What may be a while, Ellen?"

She turned to her father, still grinning. "Hello, Pa. We thought you might be talking with Mr. Norm—"

"I'm here now and hungry." He squatted down by the fire and breathed in deep before winking at his wife. "Smells good, honey."

"Thank you, dearest." Lucy glanced over at Ellen and shook her head a little. "It's just more of the same until we get to our new home."

He dipped a biscuit into the broth, wetting it before taking a bite. "Mmmm," he hummed before swallowing. "This is wonderful. You get better every day."

"Oh, well, it's just—"

"No." Jack waved her off with a spoon. "No need to be modest. Dinner is perfect, m'dear." He nodded over at his daughter. "Give Ellen lessons so she can catch a man, will ya?"

The women and children began eating. Halfway through her dinner, Lucy asked Ellen, "You won't mind watching Buster will you, dear?"

She'd much rather spend her time playing with the baby than washing up. "Not at all. It'll be nice to care for such a sweetheart. He's much cuter than the animals and dirty dishes."

Lucy frowned at first before smiling. "You're right, and look, the poor baby is sleepy. Maybe it's best I put him down for the night and let you hurry to your chores."

"I don't mind," she offered, knowing she'd already lost this battle.

Jack held up his dish and utensils for Ellen to take. "The child needs his mother. Get going and I might let you visit that Granville man. He ain't married yet so you might have a chance at him."

"Thank you, Pa." She stood and made quick work of gathering plates and the cook pot. When Lucy started to spread out their beds, Ellen almost sighed in relief that someone else did that chore. She left the light's circle, easing closer to the river.

The night insects hummed in the chilly air. Twilight lingered in the sky. She breathed in deep the fragrance of a warm breeze rising from the sun-heated ground. Every place they'd been had its own scent. Sage overpowered everything and had since Fort Laramie, she figured. But when the wagon wheels stilled, Ellen enjoyed the prairie grass and river water aromas. She blurted out a disgusted noise aloud and with "Oh, God, spare us!" when thinking of the other smells too, like fresh cow chips and rotten meat from dead animals. She glanced around to see if anyone had heard her speaking without thinking. No one was close so she finished up the wash.

She hurried back to their camp when she heard the soft music of Lucky's bugle from the Granville camp. All the Winslows were on their bedrolls, Buster asleep and Skeeter nearly so. She nodded to Pa and Lucy while easing the wash bucket to the ground. Nothing rattled and she straightened before going to Skeeter. She knelt down, giving him a kiss on the forehead. "Goodnight, little buddy."

"'Night, sis. Say hey to Mr. Do Bose for me."

"Of course." She glanced up to see her father staring daggers at her. Ellen gave him a slight shake of her head to reassure him she wouldn't talk to Del at all. Pa's expression eased.

"Be back before too long, girl. And have that Lucky boy walk you home again. I like him."

"I'll try." Ellen stood, stepping away from her brother before shaking the dirt from her skirt. "I'll ask as soon as I can." At Jack's nod, she left for Sam's camp. The further she walked, the easier she breathed. When thinking of encouraging Lucky or Sam to court her, she made a little gagging sound. She'd sooner marry Del than either of them. Ellen stopped short at the idea. Marry him? Did those people even have a marriage vow or did they just capture and enslave the woman they wanted? She looked up at the sky, wondering how to ask Del without insulting him yet again.

"Ma'am?"

She startled a little and turned to see Lefty standing with a rifle slung over his back. Ellen didn't remember the last time she'd heard him speak and replied, "Oh, yes?"

"Can I help you with something?"

"No, I'm fine." Maybe if Lefty was around more, Pa would be satisfied for the rest of the trip and stop working so hard to find prospective husbands for her. On an impulse she asked, "Are you going to Mr. Granville's campfire?"

"Afraid not, ma'am. I'm on watch duty at the moment."

She took a step forward and smiled when he did the same. "I see. I'm sorry if I've caused problems for you and everyone else at the trading post. I didn't mean to do so."

He fell in step with her. "You didn't do anything, ma'am. Some people just can't take no for an answer. Don't matter if they're us or them, I reckon."

"Thank you for saying that, Mr. Lefty."

"It's the truth, ma'am." He paused at the edge of the company's wagon and nodded at the group. "Here you are. Have a nice evening."

She said, "I appreciate the escort, sir." Lefty tipped his hat and disappeared into the night. Ellen turned to the fire where Uncle Joe whittled while Lucky polished the bugle. Del and Sam sat across from the two with Arnold up on the wagon's tailgate above them, reading. They all looked up at her when she drew closer to them. "Good evening, gentlemen. I didn't realize I'd be the only lady here."

Sam waved her over to his side of the fire. "You won't be the only one, just the first. Please have a seat."

"Take mine, mademoiselle. It's extra soft." Del slid away even further from Sam and patted the folded blanket between them. "You'll be safe here."

She accepted their offer only because she knew Pa slept. As soon as she settled in, Ellen felt much too aware of Del sitting beside her. He still wore Sam's clothes. She glanced at him as much as possible without turning her head. His skin glowed in the dim light. She stole a peek at his hands as they rested on his knees. He kept his nails short and clean. She glanced up and across the fire away from him; surprised he'd be so meticulous.

Lucky waved to Marie as she entered the fire's light. "Mrs. Warren! Come over and sit with us." Uncle Joe leaned over and said something in his ear. Lucky grinned. "If you're free to, of course."

"I am free, thank you for asking." She settled in next to Uncle Joe and opposite the fire from Sam, Del, Ellen, and Arnold.

"Thank you too, Joe, for assuming my dance card is full."

The elder man grinned at her. "You're welcome, little lady."

A rustle and Mr. Warren stepping up grabbed everyone's attention. "There you are, dearest! Thank you for cooking dinner. There's none left, it was so very good." Charles settled in beside Marie. "Hester is washing up and might join us later."

Ellen swallowed down the rising bile in her throat at Mr. Warren's mention of his sister. She would never have believed two people could be so craven until she'd encountered them. She leaned a little closer to Del. "I don't suppose siblings have improper relationships among your people, do they, Mr. Du Bois?" she asked in a quiet voice.

"*Que*? Why ask such a thing?"

She almost laughed in surprise at the disgust in his expression. "No?"

"No, it's not something I'd expect you to ask."

Sam cleared his throat and kept his voice low. "Rules and society become more lax out on the trail, I've seen."

Del also kept his tone quiet. "If Miss Winslow's curiosity is piqued, these two must take it too far, *mon ami*."

She tried resisting being loud and nosy but just couldn't keep silent. "Will you evict them from our group, Mr. Granville? Especially when everyone else learns of their crimes?"

He gave her a sad smile. "It's something I mull over during every quiet moment I have."

Ellen nodded, patting Sam's arm in reassurance. He didn't need to mention his feelings for Marie. If everyone knew what she, Sam, and Del did, Charles and Hester would be left alone to find their own way west. A movement outside the fire's circle of light caught her eye as someone approached.

"Whew! Isn't this a lovely night?" asked Hester, taking her brother's offered hand and sitting down beside him. "The river was so pretty, moonlight glinting off of it as if someone had thrown pearls." Hester sighed. "I could have stayed there at the bank all night."

Charles leaned back on his elbows, legs stretched out in front. "It was a sight."

Ellen was certain her face betrayed her disgust and tried to hide it. Not everyone knows, she chided her lapse in control. She put on a neutral expression, the one she used when hiding her anger from her father. If Marie saw Ellen's true feelings, it might hurt her and that would never do. Glancing at Sam to see his reaction, she almost laughed aloud. He shared her disgust and she patted his arm to catch his attention. She shook her head and he chuckled, putting his hand over hers. She felt his muscles relax under her touch and they both looked at Marie.

As the younger Warren disappeared into the dark, Sam asked Ellen, "Now where is she going?"

Del leaned over to his friend while tapping her shoulder. "Should one of us follow madam in case we have unexpected guests?"

"Yes, one of us should and I vote me." Sam eased to his feet.

"*Pardonez moi?*"

"*D'accord.*" He watched the other man leave for a moment. Turning his attention to Ellen, he said, "Now we are alone."

She returned his ornery grin. "In this crowd? I hardly think so."

"We can be alone here." He indicated the others with a nod. "See? They each have their own distractions."

"Maybe so, but—" A distant scream interrupted her, the sound echoing from the north. "Marie?"

Before she could say anything else, Del and Joe jumped to their feet. Joe spoke first. "Did you hear the splash too?"

"Yes," Del said. "Blankets, *si'l vous plait, immediamant.*" He didn't wait for a reply, sprinting off in Joe's direction.

Fueled by panic, Ellen hurried to the Granville wagon with Arnold close behind. She grabbed any available blankets as he took a lantern. He motioned to the remaining Warrens. "Sir, take a lantern, ma'am, you too."

She didn't hear anything but their group's footsteps while hurrying through the night. Arnold was there already, judging by how his light up ahead didn't move. Charles barreled past her and went on. Ellen struggled to catch up and as she neared, she heard him say, "What the hell were you doing, Marie?"

"I accidently fell into the river." She took the blanket Ellen gave her. "Thank you."

Charles retorted, "I know accidently; I didn't think you did this on purpose. Good thing you were headed northwest. No way am I back tracking just for you."

Marie looked at Sam with a weak smile. "There's no need to

worry about it. I'm here safe and sound." Before her husband could say anything else, she added, "You're tired and cranky. Why don't we get some sleep before tomorrow?"

"Thanks for saving her worthless hide." Charles reached out his hand to Sam.

Wrapping up in the blanket Ellen also gave him, Sam hesitated before shaking Warren's hand. "Keeping her alive is my job, sir." He shivered. "Mrs. Warren, you might consider putting on dry clothes and getting warm before catching your death."

Marie nodded. "I will, and I appreciate you saving me tonight. It might have been the Pacific before I could reach shore without your help."

"If you all will excuse me, I'm very tired and am going to bed," said Sam as he walked back to camp. Joe and Lucky fell in step behind him.

Ellen stayed with her friend and the Warrens as they walked back. No one spoke and when they passed the Granville camp she saw how Arnold and Lefty waited for them at the campfire, all their beds laid out for them. She shivered, suddenly realizing how long she'd been without warmth. Ellen turned to say goodnight to Marie, but they'd gone. Growing colder by the minute, she hurried back to her own bed.

Once back at the family campfire, she saw Pa reading in the waning light. He glanced up at her and sneered. A shock of fear raced through her. Did he know about her sitting next to Del this evening? She took another shaky step forward before seeing he held a very familiar book. "Is that my journal?"

"Yes." He turned a page. "I thought I might see how far we've been."

She began breathing again after his answer. Ellen intentionally left out a lot every evening, omitting anything that might have infuriated him during the day. If he didn't remember, he wouldn't complain or get angry all over again. Warming her hands from the fire, she offered, "Some of the writing might be poor. The embers grew dim before I could finish on a few nights or so."

He nodded his approval, handing the book back to her. "You've not written about some of the people I don't like. Good."

Ellen paused to take the journal, checking to see if her stubby pencil was still tucked in the middle. "I figured you wouldn't want to remember them once we're at our new home."

"You figured right." He sat back a little from the fire. "It'll be easier leaving them out if there's nothing to tell, correct?"

Catching his hint, she nodded. "Correct. I will always do whatever I have to do in order to have nothing of that nature to tell." Inwardly, she sighed. Every time she was nervous, she used far too many words.

"Well, good night."

"Good night." She took the dismissal and sat on her bedroll to record today's events. Ellen tried to keep from smiling. She was sure Pa had read her journal hoping to catch her in a lie. She scribbled down the day's events, drawing the distant mountains and other scenes from the day. Upon hearing her father's light snore, she tore a blank page from the back of the journal.

She turned over the little book to use the back as a smooth surface. Glancing at a sleeping Pa and Lucy every so often, she drew a small picture of Del. Ellen bit her lip when done, trying not to laugh at her effort. Ah well, drawing him was fun no matter how poorly done. She wrote his name a few times, some fancy, others in block letters. She even sketched him on his horse. When the page was full on the front and back, she poked it on the end of a stick and pushed it into the embers. The paper flared. She stirred the coals and paper, making sure every little bit burned to ashes. Once finished, she lay back on her bedroll and looked up at the stars. Infatuation with the forbidden was one thing, allowing evidence of it was quite another.

The morning dawned warmer than many before now. Ellen struggled to stand and grimaced over the picture she must present. The rocks and hills they'd traveled the day before yesterday had taken their toll on her body. The others still slept. If they felt as bad when waking as she did now, coffee and food would help. She moved slower than usual while slipping on her shoes, grabbing a pail, and limping. Others seemed tender footed too, and she almost laughed at herself and them. Who knew the term tenderfoot was a real thing? Next, they'd all be growing green horns from their skulls and be true greenhorns. She chuckled at that, kneeling on the matted reeds. Someone doing the same to her left caught Ellen's eye.

Del grinned at her while filling his own water bucket. "Good morning. It's pleasant to hear a laugh so early, especially yours."

"Thank you." She stayed at his level, returning his smile. "I was thinking what tender footed tenderfeet we are and how next we'll be green horned greenhorns too."

"No wonder you laughed. Green horns, like Vikings only without hats."

She laughed. "Exactly!" As he stood, she tried to as well. Very unsteady, she wobbled and swayed toward the water. Del held out his hand and she grabbed hold of him. "Thank you. I'm not ready for a bath just yet. Not until after breakfast anyway."

"My pleasure, *ma coeur.*" He grinned. "I could help you bathe. It's no trouble."

She gasped and then saw the humor in his eyes. Ellen said, "What a kind offer, Mr. Du Boise." His skin warmed where they touched, and she slipped from his grasp in case others watched them together. "I'll keep that in mind if I'm ever unable to bathe myself."

His eyebrows rose. "*Merci beaucoup.* Um, I mean yes, I'd be happy to help."

Ellen chuckled, taking a couple of steps back toward camp. "Sure you will, though I might be very elderly before needing you."

"I can wait, if you'll allow."

She glanced up into his face. Such a hard, lean man with a hint of vulnerability in his expression warmed her heart. She could learn to love someone like him. Realizing how others in their party passed by, Ellen knew her cheeks must be red by now. "There's no need to, not just for me."

"Only for you. Always."

His words shook her and stole the air from her lungs. He had her tongue-tied and Ellen could only mutter, "Yes, well, thank you." She turned, fleeing before Del might say anything else that kept her talking with him. Pa could read her too well and if he walked by, heaven help them both from his fury.

Once away from him, her feet hurt again. She grinned. He was quite a distraction for her to forget the aches. Everyone in her family still slept, so she worked as quickly and quietly as possible. Swinging up into the wagon, she rooted around in the bed, wincing at every loud sound she made. She found the coffee, but the sugar remained out of reach. Just as well, she almost muttered. Pa would have a break from telling her how unnecessary sugared coffee was. She eased back down to the ground. The soles of her feet tingled with pain, and she almost groaned aloud. Was every foot ache going to remind her of Del, now? She grinned at the thought and began building a fire.

She scraped away the damp wood from last night with a rock and started a small fire in the resulting pit. She placed a pail of water with coffee beans on the hook when the flames leaped to life. As low as the fire burned, she had time to milk their cows. She worked fast, breakfast aroma from other camps making her hungrier. Once done, she went back and set the full pan next to the wagon.

Her father and Lucy drank their coffee while cuddled up to the campfire. "We saved you some," Pa said between slurps.

She looked, seeing a few beans and about half a cup remaining. Taking a deep breath and working to avoid any trace of sarcasm, she said, "Oh, thank you."

Pa gave her a warning glare and retorted, "We didn't have to save you a God damned thing, so watch your tone."

"No, sir, I really do appreciate it. You didn't have to save me anything, and I can always make more." She smiled at him so he'd believe her and emptied the remains in her cup, beans too. "Or maybe not, since the fire is already out. That makes this doubly welcome this morning when there's a slight chill to the air, so thank you." She grimaced at her babbling and drank the coffee in nearly one gulp, keeping a bean to chew on as she packed up their camp.

Pa left without a word and she followed. Helping her father with the oxen, she stayed quiet while they worked. He walked away and she went to the back of the wagon to get a pail. The cows might need a little milking, even after last night's session, and having butter at dinner tonight might cheer up everyone. She settled in to work, knowing her father was right about her being grown. She also agreed that he'd done his job in raising her. Every day she stayed with him and Lucy reminded her of how she took away from his new family. Ellen sighed as she finished up with the first cow. She needed her own family or at least her own home. She went to the other cow and began work. The desperate need to marry anyone Pa chose took over her mind again but this time felt different than before. This time, her feelings for Del wouldn't stay suppressed.

Ellen stood with the pail and shook the growing affection for him from her head. How she felt about the man didn't matter. She wanted a true home. She'd not seen him carry a wigwam on his horse. Did he always sleep out in the open? Did he follow the birds and butterflies and head south for the winter? Or did he just sleep under a blanket of snow? Not for the first time was she glad they at least had a wagon in rough weather at night.

She reached camp to find her stepmother had the cooking items cleaned and packed. She grinned at the pleasant surprise then went about emptying the milk into a jar and sealing the lid. They'd have bits of butter for biscuits tonight, if the road was rough enough. Lucy washed the baby's face as Skeeter jumped up and down. Seeing Ellen, he ran to her. "Ellie! Ellie! We saw your indun friend getting water! He had his horse and it was drinking too! I said hi and he waved back at me!"

His mother took the older boy's face, wiping jelly from around his mouth. "Now, now, Skeeter, that man is not Ellen's friend. Your father doesn't want her being friends with an Indian or he'll come and steal everything we own. That's what they do."

"She's right, sweetie. He can't be my friend. Daddy said so." Ellen's breath caught at a feeling of lying to her brother. "Maybe we'll let him be an acquaintance until he rides away to his people."

"Away with our belongings and some of the women," Lucy muttered.

Ellen's temper flared a little. "We'll see. For now, we'll be polite, but not encourage him, all right? That way, we're doing as Pa says and not being so rude as to anger him into a warpath or something. All right?" She glanced at Lucy who nodded her approval.

"Yes, ma'am." A few kids running by caught his eye. "Ma?"

"Yes, of course." As he ran to catch up, Lucy turned back to Ellen and added, "I'm glad you've seen sense." The older woman picked up her baby. "Talking with a native is a very foolish thing to do. No matter how like us he seems, you have our safety to consider. I like my scalp where it is."

She chuckled at the idea of Del being so primitive. "So do I. And I do want to obey Pa. I'm not encouraging him at all but don't want to avoid Marie if she's chatting with him."

"Hmm. You might want to consider not being her friend if she continues to associate with such people."

"I'd prefer to keep our friendship no matter who she talks to, Ma."

Lucy sighed, putting a hand to her own forehead before shifting Buster to her other hip. "Don't be difficult, Ellen. Buster is sickly and I don't feel well. Besides, it doesn't matter what you'd prefer. If your father decides you need to stop being friends with someone who accepts such people, you'll stop. He'll tolerate Mr. Granville's association because being nice to the brute keeps us safe. He'll not extend the same courtesy to you."

"Very well. When Marie is near him, I'll avoid her. Otherwise, I'll keep her as a friend."

Lucy nodded. "A compromise we'll be able to live with, I'm sure. I'll talk to your father and help him see this is a good idea. He wouldn't want you to snub Marie entirely, seeing as how influential her husband is."

Ellen smirked. If she accidently saw Del once in a while, that could hardly be helped, could it? Like this morning at the creek, where his shirt hadn't been buttoned up all the way. Not that she'd noticed, of course. She'd been too busy. Besides how proper his clothes were now, hadn't his heroics at the Green River been enough? She considered him a friend after he'd saved Skeeter and Buster. Never mind her and Lucy, his hurry to jump in after the boys endeared him to her. A tickly, butterfly feeling began in the pit of her stomach. He'd looked grim when reaching for her brothers first, seeming reluctant to leave her behind. She replayed the scene in her mind, unsure if she'd seen fear for her safety in his eyes after all.

The road grew more and more rocky, disrupting her thoughts. All her concentration went to avoiding the sharper of the stones after one bruised the side of her foot. The loose rocks made going up and down the hills treacherous. Several stumbled along with her and she saw how a few inventive souls used walking sticks. By noon, the bottoms of her feet hurt even more than the scuffed side.

She heard the order to stop just as she stepped on another sharp stone. Ellen lifted her skirt and shoe. The sole was worn almost through. Another day or two and she'd be touching the ground. Lucy already had leather strips lining her shoes' soles. Ellen considered herself lucky to have gone this far without having to do the same. She hurried to their wagon for lunch, keeping a better watch of where she stepped.

Lucy had the lunch basket open on the lowered tailgate. The boys munched as if it were the last meal. She gave Ellen a couple of biscuits and began putting away the water bucket. "Have you heard anything from Mr. Granville or his friend about the trail ahead?"

Ellen's guard went up, wary the question might mean more than its surface seemed. "I didn't get a chance to really talk with anyone today. The last time I even saw Mr. Granville was a few glimpses this morning."

"I'm assuming that's when you saw that Mr. Du Boise too?"

She ignored her irritation. Ellen knew Lucy was fishing for information. She couldn't lie very well but needed to omit details. "I saw him then and a couple of times since." She shrugged. "He's ridden by a few times for some sort of reason. I don't know why because I've never spoken to him to ask."

The woman nodded in satisfaction. Once she went out of sight, Ellen sighed with relief that her stepmother didn't see through the lie about seeing him while getting water. Before she could say such things, she needed to believe them herself. Still, the twinge of guilt by lying from omission bothered her. Placing things in the wagon, she turned over the feeling in her mind. Maybe Del was the answer to her parents' problems. Maybe she should encourage him. Pa might disapprove, but marrying a savage would reduce her father's burden.

A little tremor fluttered in her heart. The feeling alarmed her a little with how appealing it was. She'd seen him shirtless, so the image of him this morning with his shirt unbuttoned captivated her yet again. Ellen shook her head a little. No, no dwelling on this now, but maybe later tonight. The flutter began again. She must be overtired. How else to explain this oddness?

The wagon began moving. From force of habit, she checked to see where Skeeter was. He walked with his mother as she carried the toddler. Ellen walked behind the wagon, lost in thought. Even if she had a suitable man courting her, she had nothing to offer. She had nothing to furnish a new home even if someone bothered to marry her. Her formerly full hope chest now held the family's rations. All of her books except for the Bible and her journal, the linens, dishes, and everything of her mother's had been sold or left behind in Ohio. Each step she took strengthened her resolve to teach school and earn her own way in life. That way, no one could ever again tell her what to keep and what to leave behind.

By late afternoon, they'd travelled only six miles to stop at what seemed an Eden in the desert. The stream deepened, flowing fast and clear, while remaining shallow. The sun shown high in the afternoon sky, causing her to wonder why the wagons set up in a semi circle around an oxbow bend in the river. She walked to the bank and knelt to take a drink. The icy water tasted refreshing. If not for the chill, Ellen would have swum off some of the dust covering her. She took off a boot, testing the water with her toe. Wincing, she tried to put in her entire foot but couldn't bear the cold.

"Ellen!" Jenny ran over to her. "Isn't this lovely? Like an oasis in the Sahara! Mr. Granville wants us to stay here for the night and fatten up the stock." Spotting Ellen putting on her shoe, she asked, "How is the water? Is it as refreshing as it looks? I'm dying for a real bath."

"It's freezing, but good. I had a drink and tried to make myself wade around" She said as her friend stripped off her shoes and socks. "Are you sure you want to do that? It's very cold."

"I won't mind. This'll feel good after all the sharp rocks I've trod on today and yesterday." The younger girl eased into the water. She squealed as each inch covered first one foot, then the other. Walking around the sandy and pebbly bottom, she said, "You'll get used to it after a little while. The ground feels good too." She bent over, putting her hands in the water. "I might try to swim or at least wash my hair."

"Washing sounds like a great idea. If we're to be here overnight, I want to wash clothes and get the musty smell out of the bedding." Ellen turned to the wagon a few steps before calling over her shoulder, "I'll be back and bring you some bath soap." She grinned hearing her friend's laughter.

Once loaded down with laundry and soap, she made her way back to the stream. A small crowd had gathered, also doing their wash. Children played upstream, ducking and splashing. Some women kneeled on the bank and scrubbed. A few, like Jenny, stood in the stream itself, letting their skirts fall into the water. Snow capped mountains provided a poetic backdrop to the scene. For Ellen, the water hadn't warmed much since flowing from the top. The sun shone hot on her back, so she peeled off her shoes.

"Just jump in!" Jenny yelled. "Don't be chicken!"

Ellen shouted back, "I'm not!" Gathering her skirt in one hand, she jumped. The sand gave way, causing her to slip and sit. She screamed a laugh, hind end flat on the creek bed. Icy water came up to her neck, too cold for her to even breathe.

"Oh my goodness!" Jenny ran over to her, splashing Ellen and hoisting her up by the arm. "Are you all right?"

After a few pants to get her breath, she laughed. "Yes, I think so. Just cold and surprised."

"Maybe I should have said ease in?"

"I think so." The girls laughed. Ellen asked, "Is it my turn to dunk you?"

"Oh no!" Jenny held up her hands in surrender. "I'll go swimming soon enough!" She scrambled to the bank. "Let me get our laundry. We can wash together, and I promise to sit like you did." She shook her head. "Poor girl!"

"Go already." Ellen waved her off, smiling. "The sooner we get started, the sooner we're done and dry." As her friend went off in search of dirty clothes, Ellen began scrubbing. Marie's dress was her top priority. She bent, dunking it and washing out the dirt. Once satisfied it was clean, she spread it out over the marsh grasses on the bank. She considered washing her hair with it still damp. Doing so now would give it time to dry by bedtime. The sun edged ever closer to the western horizon. Bedding could wait for a proper washday. Having clean clothes and hair would be such a luxury.

She pulled out the pins, putting them and her glasses in her shoes. Ellen leaned way out, setting the items as far from the bank as she could reach.

"We're back!"

Looking up, she saw Jenny and Del standing in front of her. Without her glasses, they were a blur, and Del squatted so she could see him.

"Hello, care to do my washing too?"

She laughed. "As much as I'd love to do your work as well as my own, I must decline."

He grinned at her sarcasm. "Ah, well, cannot blame me for asking." Lifting up the clothes he held and indicating Marie's dress with a nod, he said, "Our friends' needs have priorities over our own washings, no?"

"I suppose they do," agreed Ellen.

Jenny stepped gingerly into the water. "Goodness! I'll have to get used to this all over again!" She took a few steps away from Ellen. "Oh dear, I've forgotten my wash. Mr. Du Boise, I hate to trouble you, but could you bring over my laundry for me?"

"Of course." He set Jenny's basket down in front of her. "Anything else, mademoiselle? I am your servant."

She tilted her head to the side. "Well, I did notice Ellen's shoes are just sitting there. If someone should step on them, they'd crush her glasses and then where would she be?"

Ellen protested, "They're fine where they are."

He glanced at her and shrugged. "I have an idea." Del unbuttoned his shirt, pulling it off. Laying out the red gingham, he took her shoes and placed them on top. "There. No one will step on them now. The color warns them away."

Jenny went back to washing as if a half naked savage stood in front of her every day. A deep pink cast to her face gave away her embarrassment. Ellen couldn't think. Although he was out of focus, he still appealed to her. She could see the shadows his muscles made. He was slender and a little stouter than she'd expected. Ellen looked down at the water, a little panicked. In no way could she let anyone see her talking to him when he was in such a state. She felt desperate to stare at him, yet duty must win. "Excuse me, I must wash my hair."

"Good idea!" Jenny clapped her hands then grasped for the garment flowing out of reach. "I dislike sleeping on wet hair. Don't you, Mr. Du Boise?"

He chuckled. "I've never considered how I felt about such a thing. Sometimes it cannot be helped."

Ellen backed away, using his distraction with Jenny to escape. Pulling pins from her hair, she placed them on Marie's dress. She heard Del chatting and listened with half an ear. While unbraiding her hair, she walked around, enjoying the feel of the smooth stones on her feet. She sat facing the oncoming current. The water didn't feel as cold now. Leaning back, she let her hair flow downstream and closed her eyes.

"You have the fair face, but not the madness of fair Ophelia, *ma coeur.*"

Gasping, Ellen opened her eyes to see Del standing above her. "Oh my! We can't talk."

"I know." He knelt, washing Sam's shirt. "I am too busy to chat with you. And you are too busy washing your *délicieux* hair."

She laughed at his word choice. "Delicious? My hair is delicious?"

"Yes, it is." He squeezed water from his friend's shirt. "I can know this without a taste."

"You are so silly and we can't speak at all. I've been forbidden, remember?" She stood, went to the bank, and took a little bar of soap. Ellen turned to find a solid seat on the riverbed and almost ran into him. "Oh, goodness gracious! Del, honestly, if I'm seen with you like this, my father will be furious."

He shrugged. "So? Stay out of my way." The naughty glint in his eyes belied the curt words.

"How can I when you're such a mountain of a man. Honestly, you're taller than I am. How can anyone avoid you?"

"At last, maybe now you will stop trying, *ma coeur.*" He spread the shirt out to dry, taking the pants. With a wink at Jenny, who blushed and shook her head, he took a small handful of soap. "Here I am, trying to clean clothes, and you run all over, hindering my progress."

Securely seated on the stream's bed, she worked the soap into her scalp. She closed her eyes and retorted, "With me way over here, I'll not bother you. Now shush please, or it'll be both our hides." She leaned back as before, letting her hair flow in the current. Hearing him scrubbing next to her, Ellen lowered herself into the water, covering her ears and washing away all the soap from her scalp. Sounds of children playing, the muted sounds of talking, and Del's washing came through the liquid. She marveled at a man washing his own clothes. Although many did, she'd never thought of a brave doing such a thing. Every book she'd read on the subject said the men considered the women as slave labor.

The lack of Del's washing noises caught her attention. She opened her eyes to see him staring at her. "Are you done so soon?"

"Yes, sadly." He looked at the bundle in his hands and back at her. "Excuses for staring at your beauty are now washed away. Never before have clean clothes saddened me so much."

She laughed at his outrageous compliment and sat up, pressing the water out of her hair. "I don't like being forbidden from you most times. The silly things you say are nice to hear even if I don't believe them."

"Hmm." He shook his head. "Thus I need to convince you of my sincerity, but how can I when you are so certain? You give me a

lot to ponder. *Adieu, ma coeur.*" Standing, he strode to Jenny.
"*Mademoiselle, adieu.*"

"Goodbye, Mr. Du Boise." Jenny gave him a little wave.
"Thank you for dinner last night. We enjoyed it."

Though a blur, Ellen tried not to watch as he put her shoes at
the neck of Marie's dress. He put on his shirt, waved a little too big
at her and left. She liked how he'd remembered her bad eyesight.
Standing, she continued squeezing water out of her hair, and
concentrating on the lower half, she asked Jenny, "You had dinner
with Mr. Du Boise?"

"Yes, in a way. He brought over some moose, and mother
fried it in a flour and pepper batter." She sighed. "I'm hungry again
just thinking about it."

Ellen made quick work of braiding her hair, wanting to keep it
up and out of the water. Jealousy nibbled at her heart, though she
did her best to ignore the feeling. She didn't mind Jenny being
friends with Del, just that the girl and her family talked with him
while Ellen couldn't. She scrubbed a shirt. No matter what Del did
for her family, he'd always be a dirty Indian in her father's eyes. Pa
might appreciate his actions and be friendly to his face, but she
knew what hateful things he'd say once Del turned his back.

"I'm thinking the next time Mr. Du Boise brings us extra from
his hunt, I'll come and get you and Marie too. There's too much
for us to eat, and I hate the idea of the dogs getting first pick when
there's that much remaining."

"Oh goodness! Me too! Especially if it's as good as you say,"
she reassured Jenny. "Which I'm sure it is."

"It is. You'll love it." She watched as Ellen put on her glasses
and shoes. "You're finished already! I'm not even ready to wash my
hair. It's not nearly as long and full as yours. You're so lucky."

She folded the clothes loosely, stacking them. "Maybe so, but
yours is such a lovely color. Like wheat when it's ready for
harvesting."

"Thank you! I'm glad you think so! Everyone in my family has
the same color, so it's nothing special." She hopped out of the
stream.

"It would be special in my family. Do you need my hand
soap? It'll be gentler on your hair."

"Sure! How wonderful of you to offer." Jenny took and
smelled the little bar. "Ooo, this smells like roses! How very nice!

Thank you! I'll bring it back to you after dinner tonight. Will that be all right?"

"Of course, I'm sure you'll like it. See you then." Ellen waved at the girl. Jenny was preoccupied with unraveling her hair. She jumped back into the river with a splash and Ellen laughed. How like her to leap. At least Jenny had known what to expect. She carried the damp clothes to the campsite.

Seeing Lucy and Pa with the boys, she hollered to them as they approached. "I have the washing, and have loaned Jenny my hand soap. I'm betting she'll be done with it by the time you get there." Ellen smiled at the boys, putting everything in one hand to ruffle Skeeter's hair.

"Thank you, Ellen," Lucy said as she headed to the water.

Before she could pass by him, her father grabbed her arm. "Don't your friend's parents have enough soap? Did you have to give ours for her to use?" He gripped harder with each word, hurting her.

"She'll return it, Pa, I promise." She gasped at his squeeze. "Lucy is probably washing the boys with it right now." She tried to keep her face expressionless, not wanting anyone to notice his scolding.

He released her arm with a slight shove. "She'd better be. Our belongings aren't yours to give away, remember that."

She clenched her hands so her shaking wouldn't be visible to anyone else. Pa's temper always scared her, every single time. She hurried to their camp and lowered the tailgate, draping Marie's dress on top to let it drip dry. Shivering and still wet, she climbed into the wagon and found her dry clothes where she'd left them. She closed the canvas for privacy and changed into her Sunday dress. Ellen buttoned up, thinking if she hurried, she could give her every day dress a good scrubbing, this time without her wearing it. Maybe even start dinner before everyone returned. Her arm still felt hot through the fabric, and she was grateful for longer sleeves. She hopped out of the wagon, scooped up her wet clothes, and headed for the river's edge.

Avoiding her family where they were gathered, she found a place further down to wash. Ellen cleaned the grass stains from the hem of her dress. She didn't see Jenny, so she didn't loiter, opting instead to make her way quickly back to the camp. Neither Pa nor Lucy was near the wagon, and Ellen wasn't surprised to see Skeeter watching little Buster either. Her younger brother hopped up and down as much as he could with the baby leaning against him.

"Sis! Some boys from another camp want me to play with them? Can I?"

He stared with such pleading eyes, how could she say no to him? "May you? Yes you may. Remember the rule?"

"Yes, stay in sight of the wagons." He hopped in impatience. "Don't wander away, get home long before dark, right?"

"That's right. Now go before those ants in your pants carry you back here before you're even gone." She laughed when he took off like a shot. Poor boy having to stay so still for so long, Ellen grinned. She saw Little Buster sitting and almost asleep on the wagon seat with a blanket as his cushion. Ellen hoped he slept through her work.

Her father came up, hands in his pockets. "Well, well, looks like you've been busy! Very good. How's tea coming along? I've been looking forward to it happening here pretty quick."

Ellen paused, panic chilling her blood. She didn't remember a promise to make him tea. She said in an effort to placate him, "It will happen very quickly. If you could start a fire, I'll get everything else ready. It'll be done before you know it."

His jaw clenched as he ground out, "Fine. I'll do your chores for you."

Swallowing down her own anger, she hopped to the ground and began gathering the food items. "Please don't, Pa, I'll hurry." Ellen turned around for his response to see him gone. She sighed in relief, knowing every little bit of work from Pa helped, even with the bad attitude. He'd get his small meal that much faster. Buster snored behind her, reminding her she needed to block him in. She set up a makeshift shelter from blankets and the tailgate, placing him on a layer of quilts.

She reached into the wagon and gathered food for a small and quick meal for Pa. Tea, sugar, biscuits, and preserves were all she had at the moment. After a quick trip to the river for fresh water, she hurried back to where their fire pit should be. Her father stood off a ways, chatting with one of his cronies. Ellen had counted on seeing something burning, be it grass, sagebrush, buffalo chips, or even discarded furniture. She struggled to keep her frustration at bay. At least his friend would keep him busy until she finished cooking. Ellen tried to stay positive while Pa wasn't going to be happy with the delay in starting a fire. She rushed around, gathering whatever was possible to burn, started the water to boil for Pa's tea, and stirred the biscuit mixings for later.

Lucy walked up, draping her wet clothes over Marie's dress, soaking it again. "You let Buster have jam?" Her voice was shrill as she picked up her son. "Look at him! He's filthy."

Her mouth dropped when she saw Buster covered in jam. "Oh no!"

Lucy gave her stepdaughter a glare. "Do you mind starting a proper dinner while I wash up my child? It's the least you can do." She turned without another word to the river with the baby.

Ellen rummaged around in the food containers. Plenty of beans and rice, but they had only some bacon for meat and very few potatoes left for vegetables. She wished and not for the first time that her parents had left behind belongings instead of food. Back then, the wild fruits and game practically jumped up into the frying pan. Now, this desert kept away any good-sized animals. Even the scarce rabbit running from their wheels was too fast for Pa to shoot. She turned to the task at hand. The biscuits fluffed nicely as the tea brewed.

Thinking of rabbits reminded her of the wonderful stew she'd had at the Granville camp a few nights ago. She cut off some of the more spoiled portions of their hunk of bacon. Wouldn't it be nice if Del surprised her with extra meat from an earlier hunt from today?

She could just imagine it: He would stroll up, his dark hair blowing in the wind. And what would he hold for her? A jar of the finest butter, a fresh and ready to cook duck, a bowl of nearly overripe strawberries, and a bunch of tender asparagus. As she added the meat, potatoes, and a sickly onion for flavor, Ellen laughed at the thought of him so weighed down with food he sunk into the ground. Silly, yes, but it made for a very tasty fantasy. She stirred the mix and took another batch of fresh biscuits from the fire. Even better would be making a pie from the strawberries. Maybe she would even throw in a few blueberries despite how they ripened at different times. Anything was possible in a dream.

As long as she was dreaming, wouldn't it be nice if he were acceptable by her father? Ellen shook her head at the impossibility. Pa might be the best carpenter in five states, but he couldn't hunt to save their suppers. If Del was any sort of hunter, her stomach was already in love with him. She wanted a repeat of the wonderful meal he'd prepared the day they met. She glanced around, not seeing her father or his friends, wondering when everyone might return.

She looked ahead across the fire and saw Sam approach. One look at his face and her heart dropped. The mix of anger and sadness could mean a million things, but she guessed he now had proof of the Warrens and their disgusting secret.

Before she could ask, he nodded at her grim expression. "Yes, I know, and we're going to talk."

"Pa is out hunting, and Lucy is washing Skeeter and Buster. Sit nearby and we can talk about what I'm assuming are the Warrens."

He sat next to her. "How long have you known about those two?"

She didn't look at him, not wanting to admit the truth, yet she had to be honest with him. "Since the Black Hills."

Before thinking, he blurted, "That's been two months ago, and you said nothing to Marie?"

His anger both scared and irritated her. Ellen snapped back at him. "What would you have me tell her? What could I say that she'd believe without seeing with her own eyes?" She saw him shudder and added, "I know. It's deplorable and against anything decent." Ellen leaned forward to stir the pot. "As much as I've heard Mr. Warren call Del a savage, well, he has no room to talk."

He swallowed then shook his head. "We need to let Marie know. She can't go to California with them."

Ellen thought ahead to all the possibilities in her friend's future and agreed with him. "Especially if she finds out about their affair once there. She'd be alone, knowing everything, and have nowhere to turn."

"I can't let that happen." Sam stood. "And before you ask, no, I don't know what to say, but I'll have to think of something before Fort Hall."

When imagining Marie reaching California only to learn of this sordid affair, Ellen nodded. "That would be best for her."

"Thank you for the talk. See you after dinner?"

"I'll try."

"Good." He tipped his hat and left.

She turned at a sound behind her. Lucy stepped down from

the wagon. "I heard everything. What is going on with your friend? What is she doing? Does it involve that brave? Does your father know all this?"

With each question, Lucy grew so near, Ellen had to stand and back away. "I'm not sure what to answer first. It's all about the Warrens and I promised to keep quiet."

"Not to me you didn't and certainly not to Jack."

Pa walked up with Skeeter behind him. He stood toe to toe with Ellen and asked, "Not to me what?"

She took a breath and stepped back. She wanted to keep calm and not trigger his temper. "I promised Mr. Granville to say nothing about the Warrens for now. Please don't make me until he says I may."

"Since when have you taken your orders from him, young lady?" Jack grabbed her upper arm and shook her with each word he spat. "He's not the one feeding your worthless hide."

"Now, Jack." Lucy stepped in between as much as she could. "I'm sure Ellen is just following orders and will tell you everything when she can. The Warrens are none of our business anyway."

Pa let go of Ellen's arm with a shove. "I don't like her sassing me."

"I know, dear." Lucy put her arm around him, leading him to the fire.

Jack let her move him as if he were a child. "She thinks she can do whatever she wants around here, and we're to follow her tune. I don't like it, Lucy, I don't."

"I know, I know." She pulled him onto a folded blanket and gave him a plate. "Let's calm down and eat dinner." Nodding at Ellen, she said, "Would you please dish up?"

Ellen served Pa, Lucy, and Skeeter before fixing a little plate for Buster. She hesitated before getting her own dinner. Her stomach churned, and while the food smelled good, she didn't want even the smallest bite.

Watching her, Pa sighed, putting his half eaten biscuit back down. "Land's sake, Ellen, go ahead and eat. I'm sorry if you can't keep from getting your feelings hurt so easy. Eat before it gets cold."

"Yes, sir." She gave him her smile and put a scoop onto her plate. She made sure the food spread out and looked like more. Still wearing the little grin, Ellen sat down, mashing the potato first then cutting her meat with the fork. She saw Pa's frown. "I'd like to save my biscuit for dessert, maybe."

He shrugged as if to say he didn't care and turned to Lucy. They began talking about the day and Ellen stopped listening. Her arm ached and each bite stuck in her throat before going down with a hard swallow. The plate trembled while the bruised muscle ached, and her eyes stung as tears threatened to show. Horrified she might start crying, Ellen stared down at her dinner. She needed to think of something, anything, to distract her mind and stop the crying before it started. Maybe dwelling on Del might help. Had he been hunting this afternoon? Was there anything in the area good for eating? Besides all that, what made her care about him so much when she wasn't supposed to? Maybe there was a book written by someone more scholarly than her.

Lucy broke into her thoughts. "I noticed some currants ready for picking. How about tomorrow morning you and I gather some? It'll be a nice treat for breakfast or lunch."

"Sounds wonderful," she said with a gusto she didn't feel. Ellen shook the fog from her mind and stood. The sun began to set but still hovered above the west hills. Taking dishes and silver, she went to wash them for tomorrow. As she drew near the water, other men and women also cleaned their utensils. Like her, each had a bucket for carrying dishes.

Ellen brought the skirt to a little above her knees and knelt by the water. She scrubbed the dishes with clean sand, enjoying how clear the water was. Brilliant blues with hints of purple and orange reflected in the ripples. She wished her eyes were this brilliant like Jenny's, a beautiful and flashy blue. Then maybe she'd be as lovely as Del treated her. Smiling, she liked how true to his French roots he stayed. Surely Indian men weren't so poetic to their women. Otherwise, why would so many squaws marry French men? Something had to be lacking in the native male.

She traced a finger in the water, breaking up the fading colors' reflection. Ellen wanted to put her feelings into a category. This affection she held for Del must be appreciation from the Green River incident and nothing more. She didn't know his favorite color, where he was born, or even his birthday. She didn't know how he liked his eggs cooked, if he had siblings, or even his parents' names. How could this be anything more than gratitude when she knew so little about him? She picked up the bucket, now full of clean dishes. Turning around, Ellen bumped into Del as if her thoughts had conjured him from thin air. "Oh my! Excuse me, I didn't mean to run over you."

He grinned. "No harm done. I've been trampled by larger."

"Than me? You flatter me."

"*C'est flatter? Non*, no flattery, just truth. You're a willow and I've been trampled by horses."

He had a way of making her feel like a true beauty. She knew the reality, but still. Under the stars, Ellen almost believed him. "I suppose I'm tall and graceful?"

"Yes, those things plus everything else good in the world."

She laughed at his florid language. "You distract me from my work, and I really need to return to camp."

"May I escort you?" Del held out his arm for her to take.

She glanced around but saw no one nearby. Ellen rarely left the wagon circle after dark. Soon the watch would wonder where she was. "I'd like that."

He pointed to the far end of the wagon train and over to her own family's camp. "We could walk here to there and back?"

She realized Del wanted to take the longest way possible. "Let's do. It's a lovely night."

"So it is."

They strolled and Ellen enjoyed how slow both of them went. She glanced at him. He seemed even darker in the approaching night. The rising moon still hovered low on the eastern horizon, not enough to make his white shirt gleam. Most camps they passed were quiet and the fires burned low. The closer they came to her family, the further from them she wanted to be. Ellen felt sure Del would ride off soon. Right now might be her last chance to ever kiss a man without bribing or putting him in chains first. She stopped, glancing around to see if anyone around them stirred.

"Is something wrong, *ma coeur*?"

"No, I'm just wanting a rest," she whispered. Seeing no one else, Ellen looked up into his eyes. Before he could offer a refusal, she put her hands on his shoulders and leaned forward. She loved the way he smelled, like summer prairie and rain with a little bit of leather adding spice. He didn't move when their lips met and she shivered. His skin warmed hers and she pressed for more. Everywhere they touched seemed too much to bear until his hands gripped her waist. She'd been accustomed to the fading pain from

Pa's kick a few days ago.

At Del's caress, she gasped in pain. The right side still hurt. He moaned in response and she almost laughed at his misunderstanding. When his palms landed on her lower back, she sighed. He'd found a place to touch her that didn't ache.

Del growled, holding her hard against him. He moved his right hand up to the middle of her back, and holding her in place, kissed down her neck until her dress fabric stopped him. "*Mon Dieu*, I have died and met heaven with you, Ellen. I can't help but make love to you tonight."

Shame swept through her from his comment. Suddenly very embarrassed, she pushed him from her. "No, no, behave yourself." Even in the dark she saw his surprise and tried to placate him. "The blame isn't all yours. I forgot myself too. Thank you for stopping when I asked. You're French and an Indian. What else did I expect but to be attacked tonight?"

He inhaled then narrowed his eyes. "You were not attacked by me tonight. Not now, not ever."

That icy chill of saying too much and angering him raced along her nerves. She had to diffuse this and fast. Ellen lowered her voice to an even, and she hoped, calming tone. "No, of course it wasn't an honest attack. You were just being true to yourself. The civilized part of you could only keep check for so long." She smiled, trying to soften his scowl. He still looked very angry.

"Civilized part?"

"Yes, it's obviously not as strong as your other half and I'm sorry, because I knew this and tempted you anyway." She sensed he was still angry. Odd, because he'd been the one almost ravaging her. To placate him and prevent further trouble, Ellen added, "You acted so proper, gentlemanly, and even kind. I forgot just how wild you might be and pushed you too far beyond where a decent man would go. I apologize." She waited for a moment to see if he'd say anything. When he stayed silent, she said, "I'd better go."

"Please do."

At his gruff tone, she frowned, then turned and went for her family's camp. Ellen pondered his reaction. Surely he could see their rendezvous needed to stop when it did. She turned to tell him so, but found he'd already disappeared. He'd lived up to his heritage, slipping into the night without a sound. She'd do well to remember what sort of man he was at heart.

Almost running to her family's campsite, she pushed down the trembling at the same time she put down the pail. She'd crossed a serious line by kissing Del. Even worse, she didn't regret it. All the Winslows slept in their bedrolls. Ellen's lay empty a little apart from the others. Someone, either Pa or Lucy, had thought of her. She slid off her shoes and settled in for the night.

The campfire's warmth soothed her as she watched the ebbing light. Remembering her journal, Ellen knew she couldn't write anything about tonight or Pa would see. She recollected every one of Del's kisses to memorize each nuance. Her father could read anything he wanted, but he'd never know her heart.

She woke before sunrise. The beginning dawn told her going back to sleep was useless this close to morning. Ellen sat up and shivered. They needed wood and she needed coffee. She slid out of her bed and into her shoes to creep out of camp. No need in waking Pa before absolutely necessary. Not seeing the night watch, she left the semi circle of wagons and headed to the nearest grove for wood.

"You shouldn't be here. The Shoshone are angry at the whites, enough to use you to teach them a lesson."

Del's voice startled her and she turned to him. Ellen tasted fear just from his words and the images they created in her mind. "Let me get some wood and I'll hurry back." She began picking up whatever sticks and twigs lay nearby. "Del, I didn't mean to cause problems. I never do."

His fierce expression softened a little. "I know. You didn't know of the families killed in this area. Don't leave camp at dark, even this sort of dark, without one of us."

"I won't."

He began gathering sticks and twigs too. "Do you think no apology is necessary?"

Ellen shook her head. "No, I don't think you need to apologize."

He frowned. "Not me, there's no need. But you? You need to apologize to me for last night."

"I already did and you didn't accept," she replied, turning back to camp. He took hold of her arm and his grip, while not overly firm, still hurt from Pa's bruising yesterday. She yelped and dropped her bundle. "Please, Del! Let go of me."

He released her and felt along her upper arm. "You still hurt here?"

"Yes, a little from an old accident." A little embarrassed by the concern in his expression, she added, "And I am sorry for thinking you uncivilized."

"That's not important now, *ma coeur*. Either you were injured very badly then or have been reinjured since." He frowned, examining without touching her arm. "I think you need medical attention. Let's find Sam and Uncle Joe."

Ellen shook away his unease. "That's not necessary. It just aches a little."

"You cannot lie to me, which is something I adore about you." Lifting her elbow, he used his fingertips to press against her skin through the fabric. "You were well while washing yesterday, able to do chores and support your weight. My guess is you've angered your father since then."

She took her elbow from his hands, a little annoyed and uncomfortable at his accuracy. "What happens between Pa and me is none of your business and isn't open for discussion with you."

"Hmm," he said. "Who, then, can discuss this with you?"

"Who?" Her brow furrowed. "No one, actually. I'm not discussing any of this with you or anyone else. My relationship with my parents is none of your business." She walked past him towards the wagon train.

Del stepped in front of her, blocking the way. "Nor anyone else's?"

She stopped, crossing her arms. "No. Of course not."

"Then it isn't just me you avoid this subject with?"

Frowning, she retorted, "Of course not. Who would I discuss this with? No one at all."

His expression softened somewhat. "So I am not less than other friends? I like that." In a sudden move, he raised her chin suggesting a kiss. Stopping just short of their lips meeting, Del instead examined her as if committing her face to memory. After a moment, he grinned, letting her go. He looked back at the way they'd come. "You are too far from safety but too close for a kiss. I would not give your Pa a reason to hurt you again." He took her hand. Lifting it, he paused and then released it. "No, do not bother to defend him. Until later, *ma coeur*."

The man's smile could melt ice, Ellen thought as she tried to resist his charm. "No, I'm not sure you're a true friend." She glanced around them and in a voice she hoped no one else could hear, added, "I never kiss friends. In that way, you're much more than anyone else."

Like a sudden storm, Del's face clouded. *"Mon Dieu,"* he whispered. He reached out and traced the back of his hand against her cheek before taking her face in both hands. She turned to kiss his palm, and he growled a little at the touch.

Ellen answered with a hum of her own and relaxed into his arms as he enveloped her into a hug. He held her as tenderly as spun glass. She pulled back and let her hands slide from his shoulders to his arms, needing the time to clear her head. Looking up into his eyes, she said, "My goodness."

"Yes." He kissed her forehead. "Next time your father has issues with me, send him to me. I shall be glad to chat with him."

"I can't." She squeezed his biceps to emphasize his strength. "You'd hurt him, maybe even kill him."

He looked at each one of her hands before staring into her eyes. *"Non.* I'll show respect, but if he's to beat anyone for my attentions toward you, it's to be me, not you." Before she could protest, he briefly put a finger on her lips. "No more argument, *ma coeur.* Promise?"

"Oui, I promise."

He gave her a wide grin. "You've learned?" At her nod, he kissed her cheek. "I look to teach you more. But later. Go back to camp. I'll go around so we're not discovered."

She agreed and scooped up the wood she'd dropped. The early sun's rays already lifted the dew from leaves and grass. She hurried to camp and built up the fire. In record time, she got water, started coffee, and milked the cows. The biscuits and bacon cooked before Pa, Lucy, and the boys woke. None of them were in a good mood, going off to do their morning business without a word. Even Skeeter seemed puffy and cranky. Ellen made the boy a plate first, ready for him when he came back.

"Thank you, sis."

She watched for a moment, sipping her coffee as he picked at his food. "Are you still not feeling well, sweetie?"

Pa and Lucy arrived at the same time, Buster with them and fussy. Lucy worked at calming him while Pa sat. "None of us are feeling good, Ellen. Why not ask how everyone is doing and not just Skeeter?"

She hurried to fix their plates. "That was my next question, sir."

"I'm fine." He took the plate from her and began eating. "Your ma and brother aren't as good. You might need to take on extra chores to help her for the next few days."

"Of course." Ellen still wore her good girl smile as she stared down into her empty coffee cup. "I noticed ripe berries while out gathering wood."

"So?" asked Pa.

"They'd make a nice lunchtime treat. My chores are caught up, and I was thinking about going out to pick some before we leave."

Buster let out a wail, throwing his biscuit at the fire and knocking over the coffee. Pa hopped to his feet. "Damn it all to hell, woman!"

"I'm sorry, Jack. He just doesn't feel well."

"Give him to me. I'll handle him," said Jack. "Go. Leave and help Ellen pick berries. I'll show you both how a man gets things done around here." He walked off with Buster with Skeeter watching them. They heard Pa mutter, "Useless, good for nothing women."

Lucy stood. "I'll find the clean pail if you'll gather our dishes into the wash bucket."

Ellen did as requested without a word, pausing to ruffle Skeeter's hair. The boy leaned against her, his body trembling. She tried to calm him. "Don't fret, sweetie. Pa will calm down and everything will be back to normal. I promise."

"Can I go with you, sis?"

She looked down into his pleading eyes and almost said yes. Ellen felt his cheek with the back of her hand. The child was too warm to be running around, so she said, "We won't be long at all. Help me gather up the dishes, and I'll spread out a bed for you in the wagon."

"I'm not tired."

"I'm sure, but do try to rest before we leave." Before he could protest, she added, "Do it so you can play this afternoon, all right?"

"Yeah, sis." He did as asked and helped her stack plates while Ellen bundled up the bedding and laid out a pallet for him in the wagon.

Satisfied she had a nice place for him to sleep, she looked up at Lucy. "Are you ready to go?"

The two women left camp with Ellen leading the way. Pa's temper tantrum kept both quiet. They worked fast to gather as much as possible before the signal to leave sounded. Scanning the branches and seeing nothing but green fruit, Ellen said, "I think we've found everything ready to pick." She looked at the berries nearly filling her bucket. "This will make for a wonderful cobbler, don't you think?"

Lucy examined her own pail. "Hmm, I do but I'd like to push on a little further, if only to find more to preserve."

Ellen didn't like the idea of being even further from the group. She shuddered, thinking of Little Buster and Skeeter harmed. No, they needed to return to safety. "Lucy, please, let's go and find—" A hand cut off her sentence, silencing any scream. Ellen watched in horror as a brave grabbed her stepmother in the same manner. Both men held knives to their throats. She didn't know what to do: struggle and possibly get away, or stay limp and go along with whatever they wanted. What would Del recommend she do? She closed her eyes and so wished he were here to help.

The man holding her pressed the knife deeper into her skin as he let go of her mouth. She got his message, yell and they'd die. Lucy screamed and Ellen watched in horror as her step-mother's throat was cut nearly in two, stopping her cries. She couldn't even squeak as the brave drug her to his horse and pushed her on. They rode away and she clung to him, horrified at what just happened to Lucy. How would she tell Pa? She forced her eyes open to see exactly where they went. If there were any chance of escape, Ellen needed to know how to get back.

CHAPTER 4

"What do you mean gone?" asked Sam.

Uncle Joe answered, "We've searched all the brush around the body."

"I've looked to see if blood stained the bottom of their feet," Del added. He took no comfort in the suggestion they'd taken her alive. After a deep breath to help him stay calm, he pushed aside wondering if she'd caused them problems and was already dead. All he wanted to do now was run to find Ellen. After glancing at the other men gathered, he wondered if his skin matched theirs in a paled color. He clenched his hands into fists to stop their trembling.

Sam nodded. "We'll need to send out a search party for Miss Winslow. It's been recent enough, we stand a good chance of finding her."

"No. You don't want to do that." Del crossed his arms, shaking his head. "A search party is too slow and cumbersome for this. They took her into the mountains."

"How do you know for sure?" asked Uncle Joe.

Del struggled for a second with how much to admit aloud. "It's what I would do." He started to say more but Jack Winslow staggered around the wagon toward them, cutting off anything he might have added.

Winslow bellowed, "What the hell happened to my wife?" and brushed past Marie to the circle of men. "I heard she's dead. That can't be true."

"Yes, sir," Sam began. "It's my duty and regret to inform you…."

"No!" Jack lunged for Del and both Sam and Lucky grabbed hold of him. "One of you red skinned bastards killed her!" They didn't move him back far enough and he spat at Del. Ducking back didn't matter. The gob caught in Jack's beard and oozed down his chin. "I'll see you hang from the nearest tree."

"There's no need for that, Mr. Winslow," Sam said through gritted teeth.

Struggling to free himself, he continued his threats. "The hell there isn't! I'll bet the bastard raped her before slitting her throat."

An icy tremor went down Del's spine. He and Joe were the only two who knew exactly how Lucy died. Not even Sam had been told so far. "How did you know her throat was cut?" If Winslow had killed his wife, what did he do with Ellen?

Jack paled and sagged in Sam's and Lucky's arms. Sam shook the man as he began sobbing. "Answer him. I thought you didn't know how your wife died."

Leaning his head back while still limp, he gave a high, keening wail until out of breath. Before he could inhale, Sam shook him again. Jack made a gurgle sound before replying, "I guessed." He panted a few times as if the effort to say those two words exhausted him. "This animal never carries a tomahawk, just a knife."

Del folded his arms to stop his urge to beat sense into the man. If he'd wanted to kill Lucy and kidnap Ellen, he could have a hundred times over by now. He couldn't make the senseless see reason, but had to try anyway. "So I do. You carry a rifle. Does that mean every person shot in the territory has died by your hand?"

Winslow glared at him for a second before letting his head sag to his chest, his entire body deadweight. Lucky shot Sam an exasperated look and Sam nodded. They both eased Mr. Winslow down to his knees. When his shins hit the dirt, he began his wailing again. The younger men moved away from him and went to Del. Sam spoke first in a quiet voice. "We can't go on without Ellen."

He knew his friend's priority was beating the first snowfall. Sam had a set timetable for the wagon party, one that winter made non negotiable. Del's priority had changed in an instant. Now, he needed to find and return Ellen, if she was alive. The memory of Lucy's body and all of her blood wouldn't leave him. A moment passed before he swallowed the lump in his throat. "Yes, you can. Continue and we'll catch up."

"We?" asked Marie.

He tried to smile, acknowledging the hope in her ashen face. To bolster his and everyone else's confidence he said, "Yes. I will find Ellen and bring her back when I do." Del took Sam's offered hand, and the two had a brotherly hug. When they separated, Del stared down at the keening man below him. "Though I'm not sure he deserves a daughter like her." He understood the man's pain, but Winslow needed to think of his young sons now. One of the ladies sniffled and he added, "Ellen's brothers and friends need her, so I'm going."

"She'll want something familiar when you find her," offered Marie. "It'll comfort her."

Sam nodded in agreement. "We'll go and pack her some food and fresh clothes."

The sun grew warmer by the second, letting him know the day still marched forward. Ellen's kidnappers also rode further away with every minute. The need to find her hit him like the most gnawing hunger he'd ever known. "Let's get started."

Pomme dripped with sweat by the time Del slowed his pace enough to think clearly. He'd been following a small creek through a steep canyon all morning. The infrequent hoof prints he had crossed told him the kidnappers had already passed through. Both he and his horse panted while standing still. The panic inside Del subsided enough for him to realize the group taking Ellen had rode from the main Shoshone camp to the south. The others likely waited for them to the north and maybe even a little west. Del needed to stop his chase for a moment and consider the best way to go. Cutting across to the main camp meant being there when Pointed Nose arrived with Ellen.

He stared down at the hoof prints in the mud. They wanted him to follow them. At least, for now they did. If she managed to escape, he'd have a better chance of finding her by staying close to the group. He shook his head at the idea. Ellen was too sensible to run into a wilderness alone. Even so, he worried. Pointed Nose might drop her at any point, thinking she was too much trouble.

Irritated with both possibilities, he slid from his horse's back, leading him to the stream for a drink. He scooped a handful of water and drank until satisfied then waited until Pomme was finished. The pause helped him decide to head straight to Pointed Nose and Ellen's destination instead of following them. If Del talked to Chief Running Cloud first, the chief might ally with him instead of Pointed Nose. Back on Pomme, man and animal headed north.

As he climbed higher in elevation, so did the sun. Del hated running his horse so hard, but needed to beat the others. He patted his horse's neck. "We'll rest at camp, boy." Pomme snorted, tossing his head as if he understood. They eased down the mountain, every unplanned slide stopping his heart for a moment until the animal found his footing. At last the pines gave way to deciduous trees and finally a valley. By now, the sun hovered above the western mountain range. The Blackfoot River stretched out in front of him, glittering as the sun's rays scattered across the surface. The Shoshone village sat on the far side of a wide part of the river. No others approached and Del waited as the distant scouts rode to him. He knew enough of their language to speak simply and hoped they understood him despite his accent. "Hello."

The two exchanged a glance before the thinner man spoke. "Hello. What business do you have here?"

As if the men were skittish animals, Del kept his tone even. "I need to speak with Running Cloud."

One said something to his partner. After the other man's reply, the first scout said, "We will take you to wait for him."

Del nodded and the two took positions with him in between. Wanting to learn as much as possible before his arrival, he asked, "Is Pointed Nose there too?"

"No."

Any other time he might appreciate their stoic nature. This wasn't that time. "I have business with him too. Did he leave alone?"

"He went out with a hunting party yesterday."

He almost scoffed aloud at how true the term hunting was in this case. Pointed Nose had certainly made prey of Lucy Winslow. Del gritted his teeth. Even returning Ellen to the whites might not avoid a war. He needed to get her back before tempers increased.

They entered the camp. Playing children, women mending clothing, men making weapons all stopped and stared as the trio rode by them. Silent at first, they talked as Del continued past. He strained to catch snippets but heard no real words to give him any clues about Ellen. The smaller huts formed a circle. Inside was another ring of finer homes until they reached the center where the largest home of all stood. Made of skins and sturdy saplings, the richness of the beading told him the occupant was no ordinary leader. He dismounted as the other two did.

The scout who seemed most familiar with his language made a give-me motion at Del. "We will take your horse for care. You wait here until Running Cloud is ready."

Smart move, he thought, in keeping Pomme from him. Del glanced around, seeing others look away when his gaze met theirs. He let them stare, knowing they were all just as curious about him as he was about them. Unwilling to do anything else until gaining an audience with the chief, he went to the home's opening. Del sat, waiting until Running Cloud had time for him. He only hoped to have a chance to plead his case before Pointed Nose could.

At first, Del stared straight ahead and ignored the life going on around him. Eventually, curiosity drew him in and he started watching people as they went about their late day activities. The cherubic children giggled and peered around tents to stare. They soon grew bored of playing peek-a-boo this way and went to play elsewhere. He suspected those walking in front of him did so more than once. After several minutes of watching, he was sure of it and worked hard to ignore his urge to smile at their shared curiosity.

A commotion to his right caught Del's attention. Chief Running Cloud approached, flanked by the two scouts and several others. They stopped several feet away from him and spent a few moments talking. Each man spoke low enough so Del couldn't pick out the words he knew in their language. Running Cloud held up a hand to stop the chatter. His people stopped talking and scattered. The chief stared at Del. "Hello, young man. Please, be my guest inside."

He followed the man into the home as directed. The room was far bigger and more ornate than the temporary quarters Del had. Beaded fabric decorated the walls like the tapestries did in Europe. Sunlight filtered in from the top where the saplings loosely intersected. Weak embers burned and Running Cloud settled in on an ornate pillow. He gestured and Del sat opposite him.

When his guest sat still, the chief said, "I saw you at Bear River. Why are you here, my child?"

Del took in a deep breath, glad the chief spoke so kindly to him. "I have come here for a white woman taken from my friends."

Running Cloud thought for a moment before shaking his head. "There's no white woman here. You could be mistaken."

While not wanting to argue, Del had to disagree. "I'm not and wanted to be. The tracks lead away from our group and to here. Your son is also gone."

The chief tilted his head as if hearing a message meant only for him and smiled after a moment. "He's returned and his horse rides heavy. Either he has your woman or a small deer. He will come here. You and I will discuss with him his crime."

Del swallowed his heart back down his throat. He placed hands on his knees in an effort to keep still. Every ounce of him wanted to run out and find Ellen.

"Patience, child. Pointed Nose will come in to tell me what he's done in triumph."

The word the chief used irritated Del. A murder was not a triumph. He strove to keep a respectful tone. "My woman's mother was killed in the abduction. Will he be glad of that?"

Eyes narrowed to slits, Running Cloud ground out between gritted teeth, "You have certain knowledge of this?"

"Yes." He looked down at the fire, convinced the chief's words were now profane as the man swore a blue streak. Some sounded like the ones rarely said by his mother. The thought would amuse him at any other time, but now, he needed to get Ellen back to her people. "Father, the woman is mine and I'm only here to claim her."

"Enough. She will be returned to you even if I have to tie my son up to do it."

"Father! I have—" Pointed Nose burst into the home and hurried to his father. When he saw Del, the young man's face scrunched up as if he'd stepped in manure. "What are you doing here, halfwit?"

"He's here to retrieve his woman, son. Tell me what you did to get her."

"She's not his. She was married to a white man who couldn't keep her and she's mine now." He sneered at Del. "He's a white man's slave and is only here at his owner's request."

Accepting the challenge, Del stood face to face with Pointed Nose. "I'm no one's slave and am here to make sure you've only killed one woman today."

Running Cloud wore the same expression Del's father did when furious with him. "Is what this man says true? Did you kill her mother?"

"I had to do so, Father. She began screaming and—"

"Enough!" The chief held up a hand for a long while, speechless. Both younger men stood, watching and waiting. At last he said, "You've started a war that I need to end. Go to your own home until I send for you."

"No." The young man crossed his arms and leaned back. "She's my woman and I'm not a child."

"Maybe so, but you're also a fool who has begun something no one wants to finish with the death of all of us. Go before I call for you to be dragged home by your feet."

Giving Del a look that would wither stone, Pointed Nose stomped out. The air he left behind didn't ease in his absence. Running Cloud motioned to the ground. "Please be seated again and we'll discuss the woman."

Del eased back down, crossing his legs in front of him. "No one needs trouble, Father. I only want to take the woman back to her people without harm."

"My son said she's another man's wife. Why are you here and not him?"

He cursed Sam's lie and decided to tell him the truth no matter how embarrassing. "My friend misspoke in an effort to keep your son away from her for me." The chief's eyebrows rose in surprise, but not hostility. Encouraged, Del continued, "I feel for the woman but am not ready to tell her. Sam knew this and lied to Pointed Nose so I'd have time to win Ellen's heart."

"She's not married?"

"Not yet." Del looked hard at the chief, hoping he got the message.

A small smile played around the older man's lips. "So Pointed Nose can have her if she chooses?"

He breathed in sharp at the thought of her marrying anyone else. "She won't choose him."

"What if she does? You would start a bloody war over the affections of a mere woman?"

"Not a war, no, but Ellen is…." He floundered for the appropriate Shoshone word. "She is everything."

A few seconds passed before Running Cloud spoke. "I'm convinced." The chief stood, leaving the home. "Follow me."

He trailed behind the great man. Del was tall among his people on both sides, yet Running Cloud looked down on him. The chief barked out orders with Del catching only every other word. He had understood wedding.

A lovely young woman walked up to him. "Father says you

might be married today. I'm responsible for making you presentable. Others are getting Pointed Nose ready for a possible wife too."

"Who decides her husband?"

"She does. But that's for my Father to officially declare." She motioned for him to follow her into a tipi. "The woman is being bathed and dressed for this too. Your warm water is here, as are ceremonial clothes. Unless you have your own?"

"I do, with my horse."

She nodded. "I'll bring everything but the animal to you. Bathe until then." She slipped out of the small hut as gracefully as she'd entered.

He looked down at the earthen pot of hot water. The French rarely bathed, but the Natives did daily. Del grinned at how European he'd been in the past few weeks. Maybe that's what Ellen disliked about him. He undressed to his pants and began washing with a small cloth.

"Hello?" The young woman seeing to him came into the home. She held up his saddlebags. "I have both of these sacks. We can leave here what you don't take to the ceremony."

"Thank you." When the girl left him alone again, Del removed his pants and finished bathing. He opened the bag holding his clothing and took out his mother's beads, putting them around his neck. He changed into the fresh attire, liking how everything fit. The pants were a little tight, but wearable. The headdress and face paint remained left to do. The feathers felt right on his head and he carefully applied the red and black from memory, having traded his mirror long ago. Hopefully after tonight he'd have a reason to celebrate Ellen's freedom from Pointed Nose. Impatience to rescue her tugged at his conscience, and he stepped outside to see the native girl waiting for him. "Is this my home for after the ceremony?"

"Yes, no matter if you're married or not."

Del grinned at having a roof over his head. "Thank you." He put a hand on her shoulder for stability and pulled on his moccasins.

"My pleasure." Stepping away when he finished, she traced a toe in the dirt. "You might not need to spend the night alone."

Her offer surprised and pleased him in a way. If he'd not met Ellen and lost his heart, this young woman would have been worth a closer look. "Are you the chief's daughter?" She shook her head and he continued, "Then Pointed Nose is a fool for looking anywhere but here for a wife."

She smiled, her cheeks flushed. "We should leave. I hear others celebrating."

He followed her outside. The first star began its twinkle in the fading light and a waxing moon struggled to break free of the horizon. He looked and saw everyone walking to the village center. Drums began and a few beats later, so did the chants. Del and the young woman followed the others as they made their way.

Pointed Nose sat to one side of his father. Both men frowned and Del guessed they'd just finished arguing. Running Cloud motioned to his vacant side and Del went to sit beside him. The other man's glares almost made him laugh. Scowls weren't going to help Pointed plead his case with Ellen. It seemed every person in the village sat in a large circle around the fire. Lesser chiefs and leaders sat on either side of Del and Pointed Nose.

The young man leaned forward, addressing Del. "Father tells me you love this woman."

Del stared straight ahead. "I do, very much."

"Why?"

The question took him aback. He never thought about why he loved Ellen, just that he did. "She has a kind heart and cares for her family."

Pointed Nose laughed. "You've described every woman here."

"Maybe so, but why do you want her so much as to risk a war?"

The younger man sneered. "I asked you first, *metis*."

He looked away from the fire and turned to Pointed Nose, feeling his pulse pounding in anger. The French word for mixed race didn't insult him as much as the man's intent did. Using the term just confirmed what a tiny mind the chief's son had in his head. "Ellen is smart, a good cook, and beautiful," Del ground out from clenched teeth. "I've told you my reasons. Now tell me. Again, why do you want her?"

He shrugged. "I don't have a wife like her."

The few words told Del everything he needed to know. The man hadn't fallen in love with Ellen and only wanted her like a child wants a freshly made toy. He needed to make her seem unappealing to Pointed Nose without looking foolish in marrying her. "She wears glasses."

"I know."

"What happens when she loses them or they break?"

Pointed Nose waved his hand as if refusing a tray of hors d'oeuvres. "I don't care."

Del shrugged. "Fine, but she can't see without them. Do you want a wife who needs a guide every minute of the day?"

"The woman can warm my bed. I could remove her eyes with a knife and she'd still be useful."

A haze of fury clouded his vision at the cruel statement. Before Del could retort, a small ruckus began in front of them on the opposite side of the bonfire. Ellen stepped into the light, flanked by two other women. He scowled to keep his expression unfriendly. They'd dressed her in a doeskin dress. Her hair had been divided and braided, feathers tied on the ends. Even out of her element and in clothes foreign to her, she looked beautiful. She continued to stand until Running Cloud made a downward motion with his hand. The girls on each side of her sat and she followed.

Pointed Nose leaned around his father and said to Del, "She makes a good Shoshone woman, with or without eyes. I've decided I will marry her tonight."

Del's heart stopped. He ignored the statement and turned to Running Cloud. "Chief, I respect you and your son, but if you let him marry her, I will kill him."

CHAPTER 5

Mile after mile they rode, the only things visible were trees and mountainsides as far as Ellen saw. After a quick examination, she realized the futility of finding landmarks in a dense pine forest. Hopelessness replaced the lump of fear in her. Even if she escaped, how could she ever get back? She closed her eyes and let the tears fall. Everyone had heard stories of women captured and used as slaves for the savages. She'd not be rescued until years passed and she'd had several children. Her babies would be from a grunting animal. Looking through watery eyes at the ground they covered, she considered jumping from the horse. The fall might kill her, but better to die than live as an Indian's property.

The land flattened and the group took advantage by speeding up. Their full gallop jarred her bones from their joins. Ellen's glasses bounced on her nose. She pressed her cheek and ear against her captor's back in an effort to keep them on. Wincing when her face hit his skin, she recoiled from the touch and sobbed. She'd give anything if the man she held were Del taking her home instead of a stranger stealing her. Would Sam and her father start a search party? They'd have a vast wilderness to search. The odds were against her ever seeing her family again.

She opened her eyes when their pace slowed. Ahead of them lay a large Indian village. How peaceful it looked, with children playing, adults talking and laughing. Everyone stopped what they were doing and stared at the group of warriors riding up to them. Women paused their work with grinding seeds into flour. Ellen wondered how long they would wait before expecting her to do chores. If the lurid stories circulated around the campfires were true, they enjoyed torturing and sharing women among the tribe members. She shuddered. Better they kill her as quickly as they had Lucy. Fresh tears welled up and caught in her glasses' lenses before rolling down her face. A child touched her shoe, startling her, and Ellen recoiled in surprise.

The brave dismounted, grabbing her from his horse. She held onto his arm for support, getting her feet under her before letting go. He yelled at her while leading his horse to the village center. Another warrior, the one who'd killed Lucy, pulled her by the upper arm. She squeaked in pain before letting him drag her a little way until she walked along with him. Every man Ellen saw had some sort of face paint and all wore colorful clothing. She wondered if their appearance meant they were on the warpath, and if so, she feared for her little brothers. Shaking, she sought out a friendly face. All she needed was one sympathetic person to help her find a way back to her family.

Her captor stopped in front of a small hut where a woman Lucy's age stood. Ellen wiped her eyes and cleaned her glasses while the two talked. The lady motioned to her, as far as she could tell with her blurry vision. The brave walked away and the lady held open the home's door flap. Taking the cue from her, Ellen stepped inside. She went to the middle, unable to stand upright anywhere else, and looked around. She'd seen larger homes than this in the middle of the camp. Was this a single person's home and did they mean her to live here?

"Wash."

Ellen jumped when the woman spoke. "Wash?"

When the native nodded and pointed at the fire pit, she saw a pot of water. Looking back at her, the lady pantomimed scrubbing.

She had no intention of getting undressed and bathing. "No."

The woman frowned, shook her head, and left. Ellen wrapped her arms around herself, now cold. Even if she did as ordered, she had no clean clothes to wear. She walked around, still shivering while examining the walls of the home. The door opening startled her. Ellen took a deep breath, trying to ease her nerves.

The woman came in, this time with a folded bundle. She held it out with a scowl, saying, "Wash and dress."

Ellen took the item, surprised when her fingers touched the clothes. Made of the softest buckskin she'd ever felt, she caressed the dress. Beads sewn into patterns broke up the smoothness. They glittered when she tilted the fabric into the light. She nodded at the Native woman. "Yes, wash and dress. Thank you."

She backed out, leaving Ellen alone. In her distress, she'd not noticed a low cushion on the ground. It looked big enough to be a nice seat and a clean place to put the costume. She loosened her dress, not wanting to wash naked without a locking door. Finding a washrag next to the water basin, she hoped this was what the woman wanted. The warm water and scrubbing eased her sore muscles. Every part of her ached now the crisis had abated. She heard a holler outside her room and recognized the voice. She peered from a sliver of opening in the door. Her female keeper stood there, and Ellen asked, "Yes?"

She lifted another pot of water. "Wash?"

Had she been that filthy? She took the offered earthen pot. "Yes, thank you." The woman disappeared again. Once she was clean, her dress seemed unbearably dirty and stiff. She looked back at the door flap, thinking she could be out of one dress and into another in an instant. Just for now and just until she could wash her real clothes, Ellen changed out, listening for anything awry while she did so.

She gasped as the buckskin dress unfurled down her body, the fringe tickling her knees. The fabric both hugged Ellen and let her breathe. She ran her hands down the dress, surprised at the softness of it until noticing how the prior berry picking still stained her fingernails. She began shivering.

Her helper peeked in and grinned. "Yes?" She walked inside, smiling at Ellen, and barked an order. One of the men opened the door. The woman gave him one of the dirty wash waters, and he handed it to someone outside. She gave him the second and scooped up Ellen's dress.

Before the woman could give the brave her clothes, Ellen stepped between the two people. "No, give that back! It's mine!"

The woman put a hand on Ellen's arm and shook her head. She patted over her own heart while saying, "Wash, yes?" She nodded as if to get a nod from her too.

She watched the native mime sleep, wake, and bring. Understanding, Ellen nodded back. "Yes, thank you."

The lady motioned toward the cushion. Ellen went and sat, watching as the woman gave one of the men her dress. She so hoped she'd interpreted the sign language correctly. Pa would be furious if she lost her good clothes to a savage. The absurdity of everything made her laugh. If she never saw Pa again, how would he know what she'd done?

The woman had knelt beside her while she'd had been lost in her own thoughts. She held out a hand to her, showing Ellen a couple of leather shoestrings with feathers at the end. Then she lifted one of her braids, showing her the end and nodding.

Ellen patted her hair. "This?"

"Yes, please."

She didn't want to anger the woman, no matter how kind she'd seemed. Ellen sat on the cushion over far enough to share. The native woman pulled the pins from Ellen's hair before brushing and braiding the locks. The process relaxed her enough to unclench her fists. When Ellen felt the second braid tied off, she opened her eyes. When she went in front of her and smiled, Ellen asked, "Yes?"

With hands on her hips and a big grin, she replied, "Yes." She went for the door, pausing to give Ellen a let's go gesture.

The first few stars twinkled in the twilight as she stepped outside for the first time since her arrival. Shouts began in toward the center of the village. She wanted to run in the opposite direction, but two men with their arms crossed stood beside her. The girl made the let's go movement again, and Ellen fell in step behind her.

The hollering and shrieking by the festive people worried her as she examined the village's edges. They walked to the middle and the noise grew with each step she took.

At the center, her captor pushed her forward and nudged her in the ribs. She winced from the pain and looked up to see Del seated among several men. Nearly crying from relief, she wanted to run to him and beg him to take her back home. The expression on his face froze her in place. She'd never seen such a scornful stare at her from anyone, not even her father. Ellen blinked, unable to believe this man could be Del. Maybe he had a twin because the Del she knew could never scowl at her in such a way.

She glanced at the man sitting to his left. The older gentleman motioned down with his hand flat and she sat, relieved when he nodded his approval. She recognized him as the chief at the trading village from the other day. His son sat next to him on the opposite side from Del. She merely glanced at Pointed Nose, thinking he'd been too encouraged by her attention already. Ellen looked from Del to the chief and back again while clenching her hands to stop their trembling.

They talked amongst themselves, their words unintelligible. She looked at the ground and worried with a bit of skin on her chapped lips. The men spoke too fast for her to even try to understand. They certainly said no endearments. Ellen snuck a peek at the man she'd believed was a kind and friendly Del. Red and black paint covered his face, and he wore a crown of long feathers. Their ends were also stained red. He wore a few strands of multicolored beads, and the straps for a quiver holding a bow and arrows crossed his chest. Gazing at the ground below him, she saw a beaded moccasin peek out from his knee where he sat cross-legged. This savage version of Del scared her. Especially whenever he looked at her as if she were the enemy. Her lip bled a little, comforting her with the iron as she chewed.

She played with one of her shoe's laces and tried not to stare at him. He looked every bit the savage brute but a shade paler than the men flanking him. Del sat tall and relaxed, a strange mix of formal and comfortable. Whenever it seemed their gazes might meet, Ellen stared into the fire. She could almost feel the guards behind her as if they physically touched her. Glancing back, she saw they sat a few feet from her. She took a deep breath in, grateful for the space. She faced the front once more and strived to shut out all the chattering around her.

Ellen shivered despite the warmth and looked up at Del. He'd had the same hard expression, but different this time. His eyes softened and the emotion she saw gave her goose bumps. She broke their gaze, staring unseeing at the sky. He did care for her and had betrayed himself with a single glance. She realized he had come here alone for what she hoped was a rescue.

Before she could turn over this thought in her mind, women brought food to them on what looked like boards. Her stomach growled at the smells. She sat quiet, head bowed while watching Del for any hidden signals to run. Dinner for the men then the women seemed to last for hours. She ate, noticing how tender the meat was. Her family might like the food, assuming she ever saw Pa and the boys again. Her hand shook and she put the bite back down, tears filling her eyes over Lucy's death. Above all the ruckus and her musings, she heard Del's voice. Ellen swallowed hard and looked up at him.

He had stood and was now giving a speech. She closed her eyes, both enjoying hearing him talk, yet afraid of the unknown. Without the visual distractions, she heard the last words of his speech and glanced up at him. He'd said *"ma coeur."* She'd heard it as plain as anything. Still giving her a slight sneer, he shrugged, said something to the chief. The man, dressed in clothes that would blind the sun, laughed and stood also. He gestured to the braves sitting guard behind her. They scrambled to their feet and scooped up Ellen. Her legs were numb from the hard ground, but she ignored the tingly dead feeling to make herself stand up straight. The leader of the group clapped his hands while barking out a command.

A woman, young and lovely, brought a tray of three bowls to Del. He nodded his approval. After looking for and gaining permission from the chief, he and she walked around opposite sides of the fire to Ellen. Once they both faced her, he frowned. Within full sight of the entire village, he shouted something in gibberish and they all cheered. He grinned at their ruckus and turned to the young woman. She blushed, holding up the tray for him.

Ellen couldn't stop tears from forming. He dipped a finger in the red liquid and drew a line across her forehead. She didn't know if he stained or painted her skin. "Please, Del! What is happening? I want to go home."

He raised his eyebrows and shrugged as if he didn't understand. Then, Del dipped another finger in the white liquid. He drew a line from below her nose to her chin, going over her lips. Turning to the Indian woman, he winked. Ellen closed her eyes as tears fell down her cheeks. She couldn't breathe from the terror and yet he flirted right in front of her. If not for the well-armed men surrounding him, she'd love to mash all the paints in his face and see how he liked it. When he touched her cheek, she startled. He drew a line down and another on the opposite side. Wetting his finger again with yellow, he traced above the prior line on her forehead. She shook her head in a tiny motion to deny herself any more tears.

Del surveyed his handiwork before nodding to the woman. She stepped back so he stood alone in front of Ellen. He grinned at a point beyond her and she turned to see her guards still in place. He cleared his throat for her attention. She faced the front again, looking at the straps covering his chest and the colorful necklace he wore. She'd not noticed it before now, a little distracted by his stern face. The glass beads were pretty in a masculine way, she thought, and wanted to laugh at her own frivolity. He shouted out something, startling Ellen. He'd said *ma coeur* yet again and she looked into his eyes. His expression softened as he took the strands of beads from around his neck. Del turned to the chief and said something that made the older man laugh. At the chief's wave, he stared into her eyes as well, and placed the beads around her neck.

No sooner than the beads settled, a great cheer went around the fire. He took her hand and turned to speak to everyone. Ellen didn't understand a word but blushed when the adults laughed as Del led her around and past the large fire. Gripping her hand so hard her fingers hurt, he pushed her into a wigwam.

A small fire pit with embers glowing lit up the room. If not for the different decorations, she'd think he'd returned her to the first hut. A bed was already laid out beside the fire circle. The night air had stiffened her sore muscles and the furs covering the ground appealed to her with their promised warmth. She glanced at the door, hearing a rustle.

Del slid in and secured the entrance. He looked at her and shook his head. "I am so sorry for this, for everything. Are you hurt?"

His kindness undid her. She crumpled, crying. Sobbing too hard to talk, she managed to squeak out, "They killed Lucy in front of me. I couldn't do anything for her."

He wrapped his arms around her. "I know, dearest."

She melted into him, her face pressed against his neck. "If it'd been me?" His hug almost squeezed the air from her. Ellen stared up into his eyes. "Would you be here if they'd killed me instead?"

His chin jutted, his eyes watering. Del shook his head slightly and cleared his throat before saying, "I don't know. I'd be mad from grief."

Ellen relaxed into him, fresh tears falling. "I'm so glad you're here. I wasn't sure if anyone would follow me in time."

He pressed his lips against her forehead, each word a kiss. "What did you imagine? I could continue on without knowing your fate?"

"I had hoped you cared for me enough."

"More than care, my love, and I suspected they'd bring you here, thankfully."

"Thankfully." His lips continued to press against her skin. Ellen closed her eyes, drinking in the smell of him. She'd been certain on the ride here she'd be in her kidnapper's bed tonight. Instead, the one man she wanted most in the world held her. She swallowed. "What do we do now?"

"We stay tonight and maybe tomorrow as well."

His answer didn't please her. With Lucy gone, Skeeter and Buster needed her. Sure, Pa could take care of them by himself. He was their father and a grown man, after all. Still, she loved and needed to protect her little family from these savages. She put her hands on Del's face, staring into his eyes. "When can we get back to camp?"

"As soon as possible, or rather as soon as manners allow."

He wore such a guilty expression, she had to ask, "Are we expected to be here all night together?"

"Yes, all night and we're not to be disturbed for any reason." He smiled, his eyes holding a mischievous glint.

The people living here might let him do whatever he pleased with her? Surely not! "Not for any reason?"

"Not even if you beg and plead for help. If you do so, our neighbors will laugh and discount your screams as, um...."

"Discount my screams as what?" The shame didn't leave his face. "Why would I be screaming when here with you?"

"Don't be angry. It was the only way to save you." He held her by her shoulders. "I needed to claim you as mine before they gave you to Pointed Nose."

"You claimed me? As what, your slave?" He frowned so that his eyebrows met in the middle. She instantly regretted making him angry again.

"Not slave so much as wife."

Certain he'd misspoken, she couldn't breathe. "They think we're married?"

"Now they do."

She didn't like his sheepish tone and quickly surmised he wasn't being completely honest. "Now? What are you not telling me?"

"This was for your good."

"When exactly did they think we were married?"

"When I painted you as mine and put my mother's beads on you." He smiled, patting her shoulders in an attempt to placate her. "The situation, it is funny, no?"

Ellen crossed her arms. "No." This entire event made a mockery of marriage. Plus, her father must never know. He'd be furious at some Indian claiming her as his wife. "It's not funny at all."

"Once you're safe with your family it will be, I promise." He stroked her face with the back of his hand. "You being alive is very good, something to celebrate."

She softened, leaning into his touch. "Yes, being alive is good."

"Plus, our marriage has many more benefits for you than for me."

Ellen chuckled, liking the amusement in his eyes. "Excuse me?"

"I'm quite a catch."

"Really? Like a fish or maybe a rabbit? I've been catching a lot of mosquitoes lately. Are you as good a catch as that?"

He shrugged. "Well, better, I should think."

"I'd ask how so but am finding I don't care to know."

"You would not like to learn how profitable this is for you?" He traced the line on her cheek with the back of his hand. "Not learn how much esteem you now have as my wife?"

She moved away so his arms didn't reach her. "I don't care about benefiting from a marriage."

"Oh? Not even from my benefits?" He leaned forward and grinned. "I'm a very handsome man, so I've been told."

"Don't be cute. Being here with you is much better than with any other of those animals who kidnapped me. I thought I'd be sharing a bed with the chief's son tonight." She frowned, adding, "If he even has a bed. Maybe he sleeps naked on the ground."

"Pointed Nose likely does, but I would not allow his naked sleeping."

"Would you have a choice? He probably sleeps however he chooses."

"You misunderstand," he chided and then turned serious. "I will never let another man share your bed. Not now, not ever."

She tried to smile, knowing this conviction of his needed to stop before he took her back home. "Thank you, Del. You're a comfort to me and as they stole me away, I had but one regret." Ellen stepped into his embrace and felt the surprise in how his body tensed.

"I'd like to hear more about this regret you feel. It's a terrible thing, *ma coeur*."

The warmth of his skin and how close he held her distracted Ellen at first until she remembered her train of thought. "I wished

I'd kissed you earlier."

"Did we not kiss soon enough? I didn't want to attack you."

She smiled, leaning back to look at him. "You're the only man I've ever kissed, and I wanted another before I died or was kissed by one of those people."

"Who? Pointed Nose?" Del laughed. "Most girls want to be kissed by the chief's son. Did you not see all the attention they paid him?"

"I didn't. Watching for a chance to escape with you kept me busy." She pulled out of his hold. "You're not taking me seriously."

He let go without protest. "I am, but I'm also very happy he's not the one with you. Happy is not enough to describe the joy of seeing you alive. It is not enough to describe having you here safe and bound to me."

"Bound to you?"

"Yes. We are bound by my people and by their customs." He took a deep breath before continuing. "A paper in a courthouse will satisfy the whites. To me, the paper is but a formality. In my heart, you are my wife. If you prefer someone else, once we leave here the marriage can be null. I would not force you into this."

"Thank you. I'd like for my marriage to be my choice too." She watched as he removed his headdress, placing it aside. "There's only one bed here."

"We can share."

Ellen shook her head. "I don't think so."

"Nothing will happen. We'll wear clothes and may need to be close to keep warm." He took the strings of beads from her neck. "You may even keep your shoes tonight." Leaning in, Del said against her ear, "Tomorrow, you'll regret missing my love."

She went to the blankets and took off her shoes. Sliding under the blankets she added, "I only meant a kiss, not love."

He sat removing his own moccasins. "Either way, none for you."

"Good." He jostled her as he also got into bed. She smiled, knowing the contact was intentional. Once he settled in, she closed her eyes and in her mind saw Lucy's shocked eyes. Ellen shuddered. "Del?" she whispered.

"Yes?"

Her nose stung and she wanted to cry again. Laying on her back and staring at the opening above them, she said, "I have to get back as soon as possible. The boys must know about their mother by now. They need me."

"I know." Del turned over, wrapping his arms around her. "We will return to them."

She didn't think he'd believe how angry her father would be at him, although Del had seen enough of her father's bad behavior to trust her. Most people saw Pa's charm, not the temper tantrums. She turned toward Del to look in his eyes. "I don't know if you should go with me."

"No?"

"No. My father will blame you for Lucy's death. He won't think to praise you for saving me."

He let go of her to lie flat on his back, his arm tucked under his head. Closing his eyes, he stayed motionless except for breathing. Ellen glanced at him every so often. Did he sleep now? His body felt tense beside hers so she knew he had to be awake.

"Ellen?" he said so low she wasn't sure she'd heard him.

"Yes?"

"I will take you to your family tomorrow."

She snuggled against him, placing her hand on his chest. "Thank you. My returning is for my brothers, not for me."

"They have a father who can care for them himself. I'm doing this only for you."

"I appreciate you helping me. To make it easier on you, just leave me at any point the party will intersect. You don't have to wait with me there."

"*Que?*" He leaned away to stare into her eyes. "*Tu dites…? Non.* What makes you think I could do that? Do you not know? In my heart, you are my wife, my mate for life. How could I ever leave you somewhere and merely hope your people find you?"

CHAPTER 6

Ellen woke from her dream while hearing Lucy crying out "Why? Why did you let them do this to me?" Knowing how she'd had no choice in the matter didn't make the nightmare any less painful. She sat up, freezing despite the blanket. Del wasn't there but the fire burned brighter than before they'd slept. His thoughtfulness warmed more than the flames and she smiled. She stretched, testing muscles still sore from yesterday's hard ride here. Every minute she spent lazing about in this camp wasn't helping her brothers and possibly moving the group further from her. She needed to find Del and get home.

She stood and wavered on sore feet a bit before stepping outside. Her heart dropped. It had to be around noon with the sun overhead casting short shadows. He'd let her sleep far too late. She glanced around, searching for him. Despite the bustling village, no one seemed to notice her. She didn't know their language, and suddenly shy, wanted to find him. She strolled around, panicked and trying not to seem worried. Ellen searched the main campfire with no results. She went to the biggest shelter and waited outside, hoping to see him. After several minutes she wondered if he'd left her until she spied Pomme. Del had to be here somewhere since Pomme was, so she went back to the hut where they'd spent the night to wait for him.

She heard someone rustling inside and drew back the flap. Peeking in, she saw him gathering things, packing. "Del! Where have you been? I've looked everywhere for you."

"Worried, *ma coeur*?" He laughed. "No need to be. I wouldn't leave without my wife."

"Your what?" She put her hands on her hips. "That doesn't matter now. I am in an Indian village, you're the only person I know, and you're gone when I wake up. From a nightmare, I might add." Ellen paced. "I searched this whole place for you, not knowing how to talk to anyone, and you weren't anywhere to be found." She stood in front of him. He'd washed off the war paint from the previous evening. The clean handsome lines of his face distracted her for a moment. "I was saying...? Oh! And just when I think you've gone for good, you're here as if you married a woman every day."

He grinned. "Not that often, *non*. Every month maybe."

"Month?" She frowned when he chuckled. "You're horrible to tease me so."

"Too true. I should be whispering love in your ear." He paused in packing up their few belongings. "It is whispering love? My mother and father don't whisper."

"Oh." She folded her arms across her chest. "They might not talk about love much."

"Even married for as long as I've lived and they do." Del handed her a leather bag. "If you're ready, we can leave."

She peered inside the bag at her clean dress. "Leave?"

"Yes, go back to your family." He nodded to the outside. "First, they want us to parade through the village. After that, we'll be on our way."

"Oh! Thank you! Thank you so much!" She searched around her. "All right then, is this everything? I didn't have anything but a pail of berries, and I dropped that in the kidnapping." Ellen looked around at the small house. "This place isn't yours? You don't need to take it with you?"

"Non, more like a hotel. We'll leave it for others." Del opened the door. "*Allons?*"

"Um, what does that mean exactly?"

"Let's go."

His translation relieved her and Ellen grinned. "*Allons*, then. My brothers need me."

Pomme stood outside. She scratched his neck, glad to see him. Del got on the horse first with her following. When she settled in, he took her hands and wrapped her arms around him. Bystanders noticed and gave catcalls she didn't understand but could guess the meaning of. He looked back at her. "I'd like it if you pretended to be a happy bride. Just until we're clear of everyone."

Ellen gave him a squeeze. "Certainly. I'll soon be with my family, thanks to your rescue, and am very happy." She almost pulled her arms from around him until he placed one of his hands on hers. Understanding his silent message, she linked her fingers and continued to smile. Del clicked at Pomme and they began walking through the village.

People stood along each side of them as they rode through the town. She returned waves to some of the children and nodded to the chief. Pointed Nose stood a little ways down from his father, an arm wrapped around another woman. She returned his smirk before realizing what she was doing. Del cleared his throat. "Ignore him. He was laughing at me for marrying a blind woman."

"I'm not blind. Not unless I'm missing my glasses." At his raised eyebrows, she grinned. "If it means going home with you? Then yes, you're right and I'm blind."

"Ah, *ma coeur*, you speak my favorite words of love."

After the parade and leaving the last of the crowds, she stopped smiling. What she'd find back at the wagon train wouldn't leave her thoughts. The mosquitoes grew worse as they rode. He wrapped a light blanket around her to keep most of them at bay. She snuggled into him, cold, despite the warm day. She liked how the horse's motion kept her close to him, his body heat warming her comfortably, and at some point she fell asleep. The cold wind on her face woke her when they reached the mountain's peak.

"We have a ways to go yet. At the first creek, we will stop for rest."

"All right." She patted his shoulder, giving him a little caress. "I'd like that."

As promised, he stopped once they reached a small stream. The trickle of water tasted good and fresh. "When you are finished, I have something to eat," said Del.

"There's food?" She eased up the bank, taking his offered hand for help.

"Of course. I packed some for us."

Ellen ate the flat bread he gave her and the deer jerky too. The meat had a gamey taste, but she was hungry enough to not mind. He stood with an easy grace while she struggled to stand.

He pulled her to him, hugging her close. "It is difficult, I know. You walk far more than you ride."

"Yes, we lost the horse a while back, and Pa was the one always riding him anyway." She shrugged. "With the boys, it seemed a better idea to stay at their level and keep an eye on them anyway." Something in his eyes seemed sad. "Thank you for bringing me back to the wagon train, and thank you for marrying me."

He brushed a stray lock of hair from her face. "I had to; no other man can be your husband but me. I could never allow it."

She grinned, feeling ornery. "And I could never allow some other woman to be your wife."

Del leaned back to see her and asked, "So, I'm the one now captured?"

"Very much so."

He kissed her, holding her cold face in his hands. She shivered, freezing in the thin mountain air. Del pressed his lips against her forehead. "We must go. I'd like to be closer to them by nightfall."

She climbed up behind him on the horse. Her body protested and she couldn't get comfortable. She shifted around, trying to find a good seat.

Del turned to her. "Are you ready?"

"As much as I ever will be." She put her arms around him. "I don't suppose this will stop hurting anytime soon?"

Laughing, he squeezed her hands around his waist. "It will by the time we arrive."

She sighed in resignation, leaning against him as he clicked to the horse. "That's something to look forward to then."

They rode on, crossing several small creeks. The hills seemed like nothing to her while on horseback. With all the ups and downs of getting a wagon across country, a horse was a much better way to travel. Almost. She winced when the animal stumbled. Sitting down tonight would be a challenge. She closed her eyes as twilight approached. "Are we going to sleep tonight or press on?"

"I would like to be a little further before sleep. It is growing dark, however, and I must find water for us." He turned his face to her. "Will you be fine until then?"

She stretched forward, kissing his cheek. "With you? Always."

He smiled, turning to kiss her full on the lips. "I'm glad you think so." The horse stumbled a little and Del faced forward again.

Ellen leaned into his back, enjoying the feel and smell of him. He'd been right about being numb. It'd taken a few miles until she didn't feel the soreness.

Del stopped by a small stream and slid down to help her off the horse. She moved slowly, stiff from not standing for so long. He made quick work of setting up their bed. Ellen took the chance to rinse her hands and get a drink from the small creek.

"Ellen?"

She straightened with every muscle protesting. "Yes?"

"We should eat while we can still see to do so."

They ate the flat bread and jerky he'd provided. Both were quiet while eating with her wondering how to get him to say her name again. His accent left her breathless. She swallowed the last bite. "I'm rather thirsty. Do you mind coming with me since it's become darker?"

"Of course I will." He got to his feet, hauling her up as well. Del chuckled when she didn't share his graceful movements. "Don't worry, *ma coeur*, you'll get used to riding horseback soon."

She let him lead her to the stream. "I hope so." They both took the chance for a cool clean drink. "Thank you, Del."

"My pleasure."

He took her hand, his grip strong and warm. Her foot slipped on a patch of mud and she shrieked. In an instant, he lifted her into his arms and held her close. Her face pressed into his neck, Ellen couldn't breathe. Silence enveloped them, except for the songbirds calling to each other. His heartbeat pulsed under her cheek where their skin met. This, this wasn't playing, wasn't experimentation, wasn't something she could control or measure. The earlier infatuation Ellen could dismiss. But this desire, deep and dark, she felt to the marrow of her bones. Hungry for him, she gave in to the urge and kissed the hollow at the base of his neck.

He shuddered, saying, "*Non, mon Dieu, Je n'est*," just before she kissed her way up to his chin. In a fast move, Del took her lips with his own, harsh and unrelenting. He eased her to the ground, placing her down on a dry, grassy embankment.

Ellen, lost in the feel of him, welcomed the warmth of his body on hers. When he lifted her skirt, placing his leg between hers, her desire halted. Sudden sobriety splashed through her. He'd meant to take advantage of the dark and her willingness. She turned her face away from his. "No! Stop! Stop, Del!" His hand still tugged up her skirt, exposing her leg. She felt his arousal against her thigh, scaring her. "Please, please stop!"

"*Que?*" He pulled at her earlobe with his teeth.

She pushed his shoulders. "Please, please don't do this. I've never, please."

"*Mon Dieu*, I forgot myself! I am so sorry." He helped her push the hem of her skirt to below her shins. "Of course you're an innocent. I never thought otherwise."

"Don't be sorry, Adelard." Shame filled her. "I shouldn't have let you kiss me so much. It was wrong for me to encourage you that way."

He took her hand again and led her back to their camp. "No more apologies, then. We can sleep tonight under my blanket, and I promise you'll wake up fully dressed tomorrow morning."

Ellen hesitated next to the open bedroll for only a second. "I've no doubts about being safe with you." She settled in, waiting as he cuddled up next to her then made sure his wool blanket covered them both. Tingly from the kiss but too tired to think about it, she fell asleep as soon as her eyes closed.

He kept her warm through the night, his body seeming to radiate heat in their bedroll. The next morning, she woke before him. Del hadn't bothered with a fire, and now Ellen wished he had. Coffee sounded like heaven, even a few beans to chew appealed to her. She lay still, wondering if she should wake him.

"Good morning," he said in her ear. "We are almost to your family."

"How far do you think they are?"

"Guessing by their prior rate, I would say about fifteen to twenty miles from us." He nuzzled her neck. "If not so far, I would have you this morning."

"Have me what? I could fix breakfast."

He turned her to face him. "I would have you this way."

"Oh my!" She looked down as he kissed from her forehead to her lips. "You promised I'd be safe with you. Though I might like taking the time for more kisses, my brothers…."

Glancing up into her eyes, he gave her a sad smile. "I agree. They're a priority for me too."

She leaned in, bringing her lips to his till they almost touched. "I so appreciate your concern for them."

"How can I not? Even apart from being related to you, Skeeter is a good boy. Little Buster, he is a sweet child as well." He eased out of the bed.

"I'm glad you think so." Ellen sat, reluctant to do anything more.

"I do. Now, if you can stand, we need to get going." He went to his horse, opening a saddlebag for the blankets.

She tried standing, unable to get her legs to cooperate. After a little bit of struggle, Ellen rolled to her side, then stomach. She did a push up from there to get to her knees. Bracing herself and with a little grunt, she pushed herself to stand. The sound of Del snickering caught her attention. She faced him, grimacing. "I suppose you think this is funny?"

"I'm trying not to, but…." He shrugged. "Can I help that you are so adorable?"

Ellen stared up at the sky as if her patience rested up in the clouds. "If I could walk, I'd go over and show you how lovely I don't feel this morning."

"Oh, poor little *be'be*!" He went and scooped her into his arms. "You are sadly injured and here I am, mocking you." Del tossed her an inch or so out of his arms and caught her, making Ellen laugh. "You are a little *be'be*! So light and feathery."

"If you say so, I'll pretend to agree."

"I do say so." He kissed her forehead. "Now, back onto the horse you go."

"No," she whined but put her leg over the horse's back and sat.

"See? The dreading was worse than the doing." He got onto the horse, careful not to nudge her with his foot, and clicked at Pomme.

They went ten miles before seeing any sign of the trail. At last, she saw a group of wagons rolling in the distance ahead. They spent the next hour or so skirting the narrow valley caused by a thin ribbon of river. "Del." She tapped his shoulder and pointed. "Isn't that our people?"

Del glanced back at her and cleared his throat. "*Ma coeur?*"

She smiled at the endearment. "Yes?"

"Did you want to wash your face before rejoining your people?"

"I suppose so." Ellen had forgotten he wasn't really one of her kind, and his reminder set her aback. "Why?"

He traced a finger along her cheek. "You're painted in my colors. They'll announce our marriage before you do."

"Oh dear!" She rubbed her face, the chalky stripes dry beneath her fingers. "Yes, I'd better wash these off as soon as I can." At his amused look, she added, "I'll have enough to explain without tossing a wedding into the mix."

Laura Stapleton

"When we reach the river, we will break for noon, clean up your face, and go to your family." He saw her scratch a mosquito bite and reached back for a light blanket. "Here, wear this."

She let her gaze caress his smooth neck. Nothing marred the silky skin. "Why don't they bite you at all?"

"They do, then learn I have vinegar for blood."

"You?" Now protected, she settled again against him. "No, your blood must be far too sweet. They should be making a feast of you."

He stopped at the river as promised, handing her a handkerchief to wash her face.

"Imagine, an Indian brave with a hankie," she teased while dipping the cloth in water before scrubbing her face.

He grinned, and with a very Gallic shrug, said, "I have to wash my behind with something."

"What!" She held the hankie by two fingers as far away from her as possible. "Oh dear! It can't be true. It doesn't smell like your—oh dear!"

Laughing, he asked, "And how do you know what my rear smells like? Is there something I should know?"

She narrowed her eyes at him. "You have to be teasing."

"I have to be?"

"Yes, because you adore me far too much to let me wash with a hiney rag." She rinsed the cloth and continued to scrub her face, giving him a defiant look.

"Hmm, I suppose you are right. How could I kiss you if that were my 'hiney rag'?" He shook his head. "Not possible."

Rinsing the last bit of paint from the cloth, she stood. "Do you even have a hiney rag?"

"*Non*, don't be silly." He hopped onto his horse, holding his hand out to her. "I have a hiney blanket used to repel mosquitoes with its bad smell."

She laughed at his statement, secretly hoping he teased. Ellen wrapped her arms around him. She didn't want this to end. Living at the camp with him now and having no contact seemed unbearable. Not wanting to say anything for a while, she at last decided to prepare him.

"Del?"

"Hmm?"

"We need to talk. We're getting close to the others, and I need

126

to tell you a few things."

"All right, continue, ma Ellen."

Him saying her name distracted her. For a moment, she forgot what she wanted to say. The fort ahead of them jogged her memory. "Because of who you are, my father will blame you personally for Lucy's death."

"Yes, blame the French blood for everything." He glanced back at her and winked.

"I'm not even going to respond." She paused for only a moment. "Drop me off half a mile away and let me walk to Fort Hall on my own."

"Why would I do such a thing? I'm not willing to leave you alone that far from me."

Had he not heard and understood that he'd be blamed for her kidnapping? "Del, you simply must. I can walk such a short way without incident." She paused, not wanting to hurt his pride or feelings. "I'd rather you not talk with my father just yet. If he learns you think we're married, well, I don't want you to hear the nasty things he'll say about you."

"*I* think we're married?" He snorted. "There were witnesses."

"I'm glad Pa wasn't one of them." She sighed. "I don't want to hear any of the ugly things he has to say either, but I'll have to tolerate him for Skeeter and Little Buster's sake."

"You aren't telling him we're married?"

Ellen shook her head and patted him on the shoulder. "I think it's for the best. Even if we were in a real wedding, my father will never accept you."

He pulled back on the horse's reins, stopping Pomme in his tracks. "What he accepts doesn't matter. We are bound by a real marriage. The only thing lacking is a paper filed in a courthouse. I plan to visit a courthouse with you as soon as possible."

The man couldn't be serious. Ellen swallowed a lump in her throat. Pa would blow up like a powder keg if he heard a peep about her being Del's wife. He needed to understand that in no way were they together, for both of their sakes. "No, no one is filing any sort of papers. I mean, maybe a little ceremony makes a bunch of savages think we're married, but we're not."

"I cannot discuss this with you from horseback." He slid down, holding his arms out to her.

She dismounted into his arms. He felt comforting to her and

her resolve to deny him as a spouse wavered for a moment. Gathering her wits about her, she stiffened her backbone. "I'm not trying to be difficult but, Del, really. We had no minster. It's not legal, and my family wasn't there. My stepmother had just died. We aren't married, not in any binding way." As she spoke, Ellen saw his expression change from anger to hurt and back again. She tried to placate him. "Yes, in the village, we were sort of married. There was paint; I love the beads." She pulled the glass and shell beads from around her neck, holding them out for him. "And the kissing? Goodness, I'd never imagined something so wonderful. Still, you have to admit, as someone who is legally trained, we can't be considered married in any binding way."

He took what she offered and stared at the necklace. Swallowing as if he had a lump in his throat, Del stated, "It's very binding to me and very binding to my people."

"Oh, goodness." Not wanting to listen to him anymore, she wrung her hands. "My father will be furious I've spent so much time with you as it is without all this added to his anger." Ellen began pacing. "Best to just say you felt compelled to help Sam by getting me back to the group as soon as possible." Stopping, she looked at him. He stared up at the sky, still holding his beads. "Does that sound like a good story to you?"

"Yes," he said through gritted teeth. "I can say such things to others, but not to you." Del took her by the arms and stared into her eyes. "Despite what you say, I consider us very married. You are my wife and I am your husband. Whatever your father thinks of this fact is irrelevant."

"This isn't good." Ellen pulled away from his grasp, panic and bile rising in her throat from the fear. "You don't understand at all. You can't just touch me anytime you want to; you can't even talk to me any time you want to." She shook her head, scared he'd never accept what had to happen, or more precisely, what couldn't happen. "I can't be near you once we reach camp. I have to make you see that. My father will be grieving for Lucy. If he does with her like he did my mother, it'll be awful and I need to be there for him." She studied his face. "Are your parents both still alive?"

"Yes."

"Then you can't understand how upset my father will be." She clasped her hands to plead with him. "Del, please help me with this. We can't continue this marriage game. You used it to save my life and I love you for that, but it's over now. Before we get to camp, we need to agree on that."

He nodded. "We agree. No marriage."

"Good," she exhaled the word with relief and smiled at him. "Thank you so much. You don't know how much this helps. I don't have to listen to my father rail against you and blame us both for Lucy's death."

His expression seemed like stone. "Let's go. They're at noon now. We can catch them before dark."

"Thank you again." She took his hand, hopping up with a little difficulty. As before, Ellen wrapped her arms around him, melting into his warmth. Unlike every other time, she felt his body tense and remain so. "I'm sorry we have to be so distant when we arrive."

He nodded in assent but remained quiet. Weariness stole over her and all Ellen wanted to do was sleep and to do so in a real bed. She stretched her neck a little and scratched her nose against his quiver of arrows. She rather liked the idea of him in a bed with her. Smiling, she wondered what he'd do differently in such a place. "Have you ever slept in a real bed, Del? Wait, I suppose you have in France and all." She laughed. "Silly me, I'm sleepy. Of course you have; you had to at some point." Ellen snuggled against him, his body unyielding. "I'm sure your adventures with sleeping in proper beds would make a great story sometime."

"I must be clear about a few things, Miss Winslow." His voice shook with restrained rage. "I have indeed slept in a bed, drank wine from crystal glasses, and have been known to eat from plates using a fork and, yes, a knife. All of these, many times. Not only that, but I've attended an opera or two. Though, I admit, not by choice. A lady I was interested in loved Wagner. I have also a law degree and have been known to paint faces on canvas, not just faces for sport." He turned to give her a glare hard enough to stop a bull in his tracks. "I am also not the only one of my people to do such things. You would be wise to refrain from referring to us as mere savages." He gave her a tight smile that didn't reach his eyes. "Now, I hope all this sounds like a good story to you as well."

As his speech sunk in, Ellen realized she'd hurt him. Her thoughts had focused only on her father and appeasing him before they ever arrived. She'd discounted how Del might feel being set aside once there. Even worse, she'd already been just as cruel as she expected her father to be to him. Unsure of how to fix this, she asked, "Del?"

He held up a hand, shaking his head. "Non. No more. We are done talking."

She sat away from him, his anger radiating from him like body heat. Tears welled in her eyes, so she looked up to keep them from falling. Ellen's lower lip trembled as they approached the fort. Unlike Pa, Del had never hit her. She felt his fury through the air alone, and yet he'd not harmed her in any way. If anything, she sniffed, he'd saved her life twice. Tears at last escaped her eyes to roll down her cheeks and she sniffed again.

"*Non.*"

"What?" Her question came out much more watery than she'd intended.

"Crying does not work with me. I won't forgive you."

She choked back a sob. "I understand. I don't expect you to forgive me." Ellen coughed, trying not to bawl like a baby.

"You have called me a savage for the last time. I have never been brutal to you."

"No," she said in a small voice. "You haven't ever. You've been the opposite, in fact."

"I'm glad you admit it."

"I do." She wiped her eyes with her sleeve. After a while, she asked, "Del? Would you feel better if I said I was sorry for the savage comments? All of them I ever made?"

"Hmm."

"And that I'll never say such mean things again?" She leaned her forehead against his back, sad at the lack of response. Unable to help herself, Ellen started crying, soft at first, but then the more she thought about how kind he'd always been to her, the more she sobbed.

"Enough! No more crying. I'm not made of stone." He sighed. "For now, I will do as you wish. We will appease your father. But beware, later, I will want to be married to you in the open, and when I do, you won't be able to deny me."

"All right." She sniffed. "We'll cross that river when we get there." Ellen hugged him and this time, he did melt into her arms. "You are a wonderful man."

"Thank you." He waited for a moment, adding, "You might be a wonderful woman."

"Might?"

"I'm not yet happy with you."

"Oh."

The fear and shock had left her exhausted, and she spent the afternoon resting against his strong back. They topped a hill and Ellen saw Fort Hall up ahead. The place was a beehive of activity. Every step Pomme took was closer to having to deny her new feelings for Del, and she wanted to avoid the whole mess. Such a thing wasn't possible, so she thought about everything left unsaid between them.

"We are nearly at camp. In fact, the lookout has seen us and soldiers are riding this way."

Ellen wasn't ready to let him go just yet. "Where will you be?"

"My guess is explaining your whereabouts to the commander."

The men reached them, their blue uniforms faded by a tinge of dust. The lead officer addressed them. "Miss Winslow? Mr. Du Boise?"

Del responded first. "Yes we are and I'm assuming Sam Granville is at Fort Hall?"

"Yes. He told us you'd be arriving."

Del and the officer looked like complete opposites, one dark and savage, the other fair and refined. Both were handsome and that was the extent of their similarity until she listened to their polite conversation. Ellen looked from one man to the other, amazed at how they talked as if in the finest parlor. The two soldiers on their horses behind their leader squinted at Del. Did they distrust him or were the frowns a result of the sunny day? She had no way to tell until either spoke.

"I'm glad he did. We'd look suspicious with only us riding here." Del steered Pomme in step with their leader, the other two flanking them.

The officer chuckled. "Can't say I'd disagree, sir."

The respect shown had surprised them both. She glanced back at one of the guards and caught his sneer. Ellen swallowed, her mouth now dry from worry on Del's behalf. He'd been shown nothing but deference in their brief time alone among the Indians. The contrast in how whites treated him versus the natives now seemed huge to her.

At the fort, the huge wooden doors swung out to them like

welcoming arms. The soldiers rode in first, followed by several of the cavalry for their change to fresh troops.

The leader of their small group fell back as they entered the grounds. "Ma'am, your father is in a bad way."

Ellen nodded. "I expected him to be so."

He dismounted and held out his hand for her. "I can take you to him while Mr. Du Boise answers some questions. Lincoln, take my horse."

She slid down, careful not to fall due to her wobbly legs. Everyone rode away and left her with the officer. Ellen snuck a parting glance at Del, but he didn't look back at her.

"Don't worry, ma'am." He held out his arm for her to hold. "His bringing you back to us will count heavily in his favor. I don't reckon he'll hang for anything."

She couldn't stop herself before blurting, "Dear God, I hope not! If not for Mr. Du Boise, I wouldn't be here and possibly not even alive. He should be rewarded, not punished."

"Of course not, ma'am. I'll inform the commander when I return."

Realizing he still waited with an outstretched elbow, she took his arm and went with him to her family. As they passed a wagon, the Nelsons cheered to see her with the soldier. She waved, smiling and accepting their sympathies. After walking by a couple more families, they arrived at her father's wagon. "Pa?" she shouted, sliding her arm from her escort's. "Where are you?" Ellen ran to the front of the wagon when she saw Mr. Lucky caring for the team. "Mr. Lucky!"

He ran over to her and gave Ellen a bear hug. "It sure is good to see you, miss! We thought we'd have to pay a ransom for ya!"

"Thank goodness, no. Is my Pa around? I want to make sure he's all right, after Lucy's death and all."

Lucky indicated the wagon. "He's in there. Won't come out, won't eat, just drinks whisky all day and night."

"Whisky? Where is he getting it?" Too late, she realized the soldier hadn't left. "I'm sorry, sir. I didn't tell you this is my family's wagon. Thank you for bringing me home."

"It's been my duty and pleasure, ma'am. If you'll excuse me?"

She said, "Yes, certainly." He turned on his heel before leaving. Ellen asked Lucky in a quieter voice, "How is Pa getting the drink? Is there a saloon in the fort?"

Lucky looked uncomfortable, reluctant to tell her. "Well, miss, he's been trading for it at the store since we got here, maybe before then. He's been real upset since your mother died."

"Has he been drunk since then?" The other man nodded and she thought of Buster and Skeeter. "Oh no!" She looked in the wagon to see her unconscious father lying there by himself. "He didn't forget my brothers somewhere, did he? Where are they?"

"Hold on, miss, they're with Mrs. Granville and are doing good. She's spoiling them rotten, if you ask me." He led her to the front of the wagon and patted the lone ox's back. "As you can see, you still have an ox. One went to a couple of bottles of whisky at the last trading post." He glanced at her, then at the wagon. "He went through those pretty quick. So, he traded off a cow for another bottle."

"He's had three bottles of whisky in as many days?"

"Well, when you say it like that, it sounds bad, sure. To be fair, you do still have an ox and a cow. He could have traded off those as well."

"Oh dear. I suppose thank heaven for small mercies." She peeked in on him again. "He slept through all the bouncing?"

Lucky shook his head. "Yeah, and I don't see how. I'd watch out, miss. He's going to be mean when he wakes up. Especially since he's out of whisky. No more hair of the dog."

Ellen thought for a moment. "Very well. Hopefully, he'll stay asleep for a while so I can get the boys."

He waved her on. "If you see Miss Jenny, tell her I say hello."

"I will. " She walked faster to the front, looking for Marie and her brothers. Ellen didn't pause at any of the wagons she passed. She didn't want to stop and let others give her condolences for her stepmother or their congratulations for surviving an Indian attack. Their sympathy would make her cry, and she didn't feel deserving of praise for living.

Skeeter saw her before she saw him. Ellen heard him yell and turned to see him barreling toward her.

"Ellie! You're here!" He jumped up into her arms, squeezing the breath out of her. "You're here. Mama's gone, did you know?" He started crying.

Ellen's gaze met Marie's as she followed. "Yes, sweetheart, I know and I'm so sorry."

His voice muffled, he cried, "I miss her! Little Buster don't know, but I do. Pa's been sick this whole time too." He squeezed her even more. "I'm glad you're here with us."

She held him, returning his hug. "I am too, baby boy."

Little Buster leaned against Marie as she said, "Skeeter here has been the best child I've ever met. He's polite, is kind to other children, and has helped me with Little Buster's care. He's already such a little man."

A lump formed in Ellen's throat. "He's always been the best brother ever." Addressing him, she added, "Thank you, Skeeter, for helping with Little Buster. I know this can't have been easy for you and you've been so brave."

"Thank you, Ellie." He rested against her. "They buried my Ma way back there. I didn't want to leave her, but Pa made me."

She brushed away her tears. Skeeter needed her to be brave for him. "I know, sweetheart. Ma would have wanted you to stay with Pa while she went with the angels."

"But she was with us, and then we put her in the ground. Pa didn't even wrap her in a blanket. She's probably cold."

Ellen glanced at Marie. Her friend answered the question in her expression. "The men made a box from scrap lumber. It worked very well for her. We ladies put her in a Sunday dress with a lovely wrap for her neck."

She understood what Marie didn't want to say in front of Skeeter. "That sounds perfect. Thank you for taking such good care of Lucy." Ellen pulled away a little from her brother. "It sounds like everyone here did very well for our mother. Her body is in the earth but her spirit is in heaven, I'm sure."

The boy nodded, seeming happier now. "Ma doesn't know she's in the ground, I suppose."

"She doesn't," Ellen assured him. "She's somewhere else much nicer."

Sniffing, he added, "Probably she's already at where we'll be living, but as a ghost. Ma will be a good ghost, not one that scares me or anything."

"Of course not. She'll keep watch over you every day. You and Little Buster both."

"All right." He wiped his nose on his sleeve. "I can keep an eye out for Ma's ghost, just in case she's not there yet."

"You could do that, yes." Ellen looked at Marie for help. The woman shrugged, shaking her head.

134

"Can I go tell the other boys to help me watch for her?"

He looked at her with such hope in his eyes she didn't have the heart to say he might not find Lucy out here. "Of course, but keep in mind she might be at our new home waiting for us, all right?"

"All right!" Skeeter ran off, looking for his friends.

Ellen looked at Marie. "How else was I supposed to handle that? He thinks his mother is around here as a ghost. Pa is going to be so angry with me."

"Then maybe your father should have taken care of this himself. Instead, he's drunk himself sick and ignored his sons. I'm sorry. I tried not to say that."

Ellen reached out to Little Buster who ran into her arms. "Good to know he's not changed. I was worried."

"How are you? Really?" Marie hugged Ellen. "Did they hurt you?"

"No, not at all. Del was there."

"Was he really? I'm so glad. You'll have to tell me what happened. But wait until Jenny is with us, because I know she'll want to know as well." She stepped back. "I'm sure Adelard is telling Sam now. I'm so sorry about Lucy. Did you have to see them...?"

"Yes. They told us not to scream. She did and they killed her without hesitation." Ellen felt sick at the memory. "After that, I was too scared to make a sound."

Marie shook her head. "You poor dear. How about you wait until you're rested to say anything about this? The main thing is you're safe and here with us. The boys are fine and your father will sober up someday."

As if he'd overheard them, Jack moaned and hollered for her. Ellen said, "It sounds like he's already started the process."

Marie reassured her, patting her arm. "Don't worry about the boys; they're safe with me. Just get him healed up first."

"Thank you, Marie. Both you and Jenny are the best friends ever." She paused, another yell from Jack distracting her.

"I hear her! Ellen! Where are you? Get over here!" He stumbled over to her, head bleeding from a cut. "I fell out of the damned wagon. Where were you? My Lucy is dead and you weren't here to help me. I need a bucket." He staggered away and started retching.

With an odd expression on her face, Marie swallowed, saying, "I need to let you take care of him. Good luck." Aghast at her father's cursing and display, she nodded, her chin dropped a little. "Thank you. I need every bit of luck possible." She let Marie back away, stunned, with Buster still on her hip. Regrouping, Ellen went to get a pail as ordered. "Pa, here's your bucket."

"What the hell for? I don't need that. I'm fine getting sick here." He looked her up and down; eyes squinted from the bright sun. "Get the hell away from me. Can't you see I'm sick?"

"Of course." She backed away, glad to be so dismissed. "Holler when you need me."

"Eh." He waved her off and retched again.

Like a prisoner on reprieve, she nearly fled his presence. Ellen went to the back of their wagon, hopping onto the tailgate. All their things lay strewn about as if dumped and searched through. She bet Pa had been looking for whisky money. Shaking her head, she knew he'd had no luck. She'd given him everything before the trip ever started. Anything she'd earned mending clothes for others consisted of traded items, no real money.

She combed through their belongings but didn't find the other pail. Chances are it lay where she dropped it during the kidnapping. Ellen shuddered as if chilled, remembering Lucy's death and the nightmare later. Not wanting to think of the gruesome event, she scanned the mess. Just looking at the chaos tired her. Nothing seemed more appealing right now than stretching out for a nap even if only babies and the sick did so. She sighed and gathered her willpower. She crawled into the wagon and started straightening up the chaos. Jack called for her before she folded the first blanket. She peeked out. "Yes, Pa?"

"Get out of there! I have things just the way I like them, and you're probably messing it up."

"But, Pa, it's a mess, let me—"

"I said get the hell out of there!" His face reddened. "I'm hurting here and need in the wagon. I can't sleep with you banging around in there, cleaning." He jumped onto the tailgate. "Get out and stay out."

"Yes, sir." Her way out of the back blocked, Ellen went to the front as her father climbed into the wagon. She sat on the bench behind the ox until Sam approached. Happy to see his smile, she hopped from the seat and into his arms.

"First things first, Miss Winslow." He held her tight. "Words can't express how happy I am to see you whole, and how sorrowful I am about your step-mother." Sam gave her a good squeeze before letting her go.

She missed the affection from him already. First Del and now Sam's arms helped her feel safe. "Thank you, Mr. Granville. Your sentiments are greatly appreciated."

Sam dipped his chin to speak in her ear. "Adelard told me some of your adventures. I suppose there's no need for congratulations over a mock event."

"No, there is no need." She tried to smile at him and failed.

He straightened. "That's too bad. He...well, he's a good man, no matter where he is."

"I agree. My father doesn't. Maybe someday he will."

"Maybe so. At any rate, I need to keep him on as a liaison with the Shoshone, then the Nez Perce. Which reminds me of how I need to help with his defense."

"Defense?" She shook her head, disagreeing that Del had been anything but stellar in his actions. "Sam, he shouldn't need that."

"Don't worry, his hearing is just a formality."

"I hope so. They can't jail him, or even worse. He saved my life and would have saved Lucy had she been there." A moan from Jack reminded Ellen she needed to be quieter. "Do I need to give testimony as a witness?"

"Not yet and I'll be the first to retrieve you if necessary. You'll excuse me?"

"Of course," she said and he left, headed to the middle of the fort. Pa let out a healthy snore, and Ellen decided to find Buster. She soon found the Warrens' wagon.

Marie grinned when Ellen walked up to her. "There you are, young lady! Come over here and get this child. He's been crying the entire time."

"Poor little guy!" Ellen said, hurrying to where her friend pointed. She looked into the wagon and found her baby brother lying there limp. "Buster? It's Sissy." The boy jumped up and clung to her.

"I'd ask if you wanted me to continue taking care of him while you rested, but that may not be possible."

She held Buster tighter as she lifted him over the tailgate. "No, probably not." He snuggled into her as if never letting go. "I missed him as much as he did me."

"I'm so glad you're back. Go on and if you need help, please ask."

"Thank you, Marie." She carried her brother back to their wagon. Ellen envied Pa his sleep. She wanted desperately to take a brief nap. Instead, she checked on her father again to make sure he was all right. He still lay there slack jawed. A quick peek in on Skeeter reassured her he was well too. Her younger brother had all his friends in a circle around him while he told stories of a ghost who watched over her son. Buster squirmed down to sit on his brother's lap and looked at Ellen every so often as she built a campfire.

The cow needed milking most likely, so she accomplished that task. She fell asleep for a moment with her face against the animal's belly. A tail slapping at a fly hit her instead, and Ellen woke up with a start. She straightened her glasses, determined to get through chores as fast as possible. She fixed dinner in a tired haze, working around a deadweight Pa sleeping it off in the back of the wagon. The biscuits cooked nicely and she doled them out to the boys. They each got a small jar of milk and a bit of jam. Ellen spooned out the last of the jelly and tried to ignore memories of Lucy dying. If they'd not been picking berries that day, her stepmother would still be alive.

She shook the terror from her mind, determined to focus on something more controllable. "Skeeter, can you help me set up our beds, please?"

He followed her to the back of the wagon. She'd seen him play just fine with the other children. He seemed normal until near her. Then, he was far too quiet, not his usual chatty self. What had been annoying before now seemed very wrong in its absence. She set it in her mind to talk with her brother later. Right now, Buster needed changing and cleaning up, the dishes needed washing, and the animals needed staking out for the night. She'd have time after all that to visit Del, if he'd been freed by then.

She rushed, doing all her chores in record time and yet wasn't fast enough to visit Del. Stars twinkled overhead, echoing the various campfires' light. She slipped into bed, satisfied her brothers slept, and marveled at how Pa hadn't woken up with all the noise she'd made.

Ellen dreamed of a shrill bird pecking in her ear. She shook her head, trying to escape the dream. Opening her eyes, she realized Pa was saying her name over and over again. "Yes, Pa? You need coffee, don't you?"

"What the hell do you think I've been saying? Get up and get it going, I'm tired of waiting on you."

She wiped the sleep from her eyes. "Have you taken the stock to the water yet?"

"Naw, I've been trying to wake you up for my coffee and breakfast. It's almost daybreak and you're still laying around."

"All right. I'll get some water and take the stock at the same time."

"Good. Hurry it up."

She took the pail and animals to the rocky creek bank. After filling the pail, Ellen let the ox and cow drink their fill. Since the various alkali-poisoned water they'd found, she couldn't take clean, fresh water for granted ever again. If not for the heavy load on the poor remaining ox, she'd fill every pail, jar, and barrel with water. They might not ever need it, but always better safe than sorry.

At the camp, Ellen hurried through breakfast, making sure the boys had plenty. She took the last of the coffee, glad to get a couple of beans to chew. Activity in the camp increased as the sun rose higher. "Skeeter, could you keep an eye on Buster while I wash dishes?"

"Sure, sis. I could probably do more too."

Surprised at his willingness to help instead of play, Ellen smiled. "That would be wonderful. You've seen me roll up our bedding. Do you think you could as well?"

"Yep! Leave it to me," he said and began his work. "I'll show Buster so he can help when he's as old as I am."

She almost laughed at how sweet her little brother was. Skeeter was growing up too fast, while she wouldn't mind if Buster outgrew his diapers. Lucy had spared her a lot of the messy chores with him until now. She needed to go back to the Warrens' and get his diapers from Marie. She hoped for her friend's sake that she'd left the washing to Ellen and took the breakfast dishes to the river.

Jack followed her to the water while wailing, "My poor little Lucy. She's in the cold ground, in a horrible casket just cobbled together out of scrap wood."

People stared at the man crying his eyes out. Various women close to his age stopped and he hugged each one. "My poor, poor Lucy is gone, and now I have no one to take care of me. The only woman I ever loved is gone, gone forever." He looked up from the lady hugging him. "Ellen, can you get me a handkerchief? Please, darling?"

"Yes, Pa."

"No, you poor, dear man. Take my handkerchief, I insist." The woman handed him a lace trimmed, embroidered scrap of cloth.

"Thank you kindly, ma'am." He held the napkin to his nose as if overcome with grief. "My heart is so broken. Thank you for your kind words, they mean so much to me."

She hugged him again and walked on to catch up with her family. Jack watched her go and winked at Ellen. "I'm wondering when she'll want this back." He waved the handkerchief.

Ellen tried to smile at him. "Maybe we can have Skeeter deliver it for you later."

"Skeeter, hell, I'm taking this back myself. She don't want no little boy, the way she hugged me." Jack shook his head. "She ain't the only one, either. If I weren't grieving? Heck, all these women are ripe for the picking."

CHAPTER 7

Del stared out through the bars. He'd not minded sleeping on the bench he now stood on to see outside. The chill and the aches he could shrug off, unlike his need to see Ellen. He'd waited until late last night before falling asleep. Then, at the first rattle, he hoped she'd sneak away to visit him.

"Du Boise?"

He turned at the scrape of metal on stone and had to let his eyes adjust to the dark. "Yes?"

"Stay back. You have a visitor." The guard held the door open, and Sam stepped into the cell. "Keep it short because I've gotta stand here until you're done talking." He closed the door with a clang and relocked it, the noise reinforcing his impatience.

"How are you doing in here?"

He shrugged. "I've slept in worse places." Del gestured to the window. "I suppose Ellen is too busy to see me."

"Have a seat." Sam sat down, his back against the stone wall. When Del settled in, Sam began, "She won't have time to come here before we leave." He shook his head. "Save your arguments. We're already lagging behind my schedule, and I'm not delaying us another day. You can catch up to us when you get out of here much easier than we could survive spending the winter in the mountains."

Del knew he was right. Snowstorms had no schedule, and emigrants caught in them either starved or froze to death. "Practical, yes. Would you still want me to catch up with your group or find my own way?"

Sam laughed. "You'll need to join us when you can." He sobered and glanced at the guard. "It may be a while. The commander told me yesterday he wasn't sure he believed our story and doesn't trust Ellen's testimony."

"Oh? He thinks she'd lie?"

"No. He thinks she's too besotted by your saving her life."

"She doesn't seem besotted."

"She's still in shock, I think. Overwhelmed too." Sam stood

and got up on the bench to look out as Del had earlier. "Winslow has been drowning his grief, drinking whatever he can buy or trade for. The other ladies in our group have cared for the boys, My men have helped with the two animals they have left."

"Now she's the unofficial leader of her family."

"Exactly."

"She needs my help. Do you think she'd accept it?"

He grinned. "If Jack would allow it, I think she'd want whatever you had to give."

The idea of her wanting him humbled Del. His face felt hot as he thought of her asking him for anything. "I love her, Sam."

"I know. She loves you too." He hopped down from the bench. "It's too bad there's so much in your way. This cell, her father, this last third of the road, and anything could happen."

The guard rattled the barred door. "Time's up, gentlemen. Let's go."

"We're leaving at mid morning." Sam stepped out of the room. "I'll give her your regards."

"Please do, and *au revoir, mon ame.*"

The guard locked the door as Sam left. "So you got a girl waiting for you out there? It might be longer than you think before you see her again."

A metallic taste hit Del's tongue, as if someone plucked hairs from the back of his neck. "What do you mean?"

"I gotta go get your breakfast." He opened the main door, and light flooded into the dank room.

The door closed again before Del could ask anything else. This felt an awful lot like torture. Not physical pain, but mental kept him pacing as he waited. A hundred different scenarios ran through his mind on what sort of sentence or other punishment the commander might hand down. This continuous incarceration worried him. An innocent man would have been cleared yesterday and free today.

A scrape as the larger door opened startled him. The guard came in with one of Del's saddlebags and he frowned. "You have my property?"

"Only until you take it from me." The man slid the bag in sideways to him. "I went through your belongings to take out anything that might be a weapon and put them in your other bag."

Del opened it to find clothes, a comb, and his journal. He

noticed his mother's beads weren't in there. Good idea, since they'd make a great strangulation device. "Thank you for bringing this to me."

"We've had enough attacks from the natives around here that you might not get a fair trial tomorrow."

"Tomorrow? Is there a particular time?"

"Afternoon is what I heard. I'll go get your meal since it's almost midmorning."

Del nodded, preoccupied. The delay didn't bode well for him joining Sam and Ellen before they left. He opened his saddlebag to remove a crisp clean shirt, white, like one of Sam's, and a pair of new trousers. Peering close, he saw thread holes where something had been snipped off from down the side of each leg. The evidence took him aback. Were these Army issue?

The guard returned with a cloth bag and a cup. "Here's fresh bread and bacon cooked this morning. Water too." He held the items with one hand and unlocked the door. "Step back."

"These aren't my clothes."

"No, they're old ones you'll need for tomorrow." He put the meal down on the bench. "I don't know how much saving that lady's life will count in your favor tomorrow. Maybe a lot, maybe a little. I figured if you appeared a little more like us, you'd get a lighter sentence."

The implication that he'd already been found guilty before any trial angered him. "I don't deserve any sentence."

"I reckon not. Still, one of the women did die and the commander isn't sure who the killer was."

Del began to argue before remembering his audience. He needed to save his facts for tomorrow. "I appreciate your help. If dressing like my father helps prove my innocence, so be it."

"Eat. I'll be right outside until the next shift change."

He sat with the food. The bread was heaven and the meat a little salty but still good. He drank deep from the cup, smiling at how they had well water so close to the river. Del considered them such industrious people to be so lazy in their habits. He set aside the cloth and cup, digging out his journal from the saddlebag.

A few hours later, he finished updating the events. He poured over the facts like this would help with tomorrow's inquisition. He didn't want to hesitate or be tricked into saying the wrong thing. Del put everything away just as the door opened. A different guard stepped in, and the smell of dinner came in with him. The lateness of the day surprised him and he stood. "Yes?"

The man brought over another cup and a bowl with a spoon in it. "Dinner time. Reach through the bars and take it. I'm not taking a chance on an Indian trick."

The dishes fit through the bars. Del did as asked, taking the meal given. "*Merci beaucoup.*" The confused expression on the man gratified Del's soul and he continued in English, "This smells wonderful. My compliments to the chef."

"Um, yeah, sure." The man stepped backwards a little bit before leaving the jail proper.

Del snickered while breathing in the soup's aroma. It was probably too much to hope the soldier had learned anything from their exchange. Many of his mother's people spoke more French than English, thanks to the French trappers. He'd judged correctly that his current guard was from the east, maybe south, and only knew his own language.

Lunch didn't take him long. He placed everything outside the bars and settled in again to work on a defense. Del eyed the clothes sitting on the bench beside him. He stared for a while, resisting what he knew he needed to do if he ever wanted to see Ellen again.

The next day, Del stood when the outer jail door opened. He let go his pent up breath when the same guard from yesterday morning appeared. The soldier might be able to help him with one last task.

"Look at you. Except for those braids, I'd take you for white."

"That's exactly why I need your knife." He held up both braids. "I want to cut these off so the case goes in my favor."

"My knife? I can't just hand it over to you."

"Slide it over on the floor and I'll slide it back when finished."

His guard paused for a moment before taking the weapon from its holder. He did as Del instructed and it slid over to him. Del made quick work of hacking off both braids just below his ears. He ran a hand through the strands to test the feel and length. His hair was long in front, short in the back. Giving an unconscious nod of acceptance, he slid the knife back to its owner. The guard took it, his jaw still slack. "Does this look acceptable?" Del asked.

"Yeah, you look like one of my cousins."

"I'll take that as a compliment, sir."

"I meant it as one. Let's go, then." The guard sheathed his knife and unlocked the barred door. The hinges squeaked. "I wonder if I should tie you up. At least bind your hands."

"You could." Del looked around him in a deliberate way, nodding at each of the fort's walls. "Or, you could know you're safe from me in here."

The guard chuckled. "I know I am. What I don't know is how fast you can run."

Del followed him out into the blinding sunlight. "Faster than you, certainly. But faster than the US Army? No."

He laughed outright, slowing to keep Del in sight. "You're a smart man, even for an Indian." A scowl from Del and he chuckled. "C'mon. Don't let me get your dander up. Expect the commander to say worse."

They walked alongside the various buildings inside the fort's walls. He didn't know the purpose of each one, just saw how every one was a hub of activity. More than a few times, he and the other man had to pause to let someone cross in front of them. He noticed no one gave him a second glance and knew his plan to pass as white had worked. Some of these sun baked men were darker than him, even with their light hair and blue eyes.

"Quite frankly, I don't have time for you." The fort's commander sat back in his chair. "My first inclination is to toss you off a cliff and into the river, but that's rather lawless and selfish on my part. So tell me, why should I let you go free?"

The commander wanted to be a tough nut, Del thought. He narrowed his eyes, embracing the challenge. "Miss Winslow is with her family even as we speak. That should be worth something to you. If I hadn't intervened, she'd be Pointed Nose's wife."

"You managed to bring her back here without them marking her face?"

Del nodded. "Yes. I reached her in time and claimed her as my woman. They agreed to let me have her and allowed us to leave."

"Just like that? Why do I think there's more to the story?"

The honest part of him wouldn't leave Del alone. He was terrible at lying to others. It was exactly why he didn't work as a lawyer defending criminals. "They wouldn't let me take her unless we were married. We went through the ceremony, and now the Shoshone think she's mine."

"Oh? They think so, hmm? The marriage isn't legal."

"Yes. We're not married in any true sense of the word, except among the Shoshone."

"Speaking of them, let's discuss their plans. We've had several skirmishes around here, horses stolen, mostly, but no killings within a day's ride. I'd like to keep it that way."

"Of course, sir. The group I rescued Miss Winslow from is generally peaceful. They don't want to fight."

"And yet, they abduct one white woman and kill another, assuming they did it and not you."

Del sensed he was being verbally backed onto a cliff. He stared down the commander. "Let me be clear. Mrs. Winslow was dead when I found her. Ellen was gone." He realized his mistake when the other man's eyebrows rose. "I went to find Miss Winslow."

"All right. Let me assume you're the hero. Tell me what I should do to them for the murder and kidnapping."

He stared at the map on the wall behind the commander. He agreed there should be justice for Lucy's murder. He just wasn't sure war was the answer. All the deaths on both sides wouldn't bring back Mrs. Winslow. He narrowed his eyes, looking at the man across from him. "There is no way of knowing who actually killed her, sir. Three men went to get Miss Winslow, and Mrs. Winslow's death wasn't planned." Before the commander could speak, Del added, "Not that her murder is excused, but right now, you'd have to kill everyone in the village to make sure you punished the killer. Are you sure one death is worth starting a war?"

The commander laughed. "We've fought for lesser reasons." He stood. "You're right, much as I hate to admit it. This is the first problem we've ever had with tribes to the east. They leave us alone, and we leave them alone." He came around to sit on his desk. "The western natives keep us busy enough. You're free to go, but you might let the word get out: One more incident like this from Pointed Nose and we'll strike back hard. Understood?"

"Yes, sir. I'll tell my people."

"You clean up really well. I'd have taken you for white at first glance. Good tactic." At Del's surprise, he laughed and continued,

"Yes, I knew what you were doing. I may be distracted, but I'm not stupid. Your actions in saving Miss Winslow have been noted and commended. Leave whenever you choose."

Del had trouble believing the decision. Still, he didn't want to hang around and argue. "Thank you, sir. I'll be able to take my horse?"

The commander didn't look up from the paper he read. "What? Of course you may. You're an innocent hero. Take your things and horse. Be sure to stop by the mess hall and get some dinner and a little extra. Consider it your reward."

He gave a curt nod and left the room with his former guard following. Del walked out in a measured way, slow in case someone needed one last thing from him.

"Congratulations, Mr. Du Boise," the guard said.

"Thank you."

"Let's go get your saddlebag from the jailhouse first. Then I'll take you to mess hall per the Commander's orders."

He didn't need to be reminded to hurry as he went into and out of his jail cell for his belongings. "You promised food?"

"Sure did. Follow me."

Del felt like a puppy tagging along. He tried to keep up, but all the activity kept him preoccupied. Soldiers made up the majority of people there. A few plain clothed women walked by or in front of them here and there. He went through the door held open for him.

The guard went to the counter, asking, "Do we have any grub for a hero?"

A portly mess sergeant strolled up. "Who's the hero?"

"This gentleman right here. He rescued that gal and brought her back day before yesterday."

The man wiped his hands on a formerly white apron. "Well, I'll be. You did a good thing, son." He turned to the guard. "He understands English?"

Del snickered. "Not at all, sir. English makes no sense to me."

At first surprise then amusement showed on the other man's face. "You got me there, Hero. What can I do for ya?"

First the hero talk, now someone wanting to give him food made Del feel shy all of a sudden. He was far more used to giving than receiving. "I suppose whatever you have to spare." To his own ears he sounded demanding and amended his answer. "I mean, your leftover bread, maybe. Some dried out beef might be good."

He nodded. "I got it. Let me go tie you up a sack of goods." The cook disappeared into a back room.

The guard shrugged. "No tellin' how long he'll be. I'll go get your horse."

He watched the man leave and then looked around the building. The whitewashed walls seemed clean at first look. He didn't want to examine them to learn otherwise. The wood stove in the middle of the mess hall didn't radiate heat this time of year, but gusts of heat flowed from the kitchen to where he and a few others stood just outside.. Tables lined the walls with benches pushed underneath. He suspected the men's backs stayed warm in winter while they ate. A bustle at the kitchen door stopped his musing.

"Here you are, young man." The cook held up a full cotton bag.

Del took it, surprised at how heavy it was. "This feels like too much. If you're sure...?"

"I am, so go and get out of here before someone changes their mind about you being the good guy."

He gave a salute before leaving. Not seeing the guard waiting outside, Del headed toward the stables. He didn't get far before seeing Pomme being led to him, already saddled. The guard handed over the reins. "He's been fed already, brushed, had some water."

The horse nuzzled Del. "Thank the stable hands for me, please."

"Will do. Good luck in catching up to your wagon train."

Del swung up on Pomme and nodded at the man. "Thank you and au revoir." He rode through the open gate, not realizing he'd held his breath until cleared of the fort.

He gave his horse free rein as long as they headed along the road to Ellen. Pomme could gallop or walk as he wanted. Del steered him to the river whenever the bank allowed easy access. He even ate his meals on horseback. The day eased to a close, and as the sun dipped below the western horizon, he came upon a wide feeder branch of the Snake River. Several others were camped there, nearly all next to their own wagon. He kept to himself, not wanting to intrude or alarm any of the night watch. None of them were of the Granville party anyway.

Del awoke before anyone else around him. He'd not bothered

with a campfire, so he only had blankets to roll up before leaving. The clear creek water called to him, and he stopped so he and his animal could both drink. He had a dinner roll for breakfast, taking a bite of his apple before giving the rest to Pomme. "Voici votre pomme, Pomme," he said, knowing his horse didn't appreciate the pun of feeding an apple to a horse named Apple. Both had one last drink before the nine-mile trek to the Falls.

He heard the rapids far sooner than he could see them. Restraint was difficult for him, knowing each step put him closer to Ellen. Also closer to her father, he remembered and wished he hadn't. Del and his horse walked along the bank, the river crashing over the rocks impeding its progress. Pomme shook his head at the spray and Del chuckled. He slid down, getting a handful of the water and made sure his animal had a drink too.

Man and horse soon continued on, as did the day. They made good time, riding along a bluff to a rocky pass. By evening, they were alone. He figured the lack of good grazing was the reason people avoided camping along this part of the river. A couple of miles past a boulder-strewn pass, he decided to stop for the night.

He had waited too long to do much for supper in the waning daylight. The new moon kept the landscape dark as death, and he'd lived among whites too long to be used to seeing by starlight. Mostly by touch, he rolled out blankets to sleep in for the night. Here in the still and cool, he wondered what to do about Ellen.

Del considered them married, as legally as if they'd gone to a church or courthouse. He sighed, struggling to get comfortable on the rocky ground. They'd need to be married on both sides of his blood for everyone to be happy. He grinned, having no objection to marrying her again, even if unnecessary to his heart. Still, his smile faded as he remembered Mr. Winslow's frequent insults. Did she want to claim Del as her husband and risk her father's wrath? He couldn't be sure. Should he ride behind unnoticed so Winslow couldn't complain, or ride up bold as brass and claim his woman? He chuckled at the idea. If the man were any less of a hothead, Del just might.

He rolled over on his side, resting his head on an arm. His eyes closed as he decided to join the group but to keep his distance from Ellen until Oregon City. Then he'd obey her wishes on their relationship.

The next day, he and Pomme stayed along the Snake River until the ruts led to the southwest. He didn't feel comfortable veering from water, but with the road cut so deep, there had to be a reason. Sam would lead everyone over the most traveled path, he knew. Sure enough, seven miles later at Raft River, Del found his friend and the people he led.

Arnold, with his white blond hair, was easy to spot among the men on horseback. Del waved to him, catching his attention. The young man rode over to him. "Hey, Mr. Du Boise! Good to see you!"

"Thank you, it's good to see you too."

"Come on. I'll take you to the boss." Arnold turned his horse and trotted to the northernmost wagon.

Del followed, catching up to the man. "Tell me, is everyone well?"

"Sure are!"

He wanted more information, but didn't want to ask outright. Del scanned the group, looking for any sign of the Winslows. He and Arnold arrived at the Granville wagon without so much as a glimpse of Ellen.

The hired hand pulled up short. "Mr. Granville must be somewhere else. Wait here and I'll fetch him right quick."

Del dismounted. Pomme needed a drink, and both of them were hungry. Or so he heard when the horse's stomach rumbled. He petted the animal. "Soon, boy. We'll eat soon."

"Adelard!"

He turned toward Sam's voice. "Oui?"

Sam walked up to him, giving Del a hug. "I didn't expect you to catch up so soon. You must have pleaded your case quite well."

"I'd like to claim credit, but truly it was the threat of war that freed me." A movement to the left caught his eye. Ellen appeared at the front of the wagon and stared at him. He wondered at her dropped jaw before remembering his short hair. Del ran a hand through the strands, still caught by surprise when the hair dropped from his fingertips too soon. He couldn't look away from her. She seemed more fragile than when he saw her last, delicate, and her chin trembled a little. After a little nod, she took a step back and hurried away.

Sam leaned over to say, "Her father has been a handful. More so than the two boys." He motioned for Del to follow. "Come on, get a drink, stake out Pomme, and we'll talk while Uncle Joe fixes dinner."

He agreed, taking off his horse's saddle first. They followed Sam to the river and both drank their fill. "Tell me more about Ellen. How is she? Is she having nightmares still?"

"I didn't know she was in the first place. From what I've seen, everyone is good except for Winslow."

Del scooped another handful to drink, thinking. "Is he cruel to her?"

"Not that I can tell. I've not heard yelling from that side of camp in a while. Not since the kidnapping."

Silence didn't mean a lack of abuse. He straightened, staring at the western horizon. Her expression today had been happy surprise then teary. He'd love to know her thoughts when she saw him. "Maybe she'll join us around the campfire tonight."

"She's always invited."

"So do I need to congratulate you and your new wife?"

Sam laughed. "Yes, you do. We had a quick wedding at the fort with Ellen and Uncle Joe as our witnesses. We'll have a proper reception at home."

"I'm sad I missed the...what?" He couldn't remember the unusual word for taunting newlyweds. "Annoy on the wedding night?"

"The shivaree? Yep, you missed it so don't even try."

Del returned his friend's grin and shrugged. "It's fair, I suppose. You missed mine as well."

"What? I didn't know you and Miss Winslow had a real wedding."

His surprise irritated Del. The color of his skin didn't dictate the sincerity of the ceremony. Did none of these whites understand this? "Our wedding was very real. Even if to none but half my people."

"It's not that. I didn't know you and her were...."

Like a flash of lightning, he understood his friend's implication. "Oh, *non*, we're not truly married."

"Good." At Del's frown, he continued. "Her father is already angry enough. There's no need in goading him further."

"I suppose." He ignored Sam's smirk, instead taking off his shirt to rinse out the dust. His pants needed cleaning but could wait until later. He wrung out the dirty water and led Pomme to a decent patch of grass.

Later on that evening, around the campfire, Del ate without tasting. He hoped Ellen would come by if only to say hello, but the hours passed without her. Conversation flowed around him like a swift stream. He heard the words but didn't listen. Marie nudged him, breaking his trancelike stare into the dying fire.

"I have something for you. Ellen wants me to be extremely discreet." She pressed a folded piece of paper into his hand. "She's afraid you'll not read it and even more afraid her father will."

"She has nothing to fear." He opened the note and read two simple sentences that would mean little to anyone else but him: *I liked your hair before. Glad the group is now complete.* Del smiled. Warmth from his heart heated him more than the fire in front of him. For someone who had so much ill will toward his mother's people, her preference for their ways pleased him more than he could say.

He folded the note, putting it in his pants pocket. Yes, he was here, completing the group but not accepted as her husband. The clouds above them reflected brilliant oranges and reds as the sun set behind the mountains. Though difficult, he'd wait until Oregon City to claim her. Until then, he'd do whatever it took to be accepted by Jack Winslow as her husband.

The next morning, Del managed to avoid Ellen while keeping a watch over her at the same time. Every time their eyes met, she blushed and hurried off to some seemingly urgent task. He missed seeing Skeeter too. The boy kept his distance but waved every time he saw Del. The day was much like the others only the road was one of the roughest they'd been on so far. Nearly everything breakable had been left behind and in pieces along the road. He felt bad for the lost treasures and watched from a distance to see if any such mishaps befell the Winslows.

They left Marshy Creek early the next morning to return to Snake River. As they approached the water, tension rose in the group like a heavy cloud above them. Each turn of the wheel brought everyone closer to prior emigrants' graves. A hostile tribe of natives lived in the area, and while they didn't hassle every white, they attacked often enough to keep everyone wary.

The road diverted down to the river as it flowed in a wide canyon. Wagon parties ahead snaked down, high bluffs on one side, water and more cliffs on the other. Del disliked following them down onto the riverbank as he nudged Pomme down with them. Anyone could attack from above.

He breathed easier when the first of the wagon train climbed a natural ledge to the top of the bluff. Del and Lefty rode up after the last wagon. Both men looked at each other and nodded. The danger wasn't completely over, just eased for a while. They fell back behind the Granville train, avoiding the fine dust kicked up by the others. Lost in his own thoughts, he realized they'd stopped only after reaching the first wagon. The creek flowed clear and grass lined both banks. They'd found a rich oasis in the high desert. He slid down, tying Pomme to sagebrush near the water.

They'd not gone far today. He went in search of Sam or one of the boys to see if they were staying for the night. He wanted to take a break but knew they had a timetable. He found Sam first at his wagon, unsaddling Scamp. "Is this our camp?"

"Yep." He didn't pause. "I figure the stock could use the extra food."

Del unsaddled his horse. "So could we."

Sam grinned. "I'd suggest hunting, but this area makes me nervous, even for you."

"Dressed like this, I agree."

"You do look a lot more American than native."

He narrowed his eyes. "I'm unsure if that's good or bad."

"It's neither and both." Sam brushed Scamp's matted fur from where the saddle had been. "Are you wanting to talk with Miss Winslow tonight?"

Her name caused that happy feeling in Del's chest and he grinned. "Always."

"I'll talk to Jack and see if he can spare her a few minutes this evening." He knocked some of the hair from the brush and then went back to grooming his horse. "She'll be my guest."

"I'd like that." He scanned the horizon out of habit, looking for hostile people. The mere idea of seeing and possibly talking with Ellen left him feeling lighter than air. He stared off into the distance, remembering the feel of her lips against his and how good her body felt nestled into his arms. He didn't care whether she wore cotton or buckskin. Del craved her touch.

"I might get going and invite her, since it looks like you're already daydreaming about her."

"What?" He turned to his friend, realizing he'd been caught

calf eyed over a woman. "Yes, you might as well. I've missed her these past few days, and just to hear her voice would be heavenly."

Sam scratched between Scamp's ears before teasing, "Such poetry! If you'll excuse me?"

"Of course." Del shook his head. His friend had plenty to say when longing for Marie. Remembering the woman, he glanced around to see where she was. The past few days had been too hectic for one or the other of them and he missed her company. He sought out and found Sam's wagons, hearing her humming inside of them before seeing her. "Hello, Mrs. Granville?" The humming continued for a while and he grinned. She must not be used to her married name. He knocked on the side of the wagon. "Mrs. Granville?"

She yelped and peeked outside. "Adelard! You're back!" Marie climbed down and gave him a bear hug. "Sam said not to worry, but how could I not?"

"No more worry, dear coupin. They let me go and fed me besides. If the jail had a proper bed, I'd have been a king."

"Oh dear." She reached up and tugged his hair, chin length in the front and short in back. "And they trimmed you too." Marie tsked and hopped back into the wagon. "Let me get some shears and fix it for you. The fort needs a better barber because whoever did this would make a better butcher than hair dresser."

He laughed. "True, I've dressed more animal fur than people hair."

After a little more rustling inside, she handed him the scissors and climbed back down again. "You cut this yourself? Oh my. Very well, have a seat and I'll see what I can do." He did as instructed, sitting on the tailgate while Marie rested on her knees behind him. She wrapped a sheet around his neck and began snipping. "Not much, just enough to even it out. You need some refinement."

"Doesn't every man?"

She laughed outright. "Most do, yes."

Unable to resist joking with her, Del asked, "But not Sam?"

"Not him at all."

He smiled at the warmth her voice held for his friend. "You didn't answer to your name the first time I called."

"Well, I've not been Mrs. Granville very long."

"I suspected as much. Tell me what I missed."

"Since I got to hear all about your wedding with Ellen,

certainly!" She continued working in tiny little snips. "Jenny couldn't go and witness our ceremony due to her parents objections, so Ellen went in her place and was my maid of honor. Mr. Winslow almost had a fit, but Sam promised him a jug of whiskey for the trouble. Uncle Joe, Lucky, Arnold, and Lefty were all there too. None of them were willing to be left back at camp."

"I don't blame them. Your love should be celebrated."

She patted his shoulder before brushing off the stray hairs from his neck. "Thank you, mon ami. We both wanted to wait until you joined us but just couldn't."

"There was no need and I understand your impatience."

Marie chuckled. "You probably do." She carefully removed the sheet so the captured hair fell to the ground. "We could talk, if you wanted, but I suspect the subject is too intimate?"

"Very too much." He ran a hand through his hair, noting how the strands ended at the same length instead of saw-toothed like before. "Thank you for this. I feel more presentable no matter how I look."

"You look wonderful, dear friend." Marie placed the folded sheet and shears back into the wagon. "Now let's go see if Uncle Joe needs help with dinner."

He made an after you motion and followed her to the second wagon. There, all the men were sitting nearby, but not at the fire. The sun hadn't set enough for anyone to catch a chill.

"There he is!" hollered Lucky. He jumped up to greet Del with a handshake at first, then a hug. The other men crowded around, shaking his hand and settling for a slap on the back. "We thought the soldiers had you out back damming the river with a teaspoon."

"No, it still runs free like I do." He noticed Joe was the first back in his seat, tending to the stew. "Your food smells good."

"Thanks, young man. I'll share tonight if you promise to hunt tomorrow."

"Of course, I'd be glad to help."

Sam walked up, his hands still damp from washing. "Is it ready?"

Marie gave him a spoon and a cup. "Almost."

Joe stirred the food. "I reckon it's ready now."

No one needed telling twice to line up with dishes ready for his ladle. Each of them ate as fast as the hot food allowed. Too soon, the sun rested on the tops of the western mountain range, giving a hint of a chill to the air. Everyone received a second helping, even Marie. Del glanced around at each of them, enjoying the camaraderie. Their laughter and chatter reinforced how alone he'd spent his life in between the two worlds of white and red. At the last bite, he put the spoon back into the cup for good and glanced up at the sound of a feminine clearing of the throat to find Ellen standing there with Skeeter.

"I'm sorry for interrupting." She raised a hand when every man started to get to his feet. "No need to stand. Pa and Buster are asleep for the night, and we wanted to stop by for a visit."

"There's no need to fret, little lady," said Lucky. "We were just finishing up here."

Sam handed his dishes over to Del. "Adelard was just volunteering to wash up for us." He nodded at the bucket Ellen carried. "I'm sure he wouldn't mind taking care of your dishes as well."

"These? Oh, no, I couldn't impose."

Marie stood and eased the bucket out of the woman's hand. "Don't mind him, Ellen. Sam was just being ornery." She took his cup for emphasis. "See? I'm cleaning up tonight, and you can have a seat."

Del smiled at how she gave no one a chance to object before gathering everything. Soon, she left for the river and the Winslows settled in. A thousand questions came to his mind, and he resisted asking even one. He wanted her to say the first word. Otherwise, he would feel as if he had pestered her for her attentions.

Skeeter broke the ice first. "Mr. Do Bose, I'm glad you're back. Thank you for bringing Ellen home."

He looked down at the boy. "My pleasure, Skeeter."

The youngster stared at the embers. "My pa said to leave you alone, that you was as bad as those that killed ma, but he's wrong. Those that killed ma wouldn't have brought back Ellen. Not even if she was as worthless as pa says she is."

"Skeeter!" Ellen patted his leg to get his attention. "That's enough telling tales for now. He knows you're grateful. I'm sure we need to listen to Mr. Lucky's music or Uncle Joe's jokes."

Del glanced up at her, caught by her beauty. He didn't want to cause a fuss, so he asked quietly, "How are you doing, Miss Winslow? Better now with your family I hope?"

"Yes, I'm doing fine. Thank you for asking, Mr. Du Boise."

Her slight smile cheered him. Lucky began playing his bugle, the tone soft and low. Del preferred it much better than the usual strident revelry. He could almost like the instrument when played this way. Words between them seemed unnecessary, and yet he longed to hear her voice. He smiled at Ellen. "Possibly tomorrow evening you both could join us earlier for dinner?"

Both sister and brother looked at each other. Ellen visibly swallowed, while Skeeter turned back to staring at the fire. She cleared her throat. "We might later on down the road. Right now, it's important for us to spend as much time with Pa and Buster as possible." She didn't look at him. "Tonight is a rare treat, and not what we should be doing at all."

Del frowned and looked away. So they had been forbidden to talk with him, he guessed. First anger, then understanding filled him. He felt more than saw Sam's gaze on him but didn't acknowledge his friend. "I understand and am glad you could join us after all."

Skeeter leaned against her, taking his sister's arm. She bent down to kiss the top of his head. The boy snuggled into her and Ellen smiled. "Both of us wanted to take the chance to hear Mr. Lucky play and to thank you for saving me."

He stopped just short of giving any sort of response. What words could he say that told her everything and nothing at the same time? "Your wagon is close by? I'd prefer you not walk alone to your camp, even if Skeeter is here to protect you."

She chuckled. "He's the best brother ever and will keep us safe." Ellen looked at Del as the last notes faded into the night air. "I've missed you terribly."

"Likewise," he squeaked out before seeing the glint of unshed tears in her eyes.

"Goodness! The dust has been terrible since Fort Hall, hasn't it Mr. Du Boise?" She wiped her eyes with the back of her hand. "It's been bad before now, and I had hoped we were done with such a nuisance."

"Do you need a rag for your eyes?"

A choking laugh escaped Ellen before she clamped a hand over her mouth, her face reddening. "Not at the moment. I appreciate the thought."

She remembered their inside joke, then. He leaned back on his hands. "I kept the handkerchief clean just for you."

"You are so kind, sir." Skeeter snuggled against her, sleeping, and she lowered her voice. "I'll remember that for later."

"But now you need to leave and get him to bed?"

"Precisely." She smiled at him. "Good night, Mr. Du Boise."

"Good night, Mrs.—" he began as a way to tease her. Del grinned at her warning frown. "Miss Winslow."

She gently shook Skeeter awake and helped the boy to his feet. The two exchanged good nights to all the men. Del watched as they left, resisting the urge to follow and make sure they got back to their camp safely.

Nudging him, Sam said, "She'll be all right. We're due to start night watch, and I'm sure they'll be asleep by the time you take your shift."

"Don't count on it." He returned the teasing grin. "I'm wanting to be first."

"Sure. Just be sure there's no sneaking the prettier girls away with you."

Del gave him a mock salute as he left the camp. On his way to the wagons' half circle, he picked up Sam's rifle. He didn't like using such weapons, but the unrest in this area made such protection necessary.

He managed to make the first two trips without pausing to search for Ellen. The third time, Del slowed, needing to see her. Their low campfire made spotting her difficult, but she lay facing the light and him. Keeping his ears open for intruders, he stepped closer.

Her glasses reflected the flames. He wondered why she slept in them now when she hadn't when they were alone together. Del didn't blame her for wearing them now. He'd do the same, not wanting to wake up in a wilderness to blurred vision. He longed to lay down with Ellen, protect her from the night's chill. Too many days had passed since she'd been in his arms and he ached for her. Tomorrow evening, he promised himself. Then, he'd find time to talk with her alone.

Seven miles across a rocky plain dotted with sagebrush brought them to Snake River the next morning. Del and Arnold were the early scouts, and they'd found an easy way to the water. The dust choked man and animal alike. While Pomme drank, Del washed the dirt from his face and eyes. Each wagon, person, and stock diverted to the river, refreshed themselves, and continued on. All of them had hoped to find a spring fed, grassy valley. After twelve miles, Sam conceded defeat and they camped for the night.

Del's intention to pull Ellen aside for time alone never materialized. Even worse, she and Skeeter hadn't stopped by to visit with them after their dinners. He'd offered to wash up, lingering at the river to catch a glimpse of her with no luck. Now on second watch, he'd linger a little at the Winslow's camp. He used the excuse of checking on her and knew he lied to himself.

The clear creek in a wide and grassy vale made the morning's rough and dirty roads worth the effort. Sam made the decision to stay an extra hour for the stock to eat their fill. The fresh cold water refreshed as everyone drank and washed what they could. The warm day had a crisp, cool breeze. Del saw Ellen a few times, but her father hovered around her so much that even a glance couldn't pass between them. Too soon, Lucky's bugle sounded and they were on the road again.

The pebbly road they traveled ended up being a thin trail winding around huge rocks. Some were small enough to pass under wagon axles. Others weren't. Sam led them into the late afternoon and almost evening before deciding to stop for the night. By now, the Snake River lay below them at the bottom of a steep cliff. They managed to get water by climbing down a worn path.

Again, the evening and night's minutes seemed to drip like cold maple syrup, each taking twice as long to pass than the one before it. Del struggled to stay easygoing when the dishes needed cleaning and he'd not seen Ellen for most of the day. He turned to Sam. "First watch?"

"If you'd like." When Del hopped to his feet, Sam added, "Maybe I should have you wash dishes, laundry, and everything else."

"Up and down the bluff?"

"It would cure you of this restlessness."

Del laughed louder than he'd intended. "No, nothing except her could do that, but it was a good attempt to get more work from me." He left at Sam's chuckle. Too many people still stirred, not ready for sleep, for him to stop and ensure Ellen's safety as he'd done in the middle of the night. He reached the Winslows' and kept his ears open for her voice. He didn't want to move on without hearing her at least once.

Silence blanked the Winslow camp, so he continued his watch. He hadn't appreciated their time alone enough. If he'd been properly grateful, Del would have remembered every single moment. As it was, he'd allowed gaps in his memory while thinking they always had more time together. He glanced but didn't stare every time he passed the family. Ellen faced away while Jack stared straight at him. Del didn't want trouble, so he barely even glanced at them until his shift was up and Lefty took over. By then, everyone but them slept.

The wagon party spent the next day close to the river. Thanks to a northerly wind, both animal and human smelled the water. The bluffs kept everyone from drinking since not even the barest of paths had been cut into the steep rocky wall. Uncle Joe was well into telling Del and Lucky about his days as a trapper when Sam rode back to them. "Gentlemen, we'll be skirting the river all day. Lucky, Del, I'd like for you two to scout ahead a few miles."

Lucky tipped his hat and Del nodded. Both nudged their horses into a slow gallop ahead. Several miles passed with no good camp in sight. A cool breeze kept Del from sweating in the summer heat. They had gone farther than he liked without letting Pomme get a drink. "After the next hill," he murmured as a promise to the four of them.

"I hope so, or we'll have a pack of thirsty people and animals tonight." Lucky's saddle creaked as he shifted in his seat. "Reckon we should start backtracking soon?"

Del looked at the sky. The other man had a point. Another few more miles and they'd be camping by themselves. "I'd say we head back after two more miles."

Lucky nodded and both men rode on. They topped a slight hill and saw a wide creek below them. It had meandered in its path, a grass covering the two low banks. "Well, Mr. Du Boise, we've found camp for tonight."

The afternoon was young enough, so Del agreed. "Sure, but after a drink for all of us." Lucky clicked to his horse and the four went to the creek. They all drank, the animals taking bites of the grass like kids sneaking cookies.

Soon, they did a slow backtrack and intercepted the others

headed their way. Sam and Arnold rode in front and saw them first. Sam waved and trotted to them. "Camp?"

"Yep," said Lucky. "It's a ways, maybe five miles ahead."

"Good enough."

All four men headed west, the wagon party behind them. They soon reached the creek and the people prepared for staying the night. Del volunteered to take the horses for staking out by the water. He made sure they were secure before heading back to the Granville wagons for fishing line and hooks. Back at the creek, he saw it was shallow in most parts so he looked for a deeper section for good fishing. He moved the horses to fresh grass after catching a fish and quit after fishing three pounds worth. If they'd not needed to veer off from Snake River, he would have had more. He made a mental note to go the extra distance the next time they reached the larger body of water.

Uncle Joe cleared his throat behind Del, saying, "Looks like you have dinner for us."

He turned to face the older man. "I do, if you're willing to cook."

"Help me clean them and you've got a deal."

Del grinned. He was a decent cook, but Uncle Joe had him beat. The sun had tanned the man's face enough to hide his age. His hands, too, looked like smooth leather. Del suspected in another few years, Joe would bear the deep wrinkles most cowhands had. The two men filleted the fish on a flat rock nearby. They rinsed the meat in the water, making sure all the scales were gone before heading back to camp.

As they approached, Sam stood up from the fire he'd been building. "Good job, men. I'm already hungry."

"Good, because these won't take long." Joe handed his part of the meat for Del to hold before rummaging around in the company wagon. "I'd recommend y'all finish up your chores real quick."

Lucky walked up with an armload of sticks and brush he'd managed to find. "Don't need to tell me twice. I'll let the others know. You just keep on with our meal."

They scattered while Del held the fish until Joe was ready to cook. Soon, they sizzled in the pan. He didn't have time to wash clothes or take a bath but could get everything ready for doing chores later. By the time he'd finished, he heard Joe calling in everyone to eat.

The more the men gathered and talked, the more Del enjoyed being a part of this group. He had spent enough time riding alone in the past couple of years. The solitude had fed his soul, but the company now fed his heart. He glanced down at his near empty plate.

Maybe heart was the wrong word. Ellen filled that part of him, not these hooligans. Like a smudge of sap from a pine tree on his fingertips, the thought of her wouldn't leave his mind.

"So we're all agreed?" Sam asked. "We're staying here tomorrow morning and leaving out at noon tomorrow?" Each man nodded. "There's only a couple of days between us and the river, so a short delay will help more than hurt."

Lucky hopped up. "With that settled, I'll go wash up for us."

Del's eyes narrowed. He knew the kid wanted to see Jenny as much as he wanted to see Ellen. He had beat Del to the task by volunteering first. "I have other washing to do. Let me help."

"Sure."

At Lucky's knowing grin, Del felt transparent. He countered with a retort of his own. "If we hurry, we'll get to see both ladies."

"Aw, well, I'm not so sure about that, Mr. Du Boise." Lucky scuffed the ground with a toe, his face a bright red. "I'm just wanting to clean up, not see anyone in particular."

Everyone else laughed or at least chuckled at the young man's denial and Del nodded toward the creek. "Let's go, since we're not fooling anyone."

"I reckon not."

They both walked away to the hoots and hollers of their friends. Del tried not to grin at their teasing. "How is the lovely Miss Jenny?"

"She's just fine, sir. I get a chance to walk with her nearly every day. We talk about nothing much. I just like hearing her voice."

He grinned, kneeling at the water along with Lucky. "I understand." He rinsed off the few remaining spices and oil from one of the plates before putting it down on the bank. "Sometimes just breathing the same air is enough."

The young man paused. "You know, you're right." He handed over some silverware. "Miss Winslow, or, uh, Mrs. Du Boise? I'm sure you're that way about her."

Del didn't react to either name he'd used for Ellen. No matter what status those around them might think she had, she'd be his wife once they reached Oregon City. "I'm very much that way about her." As if his heart had called to her and she'd answered, he heard Ellen's voice as she approached. He turned to see both her and Buster behind them. Her step faltered when their gazes met, and Buster squealed at the sight of Del.

She walked a little ways downstream before undressing her baby brother and bathing him. Del studied her covertly. He'd catch her glancing at him before she looked away with a blush. After a while he realized Lucky hadn't ever passed him anything else to wash.

"I figured you'd notice we were done soon enough."

"*Mon Dieu!*" His face felt feverish when he realized how long he'd been distracted. "Let me rinse the sand off this bottom plate, and—"

"And nothing. Go on." He took the dishes and put them in the clean bucket. "Go on and say something to her."

"She seems busy."

"That don't matter, so are you. Your turn at first watch will come soon enough, so get over there and talk to her."

"Talk to who? Yer not talking to my daughter, and what the hell is this first watch business?" Winslow's words grew louder with each one he said until a crowd gathered to see what the fuss was about. "Don't tell me Granville has the fox guarding us chickens? Goddamn it all to hell! I'll bet he does."

Del straightened, taller than Jack even at a decline. "I am no fox. Sam trusts me because I am dependable."

Jack's jaw fell slack before he snorted. "Oh, sure you are, just like every other snaky Indian around here. Your only saving grace is bringing Ellen back, and I'm not sure why you did that unless she was no good as a wife."

"Exactly what are you saying about Miss Winslow?"

"I'm saying if yer going to kidnap my daughter, get to it. I'm tired of looking over my shoulder for you sneaking up behind me."

In his best barrister voice, Del asked, "Are you asking me to abscond with your daughter so you can rest easier knowing she's gone?"

"No, I'm asking you to take her already, instead of waiting until the dead of night to slit mine and my sons' throats."

Del's anger almost kept him from breathing. How dare this

man accuse him of laying in wait to murder him for something like this? He'd never need to kill to gain Ellen's love, and Winslow knew it. He narrowed his eyes, certain he knew his wife far better than her father did. "I will never kidnap your daughter. If she is to be mine, it will be by her choice, not yours, mine, or anyone else's." He looked over to see Ellen still standing downstream, Buster wrapped in a blanket and resting on her hip. Del narrowed his eyes and never let his gaze leave her face. "She is with you, Mr. Winslow, and will be until she decides to resume being my wife."

Like a human volcano, Jack erupted and yelled at his daughter, "Resume, Ellen? You've *lain* with him already?"

CHAPTER 8

Ellen's heart stopped cold. She took a step back as if to remove herself from the talk about intimacy and Del from her father. Something, but not everything had happened, and she wanted no one to learn of the tiniest little detail about her and Del's nights together. "Pa, there was no anything with anyone. Adelard was a gentleman and you can be sure I was a lady."

Pa went up to her, poking her just below her throat. "Can I? Because every time I see him, he's sniffing around your skirts like a hungry hound dog. You've been feeding him or he'd not be begging."

She felt the little spits from his mouth with each consonant he'd said. Ellen wanted to run as far as her legs would go, even with Buster, to get away from such crude and public talk. "I'm feeding no one anything. I was kidnapped. He rescued me. You are the only one who imagines anything more."

"More people than just me know what's going on here. First, Granville lets him trail along like a hound, then says he can defile you and bring you back, and finally lets him guard us? No. This ain't happening. I'm not letting no Indian watch me as I sleep, waiting for the best time to knife me in the heart. No sirree."

"Pa! I am not defiled in any way." She swallowed her nerves at how many people stood around them, gaping. Ellen didn't know everyone there. Had another wagon party joined them in camp? She lifted her chin. "I'm innocent. Mr. Du Boise saved my life, that's all. Please stop this show and let's go back to camp." She took his elbow, pulling him toward camp.

Jack crossed his arms and dug in his heels. "No. Not until Granville stops that mangy dog from guarding us while we sleep."

She looked around and saw Sam standing next to Del. The two men exchanged a look before Sam nodded. "All right. Adelard is no longer on night watch effective immediately." He took a step towards Winslow. "I'll need someone to take his place and nominate you, since you're much more trustworthy."

"What? I can't do that. I'm still grieving for Lucy."

"I think you can and will do a fine job to boot. In fact, I'll expect you to keep watch on the first shift so be ready."

"I'm not doing any such thing."

"Do you want to be on your own to Oregon City?" At the shake of Jack's head no, Sam went on. "Then you have first watch." He walked off, Del and Lucky following him.

Jack leaned in towards Ellen. "Be glad there's a bunch of people here, or I'd give you the smack you deserve for disgracing me."

"Yes, sir," Ellen replied, staring at her feet. She bit her tongue to keep from arguing about who'd disgraced whom. Buster let out a wail and she shifted him to her other hip.

"Here, give me my son. You're about useless in taking care of the boys."

Ellen gave him no reaction and didn't bother to argue while handing over Buster. He'd said these words or something similar ever since she'd come back. The first few days of protest had taught her nothing she said changed anything in his mind, so she kept quiet and moved on.

The lack of Buster's weight lightened her. Ellen breathed in deep, glad to be without the load, and gathered the clothes she'd been washing. She soon knelt by the water, wanting to clean a few things before the night fell. Diapers were the worst. She hadn't realized how much her stepmother had done until the job fell solely on her. She wrung out the first cloth, telling herself how fresh clothes for Buster were worth the effort.

The routine task helped her mind wander. Without the threat of Pa seeing her, she could think back and obsess over every detail. Del had been handsome with long hair in a single braid down his back. Now, with a more refined length, her heart skipped a beat every time she thought of running her fingers through his hair. Sometimes he'd worn the military pants she supposed someone at the fort gave him. The buckskins and red shirt on him today suited him better. Her hand reached for a cloth that wasn't there and Ellen realized with a start that her washing was done. Lost in thought, she'd not noticed how dark it had become.

She hurried back to camp, hoping Pa had set up bedding for the boys. She saw Skeeter and Buster already in their bedrolls, staring up at the stars.

"Hi, sis. I'm telling Buster his goodnight story about Ma."

"Thank you, Skeets. Did you set up our beds tonight too?" She smiled, laying the diapers out to dry.

"Yep! Pa didn't ask, so I figured I might help."

She wiped her hands on her skirt and got into her own bed. Ellen had heard enough in the past few days to know the younger boy had done most of the chores while she was gone. "You're the best helper ever." She curled onto her side, head resting against her arm in the usual way that didn't mash her eyeglasses. The baby slept with a slight snore while Skeeter stared up at the sky.

Ellen took the chance to do more laundry early the next day. After changing Buster's diaper, fixing breakfast, and scrubbing dishes, cleaning clothes was a welcome variation in her routine. She looked up from the water, surprised at the idea. Never in her life would she have expected washing her dresses to be enjoyable. She shook her head and went back to work.

She'd planned on enjoying some of the morning doing small tasks, but the minutes slipped by too fast. Lucky's bugle sounded and she rushed to help Pa yoke the ox. Buster hated riding in the wagon but toddled too slowly to keep up, so Ellen carried him on her hip, changing sides often during the next three miles. The wagon train bottlenecked at the top of a steep hill. One by one, wagons rolled down, their speed kept in check with a hand brake. Those on foot eased down, careful to stay upright despite the loose gravel.

Easing Buster to her right hip, Ellen carefully stepped down the incline. Each slip stopped her heart until she gained a solid footing. She'd planned it so if she fell, it'd be onto her left side and not on her baby brother.

Buster began kicking and pointing. "Skee! Sis, Skee!"

She glanced up from the ground to see Skeeter with a few of his friends taking advantage of the slope. Each boy slid down the hill on his butt, and she knew their pants would need patches after this. She shook her head. "That's right, Bus, there's Skeeter."

The baby stiffened, then became deadweight. "Go Skee, sis. Go Skee!"

"No, Buster, we can't go with Skeet—" She struggled to hold the wriggling boy until he slid down her hip and began kicking her shins. The sharp pain startled Ellen and she jumped. Rocks rolled under her feet so she leaned to her left to keep Buster safe.

Instinctively, she used her left hand to stop their fall. She felt more than heard her wrist crunch and cried out from the pain.

The hold on him loosened, Buster took the chance to slide down the hill like the big boys. Ellen tried to focus on him and getting down there. Her wrist burned, shooting tingles up to her shoulder. She stood and resumed her careful descent at a faster pace. He knew to keep away from rolling wagons, but accidents happened to even the knowledgeable sometimes. She saw him jumping up and down with his arms in the air. He made staying angry difficult for her. Ellen reached Buster and took him by the arm with her good hand. "For shame, Buster Winslow, for shame!" A wagon rolling by made a lot of racket so she almost had to holler at him. "Dang it! You're supposed to stay with me, young man!"

Pa took her arm and swung her around to face him. "Don't you talk to that baby like that! It's loud enough out here and you'll hurt his ears."

His fingers dug into her skin, almost overriding the pain in her wrist. "Pa, I didn't—" She gasped when he started shaking her, gripping harder.

"Shut up. Not another word." He let her go with a push. "I don't want to ever hear you speak to him like that again, understand?"

She bit her lip, resisting the urge to rub the bruised skin on her upper arm. Others might be watching but she didn't take the time to look around. "I won't, Pa."

He turned to Buster. "Come on, boy, go with me, not with your mean ole sister."

The boy looked back at Ellen while taking Pa's hand. He followed with a skip after she gave him a little wave. She liked the distrusting expression on her little brother's face. At least he hadn't blindly believed Ellen had been unkind to him. The two reached their family wagon and began following the others. She sought out Marie or Jenny to no avail. It was just as well. Her left arm hurt from fingertips to shoulder, and all she wanted to do was cry. Skeeter and his friends played off to the side yet close by the group.

She'd already noticed Del at the front as a scout earlier today. Ellen wanted him to hold her while she sobbed, but actually doing so would attract the wrong kind of attention. She thanked providence he'd not seen her fall or Pa's scolding. He'd ask why she didn't smile, had tears in her eyes, and cradled her arm. She couldn't lie to him and pretend nothing was wrong. She continued walking while ignoring her arm and focusing on the high desert landscape around her.

They crossed two streams slowly to give everyone a chance to drink. The late start kept them moving despite Ellen's stomach growling for an early dinner. Another mile led them to a larger creek that fed into the Snake River. This gave them a triangle of land created by swift water. Lucky's bugle signaling them to stop for the night relieved her. If she could get through the next few hours without a whimper, she planned on collapsing into bed and nursing her arm with a cloth wrap.

The isthmus they had let the men line up the wagons to create a bottom to the rivers' triangle sides. Ellen kept quiet while she helped Pa. She almost enjoyed his silent treatment, emphasized when he looked through her as if she weren't there. Sometimes, she didn't want to pretend everything was fine. Between them both, they soon had a campfire and food cooking for the little family.

"I'm going to visit the Nelsons this evening. Skeeter, you did a fine job with our blankets last night. Can I expect you to do the same tonight?"

"Yes, Pa."

"That's my boy. Help keep an eye on Buster, make sure he doesn't get into any trouble." He ruffled Skeeter's hair before walking away.

The young boy sat, staring into the fire for a while before saying, "I'm sorry, sis."

"It's all right, Skeets. He'll forget why he's mad at me soon enough." She stood, handing her plate to him and getting Pa's from where he'd set it. "If you'll do dishes for me, I'll clean up Buster. You'll save me so much time, I'll be able to tell you a bedtime story." She picked up the baby and one of his clean diaper cloths as Skeeter put the dishes in the bucket. "Don't take the cook pot. It's heavy and I can wash it later this evening."

"I can wash it."

"Probably so, but for right now, doing these dishes is enough." Skeeter followed as she led the way. Having a full tummy made Buster sleepy and he nestled into her. "Don't get too comfortable, sweetheart." At the creek bank, she took off Buster's diaper and rinsed it. He toddled over and put a foot in the water. Soon enough, he was walking in the shallows. She and Skeeter laughed when Buster began washing himself. "He's old enough to potty like a big boy, don't you think Skeeter?"

"Yeah, think I should help him know when it's time to go?"

"That's a great idea. Buster? Do you want to be a big boy like Skeeter?"

"Yep." He began hopping. "Big, big, big."

"You can begin being a big boy first thing tomorrow, all right? Come here and let me get you dressed." She held out her arms to him and he ran to her, slipping a little. Ellen tied his diaper on, swung him on her hip, and held out her hand for Skeeter. "It's getting dark."

He looked around before answering, "Sure is."

His hand felt cold in hers, thanks to the night air and wet hands. They reached the wagon and got the beds ready. When done, she asked, "Didn't I promise a bedtime story?" Both children answered at the same time and she laughed. "Quiet down, sillies. Other people might be sleeping." They both grinned at her while squirming.

"Tell us about the knights and their king."

She nodded. Buster liked everything but Skeeter loved King Arthur and his knights. She thought for a second. "I'll tell you about the brave Sir Lancelot." Ellen wove them a tale from memories of her mother's stories and whatever she could add. She'd not even given a proper ending before both children slept.

As she stood up to wash the cookpot, Pa came over and got into bed. He didn't say a word to her. Ellen waited for a moment to see if he had some sort of task for her. When he stayed silent, she took the chance to escape, even if that only meant scrubbing burnt beans and rice. The quarter to full moon gave her enough light to find her way to the creek. Shimmers glinted on the water. She began scrubbing, glad the pot was heavy enough to stay still in the shallow water. It let her clean with one hand instead of pushing through the pain by holding the pot in her left. She was almost done when a cloud covered the moon. The dark pressed in as if it was a giant unseen hand.

"Ellen?"

His voice at first startled her until a rush of love went through her. "Del." She stood, his hand on her arms helping to steady her.

"I'm glad you're here."

"So am I." He pulled her into an embrace.

She relaxed into him, wanting to absorb his warmth into her very soul. "Are you here for me, or do you need to continue on to the creek?"

"I'm here only for you, sweetheart."

Nestled into him, she breathed his scent. "I've missed you so much." She resisted a little when he pulled away but relaxed when he lifted her chin. Ellen smiled, ready for his kiss, when he wrapped his arms around her. The action pressed on the bruise Pa had left and a whimper escaped her.

He let go of her in an instant. "Your arm?" Del caressed her left arm, stopping where she ached. "This is his favorite place to hurt you, it seems. The skin is warmer here than elsewhere."

"I don't know about it being his favorite place."

"It is. He grabs you, squeezes to harm, but not enough for others to notice." Del bent to kiss her arm. "I'm sorry. Maybe I need to teach him a lesson."

"No, please don't. I don't want to start a fight among our people."

"That's noble of you." He stood straight and pressed his lips against her forehead. "Yet, unnecessary. If he hurts you again and I learn of it, I will hurt him."

"Then I won't tell you if he does." The cloud moved on, letting the moonlight fall upon them.

Del grinned. "Good. Please don't. I will do a check of you for myself."

"A what?"

"A check. Starting here," he said, kissing her cheek. "Then here." He nuzzled her ear, putting a hand behind her neck. "I'll want to check your back as well." Del ran his fingertips down her spine to the small of her back. "Feels perfect to me."

"Me too." She shivered when he traced back up to her shoulders. "Still good?"

"Still perfect." He leaned in, letting his hands caress down her arms, barely touching her left arm to the elbow. "So perfect." Del's lips brushed hers as he reached down for her hands. She gasped when he bent her hands up at the wrists and he stepped back "*Mon Dieu*! Your wrist is still injured?"

"Reinjured from a fall today." She winced, anticipating pain

when he lifted her wrist to his lips. The touch tickled and Ellen
smiled. "Such wonderful medicine, thank you."

"Your skin burns here too, *ma coeur*." He gently let go of her
arm and began unbuttoning his shirt.

"I'm certain all of me will be hot if you undress right now."

He chuckled. "I hope so, but not just yet." He ripped a strip
from the tail end of the shirt. "Let me have your hand again." She
did as asked and Del wrapped her hand and wrist.

The tight wrap compressed the joint and helped the injury feel
better. "Is your shirt still wearable? Do you have enough fabric for
every woman you meet?"

"I don't, but this is Sam's shirt. He won't mind too much."

She laughed. "He won't if we don't tell him."

Del caressed her face with the back of his hand. "What else
could we do and not tell him?" He bent to capture her lips with his
own in a kiss.

Ellen melted into him. Goosebumps covered her from the
sensual touch. She shivered and enjoyed his returning moan. He
held her closer, careful of her arm. She loved his consideration and
his strength. She leaned away to end the kiss and ran her hand
through his hair. "Care to tell me what happened? Were you caught
somehow and had to cut off your braid to get out?"

He laughed. "Something similar, yes. Cutting my hair let me
flee the fort with the Army's permission."

"I'm glad."

"Me too." Del glanced over at the camp. "Everyone is asleep
for now, but second watch will be starting soon. Let's get back
before Arnold decides to check on us." He picked up the cook pot.
"I'll escort you."

"Thank you."

He took her right hand to hold as he led her. "My pleasure."
They walked to the wagon train where no one except Arnold
stirred. "Leave me here, *ma coeur*, and I hope to see you tomorrow."

She lifted his hand and kissed him. "I hope so too." Her heart
ached at leaving him. She let his hand fall, steeling herself to walk
away from him and return to her family.

The next morning, Pa paused before sipping his coffee and
spoke to Ellen. "What's that on your arm? Some sort of bandage?"

She stopped sipping her own coffee and nodded. "It's from

Sam's shirt. Someone noticed I was favoring this hand and suggested it for my wrist."

"Didn't know you were hurt, thought maybe you weren't getting enough attention." He turned to his younger son. "Skeeter, help your sister with chores until she gets better."

Ellen had the distinct feeling from him that her injury was an affront to him personally. His words didn't say so, but his tone did. She fought the urge to insist she was fine and didn't need her brother's help. Except that she did for a few days. Even now her arm ached, and she moved her hand to check its mobility.

Skeeter leaned against her in a half hug. "Don't worry, sis. I can help just fine."

She smiled down at his earnest face. "I know you can."

"You're still changing Buster's diapers. Right?"

"Yes, I am." She chuckled. "Unless you're wanting to…?"

"Nope!" He sat up straight. "I'll wash dishes and put away the bedding. Too busy to clean poop. Sorry, sis!"

"I thought so." She gave him a final hug. "Go get started and I'll take care of our boy."

Buster walked over to her, half eaten biscuit still in one hand. "Poop." Hearing Skeeter laugh, the baby started bouncing. "Poop, poop, poop!"

"All right, that's enough." She scooped him up before setting him back down. He was wet and smelly, chanting poop for a reason. "Let's go clean you up and talk about how big boys go to the bathroom out here."

Buster followed her to the river, holding her hand. She stripped him down and let him play in the water while she cleaned up the diaper. Glancing upstream, she saw Skeeter finishing up and going back to camp. If she didn't hurry, Lucky would be sounding the signal to move out and Buster would still be half naked. She worked fast to dress him again and give his clean but wet diaper another wringing out.

Each family made their way across the creek to the Snake River ferry. Word spread quickly across the waiting families of the cost. Pa shook his head. "I ain't paying no eighteen dollars when there's bound to be some sort of crossing up ahead. They're taking advantage of the desperate."

Ellen agreed. She looked ahead to see Sam and Lefty leading one of the wagons up the river to a better crossing. Wagon ruts went in that direction for a reason, and when the Winslows followed, she saw why. The river widened here and turned relatively shallow. They approached the riverbank behind the Nelsons. She watched as Sam, Lefty, and Del approached. They were wet up to their knees. That meant their wagon's bed would be completely submerged. Ellen's mouth went dry. Green River was bad enough. "Mr. Granville, I'm not going across here. I can't."

"You don't have a choice, girl," said Pa.

Sam swung off his horse. "Lefty, get the next group ready and I'll be there in a minute." He walked over to Ellen. "Now, Miss Winslow, you know I wouldn't let anything happen to you."

"I know not intentionally." She glanced at Del and shivered, remembering how close she'd come to drowning before. "Accidents happen all the time."

Sam put an arm around her. "They do, and no one can help them. But I can promise you that we'll never cross a river unsafely again."

She returned his hug, glancing over to see Del still on Pomme and standing next to Pa. Her father said, "If Granville was a Mormon, I'd ask him to marry Ellen too. He's a good enough man for two wives."

His voice carried to Ellen and Sam. She felt more than heard him chuckle before he said, "If I were a Mormon, I'd consider it. Ellen's a wonderful young lady."

The resulting angry expression on Del's face alarmed her as much as her father's beaming. Ellen gave him a smile, hoping to lighten the mood. "No one's asked me if I like sharing and I don't. You can tell Marie I'm no competition to her."

"Ah, dear, you sell yourself short." He gave her a parting hug. "Del, I see Lucky up ahead with the next family. Shall we?"

She slipped from Sam's arm and he got back on Scamp. Both men headed to the front of the line. She'd hoped Del would look back at her with a happier face, but no. The rest of the afternoon they waited their turn. As Sam predicted, the crossing was easier than the one at Green River and every other in between. The vast stretch of dirt on either side of the banks led her to expect they'd press on for greener pastures. She was right. They rolled until nearly night and a good but small patch of grazing.

Wanting to explain away her father's comments while reassuring Del kept Ellen preoccupied for the rest of the evening.

The boys chattered with her and each other. Pa kept up his silent treatment of her. Both actions suited her just fine. She liked the happy voices of her brothers, and not having to hear Pa's complaints was refreshing.

Skeeter followed her to the creek without being asked. He talked about the games he and his friends played and told her how well Buster was doing with pottying like a big boy. She laughed at some of his tales. Soon they finished washing up and went back to camp to find the others asleep. She made a shush sound with her finger to her lips and put away their dishes before going to bed. Snuggled under the covers, she tried to stay awake and think of ways to chat with Del tomorrow morning.

The sun rose on a rare cloudy day. Ellen hurried to start a fire and their coffee. The damp chill seemed to sink into her bones. Her wrist had been improving until today as well. Lucky played his warning notes on the bugle, and everyone ate biscuits and bacon in a hurry.

Soon, they all inched down the road in single file. The damp air kept the dust down, and Ellen enjoyed the walk. She saw Del and Lefty ride toward them. They stopped at the first wagon, and she wondered what was up ahead. Word soon spread that they'd come upon a trading camp.

The ordeal of losing Lucy and being kidnapped by Pointed Nose flashed through her mind. What if something like that happened again? She had no doubt of another rescue, but no one could know who'd be killed or taken next. If one of the children strayed too far…. Ellen swallowed the lump in her throat choking her. She had to find the boys and stop the wagon.

She hurried, finding Skeeter and Buster with a group of other children. "Come on, boys."

"Aw, sis! We were having fun."

"Come with me." She held out her hands for them to take. "Let's go and hurry." They did as she'd asked and went with her to their wagon. "Pa! Pa! You have to stop. We need to hide from the Indians." At Skeeter's gasp, she added, "It's a game."

Their father snorted, snapping the reins to speed along the animals. "I don't have time for games."

"Pa, please. There's a trading post ahead. Do it for Buster and Skeeter." She almost cried in relief when understanding crossed his face. He pulled the wagon to a stop and she put the boys in first, climbing in after them. "Lay down as flat as you can." She laid down and when they followed, she hurried to cover the three of them with blankets. "Shhh, we have to be very quiet."

Skeeter pushed the bedding away from his face. "Are you sure this is a game?"

"I am. Some say that Indians can hunt any animal, even man. So we're going to play hide and seek with them. If we can roll on without them even knowing we're here, we've won."

The older boy nestled in next to his baby brother and put his arm around him. "Buster, can you be quiet so we can win?" The baby nodded and Skeeter smiled up at Ellen. "We're ready, sis."

She replaced the covers over them and waited. The wagon's bounce jarred her bones, but she stayed still. Buster whimpered and began squirming. She heard Del, then Pa talk but couldn't make out what they said.

"Ellen? Are you in here?" asked Del.

"I said she was."

She peeked out from under the blanket, as did the boys. "Yes, I am."

"You win! You win!" Buster climbed out from under the cover and went for Del.

"I do?"

"Del!" she hissed. "Go away! They'll find us here and I can't let that happen again."

A flash of hurt crossed his face. "*Non, ma coeur.* I'd never let that happen. Come with me and we'll trade for the boys some new shoes."

She loved him and how he'd noticed the ragtag shape her brothers' shoes were in. Ellen had been thinking of ways to fix their soles earlier today too. If Del went, she'd need to help him get the correct sizes. He wouldn't escort her into an unsafe place. She smiled, ignoring her worry. "Of course I'll go."

"Do you have something to trade?"

"I'm not sure. If it's for the boys, I could give them one of Lucy's dresses."

Pa's face appeared at the back opening. "You're not giving away a damned thing of my wife's! Not to those damned Indians who killed her."

"I'm not giving it to them. Just trading for the boys some new moccasins."

"Are you arguing with me? You'll hand them something of yours before giving anything of Lucy's away. It's all those boys have of their mother's."

"Yes, Pa." She turned back to Del. "I'm not sure I have anything else of value."

Her father snorted. "You could trade that dress, since you're so quick to give away clothes."

"Not this one! What would I wear on wash day?" She held up a hand to stop her father from a sarcastic reply. "It's fine, Pa. I'll find something to give them." He smirked and disappeared from view.

Ellen looked at her two brothers and they returned her gaze. Who knew what sort of terrain they'd have to walk over in the next couple of months? She had two things to give, her mother's wedding dress and silver hairbrush. Both had been hidden in the bottom of her trunk from Pa. Otherwise, he'd have considered them valuable enough to sell or let Lucy have. Del still stood there, waiting, so she opened her trunk and felt toward the bottom. The natives probably wouldn't have any use for a fancy dress, so Ellen retrieved her hairbrush. Her heart ached as she ran her hand over the bristles one last time. She held it out for him. "Take this. It's metal and should be worth enough to help the boys. I don't need to go with you, do I?"

He stared at her for a moment. "No, you don't. It'll be good if you stay here." He winked at her. "Pointed Nose might have a brother."

"Lord, I hope not." She tried to give him a smile. "Thank you."

"My pleasure. I'll catch up to you later this evening." He went to the front of the wagon. "Monsieur Winslow, you may go. Thank you for stopping."

She heard Pa mutter something before the wagon lurched forward. Before the vehicle could gain much momentum, she told Skeeter, "Skeet, hop out and I'll hand the baby to you." He scrambled out and she gave him Buster.

The older boy saw his friends and hollered to her, "Sis, we're going to play and won't be late for dinner! C'mon, Buster!"

"All right! Be careful!" She eased down, the wagon going fast enough to be scary to hop from. She stumbled but didn't fall. Ellen wasn't as lucky as her brothers. None of her friends seemed to be around, so she had a long and dusty walk by herself. Just as well, she thought. She wanted time alone to grieve for her mother's hairbrush. The thing wasn't valuable. No one would treasure such an item, but it'd been almost all that was left of the woman she remembered. Lucy had been a kind person, but not her own mother.

At least there was the dress Ma had married her Pa in. She almost snickered when remembering how Lucy had insisted on trying it on one time. The poor woman, Ellen shook her head. She'd looked like a ten-pound sausage stuffed into a five-pound bag. The second Mrs. Winslow had even split a seam in struggling her way out of it. Lucy had been round where her ma was slender and shorter.

The men decided to camp early at a good-sized stream with abundant grass. Ellen had heard mentions of Indian activity during her chores at the creek. People quieted when they saw her, so she didn't get a chance to catch everything. Their gossip worried her and she hurried to get back to the wagon. A woman's scream stopped her mid step. Her heart raced. The woman sounded like Marie. Ellen ran to the source as did several others.

Uncle Joe laid there, Marie kneeling beside him and crying. An arrow stuck out of his chest, his hands clenched around it. Ellen stared, stunned, as people from everywhere gathered. Sam, Del, and the other hired men rode up and several of them cursed. Del was the first to dismount, hurrying to Ellen and asking, "Where are your brothers?"

Memories of losing Lucy overwhelmed her, and he had to ask a second time before she answered, "I—I don't know." She couldn't take her gaze from the scuffmarks Joe's boots had made in the dirt during his death throes. Had Lucy done the same thing? She'd not thought to ask Del what her stepmother's body had looked like that morning.

"Find them and get back to your wagon. We can take care of this." He walked to where Marie openly sobbed and knelt to her level. *"Ma coupin, allons, s'il vous plait."*

"Non, Adelard. I can't just leave him here."

"You won't. The men and I will care for him. Go back to your wagon and wait for Sam."

His words seemed to wake up Sam, who wiped his eyes. "Please, Marie." He raised his voice. "Ladies, please go back to your wagons with your children and wait inside. We'll take care of Joe now and have his service in a safer place tonight."

Del turned and went to her. "*Mon amour?* Your brothers." He held her right arm, giving it a little shake as if waking her.

His action roused Ellen from her trance. "Oh, God, of course. Excuse me!" She hurried to where she'd last seen Skeeter. None of the children were there. Panic squeezed her lungs until Pa called out to her.

"Hey, get over here!"

She ran to him. "Have you seen the boys?"

"Yeah, Skeeter's back there trying to change Buster's diaper. Get back there and help him."

Ellen did as he ordered and found the boys sitting on the tailgate. "Pa said you need help with Buster?"

"Nope!" said the boys at the same time and laughed.

"I goes potty like a big boy," Buster told her, his little chest puffed with pride.

She smiled. "That's wonderful and I'm very proud of you. Now, both of you need to get into the wagon."

"Why?" asked Skeeter while Buster climbed into the back.

"I'll tell you in a minute. For now, just get in there."

Pa turned the corner and frowned. "What the hell? Didn't Granville tell you to get the boys in the wagon?"

"Yes, and I am."

"Doesn't look like it. Skeeter, get in there and stop arguing. Ellen, did you get Buster changed?"

She and her younger brother exchanged a glance before she answered. "Yes, Pa, he's good now."

"Then stop lallygaggin' around and get in there. Indians are running around massacring people, and you're out here in the open with my sons." He closed the tailgate with a slam. "Get in. Leave the animals hitched because we might be moving on."

She did as he asked, sitting with her brothers. They were too quiet and Ellen wanted to reassure them. "This is a dangerous area, but we're safe in here. Pa and the other men won't let anything happen to us."

Buster nodded and Skeeter asked, "Was someone killed?"

Ellen debated on telling him a story or the truth, and the truth won out. "I'm afraid so. An Indian shot Uncle Joe." The words hurt her to say, and she choked on a sob. Her brothers leaned against her. "He was at the creek getting a drink, I suppose." Buster snuggled into her. She patted his back. They sat in silence for what seemed like forever until Pa appeared at the tailgate.

"We're moving on to more open country, so we can see those bastards sneaking up on us." He let down the gate. "You all get down and hurry up. It'll be late before we stop tonight."

She and the boys climbed out and Pa secured the wagon again. Her brothers stayed close while they walked. The sun inched further and further down until it dipped below the horizon. Ellen wondered how they'd fix dinner in the dark if the near full moon didn't rise soon.

Pa solved her problem as soon as everyone formed the usual wagon half circle. "I'm staking out the animals and getting everyone something to drink. Stay here, set out our beds, make sure Buster is changed for the night, and we'll eat first thing tomorrow."

She opened her mouth to protest. Uncle Joe's memorial service might have already started and she wanted to attend. When her father gave her a threatening stare, Ellen did as he said, with Skeeter helping. Soon, they were all in their beds, even Pa. Ellen couldn't sleep despite being bone tired. She watched the moon rise over the eastern mountains. The light shone enough to illuminate first Lucky, then Del as they walked their paces around the group during night watch. So much for Pa's suspicion of Del serving as night watch. Ellen supposed that ended after her father's second sleepless night. She eased up, sitting. Only for a few seconds did she debate about thanking Del before slipping out of her bed and going to him.

Ellen stood next to her wagon, waiting for him to walk by. When he approached, she hissed at him to catch his attention. "Del," she whispered.

He held out his hand, saying, "Come here." When she did as he requested, he pulled her to him in a tight hug. He didn't speak, just held her in a bone-crushing embrace.

His warmth and strength fed her heart and soul. She'd not known how much she needed him until now. Hearing steps, she leaned back to leave only to find him unwilling to loosen his hold. "I think Lucky is nearby."

"You need sleep but I can't let you go, *ma coeur*. I need you."

She lifted her face to his and their lips met. He kissed her with a passion that almost frightened her. She ignored the fear and buried her hands in his hair, deepening the kiss. When he pulled away, she had to stifle a moan of protest.

"Tomorrow. We'll talk tomorrow evening. Monsieur Lucky has had to turn back twice by now and we're not being safe. Sam has your brothers' new shoes. I'll remind him before we resume traveling tomorrow." He caressed her face with the back of his hand. "Sleep well, my love," he whispered before disappearing into the night.

Ellen licked her bottom lip, aching for him. Shaking off the hunger for more, she crept to her bed and tried to sleep.

The next morning started with a shout. The sound sent terror through Ellen as she sat up. Were they under attack? She checked the boys, both also now awake and staring at her. The one yell turned into a stream of curses at the top of Pa's lungs. A lack of rest and now this rude awakening shortened Ellen's own temper. "Dear, God, what is it now with him?" she murmured before stopping herself. She looked over at her brothers, Buster not understanding her transgression while Skeeter smirked. "No telling Pa what I said, all right?"

"I won't if you don't tell him the next time I'm bad."

She chuckled. "It's a deal."

Ellen climbed out and went to see what had her father so upset. As soon as she spotted their cow on the ground, dead, she agreed with his tirade. She hurried over. The blood clotted around the animal's mouth and nose horrified her. "What happened? Was she poisoned?"

"How the hell should I know? She's just dead and our ox is sick. When he dies, we're on foot. Hope you can carry a lot because I don't think your brothers can." Pa threw down his hat in frustration and stomped off.

She picked up his hat, tears filling her eyes. As crude as he was, Pa was right. They'd be in a mess if their last animal died too. A thought occurred to her, and she glanced around to see if any other cows had died.

Arnold walked up to her. "Miss? Sorry about your cow. Is your ox doing well?" He held out a couple pairs of shoes.

She took them, the leather soft and pliable. "It seems so for now. Has anyone else lost stock today?"

"Yeah, several have. None are taking it as hard as your pa. Everyone else has more animals to lose, so I reckon he has a right to be upset."

Ellen knelt down for a closer look at her cow's face. "Did they all die the same way?"

"Yep. Mr. Granville says it's the dust cutting up their lungs or maybe they breathed in water during that last river crossing. Scary thing is, no one knows for sure."

She turned when Del cleared his throat during his approach. "Hello, Mr. Du Boise. Have you seen anything like this before now? Do you think people could catch this from the cattle?"

"No, never before now, and I have never known of people dying like this." He made a come here motion with his hand. "Why don't you step away, in case humans can become ill from this?"

The flash of fear in his eyes didn't comfort her. She did as he'd requested and moved from the animal's side. "I don't suppose we should bury or butcher her."

"No, ma'am," replied Arnold. "It's best to just leave her here."

"I agree." Del addressed the other man. "Sam wants to get started soon. He also wants your help in delivering a message to Fort Hall about Joe's death."

"Yes, sir." The hired hand ambled off in the Granville wagon's direction.

Del glanced at her before staring off into the western horizon. "Mademoiselle, good day, and leave the cow alone."

She smiled a little at his concern. "Very well, Mr. Du Boise. I'll stay healthy, just for you."

"Good." He started walking, slowly as if reluctant to leave her. "Until tonight?"

She went to gather the boys before finding Pa. With all the Winslows accounted for, Ellen looked for Marie before spotting her riding with Sam. She didn't want to intrude on the newlyweds' time together. Marie would welcome her, as would Sam, but she decided against it. Jenny was helping her mother with the new baby. And Del? He was forbidden. Everyone else being too sick, old, young, or busy, she spent the next five miles walking alone and waiting for the landscape to change. Dead animals littered the roadway, often followed by discarded furniture. Ellen had difficulty in passing by some of the lovelier pieces. She didn't miss the chance to grab some of the loose wood for the day's campfire.

The bugle sounded and she wondered why Lucky played it so soon in the day. As she approached the front of the train, Ellen saw a trickle of a creek with a thin band of grass lining either bank. Not the best place they'd ever spent a noon hour at, but not the worst either.

She had just enough time to pass out biscuits to her brothers and father, change Buster's diaper, and get everyone a drink of water. Ellen took extra time hugging her baby brother. She reassured him accidents happened to everyone, and then they were traveling again. They crossed dry creeks and wide dusty expanses. A cool wind kept them from sweating under the hot sun. Another eight miles along the road and they found a grassy area surrounding a small pond. The livestock's hooves had muddied the water, so she decided to wait until later for fresher drinking.

Pa had unhitched their ox. Ellen climbed up into the wagon and gathered everything they'd need for supper.

"I'm supposed to help you." Skeeter climbed onto the tailgate. "Pa said so."

She stifled a chuckle at his surly tone. "Good, I need someone to strain water for us. Take this and get started while I fix a fire and start things cooking."

"Is this going to take long?"

"Nope. Sooner you get started, sooner you're done." She ignored his frown. The day was still young enough; of course he wanted to be out with his friends and getting into trouble. Ellen kept an eye on him as he placed the muslin over a large jar and tied twine around the mouth to keep the cloth in place. He gingerly poured the water from small to large. She noticed the water was still cloudy. "That's good, Skeeter."

"I can go?"

"Yes, and take Buster with you."

"Aw, sis."

"Take him."

He frowned, but to his credit Skeeter was kind as he held out a hand to his baby brother. "C'mon, Bust. My friends are waiting." He glanced back at Ellen. "They probably brought their brothers too."

"I'm sure they did. Be back before dark." She watched as they ran off and wasn't too worried. They knew when dinner would be. Ellen built a fire and sifted tiny moths from the flour with a cheesecloth. She checked every so often on the water, impatiently waiting for the silt to settle. Maybe someday they'd be near a good fishing place. When that happened, she'd want clean cornmeal. Ellen checked and the jar holding the meal had kept it bug and moisture free.

At last no other tasks remained, so she poured water over the beans and rice already in the cook pot and put the lid on it. They'd need more water for coffee tomorrow, so she repeated the fetching process at the pond. After that, she was at loose ends. Pa was at another camp, and she knew the boys were still playing. She wanted to sneak away and talk with Del, but he had to be too busy to chat. Everyone had something to do, as did she. After mending their clothes, Ellen spent the time writing in her journal about Uncle Joe's death, their lost cow, and the barren land while their dinner cooked. She had to pause and stir every so often, giving her a welcome chance to stretch.

Pa walked up, breaking her concentration. "I'd like to say that smells good."

She chuckled. "So would I."

"There ain't much anyone can do about it, is there, girl?"

"No, not unless we run into an orchard." When he grinned, she soaked up the affection like the land around her absorbed rain. She wanted to keep him talking and enjoy an easy conversation but was afraid of ruining the happy mood.

"You seen any of those women in that Harper group over there?"

"Not really. Only at a distance."

"They're fine looking and some of them need husbands."

Ellen stirred their dinner again as Pa went on, telling her all about the single women and the qualities of each one. She didn't care, too dismayed at how his earlier good humor wasn't because they were getting along. She gave him the appropriate responses as he droned on. Ellen kept an ear open enough for any changes in what he said, but nothing caught her attention. She glanced up when the boys ran over to them. She welcomed the interruption and said, "There you are! Ready for dinner?"

"Dinner!" Buster hollered and grabbed a plate.

She laughed, giving him a little bit to eat. "It's hot, so be careful." Ellen served up food for everyone. They all ate quickly, the food too bland and tough to enjoy.

"Sis, do you need any help?" asked Skeeter.

Ellen knew why he asked. He wanted a pass on evening chores. "No, go ahead and play until dark, if Pa agrees."

"Sure, why not? I might mosey over to the other camp myself. One of the ladies promised me dessert if I'd visit." Pa got to his feet and stretched. "Yep, some mighty fine women in that other group. You all might be asleep when I get back."

"All right." She stopped just short of telling him to have a good time. He'd be the new rooster in a henhouse, guaranteed to have a fun night ahead. She ruffled Buster's hair. "Looks like you and me get to wash up and play games." Ellen retrieved him a fresh diaper. "Take this." She threw a bar of soap into the bucket and took her brother's hand. They walked to the water for their nightly ritual of washing dishes before bathing him.

Too soon, goopy mud clung to both of their feet and she was at a loss about what to do. Buster had already scooped up two handfuls and threw them at her. She shrieked, the mud sliding down her skirt. "Oh, good. I needed a bath too." She shook her head, set down the bucket, and picked up her brother. Soon she had him stripped bare and was hauling him closer to the middle of the shallow lake. "Stop wiggling, silly. I can't let you go or you'll drown."

Mid thigh deep to her meant he couldn't reach down for the sludge. She washed his feet, making sure to tickle him. He soon started shivering and Ellen brought him back to shore. "Here," She put his shirt on over his head. "Hold still and let me put on your diaper." He did as she asked, and she smoothed down his wet hair. "You're so handsome! You need pants, though, and they're in the wagon. Let me wash these." She picked up the dish bucket while dropping his dirty clothes. "I'll hurry and no wallowing in the mud or you get another bath, all right?"

He nodded, his teeth chattering, and Ellen rushed through the last of her chores. Her wet skirt weighed her down, but at least the road dirt was gone. They'd almost reached the wagon when Sam caught up to them.

"Miss Winslow? Do you have a moment?"

Giving him a smile, she indicated her little brother with a nod of her head. "I will as soon as Buster is dressed."

"Here, let me carry this and you can carry him." He took her dishes.

When they reached the wagon, she dug through the clothes for him a clean pair of pants. She waited until he was dressed to ask, "Is there something I can help you with?"

The man watched as the little boy ran over to a toy he'd left near the campfire. Sam turned back to Ellen and dug around in his pocket. "Yes, actually, there is. I'm rather weighed down with a hairbrush and need you to take it for me."

Her breath caught when she saw her mother's hairbrush, or at least one identical to it. "Sam, how did you find this? Del took it...."

He shrugged. "I'm not supposed to tell you how exactly."

She laughed at his sheepish face. He'd probably been sworn to secrecy, so she didn't want to tease him too much. "Very well, tell me approximately."

"I can do that. This one man in the group, I'm not sure who....Well, he noticed your brothers needed new shoes but couldn't abide by the terms of the trade. So, he interfered and traded something he says he'd never miss, just so the brush could remain yours."

Tears burned behind her eyes at Del's thoughtfulness. She already owed him more debts than she could ever repay. "That's so wonderful." She hugged Sam. "Thank him, please."

"I will. Do you want me to hug him as well?"

Ellen snickered as she let go of him. "Only if you want to do so. I'd hate to forbid you anything."

"Much obliged. I'll let you hug him yourself. He'd enjoy that more." Sam grinned. "If you'll excuse me, it is almost time for first watch. Is your family nearby?"

"They've made friends at another camp and should be along soon. Or so Pa said a while back."

He nodded and left. She looked to see Buster staring into the glowing embers, half asleep, and worked fast to put away her heirloom and to get bedding down for him.

"Story?"

"Yes, when Skeeter is here too. Rest now and he'll be back soon." She kissed his forehead then eased away to finish. Soon, she lay in her own bed, the others open and ready for Pa and Skeeter.

Ellen thought about what Del had done for her and the boys. If not so tired and needing to keep an eye on the baby, she'd thank him in person. She hoped the item he'd traded truly was something he'd not miss. Resting her hands behind her head, she wished she could write all this in her journal. Maybe she could, if she just mentioned certain things and not the person behind them. She sat up and went to get the little book. No sooner than she'd written about the pond did Pa and Skeeter return.

"Yeah, those are some fine ladies, Skeeter. How'd you like one of them to be your new Ma?"

"I'm not sure."

Ellen looked from one to the other. Pa didn't notice the stricken look on his son's face. She knew how he felt, having had Lucy as a new ma too soon after hers had passed. She glanced at Buster, glad he was a heavy little sleeper. "Seems like you both had a good time tonight."

"We did." Pa kicked off his boots and turned to her. "You writing in that tonight?"

"Just finished."

"Hand it over and let's see what all fired important thing happened to you today."

She did as asked and waited until he finished reading. No sense in settling in if something Ellen had written angered him.

"Hmph. Same ole, same ole day, huh?" He gave the journal back to her with a toss. "You should have come with us. We had a grand time tonight."

"I should have." She wore her smile, setting into bed and tucking the journal under her pillow. Considering the company Pa had kept tonight, Ellen was glad chores and Buster kept her here. She just wished they didn't keep her from Del so much.

Pa was up and at a distance, judging from the volume of his voice. The boys still slept, Ellen could tell from their soft breathing. She kept her eyes closed, not wanting to start the day so early. She heard something from Pa about more animal deaths and their ox being fine. She sighed with relief and nestled into the covers a little more. Maybe faking sleep would bring back her dreams. She tried to drift off through the increasing noise as people scrambled, moving oxen around to make sure everyone had an animal for their wagon.

"C'mon, lazybones." Pa nudged her with his foot. "Get up and get ready. Coffee's ready."

Ellen sat up, rubbing her eyes and reaching for her glasses. She must have fallen asleep because the campfire burned and her brothers were gone. "Where are the boys?"

"Off taking care of their morning business."

She nodded, taking a full cup from him. "Are they fetching water too?"

"Yeah."

"Good, that'll help me with breakfast." She got up and retrieved the breakfast fixings from the wagon. Just then, her brothers walked up, both carrying the bucket.

"We helped," said Buster.

"So you did. Thank you." She took the water from them and began making biscuits.

Pa settled in next to the fire, holding his hands out to warm. "There was talk this morning about how heavy everyone's wagon is. Several animals died last night, some of them draft animals."

Ellen nodded. She'd heard correctly, then. "That's a shame."

"Word is, the road's going to get rougher. Now'd be a good time to drop any extras." He took a sip. "We have a lot of junk in the front of the wagon we don't use. Leave it behind and our ox might live longer."

She focused on each spoonful of batter as she dropped them in the pan. "I'm not sure. We'll need everything we have for our new home."

"We will, huh? Or is it you just thinking of yourself again?"

He'd seen through her words to their true meaning and Ellen swallowed. "What? No, I'm thinking of the four of us trying to start a new life."

"Think for yourself, missy, because I have several gals lined up to be a mother to my boys. We don't need you."

"Yes, we do, Pa. We need her." Both boys had big eyes, staring at their father.

Pa glared at them before dumping his coffee in the fire and walking away. He let the cup fall behind him, and Ellen made a note to pick it up on her way to wash dishes. She smiled at her brothers. "Now then, who's ready for a biscuit and jam?"

Soon, she had them eating breakfast with their extra treat. Ellen put away some food for lunch in case they couldn't stop for noon. Too soon, the signal to move out was given. She had just enough time to throw everything into the back of the wagon.

They spent the day going up and down hills like the one she'd slipped on before. By now, all the fun was gone, even for the children. None of them slid down as they'd done earlier. With every mile, the men made a decision to go one more to find water. Twelve miles later, they'd found it.

Word drifted back that they'd reached a hot springs that wasn't good to drink. Ellen walked up to the front, finding Marie and Sam there.

"I'd like it if we could do some washing up," said Marie.

Sam leaned in toward her before waving a hand in front of his face. "So would I, Miss Smelly, but we need to make better time than we have been."

When Marie caught sight of her, she said, "Ellen! I've missed you." Back to her husband, she added, "It's Mrs. Smelly to you, and please? Even an hour or two extra would be good." She enveloped her friend in a hug.

"All right, an hour extra." Sam tipped his hat to both of them. "Let me go tell everyone the news."

She put her hands on her hips and watched her husband walk away. "Goodness, ask that man for a mile and I get a foot. Never mind him, it's good to see you."

Ellen grinned. "Likewise, and already I need to go and get washing."

"It never ends, does it? I always miss having help with daily tasks." Marie shook her head. "Never mind that! Here I am going on about my trials when yours are so much more. Please forgive me. Can I help you with anything?"

"No, you have enough chores of your own. Let's take the chance during laundry to chat." She kept her own counsel on what sort of people had been there for Marie. The Winslows had never been wealthy enough to own slaves, but she was sure the Warrens had been.

"I'd love that. Meet you back here?"

"Certainly." Ellen turned to her wagon, running full on into Del. "Oh! Excuse me!" She looked up at him and basked in his happy expression. "I'm glad to see you too."

"You forget yourself, *ma coeur*."

A wave of horror swept her. Pa could be around any corner or even behind her, listening. What if he'd heard the affection in her voice? Ellen clenched shut her hands to stop their trembling. "I have, indeed. Please forgive me."

"*De rein.*" He stood a little straighter. "It seems we are equally pleased at this slight contact."

She nodded. "It's been too long since we've talked."

"Should I summon Pointed Nose to give me an excuse to rescue you?"

A shiver went through her. "Goodness, no. With Lucy then Uncle Joe, I'd prefer you to be the only native we see from now on."

He paused before taking a deep breath to say, "I understand and agree. How is your wrist? Is it healing?"

"Slowly, yes." She moved it to and fro, about to add more when she saw his expression. She turned to see Pa walking toward them. "Oh dear."

"Let me." He strolled up to Jack. "You've heard we're here for an extra hour or so at the ladies' request?"

"No, I ain't heard nothing."

"Sam wanted everyone to know so they'd have a chance to wash up at the springs. Good day." As if too busy for small talk, Del continued on before Winslow could reply.

She saw Marie walk nearby and took the chance to escape a temper tantrum. "Pa, do you want to watch the boys while I do laundry?"

He scratched his chin, frowning deep furrows between his eyes. "No, but I reckon I don't have a choice with you here to tell me what to do."

His voice had that edge that warned her of an impending outburst and she put on a smile. "You're busy, of course. I should have known better and will have Skeeter help me."

Scanning her face as if trying to see a lie, Pa squinted. "All right. I'll keep an eye on Buster since I can't count on you."

Later. She could be angry later. Right now, time slipped past, as did her chance to wash Buster's diapers and pants. "Thank you." She hurried to the wagon, leaving him behind, and gathered up what she needed.

Skeeter ran around the corner. "Pa said you needed me?"

"I do. Where's the baby?"

"Pa has him. I don't mind helping."

Ellen ruffled his hair instead of embarrassing him with a hug. "You don't?"

"Nope. All my friends are with their ma's, so I figured I might as well help you."

She grinned at her brother, handing him a pail with the washing soap. "I appreciate it." She picked up the full wash basket and led the way to one of the hot springs. Steam rose from it, curling in the air.

"That sure is hot!" He reached in to touch the water.

"Be careful, Skeet. It might burn you."

"I'll be fine." He resumed his reach and skimmed his fingertips across the top. "Ouch! Are we going to dip our hands in this?"

"Let's see." She tested the water's temperature and withdrew her hand in a hurry. "It feels like coffee that's almost too hot to drink." Ellen tried again, able to keep her fingertips in a little longer. "Skeeter, I want you to stay back. This is too hot for you."

"But, sis, I can't help if I'm back here." He stepped up beside her. "I need to be up here so I can reach the water." Skeeter pulled a dirty diaper out of the wash basket. "Ew! This is yucky! I'm not washing it!" He tossed it in the basket, slipping in the mud.

Ellen watched as if everything happened too slow to be real as her brother fell. He grappled for anything to keep him from hitting the ground, his arm submerged in the scalding water. Skeeter screamed and leapt to his feet. Cradling his arm, he continued crying and hollering.

Women began crowding around the boy as Ellen tried to calm him. Lefty ran up, then Pa carrying Buster. As the ladies led the boy away, Jack hollered above Skeeter's cries, "What the hell happened to him?"

"He fell, Pa, and his arm—"

"I was burned, Pa! It hurts so bad."

"Didn't I tell you to keep an eye on him?" yelled Pa.

The people around them started easing away from the scene. Ellen tried to explain to him. "I did watch out—"

"No, you didn't. How'd you like to be scalded like him?"

A jolt of horror went through her. No one stood around them, except for Lefty at a distance. She stammered, "I wouldn't. It was an accident and I—"

"An accident like this?"

Before she could react, Pa reached out and shoved her. Like when Skeeter fell, time slowed and she knew she couldn't avoid hitting the water. Ellen didn't scream until completely submerged. All the air left her lungs in a whoosh. She flailed, trying to find footing in the mushy soil. Once upright, she crawled out on her hands and knees, trembling from the shock.

"Miss, here."

She looked up to see Lefty's right hand. She took it, letting him help her up and bit her lip to keep from whimpering from the searing pain. "Thank you. I'm fine." She wiped off the mud onto her skirt. Breathing hurt, stretching scalded skin. Pa was gone but had left the laundry basket. Ellen glanced at the young man. "I'm so clumsy and fall all the time. There's no need to fuss or talk more about what happened."

He paused for a moment as if wanting to argue before saying, "No fuss, ma'am. Sorry to be so forward but I reckon you'll need help carrying your laundry."

"I'd appreciate that, Mr. Lefty." Lucky's bugle to start moving played across to them. She knew Lefty didn't believe her lie. Her skin glowed red like she'd been sunburned. She flexed her fingers, wincing. The longer she stood there, the further they'd roll down the trail without them. Her chin trembled and she ignored it.

He picked up the basket with his left hand, using his right arm to stabilize it. "My pleasure." They started for her family's wagon and he continued, "That was a painful thing back there."

Ellen shivered, her wet dress drying and pulling all the heat from her body. "It still is, I'm afraid. I'll be feeling it for a while."

"I bet so."

They hurried to her family's wagon. Skeeter and Buster were up front with Pa. When her brothers saw Ellen, both boys' jaws dropped. Skeeter recovered first, saying, "Sis, you're burned."

"Miss, I've put up your basket. Be seeing you." Lefty tipped his hat.

"Thank you very much."

He nodded and walked toward the horses. She looked at Pa. He'd not even glanced at her, or he'd be saying she was cooked too. "Skeeter, thanks for your help today, but—"

"Boy, you're not to help Ellen with chores any more. You're too young and I don't want you hurt again."

"But, sis, I wasn't—"

Pa grabbed the boy's arm. "I hope you're not arguing, son."

Ellen couldn't let him hurt her brother and said, "He's right, Skeet. It'll be fine." She caught Pa's look of satisfaction and was glad he was pleased for a while. A strong breeze accentuated the cold fabric clinging to her and she shivered. She wanted desperately to change into dry clothes, but the material scraping across her body already hurt to consider.

Their wagon started rolling and she followed until the dust became unbearable. She shivered and burned as if feverish. With nothing but steps to occupy her mind, her skin ached. Her chin trembled and hot tears burned paths down her cheeks. Quickly, before the wagon gained too much speed, Ellen retrieved her sunbonnet. She'd not worn it in ages but now needed the cover in case she couldn't stop crying. She focused on moving forward, careful to not trip and fall.

The day grew later and later. She'd peek out every so often to see if the landscape changed to find everything stayed the same. No one talked to her, thanks to Lefty keeping quiet, and she liked being left alone. Pa must have realized how badly she'd been hurt because he'd not given Buster's care over to her.

At last they stopped at a wide stream feeding a wide plain of grass. She sighed in relief. Her dress had dried, the crusty minerals from the water feeling like sandpaper on her injured skin. They were in their customary half circle along the creek bank when Ellen steeled herself to climb in to change clothes.

"Sis?" Skeeter appeared at her elbow with Buster. "Pa wants you to take care of him while he takes care of Herbert."

"Herbert?"

"Yeah, the ox. If he's got a name, maybe he won't die before we get home."

She wanted to hug him and Buster both but settled for ruffling his hair. "I'm betting since he's Herbert now, he won't even get sick." She held out her hand. "Let me check where you were burned." He gave her his hand and she looked up and down his arm.

"It don't hurt much."

"It's doesn't hurt much," she automatically corrected. The boy's hand and arm was pinkish like a mild sunburn. "I'm glad you're not in pain, dear." Ellen nodded at their wagon. "You're not supposed to help me, I know, but maybe taking Buster potty isn't really helping if you have to go too."

He grinned. "Nope! I'm not helping you at all. If we pick up sticks for firewood, it's not helping either."

"Just remember to hold them sideways, not up and down." She didn't want to think if they tripped and fell on what equaled wooden stakes. Ellen watched them go for only a moment. She hopped into the wagon and began an agonizing change of clothes. The canvas openings had been secured before she took the time to lay a cool hand on her hot skin. Her shoulders, arms, neck, all ached. She shook her head. Soon enough one of the boys would be back and wondering what she was doing in here. Ellen slipped into her clean dress. She'd lost weight during this journey and it fit loosely. The worn cloth almost felt good against the burn. She eased to her feet and out of the wagon. The boys weren't back and Pa wasn't there, so she took her dirty dress and a water bucket to the creek.

She didn't have a mirror, and the water's reflection didn't help her see how red her face was. Ellen looked around hoping to find Del. She wanted him to hug her without actually touching her. Smiling at the contrariness of the thought, she rinsed the mineral water out of her work clothes. By the time she got back to camp, the new dress had rubbed different areas than before. The boys had returned and dropped off the wood they'd found. She grinned at how sweet both of her brothers were and began cooking dinner. The beans and rice needed time, so Ellen finished up her washing. She used dirty clothes like potholders for her sore hands. Buster's efforts at being a big boy meant a lot less diapers to wash, so she finished sooner than usual. She stood, stretching her back, and saw Del across the creek. Her breath caught at the sight of him silhouetted against the sunset. She missed him. Instead of wading over to him and talking, Ellen just nodded and turned back to camp.

After dinner, with the dishes washed, the laundry drip-drying, and the boys in bed playing the quiet game, Pa motioned to her. "Let's see what you wrote in your journal."

"I've not written anything much about today."

"No? Let me see for myself."

She nodded, squelching the urge to argue. She retrieved the little book and his bedding, giving both to him. He read while she set up her bed and settled in for the night. She'd not lied. Few details had been written about today's accidents and nothing about seeing Del. She knew better.

Pa handed her back the journal. "You've twisted everything around in here, not writing anything about what happened. How it's your fault you and Skeeter are hurt. I don't want you taking care of Buster anymore." He lay down and pulled the covers up to his neck. "You got Lucy killed, and now you nearly killed my oldest son. I'm not letting you hurt my baby boy too."

Ellen nodded as she slid in between the covers. Her front hurt. So did her back. Hot tears burned across her injured cheeks until she lay on her side. Today with Skeeter had been an accident. Pa was the only one who didn't understand that.

The morning sky glowed with a brilliant sunrise. Ellen wanted nothing more than to roll over and go back to sleep, but the busy camp kept her awake so she sat up. Her brothers dozed while Pa sat where she'd last left him. His rumpled bed was the only thing that indicated he'd slept. She pushed loose hair from her face. Coffee brewed and she sighed with relief. "Smells good, Pa."

"It is." He poured her a cup and handed it over. "You look pretty sore over there. Sorry you had to fall in the springs yesterday. Maybe you know now how your brother must have felt."

"Thank you for saying so. I do know now." The steam from her cup felt uncomfortable on her face, and she blew on her coffee to cool it.

"Noticed last night how you hadn't written much about that Indian. Hope you're not leaving anything out about him. I'd hate to find out you've been rutting with him."

"What?" she exclaimed. Stunned and angry, she stood. "I've done no such thing with him or any man. Ever." The children woke up and sat, rubbing their eyes. Ellen didn't care if the whole world heard her. "Excuse me while I cook breakfast." She dumped the bucket of dishes inside the wagon, the metal clanging, and headed to the creek. A large twinge of guilt tried to intrude on her outrage. She ignored any acknowledgement of any prior longing of hers to know Del as a husband. Ellen hated how Pa had said such a crude and hateful thing about what she shared with Del.

With a start, she realized she'd been standing at the creek for a while after filling the pail. Playing statue wouldn't solve anything so she went back to her family. She hurried through breakfast, not talking to Pa unless spoken to. The boys sensed something wrong in the air and stayed quiet throughout. Soon, the bugle let them know to leave and she hurried to finish up the morning chores.

The rough road that morning kept her mind focused on not stumbling over the tracks. Her skin still hurt, but not quite as bad. Or maybe she had grown used to the ache. Either way, Ellen was glad for the cool air until noon's warmth beat down on her exposed skin. When news trickled back that they were at White Sulphur Springs, she worried about the hot water. The name misled because the springs flowed cold and clear. They nooned, letting the animals eat their fill of the lovely grass around the water. She gave the boys their biscuits, checked Buster's pants, and went to the springs. Dipping her hands into the water felt wonderful at first. She put her palms on her cheeks, forehead, and neck, trying to cool the skin. The signal to leave sounded and Ellen tried to get up but didn't want to go. She'd not had this much relief since the burning happened. She hurried for one more dip of her hands until the cold was too much, then rested her palms against the back of her neck.

"Ellen?"

She smiled, recognizing Del's voice. "I know. We're leaving and I'm just sitting here." Ellen glanced over to see him holding out a hand. She took it, letting him help her up.

He waited until she was steady on her feet before walking with her to the group. "I heard you fell in the hot springs? Sam said it was best for me not to speak to your father."

Her mouth went dry. Of course everyone had heard what happened. She prayed they'd not witnessed Pa's part in it. "He's right. It was an accident, and I wasn't seriously hurt. Skeeter is fine, so there was no need to cause trouble."

"You think I would?"

She chuckled. "You'd start it with him and I'd egg you on just by being there." Catching sight of Pa, she frowned and turned to Del. "I'm going to scowl at you."

"And I'll return your favor." He frowned and leaned in a little. "Why are we scowling?"

"Because I don't want Pa to suspect that I'm asking if I can see you at Sam's tonight."

"After dinner?"

"Yes, and before first watch, if you're willing."

He shook his head and then looked her up and down with

contempt. "Of course I'd love to see you, *ma coeur*. You have my heart and I'm an empty shell when you're not with me."

Del had said such lovely words with such a foul face, she laughed. A glance ahead showed they were within earshot of Pa. "Oh? Well, I'll see about fixing that little problem, Mr. Du Boise."

He smirked before hopping up on Pomme. "I'd like that a lot. Good day."

Pa tipped his hat back. "I don't know why he can't just stay gone."

She shook her head as if not understanding why either. Nothing she could say about wanting him gone sounded sincere enough in her mind, so she kept quiet. Pa went back to their wagon and she fell in behind them. The afternoon wore on and to her relief, the road smoothed as it climbed and dipped over rolling country. The easy walk kept her from fearing a fall and scraping her burn on rocks or gravel. She liked how the sage had thinned out. Their scarcity helped her avoid touching them when she walked by.

The signal to stop for the night sounded. This seemed a bit too early until she neared the creek. The water, wood, and grass were better here than she expected and like last night, Skeeter and Buster unofficially helped her. She could do some more laundry thanks to their help. The creek was too shallow for fish, so she gave up that idea and started dinner once back at the wagon.

The loose dress now irritated her skin more than helped it. She ate in a hurry, stacking her dishes in the bucket. Ellen's work dress had been dry and clean for a while, and she thought about changing back into it. The pressure would hurt, but not as much as what felt like holes being rubbed into her skin. She shimmied out of one dress and into the other. The fabric pressed against her skin, but she ignored it while climbing from the wagon.

As soon as Ellen reached the ground, Pa asked, "Are you getting our beds out?"

"I didn't but can." She glanced over and saw his expression. "I am." Ellen climbed back in and pulled out the quilts. She set out their beds before he had to ask, glad when he nodded his approval.

He cleared his throat, putting his thumbs in his pockets. "There're some ladies I'm sparking in the other group. I'll be over there tonight."

"All night?"

"If I want to, yes. I'm the adult here, so if I want to travel with them for the rest of the way without you, I will. Understand?"

"Of course, Pa." She took his and the boy's empty plates and the cook pot. "I only asked to know if you'd be late or not."

"It's not up to you to worry. I'll be back when I get back."

She nodded, knowing there was no chance to visit with Marie and maybe Jenny at Sam's camp right now. "I'll wash up and be right back." At his permissive nod, she took the bucket to the creek. Ellen knew her friends were just an excuse. She wanted to see Del, get sympathy from him for her burn, and just be near him. The days of unending monotony had been bad enough even without the pain. Ellen missed having him care for her.

"Hello. Are you your family's washer too?"

Ellen smiled at Del's voice. "I'm the only one for my family. And you? Were you picked or forced?"

He chuckled. "I chose, *ma coeur.*"

They cleaned up together. She stole little glances to check his progress and saw Del moved as slowly as she did. Ellen hid a smile. Now was their only chance to talk alone and might be the only time for several days. She had to make the most of it. "Pa is with another group, and I'm not sure when he'll return. He likes to catch me by surprise by coming back to us when I least expect him. Can you tell me what I'm missing by not being at Sam's camp?"

"Yes. Marie and Sam are newlyweds, so they see no one else." He paused a moment to look at her before resuming his work. "Jenny is often gone, helping her mother with the new baby. Lucky is unhappy, of course. He's with us, but his mind isn't. Or should I say his heart?" Del flicked water from his fingertips at her, grinning when she laughed. "Before you ask, Arnold and Lefty have assumed Joe's tasks."

She put the last of the utensils in her pail, done and wondering if she should offer help to him. "As the extra man, Uncle Joe's chores didn't go to you?"

"Several did, but not everything." He put a hand on hers as she reached for one of his dirty plates. "Your skin is hot and I've noticed how red you still are. Are you still in pain?"

Ellen gasped at how cool and comforting his touch felt on her skin. She pulled away after a moment to help him clean the rest of his dishes. "A little. It's getting better. I'd like you to walk me back, but Pa is still there."

He gave one of his Gallic shrugs. "I don't mind him seeing

me."

His mannerism never failed to charm her. Their fingertips brushed as both reached for the last dish with him winning. She imagined Pa's temper being taken out on her sensitive skin. Angering him wasn't worth it, so Ellen struggled to stand with both her stiff legs and the pail in hand. "I do mind and don't want to rile him up right now. So I'll say goodnight here."

Del sat back on his heels and turned to watch her leave, saying, "Goodnight."

She hesitated. Her heart hurt at leaving him, even if for only a little while. But she had to think of the boys' needs first. Shaking off the longing, she headed back to camp.

The next morning found them rolling through a better part of the road. Plenty of grass grew, they crossed several streams, and what wasn't grass or water was flat road. The miles seemed easy for everyone. Food gave the stock new life. Ellen preferred ordinary days like this with no angry outbursts, no Indian attacks, and no dying oxen.

She ached still, but the pain faded. The night was warm enough to keep Ellen hot and awake, even without covers. Everyone around her slept and she'd heard the night watch change from one pair of men to another. She both wanted to meet and not to meet Del. More than that, she wanted a cool washcloth big enough to cover her whole body. Ellen crept out of camp and snuck to the creek for cold water. Soaking her hands in icy water had helped her skin this afternoon. She started for the creek and stopped. The moon wasn't out and starlight wasn't enough to light her way.

"Ellen? What is it?"

She smiled at Del's whisper. He didn't touch her but was close enough to do so. "I'd wanted a cold poultice, but can't see my way."

"Take my hand and I'll lead you to the water." He held her hand as they walked to the creek.

"I don't know how you can see in this dark."

"It's not easy and I'm relying on memory. Now, here we are and ease down. Your feet should be wet by now."

Ellen laughed, the water tickling her toes. "You're right, they are." She squatted to reach the creek without muddying her knees by kneeling and immersed her hands. When they were too cold for her to tolerate, she shook off the water and pressed her palms to her face. She felt and heard him do the same before giving a little yelp as he touched her neck with his own frozen hands.

"If I were made of ice, would you hug me for comfort?"

"Certainly! I'd come to find you over at Sam's every night and hold you until you melted."

He put a hand to her cheek. "I'd be a puddle at your feet too soon. Here, you need this."

A flash of white shown until he dunked it in the water and Ellen realized it was his handkerchief. He wrung out the fabric, folded it, and gave it to her. "Take the poultice for tonight. Tell your father it is Sam's."

"Thank you, Del." She let him pull her to her feet. "I do have rags of my own to use. I should have brought one of them."

He led her back to the Winslows' camp, letting her hold his arm for stability instead of holding her. "No matter, dearest. I like knowing something of mine is with you. Au revoir et sweet dreams for the waning night. " He gave her the lightest of kisses before disappearing back into the night.

She took a deep breath, smiling. Pa hadn't softened toward Del, not even after the rescue, and she didn't want to admit he might never accept the French-Indian. She slid into bed and got comfortable. The damp hanky rested against her forehead, helping her. Ellen needed to work harder on changing Pa's mind about Del.

Her father didn't notice the next day when she blocked out the dust with Del's cloth tied around her face. Pa still punished her with his silence. While she couldn't take care of the boys, she was glad to see he'd put bandanas on them too. Thirteen flat miles of dirt kicked up by wheels and feet, the only distraction was the mountains she saw on either side of them.

Pa pushed Buster to her. "Here, he needs scrubbing. Something don't agree with him."

The smell caught up to Ellen, almost knocking her down. She looked down at the baby and bent to wipe away his tears. "Don't cry, sweetie. I'll clean you up and it'll be fine."

"I tried to wait, sissy."

"I'm sure you did your best." They needed water, preferably a roaring river to wash him in. She smiled. "Next time we find a pond, I'll get a stick, tie you to the end, and dunk just your behind. Sound good?"

He laughed. "Yay! Swimmin'."

"That's right. Come on." She led him to the rolling wagon. "Pa, slow a little?" Her father didn't respond, but did do as she'd asked. Ellen reached in and got Buster his diaper and an extra cloth besides. Another quick grab and she had a jar of water kept for such emergencies. "Now, let's find a quiet place and get you cleaned up."

Buster stared at the ground. "I messed again."

"That's fine. Get it all over with while you can." She led him to a sage high enough to hide him. "Even if it happens again, don't be sad. We're close to camping for the night." He took off his shoes and pants and she gagged. Ellen wanted to bury everything he wore right there, but they didn't have enough clothes to spare. She maneuvered to upwind of him and did the best she could. When he was sanitary, Ellen dressed the baby and gave him a light swat on the behind. "There you go. Try to take off your pants before any more messes." She took his hand, holding the pants and diapers in the other. "Put on your shoes and we'll go back for pants. I'll get you a rag for your pocket so you can potty and wipe up."

He nodded, his little face serious. "I had accident."

"Just now?" she asked and sighed with relief when he shook his head no. "It's fine if you did, but try not to until we're closer to water, all right?" She hurried to the wagon again, getting him an extra diaper for later. Any child as sick as he was wouldn't be able to wait. She turned around, wincing at the smell before she ever saw him.

"I'm sorry."

"Oh, Buster, what am I going to do with you?" She smiled to take the sting out of her words. Ellen knelt to clean up her brother as best she could with the unsoiled parts of the diaper he wore.

"Sis?"

She didn't need to look up to see Skeeter there. "You're sick too?"

"Yeah, but I'm not having accidents or anything. Pa wants you to take care of Buster."

"Good about not making messes and fine about your

brother."

"I might stay in case you need me."

Ellen smiled at him. "Very well. Come along. Let's catch up to the wagons."

They reached the others only after Ellen began carrying Buster. The party rolled along, closer to Boise River. Both boys seemed to have calmer digestions as the day wore on. She looked along the river. The water seemed calm on the surface, reflecting a bright blue sky overhead. Her stomach rumbled hard and she gasped. Whatever the boys had, she now had too. "Skeeter, it's my turn to be ill. Watch Buster and keep close to the wagon. I'll need a rag and to run really fast."

"Good luck!"

She hurried and hid in a quiet place until her body was done. Ellen cleaned up as best she could, deciding to just leave the cloth. She rushed back to find they'd stopped for the night where the river had ox bowed enough to green up the grass. Even with the ground cover, the dust seemed like more than usual. She reached her family's wagon to find Pa standing in the middle of a crowd.

"Oh, God help me, God help me." Pa coughed several times. "What is Granville leading us through, the very center of Hell? I'm dying over here." He coughed and grabbed for the side of the wagon as if needing the support. "He's killed off a few of us, run off several more. He has our money, now we're nothing to him, nothing." Pa leaned against a wheel, wheezing.

She looked away from the drama in front of them, worried about her brothers witnessing such a display. Ellen spotted them off at a distance, playing with children from other groups camped there. She glanced up to see Pa starting another round of woe-is-me. Before he could see her, she moved to the side so a taller person blocked Pa's view of her and stared at her feet in shame.

Del stood next to Ellen and nudged her. "You are wearing your spectacles, dearest. Is there another reason you search the ground?"

She grinned at him. "No, just looking for arrowheads and such. Coins, trinkets, anything really."

"Anything to help avoid the theatre?"

"Absolutely. This sort of thing is so embarrassing." She shook her head. "He revels in it though. I don't understand why."

"Who knows? Some like the center of attention." He leaned in a little closer to her. "Others like being wherever you are."

Laughing, Ellen retorted, "You are such a tease. I don't believe a word of your flattery, but I like it anyway."

"Ah, then I'll continue until you're convinced of my undying devotion." He listened for a moment. "I think the show is *fini*."

She couldn't hear her father's voice and glanced up to see the audience dispersing. "It seems so. I have to go do what I can for camp tonight."

"Will you need help?"

"Yes, but I can't accept it from you." The last of the people left, leaving her exposed where she stood talking to him. "It is *can't*, you understand. Not won't, so, I'll manage just fine. Besides, you've done enough to help us. More than we deserve." She didn't want to leave him before adding, "I can't imagine anyone doing more for me."

With a wicked grin, he retorted, "I can imagine more, but only with me and only for you."

"Adelard! For shame on you!" She hid her laughing behind a hand. "For shame!"

Del turned so he faced behind her as if they'd just happened to be standing near each other. "I shall try to find shame before next we meet, *ma coeur*. Since you insist."

She chuckled. "I do insist." Ellen took a halting step toward her family's wagon. "I miss you already, Del."

"Likewise. You'll visit Sam this evening? I have first watch."

"Yes, I'll do what I can to be there." She left him there, looking back to see him leaving too.

Ellen smiled to herself, still feeling thrilled after chatting with him. She'd forgotten how wonderful it felt to have his undivided attention. She took their ox's reins from Pa, returning his silent treatment. Somehow, she needed to influence his acceptance of Del. She laughed at the notion of changing Pa's mind and startled their animal with the noise. Her father wouldn't be fine with Adelard after dinner, after next week, after this lifetime.

She watched as the ox drank huge gulps. Pa had been remiss in putting on his show before caring for their one work animal. Never mind a fellow creature's suffering. They all needed to keep their only pulling source alive.

The ox cared for and staked out in a grassy patch, she fetched them water for dinner. The boys' clothes needed washing yet again and she wouldn't mind a good scrubbing herself. Pa had a fire started, thankfully, and Ellen started cooking. She added extra water to the beans and rice, and once satisfied everything looked good, she searched for and found the boys. "Hey, you two, come here!" she hollered. The children ran up to her, bringing their smell with them. "Oh, goodness! Let's go play in the river, all right?"

They both ran for the water, yelling the whole way. Buster fell but soon hopped back on his feet and followed Skeeter. They didn't even pause to remove their moccasins before plunging in. Ellen shook her head at them, laughing. She went to the water and took off her shoes. "Stay with me and don't go too deep. I don't like water too much after that dunking in the hot springs."

"You have to like this, sis. It's cold." Skeeter splashed her.

Ellen yelped when the water hit her face. "Oh! You're right! I have to because it's icy."

Buster began jumping up and down. "Ice ee iceee iceiceeeee." He'd fall under the water, hop back up, and almost start to cry before resuming his ice dance.

They laughed at his antics, she at how adorable, Skeeter at how silly. Ellen patted her younger brother on the back. "Go ahead and play a little more. You might get even cleaner."

He grabbed her hand and pulled. "I will if you will."

Glad he didn't take her by her sore arm, she grinned. "Since you insist." She followed him and grinned as the boys played. They threw their shoes onto the river bank and then laughed when minnows tickled their toes. Ellen took the chance to soak her feet and enjoy the cool water on her hot skin. She kept her eyes open and kept watch on the children while washing her face. "Let's go! Dinner's probably burning."

"Race you back to camp, Buster!"

They both took off like a shot. She almost protested they needed shoes, but they were gone. Ellen scooped up all three pairs and hiked up her skirt just enough to keep it out of the dust. Many more feet than theirs had trampled the loose soil into rock. Back at the campfire, she stirred dinner and hoped no one would notice some of it burned to the bottom of the pan. The sun had dipped below the horizon and she shivered. "Boys, find some dry clothes to change into and hurry so I can change too."

Pa strolled up and settled in next to the fire. "I stirred the food for you."

"Thanks, Pa." She set the ladle down on a plate, waiting to hear his ulterior motive.

"Against my better judgment, I'm letting you watch the boys tonight." He held his hands in front of the fire to warm them. "There're some ladies a couple of camps over that are really pretty. They invited me over for a visit and I'm going."

She stared into the flames, the heat almost reaching her cold body. Nothing she could say would stop Pa from going so she shrugged. "Of course, you have to be neighborly."

"Thought you'd see it my way. How soon is supper going to be ready? I ain't getting any younger, and those gals ain't getting any prettier."

Ellen scooped out a bean, letting it cool before mashing it with her finger. The skin broke and gave way. "It's ready. Boys, come to dinner! Hurry up! I'm cold and hungry."

Pa held out a plate, nudging her in the process. "Let me eat first. I gotta get going."

"All right." She dished him up some food. "You might take a lantern with you."

"Good idea. No sense in stumbling around in the dark all undignified like."

The boys tumbled out, the elder helping the younger. Skeeter picked up his plate first. "Wet clothes are tough to get out of, sis. Sorry it took so long."

"You're fine, sweetheart. I'll eat and then change my clothes." As she ate, the hot food warmed her up from the inside. Ellen had a full mouth and could only nod when Pa left, taking a lantern. She wished he'd wait until dishes were done but felt able to trust Skeeter. Turning to her younger brother, she asked, "After I change, could you keep an eye on Buster while I wash dishes? It'll really help and not put you in harm's way."

"Sure. I can even roll out our beds for you."

She paused before agreeing. Ellen had to first think of every possible hazard. "I don't know. If you got a blanket in the fire, it might burn you. I don't want you to take the chance."

"Sis, I'm not a baby like Buster. Let me."

"You're right, you're an older boy." She nodded. "Go ahead and set up the bedding and put Buster to bed." The baby kept nodding off. "He's about there already."

"I will and come help you wash."

"Don't worry about that, just settle in yourself and I'll be back soon."

She went to the bank and knelt on a grassy part. Her knees sank the in the mud and she grimaced. So much for the earlier cleaning. Ellen began scrubbing and heard rustling behind her. "You're supposed to be in bed, sweetie. Never mind. Come here and keep me company."

"With pleasure, dearest."

Ellen startled at Del's voice. "Oh my! I thought you were Skeeter."

He knelt beside her. "Aw, this is mud!"

"I should have warned you."

"You didn't, so now you can wash me."

All sorts of naughty possibilities came to her mind with his words and Ellen gasped. "Adelard! Voices carry over the water. Who knows who'll hear you?"

"Good point." He leaned closer to her, his breath stirring the curl against her ear. "I'll whisper from now on."

She shivered, his nearness calling to her. Ellen wanted nothing more than to throw her arms around him and give in to desire. Never mind the mud, the witnesses, and her brothers. She wanted him to hold her until the entire world fell away. "That's dangerous."

"So is loving you, yet I do."

Ellen smiled, her face being the only warm part of her. "I feel the same. Pa is out catting around, so this is our only chance to talk."

"Sis! Buster is asleep." Skeeter came over and leaned against Ellen. "Hello, Mr. Du Bose. Fine night we're having."

She stifled a laugh at how grown-up he sounded. Del replied to the boy, "Hello, Mr. Skeeter. It is a fine night. How have you been? I heard you fell in the hot springs too."

"I'm feeling lots better. Except for that sickness. You don't want to know about that."

"I don't?" He looked to Ellen.

She shook her head at his worry. "You don't. Trust me."

Del nodded. "So you're here helping your sister? You're a good brother."

"I try to be. I helped her until Pa said to stop." Skeeter picked up a rock and threw it into the water. "My fall in the springs was an accident, not like when he pushed her in." The boy smiled at Del and shrugged. "That's just what happens when Pa gets angry."

The air left her lungs when Del glared at her. Ellen barely managed to say, "Mr. Du Boise can't be interested in all this. Let's just finish up and go."

Del stood as she did to let the boy pass but stepped in to block her way back to camp. "You're going nowhere until I find out from you if Winslow meant to harm you. If so, I'll kill him with my bare hands."

CHAPTER 9

He didn't like the flash of fear in her eyes but ignored his need to comfort her. Both Winslows were looking at him, waiting as if expecting an explosion. Del knew how Jack reacted to situations. He intended on showing the brother and sister how people could be angered yet not hurt anyone else. "No, not kill. I don't mean that. I'll just give him a whooping." He smiled, grateful to see their expressions soften as he did so. "Tell me what happened."

"Nothing really. Skeeter fell in and Pa was angry because I wasn't keeping a close enough watch on him." She shrugged. "Nothing more than that. So if you'll excuse us, Buster has been alone this whole time and I don't want him to wake up scared."

"No, I don't want that, either." Del ruffled the boy's hair. "Whatever Ellen tells you later, thank you for letting me know what happened that day. You shouldn't be in trouble for honesty."

"He's not in trouble at all. Go on, Skeeter, and I'll catch up." As soon as the boy was out of earshot, she leaned against him in a halfhearted hug. "I knew you'd be angry. That's why I didn't tell you."

"I understand. I'm furious at him and am even more determined to marry you again in Oregon City."

"Well, we'll see."

He refrained from arguing, instead turning toward Sam's camp. Del glanced back but the darkness of night had swallowed her from sight. Once among the hired hands, he sat, letting the music from Lucky's bugle distract him. It didn't work very well, and he brooded over how to get Ellen and the boys into a safer environment. He was sure Jack cared for his children, but pushing his daughter into a hot spring hit a limit with Del. He'd not saved her from Pointed Nose for Winslow to boil her to death.

It took them half a day to get everyone in the Granville party across the Boise River. Del was used to this by now, coaxing people and animals alike into and through the water. He shook his head at the stragglers bringing up the rear. Sam had far more patience than he. Only Ellen and her brothers kept him here. He'd be back home or anywhere else by now.

He rode ahead, passing the Winslows, and only saw Jack. Del ignored the man, riding on, and wished he'd been able to spot Ellen nearby. His stomach rumbled. Sam didn't want to stop until Sulphur Springs, and Del hadn't had time to eat this morning. The hills were high here, but still lower than any mountains. The landscape turned more featureless except for the river slicing the valley in two. Too soon, the party left water and traveled up a wide and dry valley. Hills like huge, grass-carpeted sand dunes rose on either side of them. Even as they rolled to a higher peak, more stretched out ahead of them. They'd left both the Boise and Snake Rivers miles ago. He and Arnold scouted ahead today. When either found any sort of water, they sent word back. He loved the wide, windswept land but would be glad to have the comforting canopy of pines at home. He and Arnold rode too far apart to talk, maybe fifty yards from the road on either side.

They descended via a slow and gradual decline. Several miles passed before they caught up to the Snake again. Del saw a sparkle of blue, and soon enough they closed in on the water. The river, with bluffs on one side and gentle hills on their side, left the two scouts no choice but to ride together. He kept an eye out for good grazing, better than the hay rising up from the ground. This late in summer, their livestock would have better luck closer to the water. When he and Arnold reached the riverbank, Del saw he was right. Both men dismounted and lead their horses to drink.

Their animals would have food, but not much. Soon, everyone else caught up and Del saw Jack. He wanted to wring the scrawny man's neck for hurting Ellen. If he'd known her father was responsible for the pained way the woman had walked the first couple of days after the hot springs accident, Del would have held him under the water with his own hands and ignored the heat. He noticed Ellen favoring her left wrist while taking their ox to the river. Fury clouded his gaze and he clenched his teeth. Simmering with impotent rage, he turned and ran smack into Sam.

"Whoa there, buddy. You look like a thundercloud." His friend nodded at Ellen. "I suppose it's to do with her?"

"Yes, as always. Her scalding was no accident. Winslow pushed her in."

Sam's face blanched. "Dear God in heaven." He looked at

her, returning her wave. "She's coming over. We'll talk about this later."

Del turned and watched as she walked to them, leading her ox. "All right." He noticed she led the animal with reins in her left hand. "How is your arm, *ma coeur*? Feeling better?"

"Her arm?" asked Sam as she neared them.

"I fell and sprained it, I think. I keep bumping and reinjuring it." She waved her wrist a little. "It seems to be feeling better."

"Good. I'd noticed you wore a wrap and meant to ask why." Sam held out his hand to hold her arm to the light.

She smiled at him, the amusement reaching her eyes. "You probably forgot because it wasn't important."

Sam glanced up through his lashes before turning his attention back to her injury. "I consider injuries important."

"Not ones as small as this." She patted his arm as if to reassure him. "I'm fine and doing better."

He looked at Del, who nodded in agreement with her. "Very well, just let me know next time. I assume your whisky has run dry?"

A blush stained her cheeks. "I'm afraid so."

"Come by our camp next time, and I'll make sure you have a dose to help ease the pain. There's no sense in you suffering when I have a cure available."

"Thank you, Sam. I'll remember that for next time." She nodded at Del. "Mr. Du Boise, good night to you too."

His heart sank. He'd hoped to see her this evening, but no. Her brothers took all her time. Del had seen Winslow slinking off to other groups, catting around with the ladies there after running through the women here. He sighed when she disappeared from his sight, missing her already.

Sam nudged him, saying, "First watch, because Winslow doesn't come back until the beginning of second."

Del chuckled at his friend's intentions. "You're a romantic."

"Newlyweds are supposed to be. Which reminds me, you've kept lookout for us a few times. Should I return the favor?"

A whimper escaped him and Sam laughed until Del gave him an evil glare. "Yes, but no. Not at the moment."

Sam grinned. "Right. Not enough trees or shrubbery."

His friend's amusement was infectious and Dell couldn't help but retort, "Add to your guidebook, *Carry more topiaries in the wagon to make private time truly private."*

"Excellent idea."

A couple hours later, a full pan of fish cooked for dinner. Marie had taken over a lot of what Uncle Joe used to do. She didn't have quite the way with food that her predecessor had but continued to improve with practice. Del and every other man sat around the fire, ready to eat. He grinned at how much like begging dogs they must seem while staring at Marie as she cooked.

She glanced over at him. "What is so funny?"

"All of us waiting for dinner are."

"Not for long!" She lifted a fillet up from the pan with the crude spatula. "Who's first?" Every man held out his plate and Marie laughed. "Very well, left to right."

They all ate fast, hungry. Del tried to slow down and savor the meal. He gave his empty too soon dishes to a waiting Lefty and stood. "I'll take first watch."

"Very well," replied Sam from the fireside. "Lucky will be along with you tonight."

Del didn't bother to answer, wanting to hurry over to the Winslows' wagon. Once there, he saw her writing in a journal with both of her brothers asleep nearby. For a moment, he enjoyed how the dying embers cast a glow on her face. Impatience to hear her voice hurried him to say, "Psst. Ellen. Psst."

She blocked the firelight with a hand, and he could tell when she saw him. Ellen eased to her feet. She tiptoed to him, quiet so as not to wake the boys. "What, Adelard, what?"

He grabbed her hand, pulling her away from the campground. Looking around for witnesses, he only stopped once out of sight of the camp. He held her face in his hands and said, "Say my full name once more."

"Adelard," she whispered.

Her voice sent shivery need along every nerve in him. His entire body responded with urgent hunger as his lips captured hers. She groaned and he felt the completion their touch made too. The passion with which she returned his kiss delighted Del, and he held her hard against him. He loved her sweet face and his mouth left hers to kiss her forehead, cheeks, nose, until finally trailing down her neck.

When he returned to her lips, she let him stay until she broke away to kiss down his chin to the base of his throat. He gasped at the sensuality of her touch and she trailed her lips down to the hollow.

He tilted his head back to give her better access. *"Mon Dieu!* Your favorite place to kiss me?"

"One of them, yes."

Del moaned a little, his pants hurting him. She didn't stop her torment of him, nibbling down his chest to the bottom of the shirt's vee. If they'd had time, he'd let her remove whatever of his clothes she wanted to. "Ellen, if we had the night together…."

She explored her way back to his throat and traced a circle with her tongue, stopping only to reply, "We could do so much with each hour."

"Mon amour, la coeur du ma vie." With her body pressed so tight against his, he knew she must be aware of his hunger for her physically. He fought to keep his hands on her waist instead of reaching under her skirts and helping both of them unite. "We must stop. You're…I'm…we're both uncontrollable." He wanted to pull apart the bun her hair was in and bury his face in her tresses. Preferably while he was buried in her. Del shuddered. "No more, please."

She drew in an erratic breath. "Ma coor?"

He chuckled, pleased she'd tried to speak his language. *"Oui?"*

"I don't want to go. You feel so good against me."

"You want to stay and let me throw you to the ground? Let me take you like the hungry animal I am?"

"Yes, I would like that."

He laughed at her honesty. "As would I, but not yet. I'd hate for them to see us so ready for each other. Another few moments and I could have all of you."

"Another few and I would insist you do so."

Del pressed his lips against her ear. He needed to be sensible, but her desire for him wiped any sort of responsibility clean from his character. "Ellen, you must know how I think about you all day, dream about you at night. You're an obsession I can't escape."

She bit her lip, looking up at him. "One last kiss and we stop, or I'll let you go too far tonight."

Ellen held his face, giving him the briefest of touches before kissing him with a passion that matched his. He nearly sobbed, letting his hands fall to cup her buttocks and hold her hard against him. Her gasp let him know they'd veered too close to a limit and he stepped away from her. Unable to even think in English for a moment or two, he stammered, "*Oui, allons ou, merde*, we must go." Del held her at arm's length. "*Allons, ma cherie du coeur.*" Taking her hand, he led her towards the group.

She stopped, making him stop as well. "Adelard, what is it you're saying to me when you speak French?"

"If you must know…" He hesitated, looking toward the camp. "Very well. It is that I care very much for you. You are my heart, the dearest of all, beautiful and mine."

"Oh my."

"Indeed. And now, I've kept us away for too long."

"I'm tired of obeying my father. I've come to think he's not worth it."

Del refused to admit he agreed so stayed silent until they reached the others. "Tomorrow?"

"Yes, if I can."

He continued on to the Granville wagon before stopping midway and rethinking his return to the others. Del preferred his body calmed down enough to be in polite company. As it was, memories of her kiss kept him hungry for more so he skirted the camp and kept to his watch duties.

The smell of coffee woke Del first. He didn't want to open his eyes, but the sounds around him said everyone else's day had already begun. He ignored the activity flowing around him for a couple of minutes before climbing out of bed. First he had breakfast, then cleaned up, and soon he had Pomme fed and ready to scout ahead with him and Arnold. They led everyone north and parallel to Burnt River for most of the day. The group had no choice but to spend noon in a dry area. A few hours farther and an oasis of sorts appeared ahead of them, and what at first had seemed like brush now loomed large as trees. Not until now did Del realize how much he missed the cool shade only green leaves provided.

Other groups had the same idea and crowded around the pond at the base of the low canyon. He nodded at Arnold and they fanned out, claiming a big enough area for their group to stay. Before long, Sam and everyone else arrived, taking the usual half circle along the water's banks. Their tasks were so routine, no one needed to talk. Sam had warned him about this before Ellen was kidnapped, how at some point everyone knew everything else anyone would say, so the talking decreased to nothing. Of course visiting between groups occurred, especially between wagons going east and those going west. An understanding part of him knew why Jack went off for other company at night. The selfish part of him wished the man would stay put for the rest of the journey in any other camp and let Ellen sneak away with him more often.

Dusk fell on children playing in the woods and around the pond while the adults caught up on washing and mending. The blue sky looked grey, mountains seemed flat, and nothing interested him when he didn't see Ellen during the day. He needed to fix that problem and headed off to the river with a handful of dirty laundry.

He found her there, washing her baby brother's clothes. The smell reached him first. Del didn't envy her the chore. He scuffed his feet on approach so she wasn't startled. "Good afternoon," he said, kneeling on grass near the riverbank.

"Good afternoon!" She glanced over at him, clearly pleased he'd joined her. "Are you here to help me with Buster's clothes?"

Del laughed outright before saying, "No, thank you. I can smell them from here."

"Too bad." She gave him a teasing smile. "I figured they'd remind you of why you might like to continue your free and wild life."

He shook his head and began washing his own clothes. "They do remind me to be grateful, I'll admit."

Ellen sat back on her heels, wiping the sweat from her forehead. "Don't get me wrong. Buster is the best baby ever, but goodness, when he's sick, he doesn't do things halfway."

"Is he sick often?"

"Not too much." She grimaced when she picked up a new item to clean. "But then, even once is too often."

"I understand." He grinned at her, enjoying the warm sun, cool water, and wonderful company. "This is pleasant. Should we try to find a shade tree this evening? Or maybe you could visit me, us, at dinner tonight?"

She wrung out the last item and paused until someone from another group passed by. "I'd love that but may not be able to do anything but care for the boys tonight."

"Bring them with you. No one would mind." And so what if they did, Del added in his mind. He needed more than this brief conversation with her. His gaze followed her as she stood and looked in the direction of her family's wagon. He nudged her verbally. "At least promise to try?"

"I can do that." Ellen grinned. "If you're sure they won't mind all of us, we might visit for the music."

"Please do." He stayed on his knees, ignoring his desire to hop up and go to her. She returned his smile with a modest one of her own. "I won't sit next to you, if you'd like."

She gave a skittish search of the area before answering him. "I wouldn't like that at all. I miss you."

He almost replied about how much he missed her too. She walked away and he turned to see Jack strolling toward them. Del shrugged as if unconcerned and went back to washing clothes. He kept the splashing down, listening for Winslow's yelling in case he was angry about Ellen being near him. Hearing nothing, he wrung out the last shirt and went back to the Granville wagon.

No one was there. He assumed they were off on various chores. He wondered if anyone happened to be fishing and decided to see if the trout were biting. Several hours later, he had a string of fish, enough for the entire camp.

"You brought us supper!" said Sam when Del reached camp.

Marie left the fireside and admired the catch. "How soon can you gentlemen have these cleaned and ready for me to cook?"

"Not long, ma'am." Arnold walked up. "I don't mind helping if it means we eat sooner."

"Count me in on clean up," added Lefty.

Sam let down the tailgate, and every man settled in with a fish. Many hands made short work of the task and soon a heap of cleaned fillets lay waiting for Marie's cook pan. Del asked Sam, "Is this enough to invite others in our group to share?"

He grinned before replying, "I'd think so. Lucky, tell the Allens to join us. Lefty, can you let the Nelsons know? And Arnold, you get the Winslows."

Del nodded, pleased to have Ellen and her family asked to attend, and even more pleased about not having to ask them himself. His absence made it more likely Winslow would let them come here and get a good meal. Del realized he'd never had Ellen's cooking. He'd always assumed she could fix a good meal, but now he wondered. They all seemed on the scrawny side in her family. Maybe she was awful and he should have been inviting them over far more often.

He felt his shirts to see if they'd dried and then shook the thought from his head. Practice helped and she had to be better now after months on the road. Del sat next to the fire, watching Marie stir biscuits. Neither talked, her being busy and him thinking about Ellen. All this time, he'd still not come up with a good way to win her father over into accepting him. They had a month, maybe two more and he frowned at the lack of progress so far. He had to come up with a foolproof way to gain Jack's approval. Ellen insisted she didn't care what her Pa thought, but Del suspected her father's opinion mattered a lot to her.

"How is Ellen?"

Del looked up at Marie and smiled. The woman had an uncanny ability to know what he was thinking. Either that or he was woefully transparent. "She's perfect, as usual."

"To you, yes, but is her wrist getting any better? What about Buster? He was sick this morning. Has he improved?"

"She still favors her wrist and Buster, judging from the washing she did today, is still somewhat ill."

"I hope Arnold has luck in inviting them tonight." She set the frying pan of fillets on the fire grate. "Winslow seems more intent on finding the boys a new mother than a decent meal, but I didn't say that out loud, all right?"

"No gossip from you, ma coupin. None that I heard, anyway." He enjoyed her laugh and settled in to wait for the meal. Soon, the other men arrived.

Lucky arrived with the Allens, Sam following. Arnold and Lefty showed up with the Nelsons. Del's heart dropped at the sight of Arnold and no Winslows. Anger and hurt swirled in him like oil and water trying to mix. He stared at the fire, ignoring everyone settling in around him until Marie said his name. "Yes?"

"It may be later, dear ami."

She set aside three of the fillets, and he knew she anticipated Jack resuming his catting ways. Soon, the entire crowd quieted, eating the fresh catch. He savored every bite, sure that if Ellen didn't know how to cook, Marie could give her lessons. "C'est marvelleau poisson, ma coupin."

She blushed at his compliment. "Merci beaucoup."

Mr. Allen patted his stomach. "I couldn't eat another bite."

Del glanced over at Marie and saw she still had enough for Ellen and her brothers. He only listened with half his attention as the others chatted about their day. Lucky was the first up, collecting dishes from the Granvilles and their men. Everyone else took it as a signal to leave, and most began standing before disappearing into the night. The Allens lingered, Jenny and Marie talking for a little while. He sighed, certain Ellen couldn't break away.

"Hello, everyone. It seems we're too late for dinner."

He grinned, hearing her voice before seeing her. "But not for dessert."

Skeeter ran over to him. "We had supper. What's for dessert?" He looked over at the pan Marie placed on the fire. "Fish?"

Ellen settled in between Del and Marie. She put Buster down on her lap. "Skeet, you like fish, remember?"

"I do, but what about pie?" He peered at the fillets as they cooked. "Sure do smell good."

"Sure does, sweetheart."

"Yeah." The boy came over to Del. "So, Mr. Do Bose, how have ya been? Me and my brother have been sick some. I'm better and so is he, but we get well then back sick again."

"That's not good. I've been well." He glanced over at Sam. "You and Marie too?"

"We've all been well, Skeeter," Sam replied. Lucky walked up with the clean dishes, and Sam took them from him. "Here, take three of these, hand them out, and Mrs. Granville will dish your dessert."

Skeeter laughed before helping the men. "Fish instead of pie. That's so funny."

As soon as each Winslow took a bite, they fell silent, eating. Ellen finished first. "Perfect, Marie. I couldn't have done better."

"Thank you for showing me how. Otherwise, we'd have had fish jerky or raw."

Del couldn't help but smile, glad the woman he wanted to stay married to could cook. He wanted to tease Ellen about her keeping this skill from him. Before he could say anything, Sam stood. "I need to check on the stock. Del and Lucky, you two have first watch tonight, and Arnold and I get second."

The men all around nodded. Ellen took the boys empty plates.

"I should wash these right quick."

"It's dark. Let me go with you."

"I'm not sure."

"Oh pooh," said Marie. She took the plates and forks from Ellen. "You both stay here and I'll wash up." She also grabbed the cooling pan before heading off to the water.

"She told us," he said to Ellen.

"I suppose." She returned his grin. "She'll expect us to talk."

"That's good, because so do I." He glanced around to see who listened in on them. Lucky seemed intent on his bugle, polishing fingerprints from it. Arnold and Lefty played cards. Del noticed Sam followed Marie and grinned. They were such newlyweds, seeking out every chance they could for alone time. "I'm glad you were able to be here."

Ellen waited until Buster settled into her lap and snuggled in as if done for the night. "So am I. The meal was wonderful. We'd had something already, but the fish? I'd forgotten how good it could be."

"Where is your father?"

"Pa? He's over at Mrs. Benson's again." At his questioning look, she continued, "She's a new widow, quite lovely, that Pa is helping. Both she and her young son have been in one of the groups we keep pace with. He seems to like spending time with them."

"Does he have dinner there?"

"No, never. He always eats with us first, not taking his time so he can go to see her. Sometimes Skeeter goes with him." Lying against his sister and half asleep, Skeeter nodded. She patted his head. "He used to spend more time with Buster but since Mrs. Benson, Pa has let me take care of him again. I don't mind, really. The baby is mostly potty trained, Skeeter is an angel, and our ox is my only responsibility after dinner and cleanup."

Del surmised she must feel the heat of anger from him despite his best efforts to hide it. So Winslow had found one woman to court instead of playing the field. He was torn between welcoming the distraction and being dismayed at Jack dumping the night chores off on Ellen. "When he goes to visit, come here. I'll make sure extra is set aside for you and the boys."

"What about Pa?"

His tendency for diplomacy lost out to blunt honesty. "He's a grown man. If he wants to hunt or fish to keep you all fed, then stay there."

"Oh."

He knew his answer cut her but didn't care. She had to know her father cared to provide for his family only when it suited him. "Any time you're alone with the boys, come here and we'll all keep you company."

"I'd like that."

Her answer made him smile. "Me too." Lucky stirred and Del knew it was time for first watch. "Shall I escort you to your camp?"

"Yes, please."

He took Skeeter from her and stood. The boy snuggled into him. Del grinned at the subconscious trust. Ellen eased to her feet with Buster, and they made their way to the Winslows'. He kept hold of the older boy while Ellen used one hand to spread out the baby's bed, then her younger brother's. Del put the child into his covers and pulled Ellen off to the side and out of sight. "I'm stealing a kiss and hope you don't mind."

"It's not stealing if I give one to you."

He held her close. His lips met hers and he echoed her moan at the touch. Their kiss deepened and on some level he knew they needed to keep this short and sweet. Still, the cool night air, her warm body, and his need for her kept him there, enjoying every touch. At last he broke away first. "My love, until tomorrow?"

She kissed him quick one last time. "Tomorrow."

Del left as she went to her own bed. He began the night watch. Thinking of her and reliving their kiss, his feet never touched the ground as he walked. He could grin like a fool and the dark allowed him the chance to do so. Jack staggered into camp just as Lucky and him came off of second watch. Del figured the good widow must have plenty of whisky, giving Winslow more than one reason to sniff around her skirts. He shook his head at some men's weakness for the drink and went to his own bed.

Having first watch always threw Del off the next morning. He always seemed to sleep too long and wake up groggy. He sat up, noticing how most of them had already eaten and left.

"Good morning, sleepyhead." Marie dished up some breakfast for him.

"Good morning, belle. It's not right how lovely you are first thing in the morning."

She laughed, giving him the plate. "You scoundrel! Do you say these things to Ellen too?"

He waited until she gave him a cup of coffee before eating. "Of course I do. All the women need to hear compliments."

"She's a very lucky lady."

Del swallowed and took a drink of coffee before saying, "I'd like to think so."

"Ahem. Ma'am?"

He turned to see Jack Winslow standing there. How long had he been listening in? Del frowned. Not long or he'd be screaming about him and Ellen, he was sure. He tried not to smirk at how studiously Jack ignored him.

"Yes, Mr. Winslow? How can I help you?"

"You can't, ma'am. I need to speak to your husband."

"All right." She got to her feet. "He's around here somewhere, probably readying the stock for travel." With the cook pot in hand, she scooped up the dish bucket. "Let's go to the creek and see if we can find him."

They walked off and Del slowed his eating. He'd wash up for himself. Everyone had put up their own beds, so that wasn't left for him to do. Just as he chewed the last bite, Sam came up. Del swallowed. "Your wife and Winslow are looking for you. They're at the creek, I assume with him watching her work."

"He's good at that, almost as good as you are."

"Ha. I can't help it if you and the others creep around while I sleep."

"Consider it a reward for last night's dinner."

Del cut his gaze over at his friend as the man put the fire grate to the side for cooling. "Aren't you going to go find them?"

"Nope, they'll be back soon enough."

He saw Marie and Jack stroll back toward them. Intent on ignoring Winslow as much as Jack had him, Del kept busy with putting away his bedding. He returned to his coffee, pouring a fresh cup, and sat so he could eavesdrop.

"Granville!" Jack bellowed. "I want a word with you this morning before we start out."

"All right." Sam faced him, hands on hips. "What do you need?"

"Not me so much as a lady what needs to go along with us.

There's a poor widow and her son who want to join our group. Her husband died a while back, around Fort Hays, and she wanted to go north instead of south."

"Why does she want to join us in particular?"

"Well, I might have convinced her to. I told her that you were a great scout and leader and that she'd be a lot safer with us and under my watchful eye."

"So you'll personally vouch for her?"

"I will, particularly because I want to marry her."

"Congratulations."

"I can tell her to hitch up to my wagon?"

"Yes, if you can make sure both loads are light. We have steep hills coming up. It'd be best on your animals if you don't overwork them."

"Will do, and thank you."

Once the man was out of earshot, Marie asked, "Does Ellen know she's to have a new stepmother?"

Del shrugged. "If she did, she didn't mention it."

"My bet is she doesn't know. Ah, well, it's none of my business if Winslow has mourned Lucy enough by now."

Watching his friend walk off, Del knew Sam was furious. He didn't blame him. If it'd been Ellen that died that day, he'd still be inconsolable. Even now the thought of her potential death hurt his heart. Sam had to feel the same way about Marie. Del'd bet all his family's money he did. Marie's voice cut into his thoughts.

"Adelard? Are you finished?"

"Oh, yes, of course I am. But," he said, holding up a hand, "I'm washing up for you." Del scooped up his dishes and went to the water before she could object. He'd not seen Ellen or the boys despite keeping an eye open for them. Soon, he had Pomme ready and everyone started rolling northwest along Powder River valley. He settled in back with Lucky on one side and him on the other.

From his rear vantage point, he could see another wagon with the Winslows' and assumed it was the Bensons'. He couldn't see how many oxen they had and hoped it was more than two for the animals' sake. As Sam had warned earlier in the morning, a long slope challenged them after the first mile. The Allens and a few in other groups struggled to climb up the incline. He and Lucky passed a couple of the stragglers in the group ahead of them. The way eased up for everyone after they reached the summit. A few more hills remained as they followed a dry creek.

He filled his canteen after eating lunch near a spring fed pond. Ellen caught his eye while she topped off a couple of canning jars with water. He winked and she shook her head while wrinkling her nose. "Monsieur told you about his future plans?" Ellen nodded, still frowning, and Del laughed. "No love for your new mother?"

"I miss Lucy."

He felt bad but wanted to tease her a little. "Poor dear. You need a man to take you away from all this."

She snorted down a laugh. "Yes, I do. I wish some handsome rogue would carry me away."

Del glanced over at her to see an mischievous glare until she smiled at him. "Be careful. A wild Indian brave may make your wishes come true."

"Make sure you, I mean, *the brave* has plenty of water. I can get very thirsty."

He grinned at her, glad she'd meant him. "I will."

Ellen went back to her own wagon. He watched her walk away, wanting to follow and make good on his kidnapping promise. Before too long, they and everyone else were ready to be back on the road. The stop had allowed him to check how many oxen the Warrens now had. Four animals pulled the two wagons, and Del whistled under his breath. No wonder Jack had been sniffing around Mrs. Benson's skirts. The woman was well off. He hoped the man's choice in women would benefit Ellen and the boys. For the rest of the afternoon, he daydreamed about luring away Ellen and her brothers. No matter how he tried, he couldn't work out how to get all four of them on Pomme and laughed at how that might look.

At near twilight, they found a valley full of grass. Del had just staked out his horse when Arnold and Sam came over to him.

"Did you hear?" asked Arnold. "The group up ahead butchered a cow this afternoon and has meat left over."

Del immediately thought of Ellen and her family. "Are they willing to trade or sell?"

"Yep. They want twenty-five cents a pound."

"That's what they told you?" Sam let out a low whistle. "It's not cheap."

"No, but worth the cost." Del searched a saddlebag and found a silver dollar. "Give this to them and get us four pounds.

Barter for five if you can. I'd go myself, but they'll trust and give you more."

"Will do." Arnold hurried off.

He turned to Sam. "The meat is from you, all right? It's my contribution."

"I'm not taking credit for your good deed."

"Yes, you are. Otherwise, Winslow won't let his family eat."

Sam nodded in a silent affirmation of his friend's assertion. "Have you seen his new woman's wealth?"

"Not yet and it doesn't matter. I want them to have a chance at a good meal tonight."

"All right. I bought dinner." Sam shook his head. "If you'll excuse me, I'll tell my wife about *my* good deed for the day."

Del laughed. "You do that." He went back to taking care of Pomme, settling him in for the night. He checked on the other horses and work oxen. Too soon, the rich smell of cooking meat hung in the cool night air. His stomach growled in protest and he went to camp. He grinned at the large circle of people around the fire. No one made excuses to miss fresh beef.

He settled in the only available spot next to Lefty and Arnold. Ellen sat across from him, and it seemed as if she were miles away. A woman he assumed was Mrs. Benson sat between Jack and his daughter. Marie dished up dinner and gave plates to pass down the line. Progress came to a stop when Mrs. Benson received a plate. She didn't pass down to Ellen. Instead, she began to eat. Jack received his plate and started eating too. Ellen glanced over at Del, then the boys. He knew that pointed look and tried not to grin as he passed a plate down to Arnold. She stood and went to Marie. Taking three plates to her brothers and the young Benson boy before going back and getting her own dinner. He got his food at the same time she did and both began eating. The meat melted in his mouth, and he wondered where they'd found the potatoes. Everything tasted perfect and his toes almost wiggled when he thought of Ellen being Marie's cooking instructor. He'd be fat as a merchant in a couple of months after their wedding.

Del wanted to see what sort of woman Mrs. Benson was and if she'd be good to the Winslow children. From the corner of his eyes or from under his lashes, he examined her. She seemed to be a friendly, kind person, until he remembered her not giving food to the children first. Maybe she believed children should be seen, not heard, and only let the youngsters eat after adults but before animals. Not his personal philosophy, but he'd seen how others had adopted it.

Even without her obvious money, Del could see why Jack fancied her. She had light brown hair that glowed in the firelight. She seemed to smile a lot and from this distance, the smiled looked real. Mrs. Benson also wore a nice dress. Ellen's clothes looked dowdy and stained, though Del knew his love kept her dress clean. Mrs. Benson's fabric seemed newer and freshly made. He wondered if she was a seamstress. If so, Ellen and the boys would benefit from her skills. He'd like the woman if for no other reason than the younger Winslows might benefit.

They'd traveled a tough twenty miles today, and he wasn't surprised to see people leave soon after eating. He knew without asking that he and Lucky had first watch again. With the Bensons there, he expected to not have a chance to talk with Ellen alone. Sure enough, he spent the entire watch only catching glimpses of her as he walked by. He vowed that once done with security and in bed, he'd find a way to be alone with her tomorrow.

Del was first up the next day, so he stoked the fire and went for their coffee's water. His early bird ways didn't reward him with seeing Ellen. He smiled, ate, drank, and did all the usual breakfast things. As soon as the last forkful went in, he hopped up. "Here, I'll clean." Del began gathering plates and forks while ignoring how the look Sam gave him was too aware of his motives. He tried to be casual as he headed to the creek. Seeing Ellen and Mrs. Benson destroyed all his acts of nonchalance. "Good morning, ladies," he said while approaching. "Lovely day so far, yes?" He kept the smile plastered to his face, cursing at how he'd lapsed so easily into French influenced English. His time with Sam and the gang had improved his skills better than this.

"Monsieur Du Boise," Ellen greeted him first. "Here is a friend of my father's, Mrs. Lacy Benson."

"Lacy?" he blurted out in surprise. Had Winslow picked the woman or the name? He glanced at Ellen, who shook her head as Mrs. Benson stepped forward.

"A pleasure, Mr. Du Boise." She held out her hand with a frown. "The Winslow family speaks highly of you."

Judging by how high her nose was, Del felt sure Mrs. Benson

didn't agree with her own statement. He adopted his best imitation of Sam's charming ways to counteract her disapproving attitude. "I appreciate that, ma'am. I think highly of them as well." He took the offered hand and made a motion as if to kiss it, then nodded towards Ellen. "Mr. Winslow has done an excellent job of raising all his children."

"Hmm. It's nice of you to say so. Speaking of Jack, he's expecting us." Mrs. Benson tapped the younger woman on the shoulder. "Come, dear. We still have work to do this morning."

"Yes, ma'am." She fell in step behind and gave Del a quick smile. "Mr. Du Boise."

He grinned back, enjoying her formality. "Miss Winslow." Del watched them walk away for a few seconds before beginning his dishwashing. Mrs. Benson, Lacy, seemed nice enough despite her snobbish attitude towards him. He was more concerned with how she treated Ellen. Lucky's bugle sounded and he stifled a curse. His bedroll still needed stowing and Pomme needed saddling so he hurried back.

At the camp, he saw someone else had put away his bedding, so he packed the dishes before going to his horse. He soon rode up front with Lefty, scouting the way across the flat road. The wide valley gave all of them a much-needed rest from hauling wagons up and down hills. They crossed a couple of small creeks, and while the road became a little rough for a couple of miles, it soon smoothed out to another stretch of flat dirt. Fifteen miles from morning camp, they approached Powder River and a Nez Perce trading village. Other immigrants had packed the earth down in a wide swath on either side. Some of the best grazing grass grew around them but at a distance.

The crowds made finding a quiet camp more challenging than usual. Soon, Lefty found the best place and they all gathered there. Del noticed they were at one of the farthest points from the trading camp. Was the choice intentional based on what happened with the Shoshone? He shook his head. It didn't matter. He'd speak to Sam later about trading and keeping Ellen away from harm.

Del dismounted and led Pomme to a good place for food and water. He hurried to settle in the animal for the rest of the day. The Granville wagon had been parked and already had the makings of a campfire nearby.

Marie saw him and approached as he walked up. "Have you

talked to Sam? He wants to visit the trading post but only with you or the other men."

"I don't share his concern but do understand."

"Does that mean I can go?"

He chuckled at her eagerness and wanted to agree but didn't want to get into trouble with his friend. "I'll defer to Sam on that answer."

"You're very wise."

Sam walked up with Arnold and Lefty. He grinned at his wife. "Already arguing your way over there?"

"Trying to but failing. Adelard is just as stubborn as you are."

"Good." He turned to the two hired men. "Keep an eye out for anyone going over there from our group. If there's anything suspicious, let me know. There's no need to be militant about it, just anything out of the ordinary gets reported. All right?"

"Yes, sir," said Arnold before he and Lefty went to finish chores.

He turned to Del. "Are you ready? We have extra sugar to trade, despite Marie's protests that she needs every grain." With his friend's nod, Sam hopped on the tailgate and began digging around for the sugar. He reappeared from the back of the wagon with two wrapped packages.

The amount Sam held surprised him and he had to ask, "All that is sugar?"

"No, one is but the other is tobacco." Granville hopped down, giving a package to Del.

"You're willing to lose that?"

"Joe was the only one with the habit. I never cared for it, and the younger men never started."

Del nodded and both men started for the village. He was glad it was on their side of the river. Pomme was comfortable where he was, and Del didn't feel like a swim. Soon, they walked into the middle of the Nez Perce, two lines of people trading their wares ready to take their goods. He looked at all the items for trade, seeing so much to buy for Ellen while knowing she couldn't accept. Maybe Mrs. Benson could charm Winslow into an agreeable mood. After her attitude towards Del today, he doubted she'd want to do so.

Lost in his thoughts, he ran into Sam. "Sorry."

"Don't worry." A trade had him focused. Sam made motions

to the man sitting behind stacks of vegetables. The elder Nez Perce licked his finger and stuck it in the sugar. Licking his finger again, he grinned at the taste and nodded. The man then began to measure out a generous amount of dried peas into a fabric flour sack and another generous amount of freshly dug potatoes into a different bag. He gave them to Sam, taking the sugar, and held up a hand. Setting down his new goods, he took a folded and tanned hide, also giving it to Sam.

Del leaned over to his friend enough to nudge his shoulder for attention. "I'd take it. He can divide and sell what you gave him for a good profit."

"Very well." He thanked the man in Nez Perce. As they left, Del said, "Excellent accent. You sounded like a native speaker back there."

Sam laughed. "Don't be too impressed. That's all Nick's first wife was able to teach me."

"It was better than your French, and at least she didn't teach you anything rude."

"I'm now very glad she didn't." They walked, pausing every so often at a fine display of knives or other weapons. At last Sam said, "I want to get a good deal for Joe's tobacco, but am loathe to lose it."

"If you let it go, you've let him go?"

"Exactly. Marie already disapproves of my trading for it but can't bear to tell me so. She knows every little bit I could get for it would help."

He knew how she and Joe had forged a father daughter relationship. "So wait until a better opportunity for trade arrives. There's no need to do anything today."

"I might do that." They circled around and headed back to camp, looking at everything on the other side of the aisle. Still, nothing worth Joe's tobacco tempted them.

By mutual agreement, they went back to their own camp. Marie hurried up to them. "What did you get? Can I see?"

"Of course, dearest." Sam handed her the peas first.

"Oh my goodness! Thank you! These will be wonderful tonight!" She looked into the bag again as if not believing they were truly there. "I'll start them soaking this instant."

He held out the other sack. "Would you want to see these?"

She felt of the burlap. "Let me guess, potatoes?" Looking into the second bag, she exclaimed, "Oh, how nice! The ones I cooked last night had seen better days. These look lovely. Should I cook them as well?"

Sam shrugged. "Sure. I'll see what I can do about fishing for dinner."

"Great!" She waved him away. "Get started and bring us back some trout."

"Us?" He cut his eyes over to his friend. "Del is helping me."

He laughed at Sam's suggestion and pointed to himself. "Me? What if I have other things to do?"

"You don't."

Del had to agree, saying, "No, I don't." He went with Sam and they got their fishing lines, hooks, and old bacon for bait. Before long they were a good distance apart along the riverbank. Being alone gave Del plenty of time to think. He didn't want to wait and rely on Winslow's happiness over a new marriage to be a husband to Ellen. His thoughts went in circles, wondering if he could steal her and the boys away himself.

Several trout and a couple hours later, Del was ready to call it quits to fishing. He looked over at Sam who nodded. They pulled in their lines at the same time and pulled ashore their strings of fish. Along with Del's trout, Sam had caught several catfish. Like the time before, all the hands gathered and everyone worked to clean the day's catch. Marie soon had everything frying with the peas and potatoes cooking in another pan.

Sam looked at the food. "I'm going to invite everyone here for dinner. We have more than enough to share."

Marie nodded. "That's a good idea. Otherwise some of this will go to waste."

Lucky stood. "Let me tell the Allens."

Sam grinned, leaving with the young man. As Arnold and Lefty settled in to wait for dinner, Del grinned. Everyone, him included, had found a place downwind from the aroma. It wasn't long before Del glanced up from his journal and saw Ellen and her family approach with Mrs. Benson and the boys following. The children all seemed to get along, even if Ellen held herself apart from her father and his new lady friend. He glanced to his left at a returning Sam, knowing the group would only have a large gap in the circle between him and the Nelsons to sit in. They settled into their seats and he noticed the older two adults sat as far as possible from him. Del felt both bothered and relieved. Sure enough, Ellen, then Skeeter, the Benson child, and finally Buster sat between him and Mrs. Benson. He consciously ignored Ellen as dinner was dished out and they ate.

Others talked to him and Del responded, but two bites later he had no idea of what had been said between him and whomever else he'd answered. His entire right side seemed to hum like a tuning fork because of Ellen's presence. As people finished and set aside their plates, he noticed they all talked in smaller groups. He checked, seeing Winslow and Lacey engrossed with each other. Del tried to not grin at their preoccupation. He had the perfect chance to chat with Ellen.

She spoke first, saying, "I noticed how you and Sam went to the trading post today. Did he need you to translate for him?"

"No, not at all. Like you can't speak French, I can't speak Nez Perce."

A delicate blush stained her cheeks. "Of course not. I forget you don't know everything there is to know in the world."

"Now you flatter me, ma—" He glanced over to see Winslow staring at them. Del frowned. "My friend."

"Maybe." She scowled back at him. "And maybe your intelligence is very obvious to me."

His heart thudded hard in his chest, not from just the love, but the respect she held for him as well. All he could do was respond with, "I'm glad you think so." The words sounded tepid to even his ears.

"Hmm." She stared into the fire for a moment. In a voice almost too quiet for him to hear, Ellen said, "When Pa was leaving me and the boys alone, it was nice. I almost wished he'd stay gone."

"Oh? For good or for the night?"

"Ellen." Jack snapped his fingers at her. "Let's go."

"All right, Pa." She gathered the boys' plates and stacked them with her own in a stall for extra time, keeping her voice quiet. "For long enough to speak without fear. Maybe more."

He didn't look at her. Instead, he stared into the fire as she followed her family back to their camp. Did she truly know what she said about more? The intimacy, the kisses? He was willing to argue and fuss with her however much she pleased. Sam didn't need to tell him he had second watch tonight. He knew and already didn't like missing any chance the first watch gave him to get her alone and steal a kiss.

Enough people stood up and went off to the various chores that Del stopped his musing to help. Animals checked, bedding put down, and dishes washed, he settled in with the others. His time as guard would happen soon enough.

The next day's hard drive shortened everyone's temper. Bad enough he'd been up half the night on watch, but now they rolled over a bone shaking rough road uphill. An axle had split on one wagon and a wheel splintered on another. He didn't mind the delays as much as the cold air seeping into his bones. The group reached the summit at the same time a chilly rain reached them. Del didn't feel right about leaving Pomme out in the deluge, so he huddled against the wagon with his horse. Everyone else rode out the storm in their wagon with some of the men putting oilcloths over the horses that would let them do so. The rainclouds lasted a while and passed after soaking everyone outside. They had taken advantage of the time to eat some lunch before continuing on.

The lack of dust was refreshing and he enjoyed breathing in the fresh, clean air. A hint of evergreen scent reached him along with the wet earth and prairie grasses. Of course, a damp human and equine smell did too. He grinned, hoping Pomme and he dried quick in the afternoon sun. The landscape and sky seemed too much for his eyes to take in all at once. Deep blue mountains with snow peaks stood to the east with lower, blue green high hills circling them. A dome of sky blue encircled the world, broken up by puffy white clouds and angry grey storms rolling on to the southeast. The Grand Ronde valley below lay in front of them like a vast, mottled green blanket, divided by a blue ribbon of river. Every other part of the world he'd ever seen had its merits, but the Oregon Territory was a heaven on Earth.

He shivered. The high noon sun helped keep him warm but not enough to overpower the strong breeze from the north. The Granville party rolled down the easy sloping decline. Along with several others, they created a true wagon train with the transports snaking along the smooth road for several miles. The mud bogged them down a little or they'd have made better time, he knew. It didn't matter. They'd be at a busy campsite soon enough.

Sam must have decided to push on because they passed by the general camp. Del looked at Arnold who shrugged. He guessed they'd stop when they stopped. When Lucky finally sounded his bugle, Del figured they'd driven twenty miles. He went to the small river as the wagons settled into place. The water looked good and he didn't blame Sam for holding out. Fishing might be better, but not this late in the day. He figured they had just enough time to get everyone settled before the last of twilight faded to dark.

They all settled in one by one, laying out their bedrolls while Marie fixed ham and potatoes. Biscuits for tomorrow baked while they ate. During their meal, Del noticed Sam and Marie didn't say a word to each other the entire time. Something was definitely wrong with them, and he wondered how to get a watch with Sam.

He might chat with Marie instead. She frowned while picking up everyone's dishes to wash. He grabbed the chance to chat with her alone when she passed in front of him. Del said, "Here, ma petite. Let me escort you to the water."

She smiled at him. "Thank you, kind sir."

He led the way, wishing a full moon lit their way instead of the black new moon. Many others had beat down the grasses to where only rocks and dirt lined the riverbank. He helped her kneel on a rock set out by a former traveler. "So, is something wrong with you and Sam?"

"No, nothing at all. He's stubborn and unreasonable."

"Yes, I knew that already."

She chuckled. "He can't see that slavery exists for the slaves' own good."

Del blinked a couple of times in shock. No wonder Sam was unhappy. He was a staunch abolitionist. "And you think slavery is best for the people enslaved?"

"Most times, yes. There are cruel owners who shouldn't have the responsibility but they're the exception, not the usual."

He washed for a moment before venturing to say, "I suppose Sam has told you he thinks it's wrong for one human being to own another."

"He has, and I can see his point. What he can't seem to understand is what happens when we turn everyone out to fend for themselves? They've been cared for all their lives. None of them can or should be able to read or write. How can they function in polite society?"

Del smiled, knowing his own feelings on the subject were as strong as Sam's and she was talking to a stone. "They could learn, couldn't they?"

"Of course they could. I've seen slaves do amazing things. They're certainly trainable."

Her choice of words made him shake his head. Del considered all human beings to be intelligent in some way or another. He had to ask, "Did you explain this exactly to Sam."

"Yes, and he became unreasonable, calling them 'people' and asking how dare I say such things, and how we should have talked more before marrying." Marie bit her lip and tears swam in her eyes. "I agreed and said we needed some time away so he could see reason."

"Oh."

"Yes, he didn't react well to that idea."

He tried to give her a smile as they entered the ring of firelight. How to tell her he agreed with everything Sam said without taking sides? He put the dish bucket down and went to his own bed. Settled in, he had no doubts his two friends would work out their problems, but it made him think. What issues would he and Ellen have besides the usual one about his heritage?

Lucky woke him for second watch as Arnold did Lefty. Del did not want to open his eyes when the morning still felt like night. The fretting that pestered his sleep still dogged him. He and Lefty kept watch until daybreak. People all around them began stirring, starting their day. He grinned when the scent of coffee brewing reached him on the air and decided to get his own started. Careful to keep quiet, Del emptied the bucket of last night's stale water and headed to the river.

When he returned, Marie was cooking breakfast. "I thought that might be where you were." She had the coffee pot with beans already inside. "Hopefully this will wake up the sleepyheads."

As she went about pouring water and warming last night's biscuits, he rolled his bed into a nice seat. As predicted, the others woke when the nearby coffee started smelling good. Marie was ready for them, giving everyone a full cup as soon as they were upright and ready. Sam took his. He said nothing to her, unlike the other men. Del drank and wondered if he needed to pull Sam aside to let him vent his own irritation too. No wonder Sam had been so quiet during yesterday's fishing. He must have been angry and needed the quiet time.

Having made his decision to let Sam get his anger talked out, Del hurried to get everything ate, drank, and put away. Pomme was soon ready. Del got on and went to where Sam and Scamp were.

"I suppose you want me to say something."

Del shrugged. "It's your choice."

They rode on, leading the way up a long hill. At the summit, Sam said, "I suppose she told you how her family used to own slaves. She doesn't see anything wrong with doing so and doesn't listen to me."

He found that difficult to believe of the woman. Her kindheartedness seemed limitless and Del had to counter, "She doesn't?"

"No. I've explained to her that slavery is wrong under any circumstances. She said I was wrong and some people needed an overseer."

Finding it difficult to believe Marie used those exact words, Del asked, "Is that what she said? 'Overseer'?"

He didn't say anything, just stared ahead as they rode downhill for a little while before encountering another hill. "Not exactly, no. Marie never said 'overseer.' "

"She might have said they needed an owner for their care?"

Sam squinted and shifted in his saddle. "Something like that, yes. She doesn't think all of them deserve freedom."

Marie hadn't implied such a thing to him last night, and Del needed to dig deeper. "Not deserve or just not know what to do with freedom? She pointed out to me that slaves can't read or write."

"Of course they're illiterate. It's a crime to educate them, and it should be a crime not to do so. They're human beings. I don't think she can see that, Del." He paused. "If she can't accept that slavery is wrong under any circumstances, I don't know how we can stay married."

"There's no middle ground?"

"No."

Del nodded, knowing Sam would protest at what he said next. "Then I agree, divorce her. She wants to own slaves and you don't."

Sam frowned at him. "She doesn't want to own them. In fact,

she and her family set their help free. She personally saw that they had papers and passage to a free state."

"How do you know for sure?"

The question took Sam by surprise and he frowned at him. "I don't other than she's never expressed a desire."

"Ask her if she misses owning slaves. She might surprise you."

"All right. I'll ask next chance I get."

Del grinned, knowing Marie would win the battle by agreeing slaves deserved a chance at freedom. He understood her point of view better than Sam. She saw the newly freed people as children being turned out of their home. Del wondered how much she knew of the mistreatment slaves endured. He made a mental note to ask her more about her life on the plantation.

Right now, he wanted to enjoy the pine and fir tree smell on the cool mountain air. The miles they'd covered climbed into a mountain range, low enough to miss being snow topped but high enough for evergreens. The Grand Ronde River flowed within several yards of them all day. After going over some of the driest land he'd ever seen, Del loved the sound of the river so close.

Up ahead lay a popular campsite. The wood, grass, and water made it perfect for man and beast. He glanced over at Sam. "Here for the night?"

"Yes, let's find a clear spot."

The best place they could find was on the far side of the valley. Del stayed to claim the area while Sam rode back to lead the others there. The trees and mountains strengthened his resolve to settle down. He'd had enough of dust and sage for a lifetime. In a little while, everyone had created the usual half circle around a riverbank.

A thick grove of timber followed the washed out canyons as they wound up the hills. Some trees grew in between the ravines, not as many. A person could get lost or hide in the woods. Del grinned. Forget keeping a lookout for Sam and Marie. It was time for them to return the favor. He went searching for his friend and found him leading their horses to the water. "Sam? Are you fishing for trout this afternoon?"

"I hadn't planned to."

"Hmm. No fishing and keeping guard for a couple walking further upstream?"

"Like you do for us?" Sam sighed. "You know Jack will be

furious if he finds out."

"He won't. We're talking, spending time alone. Nothing more."

"I'm sure." He gave the reins to Del. "All right, talking only. Stake out these guys so I can get a few other things done. Then I can see if any fish are left."

Del's heart skipped a beat at the opportunity to spend time with Ellen. They'd not been truly alone in a month or so. He made sure the horses were secured in a place with plenty of food and water, taking the initiative to care for the other men's animals too. When done and having nothing left to do, Del wiped his sweaty palms on his pants. How was Sam letting her know where he'd be? He took a deep breath and slowly exhaled. Would she know how alone they'd be, how much privacy they'd have? He went back to the Granville wagon. Lefty sat on the tailgate, sewing a button on his shirt. Arnold and Lucky were rearranging things in the wagon. As he waited, the two were making Lefty lean over to let them by every so often. Just as Del was about to give up and go find Sam or Ellen, he saw Sam walking toward him.

"Let me find my fishing tackle." Sam nodded to his men. "That is, if these guys haven't cleaned it into an obscure place."

"Don't worry, boss." Lucky peeked out of the wagon. "You need to go fishing? I saw your things just a little bit ago. Let me get them." After some rustling around, he reappeared. "Del, do you want yours as well? You're mighty fine at fishing too."

"Sure." Sam answered for him. "He's going with me."

More rustling and soon Del had his tackle too. "Thank you." He wanted to nudge Sam in the ribs to get him to stop grinning like a fool. "Shall we?"

They walked up the river, stopping where a creek intersected. Del cut his eyes over at his friend. The man had more spring in his step than he did and he was the one in love. "How long did she say she'd be?"

"Not long. She worked it around to where Mrs. Benson is spending the afternoon proving to Jack what a good mother she'll make to the boys." Sam cast his line. "You might scout ahead for a comfortable place to sit and talk because I'm sure that's all you two will be doing or Jack'll have my hide."

He held up a hand as if taking an oath. "Talking is all I want to do."

Sam chuckled. "That's too bad." He stopped grinning at Del's frown, adding, "Go. She'll be here soon and if someone sees you leave together, there'll be trouble."

Del nodded his agreement and walked up the creek, discarding one place after another as he went. Some were too muddy, others too rocky. After what seemed like hours, he found the perfect place. Grass covered a place under a shady spot. He sat, assessing whether any pine needles poked him. Satisfied the ground was soft enough for Ellen, he waited.

A rustle through the leaves sounded from the camp's direction. Del looked and saw her walking to him. "Hello."

"Hello." She went to him, holding his hand as he helped her sit down beside him. "Sam said you needed to talk with me?"

"He's right, I do."

"Should I be worried?"

"*Que*? No, dearest, not at all. I needed to talk to you because I need you. Nothing more urgent than that."

She exhaled as if she'd been holding her breath for a long while. "Good. When he said need and talk in conjunction with you, I was afraid it had something to do with our crude marriage."

He frowned at how she referred to their union. Not everything had to be from the whites to be valid, and he disliked having to constantly remind her of this. Del gave himself a mental shake. "We may discuss our ceremony at the village later. First, you'd mentioned our speaking together and more. Tell me what you intended?"

"Oh." She looked down at her hands, folded in her lap. "I might have misspoken. I was rather lonely and missing you at the time."

"You don't feel the same way now that we're alone?"

"Not so much, no." She glanced up at him with a little smile. "How could I when with you?"

Her words warmed his heart like the sun on a crisp spring day. He leaned to her and ran the back of his hand along her face, her skin soft against his. She turned to kiss his palm. The sweet tickle took him by surprise, and he turned her face to his. "*Ellen, mon amore. Je t'aime.*"

"*Je t'aime too, Del.*"

He smiled. "Do you know what you're saying?"

"I asked Marie how to say it in French."

He pulled her to him, as much as their seated positions would allow, and kissed her lips, soft at first until she pressed for more from him. Ellen held onto him, pulling him to her with a hand to the back of his neck. The other hand she held against his chest. He broke their kiss first. "We should spend more time talking than kissing. Otherwise, we'll go too far."

She ran her fingers through his hair as if testing the short length. "No, no more talking. I'm tired of seeing you from afar and not being able to touch you. I regret not kissing you more when we were alone."

Her speaking of Jack reminded him of how much the man hurt her when angry. He took her left hand. "How are you feeling? Any pain?"

"I'm much better. It's healing nicely." She flexed her wrist as proof.

"Your burns? There's been no new accidents since then?"

"No." She kissed his nose. "I've been a good daughter. No talking back, no late dinner, or asking questions he doesn't want to answer." She must have seen something in his face because she said, "Don't look like that. Pa isn't bad. He just gets mad too easily. It's not my fault he's so mean when angered, but it is my fault when I do the wrong thing."

He pressed his lips against her wrist, closing his eyes as he felt her pulse against his skin. "I dream of the day we're married in everyone's eyes, and I can protect you from him. We'll need to protect Skeeter and Buster too."

"Oh, Adelard, I love you." She nuzzled his neck while working her way to his ear. "I so love how you smell. All warm sun, leather, and something else I can't quite place. It's unique and I miss it when we're apart."

Her words tickled down to his toes. He wanted her in every way. "Ellen." She took his face in her hands and kissed him. Her passion took his breath. He held her until she pulled her skirt up enough to straddle him. The feel of their torsos pressed together excited and alarmed him. He had to stop this or he'd roll over and take her like the animal he'd been called. "*Non*, please, stop and sit back down."

"I am sitting, Del, and I want this."

He held her shoulders and pushed her a little ways back. "You can't, I can't."

"You're not trying very hard to stop me." She relaxed, sitting on him fully, and he swallowed at the contact.

"You're starting something we can't finish." He knew she felt how much he wanted her now and he needed to protest. Instead, all he could do was stare into her eyes with a hunger that matched the desire he saw in hers. "*Non, cherie*, we can't."

"Yes, we can. I need you." She leaned forward again, nibbling at his lip before running her tongue back and forth along his lips. "Just a few kisses and we'll stop."

He didn't think they could quit any time soon, but her body on his forced him to at least try. "A few, yes." Del leaned back until he was laying flat. In this position, she pressed more against his chest and less against his hips. He glanced down at her cleavage and groaned. He hadn't improved things at all. He wrapped his arms around her, bringing her breasts closer to his mouth. Her gasp when he nipped at her flesh pleased him, and he took care to do the same on the other side. By then, she was used to the feeling, it seemed, because she wrapped her arms around his head in a silent plea for more.

If not for so many buttons and the unyielding cotton fabric, Del would have had her dress off a shoulder by now. He consoled his hungry lips with a slight kiss of her skin before giving Ellen another light bite. She shuddered with need and a rush of pride went through him.

Ellen sat up and away from him, pressing into his hardness. She wiggled her hips. "Do you have pockets?"

"No," he gasped. "I mean, *oui*, but that's not in my pocket."

"Oh!" She lifted to where they no longer touched before setting back down on him.

She didn't say anything, but the gleam in her eyes worried him. "We should go—" he began before she crushed his lips in a begging kiss. He froze, wanting to do everything while knowing they couldn't. Ellen ran her hands up his chest to the top button of his shirt. Before he knew it, she had the entire garment unbuttoned. He grabbed and held a hand. She moaned in protest and he understood her frustration. He broke away first, wincing when she kissed his ear and down to the hollow of his throat. "We can't do any more than this."

"Just indulge me in a few kisses. I want to feel your skin again."

"Again?" he croaked before clearing his throat. "We should wait until Oregon, married, new home…." Words were difficult at the moment, with her lips halfway down his torso. Ellen was an innocent; surely she didn't mean to continue to his beltline? He took her by the shoulders and lifted her up from what she was doing. "*Mon amour*, you're not making it easy for me to resist you."

"Would you say I'm making it hard?" She let her full weight fall on him where their hips met. "It feels like I'm making it very hard for you."

"You are. Why are you doing this?"

"I'm tired of waiting. Tired of telling us both no when we want to be together so much. We're alone for just a little while and I want to do all the things I regret not doing before Fort Hall." She whispered in his ear. "Please let me make love to you. I want you to love me like you say you do."

He took in a shuddering breath upon hearing this. Her hand caressed a path from his neck to his navel. Del wanted to roll her over and take her but resisted. She couldn't know what she was asking him to do. He gritted his teeth, determined to go slow and allow her to halt their progress if she chose. Her pushing his shirt from his shoulders made thinking even more difficult for him. Kisses shadowed fingertips and he closed his eyes. She followed him as he lay flat on his back.

"I suppose you're at my mercy?" Ellen asked against his skin.

"*Toujours*," he said without thinking before repeating in English, "Always." The warm springtime smell of her mixed with the pine surrounding them almost overpowered the sticks poking him in the back.

"I want to feel you." She tugged at his pants button.

With her attention focused on undressing him, he slid his hands under her skirt. From knees, to thighs, to hips, Del refrained from pulling her onto him just as she freed him from his fabric prison. His fingers dug into her skin as her fingers raked over his heated flesh. She settled back against him, their chests touching. Her hand still moved between them, exploring his length. He pulled her up to reach under her better. "My turn," he whispered in her ear and reached for her center. She was as ready for him as he was for her and he groaned. "You lead the way, *ma coeur*."

Ellen shifted to where her fingertips held just the end of him. He groaned at how snugly she held him, and Del wanted to take over. Later, he promised himself. There would always be later to tease until she begged and take her like the animal he wanted to be with her. She accepted him inside bit by bit. All of his self-control went towards keeping his hips from thrusting up into her. When she began to move her hand away from where they met, he said, "Not yet. Feel where we're joined."

She did and her gasp matched his when her fingertips brushed over them both. "Oh, Del. I want more of you." She began moving faster, taking in more and more until giving a pained gasp. "Ow, that feels wrong."

Del kissed the frown lines in her forehead. She didn't know it, but now she was all his. "It'll be better in a moment. Relax and let me work for you." He anchored his heels and began lifting into her. Moving his hands up, making sure her skirt covered their lovemaking, he held her to him for stability. "Ellen, reach between us again and feel where we join."

She did as he requested and buried her face in his neck. Her touch drove him insane. She too made little moans, echoing his own every time he bottomed out in her. Del couldn't think, the sensation of loving her overwhelming his mind. Closer and closer to the edge of satisfaction he neared and fought against it. He thought of chores, Pointed Nose, Jack, and Uncle Joe's death until she gave a little cry and pulsed around him. The ecstasy of completion overwhelmed Del. All he could do was hold on to her as his body took pleasure from hers. He kissed her lips, wanting to stifle them both from crying out during the release. When she kissed him as if ravenous, his body responded with harder throbs. At last, Ellen went limp against him, her body giving him a little squeeze every few seconds, that being the only motion she made. He sighed, lightheaded from the pleasure. "Thank you for such a gift, *ma coeur.*"

She didn't make a sound for a moment, not even to breathe, before a small keening moan escaped her. Del held her a little up to look into her eyes. He saw tears gathered in the lens of her glasses as she sobbed. Fear, shame, and regret filled him as he asked, *"Mon Dieu,* dearest, what's wrong? Are you hurt?"

CHAPTER 10

She gulped back tears. "Oh, Del." Her voice warbled far more than she intended. "I'm fine, wonderful." She relaxed against him, her ear pressed against his chest. Little waves still swept through her body. "I've never imagined something so perfect." She heard his heart beat.

"I'm glad."

"So am I." She'd not anticipated they'd be so damp afterward. They needed to leave, and yet she didn't want to ever leave him again. "I love you."

"Mmm," he nuzzled her hair. "I love you too and have missed you."

"It's been unbearable." Tears filled her eyes again and she sniffed. "I've tried to be a good daughter to my family and not long for you."

"Be bad, please?"

A little fissure of fear began in her heart. "I think I already have." She lifted to look him in the eyes. "We need to leave, separately, so no one suspects." Pushing up to sitting, she added, "You might need to clean up, um, down there."

He laughed. "I will." He reached into his shirt pocket. "*Voila! Le hiney rag pour tu.*"

"No! I'm not using that."

"It's yours. I keep it especially for you."

"Honest?"

"Yes. You might need a handkerchief, and do you have one now? *Non?*"

"I don't, and if you're sure it's clean?"

He laughed before tickling her chin. "It is."

"Thank you, dearest. I'll wash this before returning it." Ellen struggled to her feet, keeping her eyes averted for modesty's sake. "I miss you already."

"We've made it impossible to stay apart any longer."

"I agree." She peeked behind her to see him undressing. The shape of his body and toasted color of his skin created a hunger in her. Now that she knew how to sate this thirst between them, the desire became nearly unbearable. She faced away from him again, hearing him splash a little in the creek. "Del?"

"Yes, my love?"

She smiled at his English. "I'd like to be together again like we were." Ellen looked at him again and watched as he washed his pants. "I don't want to wait very long either."

"Neither do I." He grinned at her. "If not for the lateness already, I'd be willing to love you again."

"Oh! This soon?"

"This minute." He stepped out of the water, wringing his pants. "But no more. Clean up and go. We'll arrive at different times to avoid suspicion." While she washed, Del scrubbed the ground-in dirt from his shirt.

She went to the creek and waded in, shoes and all. She scooped up her skirt to keep it from getting too wet and began washing her tender parts. Aware of the silence, Ellen turned to see Del staring at her. The afternoon lovemaking taught her what the heated look in his eyes meant. Seeing how much he wanted her began a slow burn in Ellen's body as well and she smiled. If she didn't hurry and leave, they'd be intimate again. "I'll see you back at camp."

He took the newly washed handkerchief from her. "I hope so."

Before changing her mind, Ellen left, headed back down the path they'd followed along the creek. A little bit of regret settled in her stomach. She felt like a completely different person. Would everyone know just by her face? She'd been, for want of a better word, spoiled for less than an hour. Even so, she had no idea how to appear innocent. She passed Sam and couldn't help but blush. Had he known what would happen this afternoon? Ellen hoped not. He seemed more focused on his fishing than any passersby. She hurried on. The last thing she'd need was him teasing her in front of Pa. Even knowing how sensible her friend was, a mistake could always happen while joking around.

She slowed before reaching her family's wagon with the Bensons'. If Mrs. Benson spotted her, anything could happen. The woman might guess she was no longer innocent, or just as bad, put her in charge of the three boys. She never minded caring for her brothers, at least not most times, but Caleb Benson was a totally different story. He was a handful. As she approached, Ellen saw him sneak around their wagon with something hidden behind his back. Yesterday he'd pelted Skeeter with broken up biscuit chunks. Today might be anything else.

"Caleb!"

She cringed at Mrs. Benson's shrill voice. Never mind a glasscutter, let the woman screech and the job would be done. Pa was courting the widow with more fervor than he had Lucy. Ellen shook her head in dismay, dreading the rest of her life being like the last week or so.

"Ellen!" Mrs. Benson had her hands knotted into fists and at her hips. "Where have you been?"

A heartbeat of fear hit her like a knock to the funny bone. She knew it. The guilt beamed out, displaying everything to Lacy in an instant and soon to Pa. He'd horsewhip Del, probably do worse to her since she'd let a half breed have his way with her. "I was…went out…wanted to find berries. There were none so I didn't find any and so now I'm back and how are you?"

"Never mind that." She thrust a bucket of dirty clothes at Ellen. "We need these washed and dried. I'm tired of looking after Buster and Skeeter is a bad influence on my Caleb. Settle him down or I'll talk to your Pa about the boy."

"All right."

"Another thing, Buster has wet himself twice today and once is already too many times. I thought your father said the boy was potty trained? Did you tell him that and it wasn't true?"

"I—he was at one time." Little wonder Mrs. Benson fumed. Ellen grew tired of the baby's messes as well. "I mean Buster was potty trained. He still has accidents but not many."

"When you get done washing, let me know how many not many is, young lady. I think you'll be more accurate in your reporting next time." She waved her hands at Ellen. "Go. Get busy and get done. Do I have to lead you there?"

"No, ma'am." She walked to the river with gritted teeth. Pa and the boys might need a new woman in their lives, but Mrs. Benson wasn't the one for them. Ellen planned on having a talk with Buster to see why he was messing his pants again. He'd been such a big boy and really doing well, and this setback worried her.

Ellen scrubbed everything, an ache in her body reminding her of earlier in the afternoon. She smiled while wringing out a pair of pants. Thank goodness Mrs. Benson had been preoccupied with lecturing her. She shivered, remembering how Del had felt against her. If she defied Pa, and she was almost ready to do just that, marrying Del now sounded like heaven on Earth. Daydreaming about warm baths, slippery skin, and a hot husband gave her goose bumps as she worked.

The sun had been behind the western mountains for a while now. When she looked up from cleaning and saw how dark the sky had become, she rushed to finish washing the last shirt. More people in their family meant less time in the day. She stood and scooped up the damp clothes, ignoring how the handle on the bucket cut into her hand. Her stomach growled and Ellen hoped Mrs. Benson had thought to start dinner.

Reaching a cold and dark camp next to their wagons disappointed Ellen. Where was everyone? She sighed, knowing it didn't matter. Dinner would be late. Pa would be mad, and Mrs. Benson would be shaking her head at how Ellen hadn't taken care of the family like everyone expected. She glanced at the last bit of light in the sky. The clothes needed hanging but could wait so she set them down and rushed to collect firewood. While scooping up sticks, every little thing reminded her of Del: the soft ground under her feet, how the pine needles must have been uncomfortable for him, and how the sheltering trees hid them from everyone's view. She struggled to focus on her task instead of remembering how he'd felt against her.

Once done and back at camp, she found Pa and Lacy Benson a little ways back from the roaring fire. The three boys played with toy soldiers off to the side. Ellen laid the wood down by the wagon and stepped into the circle of firelight. "Good evening. Is dinner over already?"

"Not unless you ate it all," Pa replied. "Lacy wanted to start cooking. I wouldn't let her, sure you'd get in a snit if she did something wrong."

Ellen glanced at the dark sky. If she'd not been with Del, the beans and rice would have had all this time to cook. She had to think of something faster or they'd be eating breakfast instead of dinner. Deciding on thin sliced bacon with biscuits and jelly, she went to her family's wagon. "I promise, if Mrs. Benson ever honors us with her fine cooking, I'll be very thankful."

Pa stood, his fists clenched. "Are you getting smart with me?"

"Not at all. I really mean it. I've heard you tell us how well she cooks. I'd love any meal she has time to fix us."

Her words seemed to mollify him and he sat back down. Ellen watched from the corner of her eyes as she cut the meat and measured flour. She'd forgotten water and had very little light left to guide her. She tossed the bacon into a pan and set it on the waning fire. "If you'll excuse me for a moment." Pa waved an absent minded hand at her and she hurried to fill a jar with water.

She took a couple of spoons of bacon grease for the biscuits and soon they cooked alongside the bacon. The two families had shared supplies, trading sugar, preserves, beans, and rice between them. She smiled, thinking of how her brothers enjoyed the extra sweetness.

"You want to tell me why dinner is so late? Why I had to start the fire tonight?" He nodded at the wood she'd gathered. "Were you out in the forest, hiding from chores?"

Ellen had spent her time thinking about Del, not thinking of how to excuse being with him. "I, um, I'm not sure."

"You don't know what you were doing today?"

She started dishing out the food for everyone. "I do know, but kept so busy, I'm not sure where the time went."

"Jack, leave the poor girl alone. She's fixed us a nice supper, and looks like she washed clothes today." Lacy took her plate. "You're such a tease and I think she's taking you seriously."

"You're right, dear." Pa smiled at the older woman. "I'm just joshing her."

Both of them, she and her father, knew he hadn't been joking. Ellen still enjoyed the reprieve from his badgering and gave the younger boys their dinners. Sitting down with her own, she realized how tired and sore her body was from earlier today. She missed Del. Missed his voice, his touch, everything about him. Their lovemaking was supposed to cure her curiosity and lust, yet hadn't.

Skeeter looked down at the full bucket. "There's clothes in here, sis. What do you want us to do?"

"Oh, goodness!" Ellen took a last bite and stood. "Hold up and I'll hang these right quick." She hurried to drape the clothes over the wagon's side and tailgate before Pa started scolding her. With the last shirt secure, she turned to Skeeter. "There! Now, let me have your dishes."

"Son, why don't you gather up all our dishes for your sister?"

asked Pa. Buster let out a howl and they all looked at the baby. "What the hell? What's wrong with you, boy?"

The child continued to scream, holding his arm. "Hurt me!" Pointing at Caleb, he said again, "Hurt me!"

The older boy held up his hands. "I didn't do nothing. We were just playing."

"Ellen, take him with you." Pa shouted above the baby's crying and waved them off. "Go on and let him wail somewhere else. Don't come back until he's done."

She nodded, knowing he'd not hear anything she said, and scooped up Buster in one hand and the dish bucket in the other. He rested against her hip, his head against her shoulder. "Come on, sweetie." Too late she realized he'd peed his pants. Ellen gritted her teeth as she went to the creek with him. Now everything she wore was wet. Buster had nothing dry to wear either. "What's wrong, Buster? Hmm?" She settled in. "Tell me all about it while I clean you."

"Clebs hurt me." He pointed to his upper arm. "Hurt me here."

"He hurt you?"

The little boy nodded. "Uh huh."

"I'm sorry to hear that. I'm sure it was an accident and he didn't mean to." Stars shone in the night sky, and Ellen didn't like being this far away from camp in the dark. She could tolerate a wet spot until the morning and fresh clothes, but Buster was soaked. "Let's get you cleaned up first." She took off his pants and diaper, laughing when he jumped around, enjoying his nakedness. The small clothes took little time to rinse and wring. Her hands stiff from the cold water, she put her hand near his hurt. "This will help." She placed her chilled fingers over the place he'd said Caleb hurt him. The skin underneath his shirt felt warm, but then anything would with her hands so cold. "Better?"

"Uh huh."

"Good. Sit here and help me wash dishes." They made quick work, her scrubbing, Buster putting everything she gave him in the pail. She watched as he put the last fork in the bucket. "Now, what to do with you and me?" She struggled to her feet, limbs stiff from the rapidly cooling air. "Let's go, sweetie."

Buster took her offered hand. Back at camp, everyone was already in their bedrolls. Her little brother ran to his and snuggled in, grinning back at Ellen. Grateful that either Pa or Lacy had helped her with the task, she draped Buster's clothes and settled into her bed.

Del. She missed him now, in the quiet. He'd been so strong inside her, and now with nothing else distracting her, she needed him again. She turned over to lie on her belly, forehead resting on the crook of her elbow. If they'd made love any time before today, the wait until this afternoon would have been unbearable. Ellen stifled a frustrated groan. Even if he pulled her away into the darkness this instant, it didn't feel soon enough to her hungry body.

"Sis." Buster patted Ellen's head. "Sis."

She didn't open her eyes. It'd been far too late before her body let her mind sleep and she wasn't in the mood. "No, Buster. Find someone else."

"Sis." He tapped her again. "Peedy bed."

Ellen pulled the blanket over her head. "Tell Pa."

"Sis. Peedy."

She came out from under the covers to find everyone else still asleep. Daylight spread light rays across the sky. "All right, Buster. You need to remember to pee like Skeeter showed you and not in bed or in your pants. Understand?"

Her little brother lifted his chin and let out a long, loud wail. Ellen fought with her blankets, unable to get to him and cover his mouth before he began crying again.

"What the hell? Shut that kid up, Ellen."

"Sorry, Pa." She took the baby by the arm. "Bus, come on, Bus, don't cry." He opened his mouth again and let out an even higher pitched scream.

"God damn it all to hell!" Pa got to his feet. "I'm taking care of the animals and if that kid isn't shut up and happy by the time I get back, there'll be hell to pay."

Ellen scooped up the baby and hurried to his soaked bedding. He began squirming to get down, peeing again. She gasped when the warm wet spread through her dress, wondering how much water one child could hold. "Enough, Buster Winslow, enough." She wiggled him a little to get his attention, and he paused his wails. "Stop crying this instant. There's no sense in it. Let's get you and the clothing washed."

He stared at her with large eyes, snot bubbling from his nose. She hurried to the creek, not caring when the blankets dropped in the mud. Ellen worked to keep her voice even and anger free. "The water will be cold, all right? Just let me clean you up and you can get Skeeter or Mrs. Benson to dress you." She waded out, the creek icy, and gave him a quick dunk to his waist. His scream in her ear as she lifted him didn't surprise Ellen as much as hurt her eardrum. "Stop, Buster! I know it's bad, but settle down." He didn't, instead squirming to be let down. When he began kicking her, Ellen almost dropped him before putting him at the river's edge. "Go, already."

As he and his naked butt ran back to the camp, she shook her head. She'd be surprised if anyone within a five-mile radius had slept through the commotion. Ellen waded further out, not blaming her baby brother in the least for screaming at the cold. She went as far as her knees before scooping water over yesterday and today's wet spots. The dress needed a good cleaning, but that'd have to be later. Her teeth chattered, and not even vigorous washing of Buster's blankets warmed her back up.

Wet skirts and heavy fabric made the walk back difficult. She met others on their way for water, every one of them wearing a slight scowl. Then, she saw Del as he approached with a bucket. Her heart thudded in her chest. She'd do anything and say anything if he'd kidnap her like Pointed Nose had. For a few days alone with him, before they'd have to double back and bring the boys. She'd miss them too much to leave for good, even with Del.

"Good morning," he said.

His voice did all sorts of things to her. "Good morning, Mr. Du Boise. It's a pleasure, as always."

"Likewise. Washing so early?"

"Afraid so. Buster."

He chuckled. "I heard."

Another few people passed them, all glum. Her chin dipped as the waves of their anger reached her. "I'm so sorry. He's not cantankerous very often, but I suppose today was his day."

"He's a baby, and that's what they do." He glanced at her hands. "You've not started coffee?" She shook her head and he continued. "Wait a moment." He hurried off to fill the container and bring it back to her. "Take this and bring it back to Sam while your coffee brews."

She smiled, his thoughtfulness bringing tears to her eyes.

"Thank you, Del."

"Non, no crying and no thanks. I'm merely helping another family in our group."

Ellen nodded, wiping her cheeks and leaving only after he did. A fire burned at camp due to the firewood she'd gathered last night. Lacy shook the pan of bacon and glanced up at her. "Oh, good! You thought to bring water. Only, where did that bucket come from?"

"It's one of Sam's. I met one of his men down at the creek and he suggested I take it. Seems he'd gotten too much water for them, saw I'd forgotten our bucket, and made me bring it to camp." Lacy had gone on with adding water to the flour and then to the coffee beans. Ellen couldn't stop explaining to her, and the older woman looked up as she continued. "For us, you know, so that we could have coffee and such. I'm supposed to take whatever water is left back to Sam and his people." A knowing look dawned on Lacy's face and Ellen panicked over what she suspected. "So if you don't use all of it, I'll just do that."

"Certainly. I'm sure Arnold or Lefty might not mind seeing you again." She patted the ground next to her. "Have a seat and tell me all about the young man."

Ellen grinned at how easily a crisis had been averted. "I'd love to, Mrs. Benson, but I am freezing."

"Oh my! Of course, go change into something dry. I don't know where your Pa is for sure, and the boys are out gathering firewood. I sent them off to be rambunctious somewhere else." She waved Ellen away. "I'll keep lookout so you can switch dresses in private."

"Thank you, Mrs. Benson."

"Lacy, remember?"

"I'll try," Ellen said with a smile that faded as soon as her back was turned. She just couldn't be so familiar with the woman. Lacy and Lucy's names were too similar and she still mourned her stepmother, even if Pa didn't seem to. She scooped up her other dress from the wagon wheel and climbed aboard to change. The fabric felt stiff and cold against her, but the thoughts of seeing Del again this morning kept her warm. She buttoned the first few buttons, wondering how he'd react if with her right now. A shiver went through her when she remembered the lust she'd see in his eyes yesterday. This morning had been less intimate, but then a crying child would dampen anyone's desire. She grinned at how sexy he'd looked with his messy hair and shirt askew.

She climbed down, brining the damp dress with her. "I'll wash this and anything else you'd like, Mrs., um, Lacy."

"Thank you, Miss, um, Ellen."

Ellen grinned at the teasing. "Sorry, old habits and all."

Caleb and Skeeter came running up, pushing each other and yelling, "Tag, you're it," every other second.

"Boys!" hollered Lacy. "Settle down now and eat!" They stopped in their tracks for only an instant before doing as she'd ordered. Ellen gave Lacy the plates, and she dished up the food for all three boys. "Go ahead and get started. Jack will be here soon, and I'm sure he won't mind."

Ellen disagreed, worried Pa would be furious they ate without him, but kept quiet. She pushed around the food on her plate but didn't take a bite. A glance at Buster showed he was wearing pants, thankfully still dry. He gnawed at a biscuit in one hand and a chunk of bacon in the other.

Pa came up like a black cloud over all of them. "Granville says we're leaving early today, so it's just as well Buster screamed us awake. He says the road is through timber and rough. It'll be a while to get to good water, like every other day." He sat and took the coffee Lacy poured for him, adding, "Don't know why he thought fit to tell us that."

Ellen kept quiet, eating without a word. Lacy chatted with him and he was cordial enough with her, but Ellen didn't take the chance. Her silence meant no outbursts from him. She exchanged a glance with Skeeter and knew he felt the same way. As soon as Pa took his last bite, she began gathering plates and utensils, careful to not make him feel rushed. She waited, moving slower until ready for him. Sure enough, he handed her his dishes. "Mighty fine meal, Lacy. You're the best cook I've ever known."

"Why, thank you, Jack. I do appreciate it." She smiled at Ellen. "Dear, you don't mind washing up this once, do you?"

"Of course not, Mrs. Benson." She returned the smile and put everything gently into the wash bucket. Making a racket might lead Pa to believe she was angry and thus trigger his own temper. "I'd be glad to if it means a meal like that more often." She almost curtsied before hurrying to the river. Ellen struggled to keep a grin on her face while washing up. The meal hadn't been anything remarkable. Arguing with her father would trigger a tantrum, and she just didn't have the guts for that this morning. She hurried to clean everything, wanting enough time to return Sam's water bucket and refill theirs too.

Soon done and the dishes back in the wagon, she refilled both pails and dropped theirs off at the wagon. Everything seemed quiet. Ellen backed away, working hard to not hurry over to Sam's wagon to see Del. His camp was more active, the men running to and fro. Marie spotted her first and waved.

"Ellen! How wonderful! Sam said you'd be bringing the pail back." She peeked inside. "And full of water. Aren't you thoughtful?" Taking the pail, she set it down next to a wagon wheel.

"I'd thought you might need the water as well, since Sam recommended we bring some along." She glanced around the camp, hoping to catch sight of Del.

"He's not here."

"Hmm?" Ellen pretended not to know what she was talking about, but Marie's expression told her she'd failed in doing so. "Oh, well, I'm sure he's busy."

"He is, and he'll also be unhappy he missed you."

The knowing grin on the other woman's face made Ellen's face burn. "Well, I suppose I'm glad about that." Not knowing what to do, she wrung her hands. "Pa and Lacy are expecting me back. Buster probably needs his diaper changed or something so I'll be going."

"I'd have you stay, but Del is up front today and you've already missed him."

"See? No need for me to stay." She gave a little wave and rushed back to her family just as Lucky's bugle sounded. Hurrying, she poured a jar full of water before hanging the pail on a nail as the wagon began rolling. Ellen scooped up Buster and began following the wagon train. The baby had been heavy back at Fort Hall but by now, not so much. His clothes seemed tighter on him, reassuring her he'd been eating enough. She smiled at his wriggle to be let down. "Fine, but stay with me, all right?"

He let out a whoop when his feet hit the ground and ran in circles around her. She envied the baby his energy. Buster played hide and seek with her, running ahead whenever she'd catch up to him. Soon enough, he wanted to be carried for the rest of the afternoon. They walked through timber most of the day, following the group. No one stopped for a midday meal. Ellen and Buster made do with drinking as much fresh spring water as they wanted. When her brother was bent over the small creek, she fretted about not bringing a spare set of diapers for him. "Buss, it's going to be important to tell me when you need to go potty."

He looked up at her, wiping his face. "I can, sis." Patting her arm, he added, "I can tell you."

"Tell me before you need to go, all right? Not after. Promise?" He nodded and she smiled at him. "Then let's go and catch up."

"Carry?"

"Sure." She hoisted him up and let him sit on her hip. They left the woods and she liked being better able to see the mountains to the north and west. Ellen thought back to the home they'd left behind in eastern Missouri. Right now, all her friends would be sitting in a humid heat, fanning themselves. She breathed in deep as a cool wind swept the high meadow. The afternoon sun almost heated her to a sweat, kept at bay by the breeze. She'd seen old oaks creating a high umbrella of branches at home. The tall pines poking above the deciduous trees here were higher than anything she'd ever seen before. If she were less of a lady, she'd try to climb one just to see if she could.

The day grew later and yet they'd not stopped. She helped her brother with his bathroom needs as requested, giving him as much privacy as his inexperience would allow. Lucky's bugle sounded, giving them the signal to camp for the night just as the sun dipped behind storm clouds on the western horizon. "Oh, thank goodness! Buster! Let's gather up whatever wood we can find for dinner tonight."

None of the scrub brush seemed good for burning, especially not after the woods they'd left, so she and her brother had nothing in hand as they approached the Granville party. Plenty of willows and other thin leaved trees lined the Umatilla River, so she hoped they'd find something. Seeing her family's wagon, she hurried over to find Pa and Lacy there. Her father worked to start a fire while his new friend watched.

Buster slid down, having become dead weight in her arms. He ran up to his father. "Pa! I'm a big boy today!"

"Yeah?" Their father didn't look up from his work. "Good

deal. Now be a bigger boy and help your sister get supper ready for us."

Ellen recognized the edge in his voice. She held out her hand to Buster. "Pa's right. Help me."

He gave her a surly pout and shook his head. Before Ellen could begin arguing with him, Caleb and Skeeter came up, pushing and shoving each other. Like watching a slow motion disaster, she saw the Benson boy push her brother into Pa. The action interrupted their father's struggle to start a fire. He grabbed a hold of Skeeter and threw him like his son was a rag doll. The child landed several feet away and skid a little to a stop. As calm as though nothing had happened, Pa went back to starting a fire.

They all stood or sat statue still. Buster slid behind his sister. Some in the group were in shock, but others like Ellen and Skeeter were too afraid of causing more temper to erupt from their father. Only when certain his anger was done for the moment did Ellen go to her brother and pull him to his feet. In a soft voice, she said, "Come help me start mixing and such." He stood to the side as she let down the tailgate and began pulling ingredients from the back. She didn't know or care where the Benson wagon was. They could provide breakfast tomorrow. All Ellen wanted now was a decent dinner without a major outburst tonight.

"Do we need water?" Skeeter asked her, eyes big. "Should I take Buster?"

"Yes to both, but keep a sharp eye on him. It's getting dark." She noted his nod as he took the pail and their brother to the water. Thinking ahead, soaking beans and rice overnight might mean a good breakfast tomorrow. But now they'd have to settle for biscuits and salted pork. She peeked around the wagon to see her brothers coming back. "Here, give me the water and go sit. Try to be quiet," she said in a soft voice meant only for them. Ellen soon had biscuits mixed up and ready for cooking.

"I know!" said Lacy. "Let's have tea while Ellen cooks dinner. I have some in our wagon." She hopped up and went to retrieve the fixings.

"Sounds good." Pa looked at Ellen and nodded in Lacy's direction. "You could take lessons in how to be a proper lady from her. Maybe she'll get you a refined man for a husband instead of those lowlifes you seem to like."

"Maybe so," she agreed. Or maybe, Ellen added to herself,

she'd just wait until Pa was so attentive to Lacy that he'd not notice when she ran off with Del. She placed the pan on the fire grate. Wishful thinking was all that was, considering her father would notice and she couldn't just leave her brothers like that. She glanced at them to see the boys settled in opposite from their father. Out of arm's reach was a good idea and she stopped short of nodding in approval.

"Here I am!" Lacy stepped into the firelight. "This is exactly what we need to feel human again, don't you think?" She didn't wait for an answer but began preparing the small cookpot and tealeaf strainer. "Now then, all I need is water. Caleb? Skeeter? Water please?"

Skeeter hopped up. "Yes, ma'am. I'll get it." He hurried over to Ellen and she handed him the pail.

She saw Caleb's leg stuck out to trip Skeeter and over the boy went before Ellen could squeak a warning. Water from the pail went out in an arc, splashing down onto supper and some of the fire. The pan hissed, as did the embers, steam rising up into the night. Skeeter got up off the bucket. "Sorry, Pa," he said while trying to straighten out the bent metal. "I guess I tripped."

"You guess?" Pa stood. "I'd say you did and you ruined Miss Lacy's tea. Our dinner is soaked, and now most of the wood is wet. We're getting nothing tonight and it's all thanks to you." He stepped up to the boy. "If we'd not had to wait on your good for nothing sister, dinner might have been a little earlier. Early enough so's you'd not ruin it with your goofing off."

Ellen glanced at the food, seeing the water was already boiling away. She eased over to the pan and flipped the biscuits over so they'd not burn. A little stir of the bacon and she sat down on a dry patch of dirt.

"I don't want to look at either of you. Go on, get out of my sight for a while."

"Now, Jack, there's no need to be upset. I'm sure Caleb would be glad to get more water for our tea, and look." She nodded at the food. "Our dinner is almost ready. Looks like nothing is too far gone, and we'll have a nice treat before bed." Her son came up and carefully gave his mother the bucket. "Thank you, dear." She filled the teapot. "Dinner smells wonderful, and I'm sure Ellen's almost ready to pass out our plates so we can dish up, isn't that right, dear?"

She nodded, glad Mrs. Benson could calm down Pa. Ellen hurried and soon everyone had a plate of food. She half listened to the older adults talk about the Winslow children as if they weren't there. She expected the useless older daughter talk, but the "Skeeter is a problem" refrain was new. She glanced at her younger brother, but he wasn't looking anywhere but his half full plate. Checking on Buster showed he sported a huge wet spot in his pants. Ellen swallowed, hoping she could get the baby down to the water and cleaned up before her father noticed and complained.

Pa continued on his speech, this time not stopping with what had been wrong with Ellen's mother and now with her. He went on to include Lucy and the boys. Ellen gritted her teeth when she saw Skeeter's stricken look. She bent to say only to him, "One more bite, then we'll leave him to it."

"I can't. I'm not hungry."

She saw how little he'd eaten and had to prod him a little. "Just one more?"

He did as she'd asked, chewing slow and swallowing as if his throat wouldn't cooperate. "You'll need help with Buster, won't you?"

"Afraid so. You take him and the dishes, and I'll get him clean clothes, all right?"

Skeeter nodded and grabbed hold of Buster's hand. "Let's go, Bus, and play in the water."

The adults and Caleb watched without comment or interrupting Pa. Ellen took the chance to gather plates and the baby's fresh clothes.

"Ellen, you must have tea with us."

"I'd love to, Mrs. Benson, but it'll be cold by the time I get back. Please, enjoy some for me and I'll have some next time for sure."

"Very well," said Lacy, giving her a little wave.

She escaped to the river, the darkness making it seem inky black. Skeeter sat on the bank, silently crying. Buster clung to him, trying to pull his brother's forehead off his knees. "No cry, Skee. No cry."

"Hey, Skeeter, come on." Ellen sat beside him, putting her arm around his shoulders. "You know how Pa is. He's just angry and wanting to complain about everything. My mom was wonderful, yours was too. He misses them so much, it's better to say he hates them instead." Skeeter didn't react, but his sobs stopped. Buster still leaned against him. Ellen reached out to pat her youngest brother. "Bus, try playing in the water without your pants."

She shook her head as the boy stripped down to just his shirt and ran to the water. His love for the cold amazed her. She tried not to laugh at his jumping in a bit at a time. He danced around, slipping and landing on his butt once. The river's edge was shallow enough that all three of them laughed. She had to get him out of there soon, or he'd stir up enough dirt to make mud. "Come on, let's get dressed. You don't want to freeze to death."

He ran up the bank to her, teeth chattering. The sound made him laugh until the chattering resumed. While he and Skeeter had fun listening, Ellen got him dressed and ready for bed. She hugged him to warm him up. "Listen, Buster. If you need to go potty, wake me and I'll take you. All right?" Feeling him nod while shivering, she chuckled. "Another thing, if you mess the bed, just wake me up with your quiet voice and I'll fix it. No yelling."

"My quiet voice?" he asked in a loud, whispery tone.

"Quieter."

"Is this quiet?"

"Perfect. If you wake only me up and no one else, I'll give you a prize." She gave him one last hug before letting him go. "Now run along and help Skeeter set up our beds."

The younger boy froze. "What if I make a mistake?"

"Just keep the blankets away from the fire and you'll do just fine. Stay away from Caleb's feet too. I think he likes tripping people." She grinned. "You'd better hurry or Buster will have it all done for you."

He hopped up and followed the child back to camp. Not even starlight gave her enough light to wash by. She rinsed Busters clothes and cleaned the dishes by touch until the cold water numbed her fingers. It'd have to do and she could always wipe them in the morning. She gathered up everything for the return to camp. Pa and Lacy sat together, their bedrolls side by side. All the boys were in bed already, the Winslows asleep. Ellen set everything in its place and slid into bed before Pa or Lacy could draw her into a conversation. The day had been too long and her father's temper too quick for her to play nice now.

Tap, tap.

"Sis."

No, not yet, she thought, still wrapped up in a dream. The apricots were ripe and warm. She didn't want to stop eating them now. Another few taps from Buster pulled her away and into consciousness. "Yes, sweetie?"

"Didn't pee."

She grinned at how he used his quiet voice. "Very good! I promised you a prize, didn't I?" He nodded, his eyes big. She sat up. "Let's see, what's a good prize for you?"

"Toy?"

"Oh, that's a good idea. I'll make you a new toy. Is there anything in particular you want?"

He nestled in beside her. "A lil brother."

Ellen wanted to retch. Pa and Lacy having another child would keep her from leaving with Del. She wanted anything but that. "A little brother? Why?"

"I'm a big boy. Big boys have lil brothers."

She laughed, putting a hand over her mouth so no one would hear. "You're right. You need a little brother. He may be really little, but I'll make you one."

"Now?"

"I'll start work on it today."

He gave her a hug. "Thank you, sis."

Ellen grinned when he went back to his bedroll and got in under the covers. A new day's dawn spread across the sky, guaranteeing she'd get no more sleep. Everyone else except her and the baby slept, so she crept about, getting beans and a pail for coffee. She managed to see everyone on the way to the river and back without catching a glimpse of Del. Despite her efforts, the noise of breakfast woke her family and friends. Soon they were all awake and tending to first of the morning chores.

Her mental note to soak beans and rice overnight had slipped her mind. Pa wouldn't like a repeat of last night's dinner for breakfast, she guessed. Sure enough, when he complained and groused, she tuned him out. The bugle sounded as she washed up. Skeeter helped her fold the last bedroll while the other adults readied the oxen for travel. The three boys ran off to find friends, Buster toddling behind. Ellen thought about seeking out company from Jenny or Marie but didn't feel hospitable enough for polite company.

She looked around at the rolling hills stretching out in every direction and realized she hated Oregon Territory so far, hated everything: the too blue sky, the never-ending sage, and the rolling flat of it all. The forests of less than a week ago had spoiled her. The shade and just the comforting canopy of leaves had felt a lot like home. Now, she was back in the wide nothing of a high desert. She wanted to write her friends, telling them to enjoy the moist heat. The cold dry stung her eyes and burned her nose.

Ellen kicked at a dead sagebrush in despair. She'd never be able to swim in warm water, just the ice baths of rivers and such. A warm bath meant heating up water by the buckets. That was a waste. The bath would be stone cold by the time she'd dump the last bucket of hot water into it. She stared ahead, wondering when something might break up the monotony. Scanning the horizon didn't help. Del was nowhere around, and even if he were, she couldn't hold or even talk to him without someone seeing and riling up Pa. It might have been better if they'd not made love in the woods. Then, she'd not know now what she was missing.

The river provided a bit of interest in an otherwise gently rolling plain, but only a bit. The day passed quickly, mainly because they stopped hours early. For most of the way, a long sloping canyon had kept them a good distance from the Umatilla River. They found a wide flood plain to camp on. The slope there was easy enough to lead the animals down and assemble the wagons in their half circle. She hurried to her family's wagon, glad to see some sort of scrubby trees growing along the river.

Lacy saw her. "Oh, there you are! Buster needs changing and you'll need to start the soak for dinner. I have other errands to tend to, so if you'll excuse me?"

Ellen nodded as if she'd had a choice. Mrs. Benson being with them and sharing her provisions was a blessing, even if it meant dealing with Caleb. She tried to pin down why she disliked him but couldn't. It didn't matter. Pa liked the boy's mother and that was that. She smiled at a worried Buster. "An accident, huh?"

He stared at the ground. "Yeah. I don't get my brother?"

"You do get him, just a little later when I'm done with chores, all right?"

"Yay!"

"No, no cheering just yet. Let's get you cleaned up." She

chuckled when he ran to the river as if chased by a bear. She grabbed his spare clothes and a water pail. Soon he was clean and the beans and rice were soaking for dinner. "How about you help me gather firewood? It's what the older boys do too."

He let out a whoop and ran ahead. They passed others in their group and then some who they'd seen intermittently on the trip. This looked like a popular camp. She fretted a little, hoping she and Buster might find enough fuel for dinner tonight and maybe breakfast tomorrow. They wound their way through the trees. She wondered if being in a grove would always remind her of Del. Probably so, because everything else seemed to. With a bit of a start, she realized they were walking along a riverbank lined with washed up wood. "Bus, stay with me. There's plenty here for us."

Buster turned around and ran back to her. While today hadn't been a long one, she still felt yesterday's miles in her bones. Soon, she and her brother had as much wood as they could carry. Others saw them and headed off to gather their own fuel, leaving her grateful they'd been there first.

Before too long, she had a fire built and the pot sitting on the grate. Her chores being done so soon left her at loose ends. She'd forgotten what to do when having nothing important looming ahead in the day. Ellen glanced at Buster. She'd promised him a toy and it'd been a while since she'd written anything in her journal. She climbed in the wagon to retrieve her sewing kit, rags, and the journal.

"Ellen!"

Pa's voice right outside startled her. She peeked out of the back. "Yes, Pa?"

"There you are! Dinner ain't gonna be late tonight, is it? I don't like starving to death."

"It's not." She hopped down. "See? It's already cooking."

"Hmm." He leaned over, peering into the cook pot. "As long as it doesn't take all night to cook up...."

"It won't, I promise." She almost crossed her fingers behind her back. Promising meant something random would happen to knock everything into the fire, have dirt thrown in the pot, or any other minor catastrophe. Lacy walked up just then, taking Pa's attention from Ellen. She tried not to listen as they gossiped about people in Lacy's former group that she'd never met. Being left out didn't bother her. It seemed to her that Pa would be marrying the woman soon enough. She hoped to be out of the house by the time Lacy threw socials or some other such events.

Ellen retrieved her bedroll and laid it out next to her supplies. She sat and leaned forward to stir the food before settling back down. Socials sounded fun in a way, especially if Pa wasn't there. She loved her father, but feared him more. Something about the frontier had led him to hit her more times in front of others than he'd done in her entire life. She pawed through the rags, looking for light cloth for the face. Ellen smiled. Or maybe a beautiful toasted bread color like Del. She could use Mrs. Benson's tea to stain white muslin.

And then watch as Pa threw a fit about the skin color. She shook her head, searching for the lightest possible cloth. It was better to make the baby as close to Buster as possible. Ellen spent the afternoon sewing patches together enough to make a deflated body with flattened limbs and head attached. She'd look up every so often when someone walked by or one of her family members needed something out of the wagon. The break gave her a chance to stretch and stir the food. Each time, she took a hard look around, hoping to see Del.

Both families of Winslows and Bensons gathered around, staring at the food. Pa and Lacy chatted in quiet tones. Ellen tried to not listen in and the boys made it easy by being loud and playful. She bit the last thread, careful to put the needle back into the pincushion. Holding out the doll, she smiled. The toy didn't look too bad at all. All it needed were eyes, a mouth, and nose. She stood, stretching her stiff legs. She exchanged the sewing kit and rags for dishes, passing them out to everyone.

Pa helped by serving up everyone's dinner. Ellen smiled. She was glad he was in a good mood and playing gracious host. She glanced over at Lacy. Despite her sometimes sharp tongue, the woman had been a benefit to them for sure. Ellen welcomed her provisions, the extra ox, and her distracting Pa. She took the plate from her father. "Thank you."

He gave her a regal nod and dished himself up last, setting the cook pan aside to cool for washing. In between bites, he gave them a monologue of his day. Certain words would capture her attention. She'd listen for a while, realize she didn't know whom he was talking about, and go back to eating her dinner. Maybe she should pay better attention for the journal's sake, but that was just not possible. All the names ran together, and she was far more interested in the food. A couple of days without beans and rice made dinner a lot tastier than what it had been. Or maybe it was the extra salt she'd added. Either way, dinner was much better tonight than usual.

"I see you have your journal. About time you started updating it again."

"Sorry, Pa. I've been distracted with getting Buster into big boy pants."

"No excuse. Be sure to add in all the days you missed."

"I will, I promise."

At the word "promise," Buster looked over at her. "Sis! Where's my toy?"

Ellen grinned at him and brought the doll out from under her bedroll. "Right here!"

The boy's eyes were huge in his little face, his amazement clear. "My own little brother!" He reached for the toy and hugged it to him. "I want his name to be Buster too."

Caleb laughing got everyone's attention. "You have a dolly? You're a boy with a girl's dolly!" He nudged Skeeter. "You didn't tell me you had a little sister, Skeet. She's pretty."

Buster's lip pouted. "I'm not sister, I'm brother."

"Nope," Skeeter retorted. "You're my little sister now."

Before Ellen could react, Buster threw the doll into the fire. Sparks flew, several landing on Lacy's dress. She screamed, jumping up, dumping her food, and brushing the tiny embers from her dress. All Ellen could do was stare at the mess with her mouth agape. Of all the reactions Buster might have, she never expected this one.

"What the hell!" Pa ran over to Lacy. "Sweetheart!" He helped brush off imaginary cinders. "Calm down, you're fine." Taking her in his arms, Jack held her. "There, there, dear, it's all over now. Nothing happened."

She pulled away from him. "Excuse me? Something did in fact happen. Look at my dress." Lacy held out her skirt. "It's ruined, thanks to your hellions."

Ellen saw Pa turn to Buster. The expression on her father's face scared her, and she stepped in between the two. "Pa, it was an accident. Buster didn't think what he was doing."

"Yeah, but you could have!" He gripped her arm. "What were

you thinking, giving the boy a doll? What do you think he is, some sissy girl?" Before she could say anything, he gave her a little shove. "Go on, start chores and get out of here. I don't want to see you before morning and if that means you skulk around all night until I'm asleep, so be it."

She picked up the dish bucket. Arguing would get them all in bigger trouble. Better to just let him play hero to Mrs. Benson and hide until everyone was asleep. She headed to the river, unable to enjoy the glorious sunset spreading out in front of her. The water reflected the brilliance. The beauty and mix of warmth from the ground and cool air calmed her. Washing up took very little time. She had the rest of the evening light free, but what to do?

No one else was there. The livestock had been swum over to an island in the river. Most of them grazed while others rested. She regretted not having pockets to keep her journal in. The twilight glowed bright enough to write at least a page before dark. They'd need firewood tomorrow. She might as well see what could be gathered before dark. For that, though, she'd need free hands. Ellen went closer to the wagons and left her pail in an easy to find place before heading to the thicket. Almost there, she heard a twig snap behind her. She turned and saw Del standing there with a broken stick. She chuckled. "Isn't part of your nature to be swift and silent?"

"Yes, just as it's yours to be sweet and beautiful." He stepped up to her.

Ellen could feel his uncertainty over reaching out for her as if his desire was a physical thing. "Del?" She melted into his arms, silent sobs overtaking her.

He held her close. "I heard him yell, but nothing else. He didn't hurt you?"

"No." She snuggled into him, realizing her arm didn't ache like usual. "Pa must be on his best behavior in front of Lacy."

He sighed. "If something happened to you, the earth would die before I'd love another woman."

She looked up at him. "That's easy to say when you're hugging me."

In a sudden movement, he kissed her. The swiftness startled her at first until the sweet warmth of him took over her senses. He groaned when she relaxed into him and she almost shivered. His lips held a trace of whiskey. A laugh escaped her. She pulled away and smiled. "No wonder the sweet words. You've been drinking."

"A sip when it was passed around and all it does is reminds me of how much I miss you."

Del's words felt like a cooling balm on inflamed wounds. "Maybe I should sneak some into your coffee every morning so you remember to miss me more often."

"Ah, that's not possible." He began kissing her cheek to her ear and whispered, "I miss you every minute of the day. I remember our afternoon together far too often for my own comfort." He traced his fingertips from her chin to her cleavage. "Whiskey merely loosens my lips and good sense, leading me to follow you into trouble."

His words reminded her of earlier. She glanced around, dismayed at how dark it'd become. "I suppose Pa has cooled off by now. I should go back to camp but would rather stay here and, um, be close again."

"*Mon Dieu*, so would I, but not in the dark on the ground. The next time is in a bed in our own home."

"Sounds heavenly but I don't want to wait that long." Ellen relaxed again, wanting to soak up all the love possible before returning to her family. She would have laughed if anyone implied such a strong man like Del could have made the whimper he did before kissing her again. He kissed her entire face as if memorizing her features with his lips. She chuckled when his lips pressed against the bridge of her glasses. "I suppose I'll want to remove them."

"One day, yes. But not right now." He gave her a squeeze before letting go of her only enough to hold her hand. "Now, we need to go. I'm on watch. Keeping you safe includes safe from me."

She followed him, amazed at how surefooted he was in the darkness. Del led them back to her dishes without a mishap. "I'd ask for another kiss, but…."

He swung her around and gave her one, quick on the lips. "Now go before I'm tempted anymore."

"If you insist." She picked up her pail, smiling at the forlorn expression on his face. "See you tomorrow?"

"Yes. Goodnight."

Ellen went to camp. She took a peek back to find him gone already. Emptiness settled into her heart. She placed the pail down gently so the plates didn't rattle anyone awake. She smiled seeing her bedroll ready. Skeeter must have done that, possibly against Pa's orders. He was the best brother. Both he and Buster made staying with them and away from Del a little more bearable.

"God damn it all to hell!"

Ellen woke with a start, almost leaping to her feet at Pa's shout. Her heart thudded in her chest so hard she felt the pulse in her fingertips. The others woke more slowly than her, the older boys wiping sleep from their eyes. Buster grunted and rolled over, away from the noise. Unable to decide whether to run or hide under her covers, she stayed rooted to the spot.

Lacy stretched, giving Pa a sleepy smile before asking, "What is it, darling?"

"It's your cattle. They're gone."

"Excuse me?" she said in a shrill tone and stood. "What do you mean MY cattle are gone? I thought you'd secured them on that island last night."

"I did. Yours aren't the only ones missing. Plenty of other livestock ain't there anymore. Some of Granville's men are out looking for them."

"Oh. Very well. As long as we're up, you might as well build a fire, Jack." Lacy motioned to Ellen. "You can fetch water for coffee while I start breakfast."

She nodded, going for the pail. As she left, Ellen heard Pa say, "Thanks for cooking, darling. Now we'll get something decent to eat."

After a calming breath, she brushed off the fear. Her body still quaked from Pa's yelling. Even with a full water bucket, Ellen didn't hurry back to camp. She wanted to see Del but knew he and Pomme would be with the men as they hunted down the wandering stock. She scanned the horizon for him but saw no one. Not even a stray emigrant wandered between them and the western horizon.

Everything at camp seemed to be fine as she approached. Lacy reached for the water, not interrupting Pa mid-story to ask outright. Caleb was the only boy there. She looked over at Buster's bedroll and smiled when seeing it dry. So that's where her brothers were. Maybe now the baby wasn't such a little boy.

"So, you going to stand there all day or help Mrs. Benson with breakfast?"

Pa's question broke her train of thought. "I'd be glad to help, of course."

"It's too late to do anything, looks like."

"Come on, Jack, don't tease the poor girl." Skeeter and Buster walked up before Pa could open his mouth, and Lacy took the opportunity to divert his attention. "Ellen, could you get us the dishes, please? Buster, you don't look happy. What's wrong, sweetie?"

Ellen gave everyone a plate, but Buster crossed his arms and not taking one from her. Skeeter took both dishes and replied for his brother. "He's mad about last night. His bed is dry but there's no toy like sis promised."

"Oh damn it, is that all he has to worry about?" Pa took his plate from Lacy. "I can find him some toy another kid dropped along the way." He pointed a fork at his youngest son. "Straighten up and stop this nonsense, or I'll give you something to be angry about."

Lacy held a full coffee cup out to Jack. "Dear, would you like sugar?"

"Sure, honey." He winked. "Maybe a spoonful or two."

"Very well." She measured and stirred his drink before giving it to him. "Ellen, how about you? Would you like some sugar in your coffee?"

Ellen looked at Pa then Lacy. "Um, no thank you. I like it plain, please." She took the steaming cup, not daring to look at her father. Had this been a test, something he and Mrs. Benson discussed before this morning? The Bensons had plenty of sugar, certainly enough to spare for coffee from here to Oregon City. Still, Ellen had been unnerved by this morning enough.

Half the morning passed before all the cattle were found. By then, she'd washed dishes and a few other things besides. Cleaning helped with her nervous energy and gave Buster clean clothes as well. Ellen smiled at the double success as Lucky's bugle sounded to start them rolling. They followed the river with its trees lining the banks for most of the day. Noon ended up being later than usual. For the first time since Fort Hall, she and the others saw real buildings. Some were homes, not military forts. Ellen slowed, wondering what sort of person could live out here in the wilderness. Civilization had to be closer than she thought, with so many ordinary houses here. A rush of motivation put a spring in her step just in time for them to stop after crossing the Umatilla River. She chuckled at how easy it was to cross. No capsizing, no one drowning, and she liked it that way.

They camped opposite an abandoned fort. Ellen agreed with Sam's decision, even if they had fewer trees to find wood under. Nearly everyone else stayed on the ruins' side, and she almost wanted to join them. She wanted to poke around in the foundations to see what sort of trinkets had been left behind. People and wagons milled around, obscuring the view from her sometimes. She shook her head. Nothing probably remained, thanks to all the scavengers before now. Ellen looked around for her family, wanting to make sure her brothers got something to eat before they continued on. The wagons pulled into their nightly semicircle as if camping there. She frowned, knowing it was too early for that.

"Ellen!"

She turned to see Marie waving at her. The leader's wife might know the plans for today. "Hello! Are we stopping for the night, then?"

Giving her a brief hug, she replied, "Yes. Sam says this is the best camp for the next thirty miles or so. He said something about a creek between here and the John Day River, but it's not reliable."

She walked with her friend and stayed quiet instead of arguing. Ellen would rather they press on from here and not waste nearly half a day. She had to concede that her impatience to marry Del clouded her judgment and that Sam might know better than her.

"He's just as unhappy as you about the delay."

"What? I didn't say anything."

Marie laughed. "You didn't have to, dear. It's all right. Del is still moping about having to wait an entire half day before moving on too." She patted Ellen's arm. "Your family is up ahead. Could you join us for dinner tonight? We've not talked properly in days and I miss you."

"I miss you too." She gave the woman a hug. "Yes, I'll be there tonight just because you asked me." Her friend's smirk made her chuckle. "Not for any other reason, much."

"All right. See you then."

With a little wave, Marie went to her husband's camp. Ellen

shook her head, still grinning over the other woman's perception. Sure, seeing Del was a motivation, but she missed her friend too. At her own family's wagon, Lacy stood at the tailgate with Buster.

"Ellen! Your brother wet himself again. I don't know where Skeeter is, probably out playing with Caleb." She motioned her over. "Come here and clean him up while I help Jack with the livestock."

She drew closer and Buster took the chance to jump into her arms. The wet from his clothes soaking into hers frustrated Ellen. She kept from grimacing; knowing her dress needed a good scrubbing anyway. "Do you and your son have washing for me to do too? I could be doing that while you all gather firewood."

"Oh, that's right. I think Jack wanted you to fetch wood this afternoon for us." Lacy patted her on the shoulder. "You have time and can gather while the clothes dry."

"Very well," she said while despairing of having any time with Del this afternoon. He'd understand how her family needed her. "I'll start by scrubbing down this little man." She scooped him up like a little sack of potatoes, pausing only to grab clean clothes for him. Pa's new woman was right, she thought while headed down to the river. Never mind her dress. She held the last clean diaper Buster had.

They did their usual ritual of him playing in the water and her washing his wet pants. By the time she was done, Ellen was drenched and Buster dry. She laughed as he ran up the bank. Her soaked skirt slowed her down and would until she could change into dry clothes too. No sense in doing so until everything was drip-drying. Soon, she had every surface used as a clothesline of sorts.

Ellen hopped into and secured the wagon before she shrugged out of her wet dress and into a dry one. Most of the people she'd seen with firewood had brought it up from the south. Exploring to the north while completing a chore sounded fun, especially when shaded by trees and serenaded by a river. She followed a path along the bank, picking up broken branches along the way. So absorbed in her task, she gave a little yelp when she noticed Del in front of her leaning against a tree.

"Hello, *ma coeur*."

Happiness bubbled out of her in a chuckle. "Hello, my handsome man."

He pushed off to walk up to her. "I like that." Nodding at her armload, he asked, "Do you need help?"

Looking down, Ellen realized she'd overloaded herself with branches and twigs. "I suppose so." He began unbuttoning his shirt and she swallowed. "Um, what were you doing out here and what are you doing now?"

Del laid his shirt on the ground, open with the sleeves outstretched. "I was hunting until a herd of buffalo in the form of one petite woman walked up to me. Now, I'm helping her carry wood back to her family." He smiled at her. "You act as if you've never seen me shirtless before. Place your bundle here and I'll tie it up for you."

"Oh." Her face burned because he was right. She had been staring. His skin was so smooth and she struggled to keep from touching him. Memories of how he felt in her arms wouldn't let her go. She put down the bundle, watching as he tied the sleeves. A slight reach out and she'd be able to run her fingers through his short black hair. "Del."

He straightened and pulled her to him, taking her lips with his. One of them moaned, but she couldn't be sure who. His arms wrapped around her body and trapped her against him. Ellen snuggled into him, running her hands down his bare back and up again. His lips left hers to trail down her throat and to her shoulder. He growled, "I could rip this from you right now."

"I could let you if I had a dress nearby." She grinned at the shudder sweeping him, glad to not be the only one suffering from such temptation. "We might only do what we did the last time we were alone."

Del paused only for a second on his way back to her ear. "You tempt me, *coeur*. But no, not today." He chuckled at her whimper. "I know and feel the same. This is a popular trail and we have no lookout."

She pulled away from him. "You mean Sam knew what we were doing? Del! I'm so ashamed."

"He didn't know exactly." He picked up her bundle. "I told him nothing, only that I wanted time alone with you."

"We're the only ones who…?"

"Yes, and I would keep it that way." Del led them back toward camp.

"So would I." She reached out and traced a finger down the

middle of his back; enjoying the goose bumps she gave him. "I care about my reputation, certainly, but also want you all to myself." He stopped in midstride and Ellen ran into him. "Oh! What's wrong?"

"Nothing. I just wanted your touch one last time."

Hidden behind his back, she kissed him between his shoulder blades. "Thank you."

"Could you hand this over to your family?" He held up the bundle. "Then run away with me?"

"I could, yes, but would you want a wife who found abandoning her family so easy to do?"

"*Merde.*" Despite the swear word, he grinned and gestured forward. "*Allons, mon amour,*" he said as they continued back to camp.

Ellen wanted to reach out and touch his skin again. The muscles underneath moved gracefully under the smoothness. She smiled, enjoying his tensed arm from behind as he carried her firewood. Too soon, they reached the clearing and she stepped up to walk beside him. "Marie has asked me to dinner this evening. I'm hoping you'll be there as well."

"I'd planned on it."

She grinned at him. "Will you be hunting or fishing for this evening?"

"That depends on what you w—"

"Stop right there!" hollered Pa.

They did as he'd ordered and Ellen gasped. Jack held a rifle that was aimed at Del's chest. "Pa, no! He was just helping me carry firewood."

"I know what he was helping you with, young lady." He pulled the hammer back two clicks. "Skeeter and Caleb told me everything. For an Indian, your lover isn't very good at noticing things." Pa took a couple of steps forward. "Like noticing where he's not wanted."

The bundle Del held between them kept Ellen from stepping in front. Pa might smack her around, but he'd never kill her in broad daylight. "Come on, Pa. The boys couldn't have told you about something that didn't happen. Mr. Du Boise was just helping me back to camp." She thought about leaping before deciding any sudden moves might itch his trigger finger. The rifle's hammer had clicked twice. A sneeze might fire the shot.

"What do you say, Mister Du Boise? Or do you let squaws

speak for you?"

Del's eyes narrowed. "No one speaks for me when I have a voice of my own. Miss Winslow merely stated facts. She needed help so I helped her."

Ellen glanced around at the crowd forming around them. Pa loved nothing more than an audience. Even worse, she saw a glint of light from a cap on his rifle. He wasn't making an empty threat, and she moved to get in front of Del.

"Here." He gave her the firewood. "Take this to your camp, now."

"No, I need to stay with—"

"Go." Del shoved the bundle at her and she stumbled a little.

Pa raised the rifle, eye to the sights. "Now then, it seems you need a little lesson that I mean what I say." Before Ellen could protest, Pa's rifle shot exploded in the summer air. The noise startled a scream from her. Del's eyes were closed until Jack began laughing. "Check his pants. See if he soiled them, Ellen. You're always cleaning up Buster. This big baby shouldn't be a problem."

She went to Del, holding him close. He wrapped his arms around her, slow as if forgetting how to move properly. Ellen rested her cheek against his clean chest and sobbed. Had Pa missed him entirely? Thanking God and every saint who would listen, she leaned back to look at his intact body. She glanced up at him and trembled. A hard fury had turned his face to granite. "Del, are you hurt?"

Sam walked up to them, Lucky and Arnold behind him. "What in hell is going on here? Are you shooting within sight of camp, Mr. Winslow? Tell me I didn't hear a rifle." He nodded at Jack's weapon. "Not this particular rifle."

"Yeah, it was me." Pa rested the butt of the gun against the ground, still grinning. "I just wanted to teach him a lesson to leave my daughter alone. Boys told me he and Ellen were kissing and I can't abide that."

Del cleared his throat before speaking. "He's a horrible shot. No wonder his family starves."

"Shows what you know. I don't have any powder or shot."

Giving his friend a warning glare, Sam stepped between the two. "Nevertheless, Mr. Winslow, no more shooting from so close to the camps. Not unless your life is in danger. Adelard, we need to talk." He looked at the bundle. "That's your shirt, I presume?" He motioned to Caleb and Skeeter before squatting to untie Del's shirt from around the firewood. "Boys? Take this wood back to your camp." Sam straightened and took a couple of steps over to Winslow. "I'd suggest you supervise your son for the moment. Build a fire, clean your rifle, do anything except let me see your face for the next couple of days, got it?"

Jack nodded, his face paling at the younger man's tone. "Yeah, I have chores to do anyway. Ellen, come on."

Sam shook his head and went to the couple. "She'll be there in a moment. I need to have a talk with her as well." He wiped his forehead with the back of his hand as Jack slunk off as ordered.

"Sam—" Del began.

"No, you don't need to explain or argue anything." He held up a hand. "I don't care what you were doing. You're both adults." He turned to Ellen. "Mostly adults, anyway."

"I am an adult, Mr. Granville."

"I understand that, Miss Winslow, but I can't have this sort of occurrence again. We're two weeks from home, and I'd rather not have a shootout among my people." He handed over Del's shirt. "And you. I'm glad he didn't kill you."

"Me too."

Sam ran a hand through his hair. "Del, you can't stay with us anymore. I don't want you to leave, but I can't have Winslow shooting at you. He didn't think to raid Mrs. Benson's wagon for buckshot, thank God, or you'd be dead right now."

He shrugged into his shirt. "I've never been so glad for someone's ineptitude."

"Me neither." Sam paused for a moment. "So, I'll see you in Oregon City?"

Del looked down at Ellen before nodding. "Yes, I'll be there."

"No," she whispered and then cleared her throat when tears filled her eyes. "I don't want you to go just yet."

"Could you come with me?" Del took her hand. "You know how well Pomme rides two."

She opened her mouth to say yes as a movement caught her eye. Skeeter and Buster came out from behind a wagon, a dark spot showing in front of his pants where the little boy had had an accident. A sob escaped her before she said, "I can't. They need me too much."

He glanced over at them and smiled. "I understand how that

feels. I need you too, but I can wait until you catch up." His chin trembled before he looked back at her. "Take care of yourself and them, please." He took her in his arms when she began crying. "*Mon coeur*, I know. *Je t'amie*. So much."

Ellen wiped her eyes and sniffled. "I love you too, Del. Promise me we'll find each other again."

"Of course we will." He leaned back from her and tilted up her chin. "Here you are with a wet face and no handkerchief, I'll bet." He took a soft cloth from his pocket and wiped her tears. "No, not a hiney rag and not yours to keep. You'll return it when we next meet."

She accepted his gift and gave him a watery smile. "It's rather small when I want a hug from you. This can't wrap around me like your arms do."

He bit his lip as if thinking. Giving her a wry grin, Del tore the pocket loose from his shirt. "It won't be enough, I know. But take this and sew it to your skirt. When you need me, put your hand in my pocket and it'll be like I'm holding you too."

The idea made her chuckle. "As if anything could replace you."

"I hope not." He glanced to the west before looking back at her. "It's merely a token, a reminder of how much I love you. Keep the handkerchief in your pocket for when you cry. Return it when you're ready to marry me."

She laughed with a little cough. "If I were an only child, we'd be married already."

He took her in his arms, holding her close. "It will happen, I promise. Reach me safely, my love. If I don't leave now, I never will and your father will have to kill me."

"Not while I'm alive." Ellen pressed her lips against his neck before releasing him. "Good bye, Del."

"Non, it's au revoir. Until we meet again."

She nodded, her heart aching as Sam led him away. Her brothers still stood next to a wagon and she went to them. "So, it seems someone needs to play in the water again."

"I'm sorry, sis. It was Caleb who—"

"Skeeter, I don't want to hear anything from you right now." Her voice came out sharper than expected. "Let's just get Buster clean and dry. I'm hungry and I'm sure you are too."

All through dinner, she ignored the little jabs Pa made at her. Grapevine gossips had already spread word that Del had left not long after Pa's trick. Reacting to his taunts only fed his ego, and she refused to do that. Instead, she ate dinner with a smile on her face. No matter that it couldn't reach her eyes. Pa was too full of himself to notice anything as insignificant as her sorrow. Without a word, she finished eating and waited until everyone else was done as well. Her desire to be alone grew so strong that she struggled to keep from taking half empty plates from everyone's hands. At long last, when the last bite had been taken, Ellen gathered everything for washing.

The riverbank seemed to swarm with other ladies and a few men washing dinner dishes. She waited for a little while before a place for her opened up next to Jenny. She smiled at her friend before settling in to clean.

"Ellen! I heard about today's excitement. Are you all right? No one was really shot, right?"

"No, Pa was just joking with Del."

"Someone told me, probably Lucky, that he left us entirely."

Ellen struggled to stay civil. "Mr. Lucky is correct. Del went on without us."

"That's too bad. Still, I'm rather glad he's gone. He seemed like a nice man, rescuing you and all. But he's an Indian, partly, and no one can really trust him."

"Oh," said Ellen through clenched teeth. Learning a juicy bit of gossip was the only reason the girl talked so much now, she suspected.

"I mean, you could, yes, but not all of us could. He didn't rescue us." Jenny laughed. "He couldn't carry all of us back here on his horse."

"No, I suppose not." She glanced over at Jenny's washing, hoping the other girl finished up and left soon. The woman needed a change of subject before truly angering Ellen with her prejudice. "Enough about my drama. How about your family? How is everyone?"

Her friend began a monologue that lasted until Ellen's last dish was clean and nearly dry, yet she didn't interrupt Jenny for fear of another rant against Del and his people. She just couldn't bear hearing another bad thing said about him right now. When Jenny made a comment about seeing her later, Ellen nodded and said something appropriate. She waved and took the long way back to camp only to find everyone still awake. The two adults talked, heads close together, while the boys played with rocks like they were toy soldiers.

Bedrolls had already been laid out despite the early hour. They'd been going into the late afternoon for so long, she'd forgotten what it was like to bed down before twilight. The waning day gave her enough light to write in the journal without squinting and maybe enough time to sew Del's pocket onto her dress. She climbed into the wagon and put away the dishes before retrieving the little book and a threaded needle. Back on solid ground, Ellen sat on her bedroll, giving a nod to Skeeter for setting it out for her. He returned her smile and she settled in. She made quick work of sewing on the pocket before starting to write the day's events.

"You better put in how I scared away that redskin."

She glanced up at Pa. "I will."

"It's the best part of this whole mess so far."

"Of course." She gave him a wan smile before finding the last page. Counting the dates on her fingers, Ellen wrote the date and stopped. How to write down losing your heart and soul without specifically saying such a thing? She shook her head, deciding to transcribe the events in anyone else's point of view but her own or her father's. Pa wouldn't get his heroic tale of running off an Indian.

"You done yet?"

She noted with a start that he was reading over her shoulder. "Almost."

His lips moved as he read the words until at last he straightened with a scowl. "I don't like it. You're not telling how I scared him off."

"No." Temper rose in her and she gripped the pencil hard. She'd transcribed the facts to the best of her ability and didn't like him second-guessing her. Before Ellen could rethink her words, she blurted, "You didn't scare Mr. Du Boise off so much as just scare him. I think Mr. Granville had to tell him to go."

"Huh. Well, he wouldn't have left if I'd not shot him."

Remembering the pain in Del's eyes before they parted fueled her anger. She had to admit Pa was correct. "You're right. It took your prank to do it."

"Ha! Wouldn't have been a prank if my powder hadn't gotten

dunked in the Green that day."

"Ah, that day Mr. Du Boise saved me and the boys from drowning? That day, specifically?"

"Yeah, that's the one."

Lacy clung to Pa's arm. "Jack! You didn't say anything to me about this. Ellen, you must tell me what happened."

With a look at Pa first, and seeing his nod, she gave him the journal to inspect. "Our wagon tipped over in the Green River and washed everyone overboard. Pa had the top down that day, or I suppose we'd have been trapped and drown."

"Thank Providence he'd removed it!"

Jack looked up from the journal. "Yes, and I do thank God every day."

"Then, the boys and I were swept away until Del, I mean, Mr. Du Boise and Mr. Granville saved us."

"How romantic! He rescued you three then brought you back from being kidnapped? Jack, how could you not like the man? He's saved your daughter's life twice and your sons' once."

"I hate him and his people for killing Lucy."

"He killed her?"

"Not directly, no." He pinched the bridge of his nose. "Look, he's half French but he's also half red. You know what that means. We can't trust those animals as far as we can throw them." Pa stood, tossing the journal back at Ellen. "Fill in those days you were too lazy to write down, and we're done talking about that red bastard, done."

She recognized the signs of an impending temper tantrum and stayed quiet. A glance at the boys told her they were already asleep. She soon had the journal updated as Pa had demanded. With her movements slow and deliberate, she slid down into her covers for the night.

The next morning, Ellen caught herself searching for Del out of habit. Each time she remembered he was gone hurt a little more than the time before. The cold metal pail handle dug into her hand as she went for water. Everyone she saw looked the same, chilled through and miserable. Only once beside the campfire did she look at the clear sky as it brightened overhead. No clouds reflected the brilliance of dawn and she shivered.

Pa slurped his coffee and nodded at Lacy. "Ellen, you'd better watch Mrs. Benson fix breakfast. See how she makes the best biscuits this side of the Mississippi."

"Oh, pshaw, Jack. It's just a little cornmeal and sugar added to the mix. Helps make it taste a little different is all."

Buster woke up and crawled into Ellen's lap. She lifted her coffee out of his way and quietly asked, "Do you need to potty?" He shook his head, still rubbing his eyes, giving her hope he could go later and not mess himself.

The coffee sat heavy on her stomach and the cooking smells turned her insides further. Food sounded both good and bad, and she debated on skipping breakfast. Hunger soon won out over nausea as she passed a biscuit to her baby brother and kept one for herself. Pa was right; the cornmeal and sugar added a lot to the usual meal. Ellen smiled when Lacy set aside more for noon. The woman must be feeling more a part of the family from the way she corralled the boys, having them help Buster with his bathroom tasks. "Ellen, would you mind washing up while your father and I tend to the animals?"

"I'll be glad to, ma'am." She took the cook pan, now cooled, and the coffee pot for cleaning. Again, she searched for Del out of habit, and again, he wasn't there.

Before long, the bugle sounded and they rolled on over a hilly stretch of land. She tried to imagine Del and Pomme going this way. How far did the rolling plain stretch to the west, Ellen wondered? Were they through this flat or in another part of the country entirely? She both didn't want and wanted to think about nothing but him. Taking the handkerchief he'd given her, she unfolded and refolded it before putting it in her new dress pocket. He'd been right. The small token worked like a talisman and reassured her.

They rolled on for what seemed like forever. The sun shone overhead before casting longer shadows to the east. Mrs. Benson had taken Buster under her wing, helping him with his bathroom breaks and keeping him dry. Ellen questioned her motives in being nice all of a sudden, but didn't object. She enjoyed the reprieve from her brother's toilet habits.

The only creek they crossed had been more of a wide dry bed with patches of mud. Everyone went without a drink. For lunch, her biscuit from breakfast hung in Ellen's throat. The party rolled on after the meal, not reaching a good creek until near dark. The spring water satisfied everyone. Most people, including Pa and Lacy, decided to stake out the animals and just head to bed.

Ellen dreamed about Pa shooting Del again, each gunfire sounding oddly like Buster saying "Sis!" She opened her eyes to find her little brother doing just that while shaking her awake. "What, Bus? Do you need to go potty?"

"Yeah, I needa help."

She sat up to see and sure enough, they were alone. A glance over showed the water pail was gone too. No fire burned just yet in the stone circle either Pa or Lacy had made. "All right. You can help me gather firewood and I'll help you potty."

While giving her brother his privacy, she glanced over the sage. It'd been dry enough long enough that she could burn it. The stink of the weed while burning didn't appeal. She'd rather scavenge from broken down carts along the road. Buster chattered while they walked along the ruts. Wondering what Del was doing at the moment kept her mind more occupied. She stopped every so often to pry apart a broken wheel. Spokes were the perfect size and if old enough, didn't have splinters. She thought about Del having to build a fire the same way. Unless he rode straight through to his home? She'd have to ask if Sam knew where he lived.

They soon had enough for a decent fire and Ellen turned them back to camp. She felt a little guilty for not paying attention to Buster's stories. "Thank you for helping me. You're such a good boy."

"Caleb stupid. I not pottying pants like a baby."

"Buster!" She almost started arguing with him. "Bus, is he teasing you and calling you a baby?"

"Yeah. I not."

She stifled a smile over his adorable little pout. "You're right. Caleb is just having fun. You're not a baby anymore, I promise." As soon as she promised, Ellen realized she'd left him no room for mistakes. "Although, you might have accidents. Even big boys have accidents. They won't tell you so, but they do."

"Caleb too?"

"Even him."

"Mr. Granville or Pa?"

"Oh, goodness, no!" She ruffled his hair. "They're men, not

boys, and once you're a man, you're finished with accidents too." They reached camp as she finished explaining. Ellen so hoped this discussion was over. Next they would be discussing the differences between boys and men, a topic for Pa to address. Not her.

"Well, look at you!" said Lacy. "Such a young man helping your sister."

Buster gave Ellen a worried look, and she knew what he was thinking. "He is a big boy, for sure. Let's put the wood in here, Bus, and you can go play until breakfast." She loved the relieved look on his little face before he ran off to find his brother.

"I love cooking in the mornings when it's so cold. I hope you don't mind." Lacy already had biscuits cooking in bacon grease. "You can wash up after and we can switch chores this evening for dinner."

"I'd like that, thank you." Ellen liked breakfast for the same reason Mrs. Benson did. Most times, evening was still hot enough to make fixing dinner unpleasant. Still, with the other woman to share chores with, she'd suffer through just fine. When the meal was finished and Lacy began plating up the food, everyone arrived as if given a silent signal. Ellen smiled. Maybe the aroma of breakfast was the reason. She sipped her coffee, taking her plate last.

"So, seems your man done left after all." Pa settled in to eat. "Granville says he's gone for good, not skulking around in the bushes. Also said to bring extra water because there's a long dry day ahead of us."

"Yes, Pa." His reminder of Del's absence crushed her appetite. She'd not realized how much hope she'd had of him leading or trailing them. Ellen glanced around at her family, glad they were too wrapped up in their meals to be watching her. The food didn't appeal at all, but she ate anyway, finishing first. Putting her dishes in the wash pail, she set it by her bedroll and climbed in the wagon.

"Ellen? You're washing up, aren't you, dear?"

"Yes, Mrs. Benson," she called from inside. "I'm finding a water jar for later."

"Very well, I'll make sure our plates are ready for you."

"Thank you." She hopped down with the biggest canning jar they had. Washing up and getting today's water meant two trips to the muddy creek. The dishes took up less time to clean than did straining silt from the water. She wasn't quite done when Lucky played the signal to go. She hurried, getting to the wagon with the jar just before it started rolling.

They rolled over ten miles of rolling hills. The landscape had a yellow cast from dried grass, broken up by the infernal sage. A stiff wind kept her cool, drying sweat almost before it formed. Buster walked with her, let her carry him, or played with the bigger kids until noon when they all stopped for a lunch and drink from the water jar. Jostling kept the silt stirred up and Ellen hated the grit.

Another ten miles passed and they rolled on into the evening before they stopped at last. She knew Lacy would rely on her to cook tonight. After the day's dusty wind, Ellen's stomach protested. The usual routine of chores after the wagons were circled, the smell of fires started in the cool twilight air, and none of it helped. She'd not seen wood, even discarded or broken, in the last five miles walking.

She shrugged off her lethargy. Laziness never finished anything, so Ellen grabbed the water pail for something to drink and followed a line of people down a long gully to a river. It flowed faster than some she'd seen in a while. Blue and orange from the last of the sunset reflected from the waves, giving them a target. A few had thought to bring lanterns. She shook her head. They'd run out of kerosene a while back, something she missed in times like this. She followed Mr. Nelson out by staying close to him and his wife as they walked back up the crevice.

Pa saw her first. "Good! You weren't sitting around mooning over that man." He took the water pail from her. "Lacy is waiting for you to start supper. I got a fire going from some of the scrub and she's wanting tea."

Having some of her tasks done for her bolstered Ellen a bit. She stared at the wagon after letting down the tailgate. What could she fix that they'd not eaten a hundred times before? She remembered the fish Del caught and the meat he'd brought them. No wonder Pa hadn't been hunting. She'd not known until his rotten prank that he'd been anything but indifferent to providing. The recollection of what Pa had done to Del sickened her. Her father deserved his never ending supply of bacon and biscuits. She soon gathered dinner's ingredients and began cooking.

Lacy and Pa talked quietly as Ellen wrote in her journal. The boys played a game of Caleb's and she smiled proudly over how dry Buster had been all day. If she'd had wood and any sort of talent, she'd whittle him a horse. Just no more dolls or pretend little brothers.

"Dinner's ready," she said after poking a biscuit to find it cooked through. They scrambled, hunger making them happy for anything. She settled in on her own blanket. "Would you want to wash up first thing in the morning?"

"Of course, child. No need in wandering around in the dark. Dawn'll be here soon enough."

"Wonder why Granville is grinding us so hard. Most people's animals can't take these twenty mile days." Pa shook his head and took another bite.

Lacy patted his arm. "I've no complaints, dear. The sooner we get there, the sooner we're married."

"I reckon so." Pa grinned at her and the boys. "You kids are getting a proper mother. Ellen's been fine and all, but we needed a real lady who can cook and teach us manners."

She smiled at his words, hoping to hide her inner seething. He'd not starved despite his inability to bring food to the table since Lucy's death. Ellen glanced at Buster and Skeeter. They didn't seem too upset, though Skeeter didn't look happy. If it'd been her in their place, she'd be furious at how quickly Pa and Mrs. Benson had replaced their mother. "That sounds lovely, Pa. You're a lucky man. Mrs. Benson is a catch."

"Thank you, darlin'. That's the first sensible thing you've said in a while."

His backhanded compliment made her smile, even if she didn't quite like it. "If you don't mind, I'm really tired for some reason."

"Certainly. I'll look over your journal while you get some shuteye. Buster, have Caleb or Skeeter take you potty before bed."

She noticed her baby brother clung to Skeeter. Poor Skeeter, she thought, settling in and falling asleep.

Ellen shivered herself awake. The cold air clung to her bones, the chilliest she'd felt since their trip started. She got up to get water for coffee and realized dinner dishes still needed washing. Dishes in the pail rattled a little when she picked it up. They made a little noise with each step as she crept down the crevasse to the river. Arnold caught up to her with his own bucket and she smiled at him. "Good morning. It's nice to see you."

"Good to see you too, miss. I've been out at the back most times, keeping us safe."

"And doing a good job at that, sir."

"Thank you, miss."

She grinned at him as he held out his hand to help her over a rocky place. Ellen had tripped over it last night and liked how Arnold steadied her. "How much more do we have before reaching Oregon City? Does anyone know?"

"Well, this here's the John Day and it usually takes a good two weeks after this."

She scooped up some water. "That's not very long at all, Mr. Arnold."

"It's a long while considering the distance, miss. We've gone further faster. The Barlow Road just takes a while, more than most people expect. There's been trouble with the Indians lately and with Mr. Du Boise gone—sorry again, miss—Mr. Granville decided to take the safer route."

Somehow, the canyon bathed in golden light from sunrise mirrored the happiness in her heart. "Do you suppose Mr. Du Boise would be safe going the more northern route?"

Arnold dipped his bucket into the river and stepped aside to let a waiting Mr. Allen get water as well. "I don't know for sure. I imagine so. Mr. Granville said Do Boise is like a cat, always landing on his feet no matter how far you throw him."

Ellen laughed. "I hope so. I'd like to be that way too." She turned away from the river and its gleaming canyon with a lot of reluctance. "Thank you for telling me about the travel ahead." She smiled at him as he helped her through the rocky spots again. "I'd not realized we were so close in distance to the finish."

"I understand, miss. We've been crossing a whole lot of flat in the past several days. Soon enough, you'll be wishing our road was as flat as now."

"Oh?" She hoped he'd take her urging to say more.

"Yeah, we have the worst road ahead of us. Mr. Granville has wanted to get to it as soon as possible so we can take it slower. But not so slow we're caught in a snowstorm."

Ellen nodded. "I understand." Enough people had been snowed in and barely rescued to tell everyone of the dangers of not taking the mountains seriously.

Lacy, her future stepmother, fixed breakfast while Ellen folded the bedrolls into seats for everyone. Buster's was thankfully dry and she thanked heaven for it. She drank her coffee, black to Pa and his fiancée's sugared, and hurried through eating. "I'll clean up right quick," she volunteered and headed to the river with the water jar. Washing everything, including the silt from the jar, she returned with clean dishes and a half-gallon of water for the day. Lucky's signal sounded and she rushed to put everything away.

They skirted a rocky and sandy canyon until noon. Ellen despaired of them reaching a new home in only two weeks if this were part of the best roads they'd see. Lunch was eaten next to a tepid and stagnant pond. They continued on until the canyon flattened to nothing. The road seemed so rough that she wondered how anything in their wagon was still in one piece. The hot, dry, and dusty land continued on until they reached the rim of a river canyon. She wasn't surprised to hear the signal to stop for the night. Standing at the edge of the ravine, she saw a ribbon of water gleamed in the dusk.

"It's about a mile and a half away still," said Sam.

She turned, glad to see him. "So no traipsing around at night for a little drink?"

"I'd prefer you didn't without an escort."

Ellen sighed, staring at the western horizon. "Too bad he's miles from here."

Sam grinned. "I'd say so. I'd also say don't get too used to him being gone."

"Oh? Is he nearby? Can I see him?"

"No, he's headed home."

"I see." Tears welled up in her eyes. "It sounds like I'm not as married as I thought I was."

Sam laughed. "Good thing you love to argue, because he'd rebut that until you gave in."

"I don't love to argue, Mr. Granville. You just make it easy for me to do so."

"Uh huh. Be that as it may, I've been given instructions to deliver you to him once we reach Oregon City."

"What about Pa and the boys?"

"I think I'm supposed to leave Jack wherever he'd like to be, and your brothers—I don't know, Ellen." He sighed. "Your father has chosen Mrs. Benson to be the boys' mother. Where does that leave you?"

She smiled. "Wherever I want to be that's also near Buster and Skeeter."

"That's what I imagined." He tipped his hat. "Until later, my dear?"

"Of course." Ellen watched him walk away and then turned to the glorious sunset. She had a list of chores she needed to do, yet the clouds in the west glowed with oranges, yellows, and reds, compelling her to stay. She enjoyed a couple minutes more of selfishness before going back to camp, her family, and the usual night spent with them.

Despite Ellen's rushing around, the morning meal and long drive seemed to last forever. She pushed through, knowing every minute that passed, every step walked was one more closer to reuniting with Del. A few times during the day, she'd get a good look at the De Chute River. The water teased her before the wagon train would turn away to avoid a canyon as it sloped down to the river. The road going south frustrated her. They went ten miles to a flat, grassy valley with a trickle of a creek.

Time lagged there too, and it seemed to be mid afternoon before the order was given to continue. She double-checked that Buster had stayed dry and then let him run free. Much to her relief, the road angled southwest. With the wind from the northwest, walking behind meant missing most of the dust kicked up by the stock. Ellen smelled the rain only long enough to still be surprised when fat drops began pelting her. They felt more like hailstones than water, and she hurried to her family's wagon to escape them.

"There you are!" Pa hollered, giving her a hand up and inside.

"Thank you. I avoided the dirt but not the shower."

"Mr. Lucky came by a moment ago saying we're staying put until the weather clears," Lacy said, giving her a dry blanket to wrap up in. "I hope that this won't last all night."

Pa answered for Ellen, saying, "Naw, as fast as this moved in, it'll be over soon."

Thunder shook the canvas top while it rumbled through as if to punctuate Pa's words. Buster clung to her. The storm's noise kept any of them from talking much until it was over. Afterward, she stepped out into the sunshine of late afternoon. The world seemed more colorful and freshly washed. Ellen smiled, thinking now was a perfect time to go another ten miles or so. At the signal, wagons resumed their rolling and she saw the men who still had horses ride out in search of missing cattle. Buster came over to her, shivering. "How about I hold you?" He nodded and she ignored his muddy feet to hoist him onto her hip and under the blanket she wore like a cape. Buster soon became dead weight when he overheard other children, slipping down to the ground to go play.

Lucky gave the signal to stop for the night. Not enough time had passed, in her opinion, for them to get anywhere today. The wagons drew into a semi circle around a dirty pond. Runoff from the rain had filled it full of muddy water, and she dreaded cooking with such muck. Ellen went to their wagon, getting a cheesecloth and their biggest jar. The damp land lacked any sort of decent fuel, giving her time to strain their water instead of looking for firewood.

"Damn it all! I wanted a decent meal tonight, not some dry beans and water!"

Pa's yelling stopped her in her tracks. She needed to help fix something for dinner, but not now. Not in the middle of his temper fit. He had not hit Ellen in front of Mrs. Benson, and she didn't want to start such an embarrassment now.

"I don't care, woman! I'm hungry now!"

Lacy must have been trying to placate him, judging by their conversation, or rather, his part yelled at the top of his lungs to her quieter tones. Ellen squared her shoulders, preparing to go into battle. He'd not dare hit her before his marriage to Mrs. Benson. Otherwise, he'd scare the woman away and they both knew it. She turned the wagon corner to find him sulking on the lowered tailgate.

"Ellen, dear, could you talk some sense into your father? He insists on a hot meal tonight and it's just not possible."

"I'm afraid it isn't," she agreed. "But we can have a nice breakfast or lunch tomorrow."

"Oh? You think so?" Pa gestured, flinging his arms open. "Look around you, dim wit. See anything dry enough to burn? I don't."

"Jack Winslow!"

He had the grace to look shamefaced at Lacy's admonishment. "Well, it's true. Even a fool could see everything's wet."

"Still! For shame." She patted Ellen's shoulder. "Thank you, dear, for getting us water." She ignored Pa's "Humph," to continue, "We'll scrounge around in my wagon. There's pickles, dried fruits, and we'll see if the nuts are still good." Lacy took Pa's hand. "Come on, Jack, and help me find something for us. We'll clear a place in the wagon to sleep tonight, high and dry." She pulled him to her wagon. "Maybe we'll turn in early too."

They soon rustled around, doing what Lacy wanted. Ellen looked at the boys staring at her. "All right, while they're getting their wagon ready to sleep in, let's see what we can do about sleeping here for the night." She hopped up on the tailgate. "Be sure to leave your dirty shoes outside of the wagon." The boys helped her move things, putting some belongings into her mother's trunk as much as they could pack in. They spread blankets down and shimmied down to the tailgate for their moccasins.

"Ellen, dear?"

She looked back to see Lacy standing there with an armload of clothes and blankets. "Yes, Mrs. Benson?"

"Could you please put some of my things in your wagon? Your Pa needs the space, and I know you have room."

She bit her lip while searching for more space. The boys and her would already have close quarters tonight. "I will but don't know if I can find any."

Pa stepped into view. "What? We have plenty of area back there. You kids don't need much. Here." He hopped up onto the tailgate. "Boys, go on and play. Let the adults work."

A flush of pride went through Ellen at being referred to as an adult. "I don't know how to get any more from what we've got without dumping things."

"We could get rid of your trunk. It takes up a lot."

"No, we can't Pa, I'm sorry." Before he could turn on her and start a fight, she added, "It's the perfect place for Buster to sleep on and I stuffed it full to make more room for everything else."

His eyes narrowed. "That's a good idea. I'll stack things up on one side so you children have a place to sleep on the wagon bed and we adults have room in our wagon. Get out and let me work."

Ellen smiled, though not happy at being demoted in status. She did as he ordered, taking the journal with her to the wagon seat in front. By the time she finished writing the dreary day's events, Pa and Lacy were done rearranging their belongings. She went around back to see how much sleep area they had. The two had stacked everything up on the right side of the wagon. A few of the heavier items counter balanced on the left. Even with that, she could see how the vehicle listed slightly to the right. "Looks great for tonight."

Lacy went to Pa and hugged him. "I think so. Jack did a wonderful job."

"I had a good helper, ma'am."

The entire mutual admiration conversation irritated Ellen. "Should we be thinking about feeding the boys and staking down the animals for the night?"

She smiled at Ellen. "Of course, dear. Why don't you help your father with the oxen and I'll get supper ready."

After a quick nod, Ellen did as the woman asked. Pa didn't talk to her as they worked. She didn't offer any conversation, not wanting to start an argument. Too bad Sam wasn't here. Ellen almost laughed aloud. He'd love her quiet acceptance for a change.

They ate the pickles and dried fruit for dinner, Lacy having deemed the nuts too rancid. She laughed at Buster's sour face when he bit into the first pickle. "The first taste is the worst, I promise." He gave her a dubious stare and then took another bite. "See?"

Pa ate the last of his fruit. "If you don't want your dinner, boy, give it to someone else. Don't waste Mrs. Benson's food."

Buster shook his head and ate the rest of his food. They all washed down the dinner with murky water. The larger grains had settled until the last person, Lacy, needed a drink. "I might just wait until tomorrow."

"Ellen, go get Mrs. Benson some fresh water."

"Oh, Jack, no. I don't want to trouble her."

"It's fine, Mrs. Benson. I'd be happy to do it." She took the jar and hurried to the pond. No one else was there, and the water was still full of silt. She filled their jar and went back to find everyone in their wagons already. Securing the water for the night, Ellen climbed up, jostling Caleb and Skeeter.

"Sis, watch out!"

"Sorry. It seems we're packed in here pretty tight. Buster, sweetie, why don't you sleep on the trunk?" Ellen took one of the quilts and folded it into a cushion for him. A thin blanket served as his cover. "See? A proper bed just for you."

"I want a proper bed for me too," said Caleb.

"Sure, I can do that." Ellen fixed him a bed like Buster's, only on top of his mother's belongings. "Skeeter? You too?"

"Naw, I'm good here on the floor with you."

Caleb snickered. "He's a baby sleeping with his sister."

"Am not. There's not many blankets left is all."

"Baby."

"It's ok, Skeeter." She began folding two of the remaining three blankets. "Here. You can sleep with these and I'll wrap up in the heaviest one. Everyone gets their own bed."

He climbed up to sleep on top of the Winslows' possessions when Ellen was done. Satisfied he was up there safely, she folded her own bed, leaving a flap open as a cover. Settled in for the night, they laid in bed for a few moments before hearing the wagon next to them squeak. Her eyes opened into the inky blackness as the noise grew louder and more rhythmic. "No!" she whispered when she realized what Pa and Lacy were doing. She could have lived the rest of her life just fine with never hearing such goings on.

"Sis?"

"You don't want to know, Skeeter. I promise I'll tell you someday, just not right now."

The next morning, Ellen lay in her cocoon for a while longer than necessary. Pa would have the fire going, and Lacy would have breakfast ready for a quick bite. With any luck, of course, and she had none. The wood, if there were any, would still be wet and the provisions still low. Oh, and the water still dirty. She closed her eyes and groaned. That was the gild to the lily.

She sat up when hearing Pa and Lacy hitch up the oxen. "That late already?" she whispered. Ellen scrambled out of the wagon.

"There you are, lazy bones!" Pa grinned at her. "Up and at 'em, young lady. This time tomorrow, we'll be at the Barlow Gate."

His good mood bolstered her own until she remembered last night's shenanigans. No wonder he was so happy. He stood there as if expecting a reply, so she said, "Wonderful!" She'd prefer to focus on getting to the Gate instead of knowing too much about her father's love life.

They began rolling at the signal and Ellen got a quick drink from the water jar before dumping out the mud. She carried it for a mile or so before giving up on finding any clear springs between here and the Des Chutes. The early start to the day meant they'd be at the river at noon or so. If not for skipping breakfast and coffee, she'd be happy to run there just to see Del sooner.

Five miles later and she was worn out just from walking. At a slight pause, she dug in and found a coffee bean to chew on for a while. She tested the toughness and decided holding it like a tobacco chaw might be best for her teeth. The Granville party wound their way down a long hill before reaching the Des Chutes River. Ellen hung back, the boys with her, watching the others cross first. Second to last, the Benson wagon crossed on a makeshift bridge. Ahead of her, the Nelsons, Allens, and Granvilles began climbing up a steeper but smaller hill.

From where she was, Ellen could hear Pa shouting and hawing at their ox. The wagon would begin rolling then stop as if the animal loathed crossing the bridge. More yelling floated up to them on the wind, along with a few choice words. She covered Buster's ears and he shrugged out of her hands. They saw Pa hit the ox before hearing the loud crack against the animal's flesh. By then, the wagon leaped ahead as if by a giant hand, hurtling toward the bridge. It wobbled side to side, listing harder to the right each time. She held her breath as the wagon laid over in agonizing slowness. A scream escaped her as she watched the canvas top collapse in the river, followed by the wagon bed, their ox, and Pa.

CHAPTER 11

Ellen and her brothers watched, frozen, as everything they had in the world floated down the Des Chutes with their father. She heard distant shouts from the others as they realized what had happened, yet she couldn't move. Winslow and his flotsam drifted downriver until hidden by a bend in the canyon. Only then did a whimper escape her.

"Sis?" Skeeter tugged on her arm. "Pa?"

She knew what he couldn't ask. "I don't know." Her eyes filled with tears. "I hope they do find him."

He buried his face in her arm and she hugged him. Buster took a cue from his big brother and did the same, hiding his face in her skirts. She wrapped an arm around her younger sibling and picked up Buster to hold. Somehow she noticed Caleb leaving, running to his mother at the top of the hill across the river. When they met, she heard the woman's screams but not the words.

A group of men on horseback also disappeared around the bend. She watched a thin cloud rise from their animals' hooves until the afternoon wind blew the dust away. The boys clung to her so hard she could only debate for a moment on running after the men and her father. "They'll find him," she murmured more to herself than her brothers. They had to. Pa was all they had in the world besides their wagon. They needed him.

"Miss?"

Ellen woke from her trance like stare at the vanishing point of the river and horizon. Lefty stood at her side. "Yes?"

"Come along with us. We'll get you across the river, you and the boys. Mr. Granville and the others will find your Pa."

"I don't know...."

He took her elbow. "Miss, come along. It might be a while, and you'll want to stay with the others."

She nodded, glad someone could think at a time like this. Ellen gave her brothers a little hug before turning them toward the wagon train. "Let's go, boys, and see Mrs. Benson and Caleb." The three of them followed Lefty down the hill. Each one slipped a couple of times on the rocks before catching themselves. The closer they got to the stone bridge, the louder she heard Mrs. Benson's crying.

"They have to find him, they have to!" Lacy sagged against Marie. "Please tell me Sam and the others are doing everything they can!"

Marie patted her back when the woman enveloped her in a bear hug. "Um, of course they are, Mrs. Benson. They're doing everything possible to retrieve Mr. Winslow." She glanced up at Ellen and the boys. "They'll find him. Come on, everyone, and have a seat in the shade while we wait." Marie quickly pulled down the Granville wagon's tailgate.

Lacy was the first to hop on. Caleb shook his head and walked away. Ellen didn't want to sit but had nothing else to do, so she found a seat and nestled Buster beside her. Skeeter climbed up too and settled in. The three of them watched for signs of the men riding back with their Pa. None of the Winslows made a sound. Ellen kept quiet because she wasn't sure what to say. Then too, Lacy kept wailing and crying so much, there was no point in even trying to talk.

"Buster? Skeeter?" Marie held her hands out to the boys. "Come with me and let's see if I can find something tasty for lunch."

The boys followed and Ellen winced when Lacy began another round of wailing. "Mrs. Benson!" she hollered to get the other woman's attention. "There's no need to keep crying. They have probably found Pa by now."

"I hope so." She sniffled. "But what about all my things? Jack and I had divided up my provisions equally for the oxen's sake. He'll survive, but my jellies won't."

Ellen didn't know what to say without sounding rude. She sat still for a moment, thinking of responses and discarding them just as fast. Had Lacy never known of anyone drowning from an overturned wagon? Maybe she had supreme faith in Pa, something Ellen couldn't share. "Pa loves you. He'll make sure your jellies are replaced by ones even better, I'm sure."

"I hope so." Lacy continued in a teary voice. "Do you suppose Oregon Territory has strawberries?"

She continued to stare at the place she last saw Pa. Her and the boys' father might be dead and the woman cared about strawberries? People showed grief in odd ways, Ellen thought as she replied, "I'm sure settlers have planted some by now."

"I hope so. Good thing I didn't let him take my good Irish linens. No one else in the Territory will have those." She sighed. "When do you suppose they'll come back with him? I suppose it's too much to ask for an intact wagon."

Ellen turned to her as two fat tears rolled down the woman's cheeks. "Pa can cobble together another wagon, if he's alive."

A movement of one rider galloping along the riverbank caught Ellen's eye. All the men wore hats, so she couldn't tell who it was. From this distance, the shirts, horses, and people looked the same. She sat up, straining at first to see before removing her glasses to clean them. Arnold was the man. She could see his horse. Ellen slid off the tailgate to her feet.

Lacy also hopped to her feet. "Is that Sam? Have they found my Jack? Why is only one man returning?"

"I don't know. Maybe Pa is hurt and needs us. I'll get the medical kit." She stopped cold. No, she couldn't get anything. Everything they owned now lay at the bottom or along a river's banks.

"Never mind that." Lacy dusted her hands on her skirt as if getting ready to work. "Let's find out what we can do to get Jack and my belongings back into my wagon."

Arnold and his horse went over the bridge to them. He pulled the animal up short and dismounted. "Ma'am, miss."

Ellen's throat closed in at his expression and tears filled her eyes. He didn't need to say anything else. She knew Pa wouldn't be coming back to them.

"Well?" The older woman gestured down the river. "Let's get started, young man! With all of us, I'm sure we can help you all load up my things again."

"Ma'am, I don't rightly know how to tell you this, but Mr. Winslow didn't survive the fall. We found him washed up on a sandbar." He took off his hat and nodded at Ellen. "Your trunk and a few things of Mrs. Bensons were there too, along with some busted up wood. I reckon it's from the wagon proper, miss."

"No!" Lacy's hands were fisted and on her hips. "Are you telling me my fiancée is dead and half my provisions are floating to the Columbia?"

"I'm afraid so, ma'am."

"Damnation all to hell!"

The woman's cursing at the top of her lungs startled Ellen. She stood in shock as Lacy stomped off toward where Jack had been found. Various words and phrases floated back to them on the wind, none of them repeatable in polite society.

"I'll confess, I'm at a loss over what to do with Pa," Ellen murmured.

"Don't worry about it, miss. The boss and them are taking care of your pa. They'll be bringing back what he had in his pockets for you and the boys."

"I should go back with you to make sure he's had prayers said over him." She swallowed the lump in her throat. "Was my family trunk intact? There are things inside that I'd planned on giving to my brothers."

"Mostly. We found it on its side a ways from your pa. The lid was open but Lucky scooped everything back in." He put his hat on before getting on his horse. "Mr. Granville wants you to stay with his missus for now. She'll help you. I'm going to find a pushcart for your trunk and need to get shovels to the men. Little ole Skeeter will want to know what has happened to your pa. It'd be best if he heard it from you."

"You're right. Thank you, Mr. Arnold."

"Sorry for your loss, miss." He saluted and rode forward to the rest of their group. Ellen took in a deep shuddering breath before taking the oxen's reins to lead them to the others. The walk to their new gathering spot seemed so long in the dry heat of the valley. Arnold soon met her and went on with a pushcart instead of his horse. Tears filled her eyes when she saw he had shovels with him. She couldn't pretend Pa might still be alive, now.

She plodded along with the ox, each step difficult. While the men might have relieved her from the gruesome chore of burying Pa, they couldn't take away the effect the death would have on her brothers. The boys had only her and maybe Del to care for them. She looked up from the ground with a start. Del. He waited for her in Oregon City, but would he accept her brothers as well? He had to. She couldn't put them up for adoption. Not now, not ever.

Fresh tears formed and spilled. He just had to love and take all of them in. Otherwise, she'd need to find a way to support the three of them. A tiny cold lump of fear settled in her stomach. Adelard Du Boise didn't have to do anything. She couldn't make him. Ellen swallowed down the rising lump in her throat. The campsite loomed ever closer and she decided her family needed a backup plan. Marrying Del was her first choice, of course. But if life had taught her anything, it was that she couldn't count on anything being permanent. Teaching school, sewing, even being a maid to a wealthy family went on her mental list of possibilities to keep the boys fed and clothed.

She'd been walking along with different wagon parties on either side of the road for just a little while before spotting Marie with the Allen family. Ellen hesitated to approach, not willing to listen to anything bad Jenny might have to say. She shook her head and knew one of the worst things possible had already happened. Her brothers were orphans.

Once Marie saw her, she ran up to Ellen, giving her a hug before taking the reins to the Bensons' wagon. "There you are! I was worried you'd not find us in all this mess. Arnold has been and gone. Did you see him?"

"Yes."

"Good. I've not said anything to the boys yet. They're playing with the Allen children right now. I wanted you to decide how and when to talk to them about your father."

"Thank you. I'd prefer to never have to admit what happened to anyone."

"I know, dear, and I'm so sorry." She hugged Ellen. "I can't undo what happened, but I can help however you need me to."

She couldn't speak without sobbing and settled on nodding. Marie led the wagon into the semi circle with the others. Ellen swallowed down some tears before managing to say, "There's no sense in you doing my work for me."

"Don't worry about it. I need to check on the other animals anyway." She unhitched the ox and led the animal away with a wave.

What was there to do next? Looking around for the boys? Ellen searched the landscape as if looking hard enough could bring Pa back. Arnold walked up with a handcart, Lacy following, and then the men on horseback behind her.

The older woman stomped up to her, saying, "Well, here's my wagon. What have you done with my ox?"

"He's staked out, getting a bite to eat and Caleb is some—"

"I don't care!" exploded Lacy with a fury matching any Pa had ever had. "Get him back here this instant! I suppose I'm lucky you didn't just take off with all my belongings and go to that half-breed you're so enamored of! Your Pa always warned me about you and he was right! You take what you want and don't give two figs about anyone else."

Hurt and anger filled Ellen so much she couldn't breathe. All of it, what Pa had said against her, Lacy's rudeness, and the grief and worry for the boys swirled in her like a mix of acid and poison. Her heart hurt as if clenched by an iron fist. "I do? Thank you for informing me. I'll go get your ox."

"You do that, young lady."

Ellen went in the direction she'd seen Marie go. The Winslow animal had been more familiar to her, but hopefully she'd recognized the Bensons' ox. She'd noticed how Lacy hadn't mentioned Caleb. He was on his own. His mother obviously didn't care as much for him as she did that beast. Let the boy come back when he got hungry. Ellen didn't care.

The Benson ox stood out from the others and she thanked her memory. "C'mon, boy, let's go," she said, scooping up the animal's rope. The placid beast followed her like a huge puppy. As they neared camp, she saw Marie talking with Lacy. From her friend's body language, Ellen guessed Lacy had stepped on her friend's last nerve.

"You're free to go any time, Mrs. Benson. I'm sure Sam would agree."

"Excuse me? I don't need to stay with this horrible group one second more! Letting people die all the time, I never!" She spotted Ellen leading the ox. "There you are! About time you decided to bring back my animal." Lacy grabbed the leather straps from the younger woman's hands and stomped away.

Marie patted her friend on the back. "Dear, shall I go talk with her? Tell her you all need to stay together?"

"No. I'm fine with never seeing her again. She was Pa's friend more than mine or the boys'."

"Ma'am, miss?" Lucky rode up first with Sam. The younger man stopped his horse and hopped down behind them. "Miss Ellen? We buried your pa. Arnold is bringing what's left of your belongings with him."

Sam stepped up to her. "He had a few things in his pockets that I thought you'd want." He dug in his pants pocket for a moment before giving her twenty dollars in bills and coins. After another rummage around in the opposite pants pocket, he held out caps for a rifle, still wet, and a pocketknife.

The money would come in handy. The caps meant something only because they'd belonged to Pa. She could split them with the boys. Ellen might need the pocketknife in the future. Skeeter would want it or maybe Buster would when he grew old enough to value such a thing. "Thank you, Sam, Mr. Lucky."

Arnold came up before she could add anything more. The pushcart ahead of him was full of her busted up trunk and muddy shovels. "Hey, Miss Winslow. We found a few more things on the way back here. Most everything's wet, but it'll dry." He set down the cart on its back legs. "I can roll this on over to the company wagon, and you can go through everything yourself."

"Thank you, Mr. Arnold." She watched as he continued on with everything they had in the world. Ellen wondered how she and the boys would manage. To no one in particular, she said, "I need to go through everything, find out what we can carry."

"Sam?" began Marie. At his nod, she continued, "Ellen, you can have the pushcart if you like or keep your things in the company wagon. Whichever you prefer, dear."

"I appreciate that." Tears filled her eyes again. "If you'll excuse me?"

"Of course."

She hurried off to where Arnold had parked their things. The lid fell off completely as she opened her trunk. All the linens and blankets she'd embroidered were drenched. When she lifted up the cloth cushioning the china from her mother, she found most of it cracked or in pieces. She set aside the intact dishes and mourned the loss of the broken ones. The shards had their own pile. Ellen couldn't bear to throw them out. Setting some down on the upturned lid, she spotted her family Bible and journal. Both were soaked through. She opened the journal before closing it to press as much water from it as her strength allowed. Pa had relied on her to write down their journey, and now she regretted him doing so. If he'd been the one to make the entries, she'd have his writing. Not a large legacy from her father, but more than the nothing she now had. A movement to her left caught Ellen's eye and she saw Skeeter and Buster walking toward her. "Hello, boys. I have something to tell you."

They held hands and as soon as her younger brother saw her, awareness dawned on his face. Her eyes filled again as his steps faltered before the boy soldiered on to her. "Pa's gone."

She nodded confirmation of Skeeter's statement. "He is."

"Can we see him?"

"No, because they've taken care of him already."

He let out a wail before crying, "I didn't get to say goodbye."

Ellen took him in her arms. "None of us did. He died too fast. We'll need to say goodbye in our hearts and know he'll hear us in heaven." She glanced down at Buster to see a big wet spot on the front of his pants. He needed cleaning and a bath. She also needed to find a fresh pair of pants for him and something for them to eat. A sob escaped her at the enormity of her new responsibilities. "I can't do this." She leaned against the cart, putting her head on her arms and cried.

The little voice in the back of her mind chastised her to be the adult. It sounded suspiciously like Pa as it told her to straighten up and stop this nonsense, but she couldn't. The fact she was alone and responsible for two young children scared her. Even if she could count on Del's help, days and miles were between them. She felt able to do without, but what about the boys? They couldn't starve and she couldn't let them.

The more she tried to stop crying, the harder the sobs overtook her. She felt more than saw as Marie whisked away Buster. Skeeter patted her on the back in comfort until Lefty led him away too. Ellen heard the talking but didn't listen. When Sam turned her around and held her, she let him. Her sobbing slowed and she drew strength from him as they stood there.

He gave her a little squeeze. "Feeling better?"

"A little." She sniffed before reaching in her pocket for Del's handkerchief. "Thank you for letting me cry it out. It's childish, I know, but maybe I'm done for a good while."

"Any time." He shuffled his feet a little. "Let me know when you're ready to think about the future. I have some ideas. Until then, you're free to keep what you want in our wagon."

She nodded, knowing he was aware of how little they had. "It won't be much. I have half a mind to turn around and go back home to Missouri. If it weren't so far away or if I had family there, I would."

"So Del doesn't matter?"

Ellen saw the beginning glint of anger in his eyes. "He does, very much. But what if he doesn't want an instant family? I can't abandon the boys, so we're a package deal." His expression softened and she continued, "He's used to being a single man, able to do as he pleases. We would just complicate his life. I have to think about the possibility of us arriving on his doorstep and being turned away."

Sam's jaw dropped a little in surprise before he grinned. "You underestimate his love for you. Invent reasons and alternate plans if that reassures you. Otherwise, they're not necessary." He picked up the pushcart by the handles and lifted it. "Let's go see how your brothers are. I'm sure my lovely wife has the baby cleaned up and his clothes drying by now."

She followed him to camp. Her brothers sat with Marie and Lucky as she cooked over the open fire. Buster wore a long shirt, and Skeeter drew in a journal with Arnold watching and correcting his scribbles. The scene looked so normal and peaceful. Ellen took her own seat, a little stunned at how life was continuing on without Pa.

Numb through supper, she ate the potatoes and rabbit stew without really tasting them. Sam's earlier reassurances helped. Still, she fretted inside over what sort of home Del could provide them, if any. When done, she stood to wash up out of habit until Sam gathered the dishes from her. He was soon gone and back, taking no time at all. She shook her head at his speed and wondered if it was truly him being in a hurry or her being in a slower world.

Lefty and Arnold retrieved the bedrolls, passing them to others. Marie led Buster off for one last potty break. Ellen caught Skeeter staring at her and smiled. He returned her grin as weakly as she felt her own. She looked down at her hands in her lap to keep the sadness at bay.

"Ellen?"

She looked up at Sam. "Yes?"

He knelt. "We have a limited number of blankets, so Marie and I will share a bedroll. Lucky and Arnold will have one each during Lefty's watch, and Lefty gets Lucky's bed during second watch. Are you fine with sharing a bed with your brothers until some of the blankets in your trunk dry?"

His kindness added to the others touched her heart. "Yes, thank you," she squeaked. "I suppose we need to give Pa a proper funeral service."

"We can, whenever you like," said Sam. "The boys and I had a small ceremony after we buried him."

She cleared her throat. "I can never repay your generosity, Sam, you or your men."

"No payment needed, dear." He stepped aside as Lefty spread out a thick blanket on the ground for her. Soon, the three Winslows lay together under a blanket and fell asleep staring at the stars.

Ellen felt like a ghost the next morning, drifting around while helping with breakfast, cleaning up, and caring for her brothers. While she folded her dried blankets and mother's belongings, people talked to her. She answered them even though she couldn't recollect what anyone had said. Yesterday had been a fog and today promised to be more of the same.

The country distracted her for an hour or two with its brilliant yellow of summer grasses and the deep blue of the high desert sky. She tilted her head at the idea this was an arid region. The dust and sagebrush said wasteland while the ever-increasing pines and deciduous trees contradicted it. Mount Hood shone ahead in its snow-covered gleam. The peak called to her, saying just a few steps more. Last night she'd learned it was their last landmark before reaching their new home. Had Sam told them or Lucky? She shook her head. It didn't matter. With Pa gone, she had no reason to update the damp journal.

She looked for Marie among the people walking west and avoided her. Ellen knew she needed to be more sociable. Later today, she promised her guilty conscience. She just wanted to be alone in the crowd.

"Ellen!"

Marie's voice took her out of her own mind. Ellen smiled at her friend, pushing away the irritation at having her musings interrupted. "Yes?"

"Come here and eat a little. Sam went ahead to the post and traded for some dried fruit and it's divine." She held out a sack. "Show me your hands." Ellen cupped her palms together and her friend poured out a few flattened apples and apricots. "There, that should tide you over until supper tonight."

"Hmm." She took a bite of the apricot. The fresh flavor of

summer danced along her taste buds as she chewed. Ellen swallowed, saying, "I might have to stop in and see what else the post has. Buster needs more clothes for sure, Skeeter too." She nibbled on a chewy apple ring, already wishing Marie had more to share.

"We'll be rolling by there soon. I can have Lefty stop the wagon for you."

"That would be perfect. Thank you." She held up the last apricot and a raisin. "And for these as well."

"My pleasure. I think Buster is still gnawing on his and Skeeter didn't take long to finish. I might give them extra in a little while."

She nodded, not trusting her voice as Marie went off to her new tasks. Ellen hurried to the Granville wagon as it slowed. "Hello, Mr. Lefty."

"Howdy, Miss. Let me know when you're done hunting around back there."

"Will do." She climbed over the tailgate and went for her trunk. The lid flopped off when she lifted it. Ellen made a mental note to fix the strap later. Now, she hunted through the blankets, looking for an entire dish set she could trade. She had a little of everything and a lot of nothing. What man or even woman out here would swap clothes for fancy dishes? Ellen couldn't imagine. She set down a plate and heard a metallic clink. Silverware. She dug into the trunk and found a few tarnished forks, knives, and spoons. People could use these as is or melt them down for the metal. Ellen separated out four of each for her, Del, and the boys before taking the rest and climbing down. "Thank you, Mr. Lefty!" She returned his wave before hurrying to the trading post.

An orderly crowd choked the doorway. She eased in, clutching the utensils close to her. A multitude of language sounded around her, and she picked up on French immediately. It wasn't in Del's voice, certainly, and yet the words' melody hit her heart. She swallowed against the threat of tears from missing him. Ellen stepped up to the front for her turn. "Hello, what can I get for these?" She held out the metal.

The grizzled man rubbed his chin. "It depends, young lady. What do you want?"

"Clothes. I need them for a small boy around two years old. Then, if I can, clothes for a ten year old boy."

"I might have something back here. Lemme check right quick, ma'am." He turned and slipped into a back room.

Other people helped customers around her. He'd probably expected Ellen to be asking on behalf of her children, thus called her "ma'am." She sighed, not realizing she'd been holding her breath while waiting for his return. People on either side jostled her, and she didn't care for the physical contact. Was that the way things were out here? Wide-open spaces were truly wide and open. But indoors? Not so much, it seemed.

"Here we are, young lady." He held up a small pair of pants. "This'll be good for the small fry. While this…." The man spread out a larger pair and a shirt. "This is a whole outfit for your ten year old." He shrugged. "I found a shirt for the baby, but it's all boogered up. You throw in another knife or two, and I'll throw in a sewing kit."

Ellen shook her head, unwilling to give up anything else. "I can't. This is all I have. I will take the bad shirt, if you'd like."

He frowned. "It ain't so much bad as torn up. Let me go get it and you can see for yourself." The trader went back for only a moment before returning with a small shirt. The clothing had a rip down the front and no buttons. He laid it down on the counter. "If you had that knife, I could throw in some fasteners."

She smiled. "I truly can't, but I will take the pants and good shirt, sir."

"Aw heck, ma'am. Go ahead and take all of it." He pushed the clothes to her and took the silverware she pushed at him. "No one's been interested in it before now. Reckon no one will be after this, either."

"Thank you, sir."

"Eh." He waved a handful of utensils at her, grinning. "Go on with ya."

Ellen turned, smiling. She felt bad how the man missed out on getting a knife for his troubles but knew someone else would oblige him. Besides, she wasn't giving up Pa's pocketknife for no one and nothing.

She hurried back to camp, tentatively smelling the clothes to see how clean they were. Dusty, but not unbearable. She saw Marie first at the wagon, rearranging the supplies.

Her friend spotted her approaching and smiled. "There you are! Skeeter was asking about you and I said you were at the post."

She nodded at the clothes. "I'm betting the Winslows will be the best dressed at dinner tonight."

"I hope so." Ellen held up the torn shirt. "Buster will have to wear the same shirt for now, but these pants look nice. He'll be able to grow into them a little too."

"What? Let me see." Marie took the defective shirt. "Oh, this isn't bad at all. I'll trust your sewing kit didn't survive? No? Well, then, I'll scare up some buttons and work on this tonight after supper."

The kindness touched her and her eyes filled with tears. Just letting them tag along had been so reassuring. Then with this good deed, she sniffled back a sob. "The trader offered to sell me a sewing kit, but I didn't want to give up what I had left."

"Darling!" Her friend hugged her. "No! What did you trade for these? I never even thought of what you'd have to do." She patted Ellen's back. "Silly me, I should have asked before you left for the post." Holding her at arm's length, she added, "No more trading for you, young lady. Sam says we have six, maybe seven days left. We'll take care of everything until then and you're not to worry."

The words "until then" caused a little current of fear to race through her. "All right. I won't worry for the next six, maybe seven days."

"Good." She gave Ellen another hug before letting her go. "After that, Del will see to it you'll never want for anything again."

She wanted to give in and completely believe her friend's opinion. Still, life had taught her nothing is ever certain. "Can I rely on him?" she asked in a small voice.

Marie's jaw dropped for a moment until she recovered. "I don't know what to say to that." Lucky's bugle interrupted for a moment, giving them the signal to move on. "I suppose you'll just see when you see, Ellen."

The woman walked away as Buster and Skeeter ran up to Ellen. Their presence distracted her from the unpleasant feeling of having overstepped her bounds. "Hello, you two! Look what I found for you." She held out the clothes for each boy.

Skeeter took his first. "Huh." He flung the shirt over his shoulder like a cup towel and held out the pants. "Do you want me to wear them now?"

Buster draped his pants over his shoulder like his brother had done. The baby looked for the buttons while Ellen replied, "No, not unless you want to. I'll need to wash your current clothes this evening." She nodded at the wagons rolling away from them. "Let's get going for now and change out later. Buster?" She held out her hand for him. "Come with me and I'll tell you how I'm sewing up your shirt."

By the time they'd eaten their venison stew for supper, Marie was back to her usual chatty self. The lapse in good humor had been odd. Ellen couldn't remember another time when her friend had stopped speaking to her specifically. She licked her lips. At least now she knew to keep her worries about Del to herself. Marie was firmly in his corner.

"I know when I get home, the first thing I want is a hot bath." Sam set his empty dish aside and leaned back. "How about you, Ellen?"

She'd not expected him to ask her first and tapped her plate a few times, thinking. "My wish is I'd like a hot bath too, but I don't want to copy you."

Lucky took both their dishes, clanking them into the wash pail. "I'd like to marry a pretty lady and her do all my washing for the rest of my life." He waved off the catcalls from the other men about him and Jenny. Even Skeeter joined in teasing the young man until he blushed. "What about you, Lefty? You got any special plans?"

"I'd like to see my Pa. He said get out and travel the country while I was young." Lefty shrugged. "He knows about my hurt arm but said it don't bother him none and come home so I can help farm. Come spring, I might just do that."

Lucky set the full pail in front of Arnold. "You're washing up tonight, right?"

Stretching, Arnold said, "I guess so. A nice bed is going to feel good once I'm back."

Marie smiled. "That's my choice. At this point, I don't care if it's straw tick or goose down, I'd like a real bed."

Buster crawled into Ellen's lap. She held him, rocking a little so he'd relax and sleep. Skeeter helped Lefty spread out the beds before settling down with him. She kept an eye on the two, soon joined by Lucky, as they began playing cards. When her little brother began snoring, Ellen eased over to their bed. She snuggled in under the cover and fell asleep to her younger brother's giggling.

Hissing whispers woke Ellen.

"What? How many?"

"Two. No one's seen them."

"All right." Sam sighed before rustling around. "They couldn't have gone far. Start searching and I'll join you."

Ellen peeked to see him putting on his boots as Lucky went toward the creek. She sat up. "Do you need my help?"

"No." He pulled on his second boot. "Though if you'd start our coffee, we'd all be grateful to you."

She smiled. "I'd be glad to." As soon as he left, she stoked the fire and hoped everything might be easy to find. She'd been rustling around in the wagon for a little while, trying to be quiet.

"Looking for the coffee pot?" asked Marie. At Ellen's nod, she pointed to a small trunk. "I put it in there to keep the dry goods dryer."

Ellen opened it and found everything she needed, plus breakfast fixings besides. "Should we start cooking, or wait for them to return?"

"The boys will be hungry, so we can at least get them fed first." Marie hopped into the wagon as Ellen got down from it. "If you get water, I can start everything else."

"All right." She scooped up the pail, taking out the dishes. On her way to the river, Ellen realized she was looking for Del. She smiled at her habit. He was probably living the high life in Oregon City, eating stove-cooked food after having had a hot bath and sleeping the night in a feather bed.

Her steps faltered when remembering how close she'd been to running away with him that day. If she'd left before Pa died? She shuddered, happy with the choice she'd made for her brothers' sake. Back at camp, she poured water for coffee and biscuits.

"It's a bit cold this morning." Marie took a blanket and wrapped it around her like a shawl. "Sam assures me summers are warmer than this usually. I think he's just trying to appease me."

"Maybe so." Ellen knelt by the fire. "We seem higher in elevation here than at home. The air is thinner and drier."

"He said the valley is lower and rainier. I can only hope his idea of warmer and wetter is my idea too."

She smiled at Marie, glad the silence was over between them, yet like a loose tooth she couldn't leave alone, Ellen had to say something. "Marie, I know you have an affection for Del and I'm sorry for what I said earlier. He's a wonderful man and I have no doubts about him."

"I understand. Later, when thinking about your situation, I realized you might not have much confidence in people staying alive for you." She looked up at her friend. "I hope that came out as caring as I'd intended."

"It did. Or at least, I took it as such."

"Good."

"Is breakfast ready, ma'am?"

Ellen turned to see Lefty behind her, tying his horse to their wagon. A sound from Skeeter caught her attention as he sat up and rubbed his eyes. Marie spoke first. "Not quite. You have time for your morning toiletries if you like."

The young man grinned. "Sure thing, ma'am."

Before she could say anything, Skeeter had their little brother up and out of bed. "Come on, Bust, let's go."

"Don't stray far; it's about time to eat," hollered Ellen after them. The trees weren't as thick as Missouri's forests, but a couple of boys could get lost. She breathed easier when they returned and wolfed down their meals.

The excitement buzzing in the air dimmed only while people ate. Barlow's Gate was on everyone's mind and in all the conversations. She imagined it to be like Devil's Gate but with a pathway through it instead of a river. It had to be something grand, a gateway to fertile land and civilization.

"We might as well get started. I'm expecting a wait at Barlow's." Sam shook the dust from first himself then his seat. "I'll tell the others and let them get ready to go."

She hopped up, pulling Buster to his feet also. They had folded bedrolls, washed dishes, and saddled or yoked animals by the time Sam came back. The wagon party began rolling, stopping early in a line of other groups. Ellen strained to see the huge gates and figured the landmark must be too far ahead to see from here.

Buster tugged at her skirts with a guilty look on his face. She grimaced, checking his pants to find them dry. "Potty time?" The little boy nodded and she led him off the road to a more private area in the trees. She kept an eye out for the Granvilles, hurrying back once her brother was done. The wagon had already gone between two posts guarded by two men. Others milled around and she saw the Allens and Nelsons behind them.

Past the posts, the road smoothed out and made walking easy. She glanced behind to check. That had to have been Barlow's Gate. Ellen hurried ahead to see Skeeter and Marie walking together.

"Your brother said the most adorable thing. He expected the Gate to be made of gold and silver with a *Welcome to Oregon Territory* sign." She patted the boys back. "It's a grand idea. I think he should write a letter suggesting that very thing."

Before she could think of how foolish it might sound, Ellen said, "I'd expected a canyon with tall spires on each side. Not two hitching posts."

Marie laughed. "It sounded that magnificent, certainly!" She nodded ahead. "I'm to take over for Lefty in a little bit. Sam and the men will need to guard the Allens' cattle. As often as livestock gets lost in the timber, they're expecting to bring back more than we started with."

"That will be handy."

"Yes, until we find their true owners."

Both women caught sight of Lefty's wave, and Marie hurried to lead the oxen. Ellen stayed back with her brothers. The forest became denser with each mile, the blue sky peeking in between leaves and pine needles. The road descended into a valley, flanked by gentle cliffs caused by the river beside them. The narrow path barely allowed two wagons to pass each other.

"I'm going to find the Allens," said Skeeter.

"All right. Stay close to us. No getting lost or hurt." She smiled as he waved and ran off. Ellen looked to see one of the twins—she never knew which one—motioning to her brother. She scooped up Buster and settled him on her hip. No one stopped for the noon meal, and both Ellen and the baby grew cranky from missing lunch. She had to let him walk a little while, otherwise, he'd not stop untying her sunbonnet or smearing her glasses. He thought it great fun to mess up the lenses so she'd stop and clean them. As soon as she sat him down, his feet hit the road and he hid behind a tree. She grinned, having figured out a game to play with him. "Goodbye, Buster. It's been good being your sister. So long."

He ran up to her. "Sis! Hi! Here I am!"

"What? Why, hello little boy. Have we met?

"I'm Busser! Your brother!"

She hid a smile. "Oh, I don't know. I said goodbye to him a

long while back."

"I'm him! I'm me!"

Ellen laughed. "No, I'm pretty sure you're not Buster." She kept up the game for a while, letting him try to convince her of who he was. When the boy stopped to yawn, Ellen picked him up and tickled him. "You giggle like my brother. Why! I think you are my brother!"

He gave her a hug, burying his face in her neck. "I told you!"

The hills seemed more like mountains as they climbed up and then braced for going down. Just when Ellen didn't think she could take one more step, it always seemed like they'd reach a peak of some sort. The view of Mount Hood's beauty rewarded her. Plus, going downhill appealed to everyone but those responsible for braking the wagons. The sun was still well above the mountaintops when they rolled into a small valley. The sudden width and absence of trees felt good. With months out on the open prairie, she'd not realized how closed in the timber seemed.

The grass spread out like a blanket either side from the road. After what had seemed like a lifetime without fuel, wood was everywhere for the gathering. She marveled at the water's clearness every time they crossed the creek. Ellen wondered if Del lived in such a place and knew he had to have a home in a similar valley. As the wagons formed their semicircle, she grinned. Now she'd have time to wash clothes, fix Buster's new shirt, and maybe write in the family journal. Their blankets from the trunk smelled musty. They'd get a good scrubbing too. She shook her head at the thought of being happy to do laundry in the wilderness.

She found Skeeter on her way back to the Granville wagon. "Would you please watch out for Bust while I do chores?"

"Sure, sis!" He held out a hand to the little boy. "Come on. Let's see if anyone else wants to play train robbers with us."

Ellen saw Marie leading the oxen to water, so she took the chance to let down the tailgate. She piled the dirty clothes and blankets on the ground. There was a moment's hesitation before she added everyone else's laundry. Would they mind her taking initiative? She wondered as she piled them all on. Hopefully not, because washing was the least she could do for the group taking in her and the boys.

The dappled sunlight danced along the water as she scrubbed. The woods were lovely and reminded her of Del. She shook off the longing for him and worked harder on the dirt stains. Every so often, she'd have to stand and stretch, giving her time to see who else lined the creek. Sam had been far upstream at a swimming hole. His fishing pole meant they'd have a good meal tonight. She went back to cleaning his shirt. The amount of laundry for Sam's group was a lot more than the Winslows'.

She laid out the lighter things on the taller grasses. The blankets were heavy enough on their own without being damp too. Ellen draped them over the wagon wheels, stopping when she saw Marie with Buster's new shirt. "What are you doing?"

Her friend held up the little garment. "I was done staking out the animals and thought I'd help you. I noticed all our clothes were gone. With you busy there, I decided to be busy here." Marie bit her lip before saying, "What do you think? I used all the white buttons we had. Lucky might need to whittle us more for the shirttail."

"It's perfect!" She checked the rip. "You've even fixed the tear. He can wear this tonight." Ellen gave the woman a hug. "Thank you!"

"It was my pleasure. He'll look smart in it for sure."

"All due to you. I'll get the rest of the clothes and help you with dinner." She strolled down to the creek bed and scooped up their dripping laundry. Headed back, she saw Skeeter run up with the Allen boys and Buster.

They all breathed heavy while the older Winslow boy asked, "We're hungry. When is supper?"

Marie spoke first. "Not for a while. Would you like something to tide you over till then?" She stood, headed for the wagon. "How about some dried fruit? I'm planning on a peach cobbler tonight, but there are some apple slices in here." She gathered up the dried rings, giving a few to each child. "There's fresh water at the creek when you're thirsty."

"Thanks, Miz Granville."

"You're welcome, Henry." Marie went back to picking out the flattened peaches while Ellen began draping the clothes over anything possible. Her friend paused in her sorting and she felt Marie's stare. "Remember that dress you borrowed after that dunking in the Green River? I've not worn it since, and it suits you much better." She climbed up in the wagon, her voice muffled by the dingy canvas top. "You'll be doing me a favor by taking it off my hands. Otherwise, moths will eat it right up." She hopped down with the folded dress in hand. "I hope this will still fit."

Ellen fluffed out the fabric and held it against her. "I'm sure it does."

"I'm glad. Now, you'll have something clean for when we reach Oregon City." Marie moved her fruit and jars to the wagon seat in front. "I'll guard up here if you'll tie up the back."

"All right." She pulled up the tailgate first. Aware that Sam or one of his men might wander by and need something, she changed out in a hurry. The gifted dress seemed looser now than the time before. She might need to take it in, depending on how well Del provided for them. Ellen shook her head at the assumption. It'd be better to wait and see if he truly would welcome her and the boys. Even if he might have been willing to at some point, any number of things might have happened in two weeks. She opened up the back of the wagon and eased to the ground.

Marie walked from the front. "You look lovely!" She nodded at the tailgate. "If you'll let that down, I'll get started on dinner."

"Wait, you were guarding the front, weren't you?"

"Of course! I heard you open the canvas before coming over." She patted Ellen's arm. "Don't worry. I did keep a look out for you."

Ellen laughed as she went to the creek yet again. All the people were different, yet the chores were the same. She scrubbed the skirt extra until the water ran clear. This time, she didn't linger. Dinner required cooking, and while Marie said she didn't need help, Ellen wanted to sneak bites when she could. Soon, the dress hung over the last bit of space on the wagon's tongue.

Marie had seats ready for them and a fire pit made. She must have seen Ellen's surprise because she laughed. "It wasn't all me. Lucky and Arnold came by, fixed all this, and then went off to see if Sam's caught dinner." She patted one of the folded blankets. "Have a seat and help me peel."

She did as requested, both women working. "These are really good quality. Were these in your wagon all this time?"

"No, Sam traded for them at the Frenchman's post. We had extra rice and everyone here decided potatoes would be a welcome change. He also traded beans for peas, but we'll have them tomorrow night."

Ellen smiled. "Thank you for taking us in, especially after

hearing all this."

"It's our pleasure. Sam will be especially glad we did after he sees his clean shirts."

"They're not perfect."

"At this point, I don't know how they can be." Marie stood, stretching her fingers. "It'll take a good boiling and bluing to get them back to white. Maybe I'll just dye them brown and be done with it."

"No!" Sam came up with four large salmon fillets. "How dare you suggest such a thing? My white shirts let the world know how erudite I am."

His wife laughed, taking the fish from him. "Oh, I see. You're so erudite that you can't say cultured or well-educated instead?"

"Exactly. A brown shirt would render me banal."

"Instead of just ordinary? Very well, I hope your mother has bluing or knows where I can find some."

Their banter gave Ellen something to think on while she cut up potatoes. She knew Del had parents, but where did they live? Did he see them very often? Did they live in a little log cabin or a teepee like the plains Indians? She'd not seen enough of the natives in a while to know what sort of houses they had. Somewhat shamefully, she realized in all their time together, she'd never asked about his permanent home.

Her imagination followed several twisty paths, imagining where a Métis like him might live. Everything from a cave to a ramshackle hut was possible. She helped with the last bit of dinner, listened to her brothers first, then the other men about their days, all the while not really paying attention. Instead, she went back over every scrap of conversation she'd had with Del for clues about his true lifestyle.

"Help, sis."

Buster shook her out of her musings. He stood there with his new shirt on but unfastened. "Don't you look nice!" she said while buttoning him up. "Did you thank Mrs. Granville?"

He leaned against her, looking at Marie. "Thank you."

"You're welcome, sweetheart. Now come here and get your supper."

The little boy toddled over and sat with his hands out. Marie served the freshly caught salmon, potatoes, and peach cobbler to everyone. The peaches tasted like heaven to Ellen, almost blotting out how wonderful everything else was. If this was Oregon's campfire food, she was eager to try something from a real stove. "How much longer do we have before this journey's end, Sam?"

"Let's see, four days if we're lucky. If another ox dies or a wagon axel breaks, longer."

Four days seemed like both nothing and forever when it came to seeing Del again. She glanced up from her plate, seeing Lucky collecting dishes. Ellen ate the last couple of bites before handing him hers. A quick check of her brothers showed they were already wandering around, playing among the wagon wheels. Arnold got out his diary while Lefty and Sam spread out the bed, reminding her of the Winslow journal. She'd not written anything since Pa's death.

Ellen helped with the beds before climbing in and searching her trunk. It'd not taken long in the dry air for her books to dry. She retrieved both since they needed updating with Jack Winslow's death. Back fireside, she opened the Bible to find that Pa had never entered in Lucy's death. She sighed in frustration, not remembering the exact date. The clank from their dinner pail caught her attention, and she looked up to find Lucky had returned from cleaning.

Others in the group worked on their own projects. Sam and Arnold wrote, though it looked like the younger man was sketching. Lucky had his bugle out and wiped away fingerprints from the brass. Marie was sewing while Lefty quietly read to her from the Bible. Which reminded Ellen of her start in updating theirs. Finding their family record in the middle, she guessed at Lucy's death and entered in Pa's. She tapped her finger against the page, wondering if she should include her wedding to Del. It hadn't happened in a church, so she closed the book and set it aside in favor of the journal.

The pages crackled open, thanks to their dunking. The pencil marks still seemed strong, so she thumbed her way to the last blank page. Not much space was left in the little book. She smiled. Just enough to write about the prior few days and the next week, then, Pa would....

Ellen stopped her thoughts right there. Pa would nothing. He'd never be able to read her thoughts ever again. Maybe the boys would later after they learned to read, but now she could write what she wanted. Not freely and not everything, but certainly about how Del had saved them from drowning and rescued her from Pointed Nose. She bit her lip, certain she'd need a new book for all the additional information. Ellen wrote far into the evening, only stopping when Lucky snored loudly enough to jar her from her thoughts. She smiled before setting the journal on top of their Bible and settling in for the night.

Rain woke up everyone. Ellen rushed to gather clothes before they were any more drenched. No one complained about the wet, she suspected due to the vast desert they'd lived through in the prior months. Coffee and breakfast were skipped in favor of getting on the road. They descended with her carrying Buster most of the way, weaving around huge rocks as the wagons bounced over smaller ones. The wet ground made traction tough, so most on foot walked along the sides. The loamy soil helped keep them from falling.

First hers then Buster's stomach growled. He whimpered before leaning into her to avoid the rain. She'd heard something about snow as everyone rushed around but never got the chance to ask. If Sam suspected flurries, she agreed; they needed to hurry like they were. They passed a wide boggy part on the way, and she wanted to stop for a noon meal. No one even paused as they continued, so Ellen hurried up to Marie and asked, "When will we camp?"

"Not for a while. Sam said with the road narrowing, we would have plenty of time for eating while we wait for the jam to clear." She shook her head. "He's warned me there won't be much room to walk alongside the animals. The road is too narrow."

"What if someone is coming east?"

"He didn't say."

"Goodness." She shifted Buster to the other hip. He squirmed, trying to slide down. "No, you need to let me carry you for now." Ellen turned to the wheels behind them so he could see. "You don't want those rolling over you." She tickled his neck to distract him. "I'll let you run free as soon as it's safe, all right? Just be good until then."

"I want to go with Skeets."

"He needs to be with us too." She peered down the side of the hill. "It's a steep fall down there." Buster looked where she did then at Ellen, nodding. "See? So let's find him."

Marie hollered to them. "I saw him with the Allen twins earlier. He's probably walking with them still."

"We'll go look for him there." She boosted her brother back onto her hip and fell back. The road was still wide enough for her to walk east. Ellen didn't feel like backtracking, so she waited until first the Nelsons passed her and then the Allens rolled by. All the children were following with Jenny, her mother, and Mrs. Allen herding them along. She fell in step with Jenny. "How have you been?" Mrs. Allen glanced at Ellen without turning her head.

Jenny looked to her mother before responding. "I've been fine, and you?"

She stifled a frustrated sigh. "I've been good despite losing Pa."

"I'm sorry for your loss."

The short answer, while not curt, still irritated Ellen. She smiled instead of frowning and worked on being civil. "Skeeter has been playing with the twins a lot. Send him to me if he's overstaying his welcome."

Mrs. Allen leaned over to her a little. "He's a fine young man, and we're glad to see him. Your baby brother is welcome too."

The woman's nose wrinkled in such a way that Ellen knew she wasn't included in the invitation. She didn't trust herself to speak calmly, so she merely nodded. This time when Buster squirmed, she let him go play. She had a few moments of walking without his weight before the wagon in front of them came to a full halt. Going to the side and looking down the line, she discovered everyone had stopped. Sam and Arnold rode uphill to them, pausing at each wagon before reaching them.

Sam turned back to his company wagon and Arnold tipped his hat at them. "Ladies. We've had to stop. Not sure why, but we'll get going as soon as possible. Boss says to grab your noon meal while you can."

Ellen pounced on the excuse to flee from the Allens and called out to her brothers. "Boys, let's go find Mrs. Granville." They ran up to her and followed down to the wagon.

Marie was letting down the tailgate and climbing inside when they arrived. "I think we have some fruit left." She reemerged from the back. "Not a lot, but it'll tide us over until supper tonight."

Each of them took the handful she gave. Ellen noticed how little remained in the jar. "What about the men? Won't they want some? Maybe we should put some of ours back in there."

"Goodness no. Sam and the boys have hardtack and jerky in case they need it." She retrieved the rest for herself before putting the lid back on. "They'll want to eat what they're carrying."

Ellen nodded, her mouth too busy chewing the leathery food to speak. She'd have to learn how to dry fruit like this for meals during the winter. The boys, she noticed, didn't waste time eating. "I suppose we'd better get moving," said Marie. "I hear creaking from the wagons in front of us." She hurried to put up the jar and secure the tailgate before leading the animals.

Skeeter pulled on Ellen's arm. "Sis! Can I go play with the twins?"

"Yes, if you take Buster with you."

"Aw, do I have to? He's kind of little."

She smiled at him. "You don't have to, but he'd like playing games with you and the others."

"We have to stop all the time and let him go."

"So have him go before you start playing."

"Will that work?"

"Try it and see," she said. He held out his hand and Buster took it. "Watch out for the wagon wheels, both of you." Skeeter's absentminded wave didn't completely reassure her. Still, she knew her brother had heard enough about tragic accidents that he'd be careful. He might protest bringing Buster along, but she saw the affection the older boy had for the baby of their family.

They crept along through the forest. Most times, they hugged the hillside so much that everyone walked in single file. Needing to slow now seemed almost cruel after the breakneck speeds they'd rolled along on the flat prairie. The sun inched its way down to the horizon. It was early evening before they entered a wide valley. Foothills rose up north and south of them while the west was clear and flat ahead. The wide green expanse seemed like a dream or some paradise. Ellen knew now why so many risked so much to travel here. The afternoon rains, the rich soil, and the cool temperatures left her feeling joyful and at home.

The boys straggled back to her, worn out from all the playing. Buster didn't fuss and let her hold him while Skeeter stayed close. The road widened with each foot they descended into the valley. She marveled at her brothers' patience. They didn't ask about supper, knowing they'd eat when the wagon stopped. Meanwhile, she daydreamed about eating as much as anyone could fish or hunt for her.

She almost cheered when the lead wagon left the trail and headed toward a grassy meadow. The dim light cast long shadows over everything. She ignored her exhaustion and put one foot in front of the other until at last the wagon stopped rolling. Sam and his men rode up and started unsaddling horses and unhitching oxen. She let Buster slide down and stretched that side of her body. Before she could begin chores, Mr. Allen and Mr. Nelson walked up to Sam.

Nelson squinted at him and pointed a finger at the younger man. "Look, Granville, you've been pushing us mighty hard this past week, and we're tired of it."

"That's right," said Allen. "We either stay here a couple of days, or we're not a part of this group anymore."

Sam took off his hat and ran a hand through his hair. "You paid for me to take you to Willamette Valley and we're not there yet. No one is going anywhere until we arrive."

Mr. Allen took a step forward, standing toe to toe with Sam. "See, young man? You've had that wrong attitude all along."

Pushing Allen aside, Nelson added, "We all listened to you until now because you seemed to know what you were doing out there in the wilderness. We're in civilization now and Allen and I agree. We can go on from here."

Sam lifted his chin, looking down his nose at them. "I'd prefer you didn't."

Nelson smirked. "That don't matter. We're staying a couple of days and that's that."

"It seems we're all overtired." Sam slapped his gloves against his leg. "Fine. Let's agree to talk about this tomorrow morning after a good night's rest."

A look passed between the dissenters before Nelson said, "Won't make any difference, but if you insist."

Both men wandered back to their wagons and Ellen relaxed a little. They'd looked furious enough to erupt in anger like Pa often did. She hadn't realized until just now how nice life was, out from under someone else's bad temper. When she glanced down at Skeeter, she saw him looking up at her with wide eyes. "It's all right, sweetheart. They were just discussing, not fighting."

"I'm glad. I might help you with chores in case anything

happens to make them mad again."

"Certainly, I'll let you." She and Skeeter retrieved and spread out the beds for everyone. Lucky built the fire, and when he was done, Marie hurried to start supper. Ellen was taking Buster for a potty when Lefty walked up with a pail of water. She smiled, knowing they'd be eating soon.

They returned to find everyone seated. The men worked on the same projects tonight as last night, and Marie stirred the potatoes and peas. Ellen fretted a little, hoping they'd have enough provisions to reach either Del's or Sam's home. Her brothers were playing soldiers using whittled men Arnold had made, so she retrieved her journal. She'd poured her heart out about Del on most of the pages left. The inside back cover was all that remained. She wrote in small letters about the beautiful green valley.

No one tarried in eating dinner and piling the dishes in the pail. Their meal might have been plain, but each one imagined the better suppers they'd have in just a few days. A sleepy satisfaction settled everyone as each nestled into their beds. Even the boys didn't need to be told to go to sleep.

Quiet but insistent talking woke Ellen. She squeezed her eyes closed, not wanting to listen to a private conversation. Yesterday's rocks and walking downhill had been tougher than she'd thought. She turned over and felt every achy muscle.

"They're just sitting there, boss. I tried telling them you'd leave, and Nelson said he didn't mind," whispered Lucky

"All right. I've said what I'll do and so has he. So, just get ready for leaving."

Ellen kept her eyes closed. She wondered if the Allens would go or stay. Jenny might tell her if she asked. She reconsidered talking to her former friend. No, Ellen would prefer to not speak to any of them for a while. She didn't blame anyone for their prejudice, even if she thought it very wrong. However, she knew that if Del had proved nothing to a person by rescuing her from the kidnapping, he'd never be able to convince them.

She stared up at the sky. High clouds caught the sun's first colors of the day. She slid off her glasses and wiped the lenses with the blanket's edge. The frames were a little bent, a hazard of sleeping with them on. It was a habit she'd started while on the trail and needed to stop. Otherwise the metal would weaken every time she bent them back into shape. Ellen rested the glasses on her chest and put her hands behind her head.

The sky really was lovely. The forests they'd been through in the past few days kept the blue from her. Ellen tilted her head a little, thinking of how similar the forests of Missouri and Oregon Territory were. The only differences so far were the amount of rainfall and number of pine trees. Except for the mountains, it felt like home. She sighed. It'd not be a home if Del weren't there with her and the boys. She knew they all liked each other, but was it enough to make them a family? It had to be.

She sat up, the nearby noises too loud to let her sleep. Ellen saw a man in a white shirt nearby and smiled since he had to be Sam. He sat down beside her and she said, "I suppose we'll be missing the Nelsons. Such a shame but I'm sure they'll be fine. You've led them close enough. They'll find their way just fine even now, thanks to your expertise."

"*Merci*, but the credit goes to Sam."

"Del!" she squealed and sat up.

"*Un moment, ma coeur.*" He picked up her glasses. "Don't crush these or you'll think any other man might be me, too."

She put on her glasses as fast as possible and saw his dear face. Had he always looked at her with such love? "What are you doing here so soon? I thought it'd be days yet."

"I couldn't resist you any longer. An entire day at home and *maman* threw me out for my gloom without you."

Her heart sank. He might live in a teepee, but it was the only home he might have. "Oh no! Are you gone for good, or will she take you back if you want?"

He chuckled, kissing her forehead. "I'm not to come back home without you. She insists."

A warm feeling spread through her, as if she'd drank a dose of cough medicine too fast. "My goodness. I'd better start packing."

"Are we going with you?" Skeeter asked.

Both adults turned to him. Del spoke first. "Of course. Where else would you go?"

The boy sat up but didn't look at either of them. "I don't know for sure. Robert said sisters didn't take their brothers home when they married."

"Robert?" asked Del.

"One of the Allen twins," supplied Ellen.

"Ah." In a louder voice, he continued, "Your sister does. You and Buster are to live with us for as long as you like."

"What if it's for forever? Will you let us then?"

Del nodded. "Yes."

Skeeter went and hugged Del. Buster followed, both boys clinging like they'd never let go. Ellen got out from under her blankets. "Are you hungry?" She looked around and found the camp deserted. "I can start breakfast for you."

"I can't. I'm not staying here long." He grinned as the boys let go of him. "No, it's nothing. I'm leaving to get a wagon and oxen for us. Sam told me what happened to yours. He and his men are sending the word out about how you need a new one."

"We don't. All we need is you." She laughed when the boys scooted next to him as if they were his own children. "We don't mind staying with the group until Oregon City as long as you're with us. Once we're all there, it might be a good time for a wedding."

"A wedding there? No, Ellen, we're not getting married in Oregon City. In fact, I don't want to stay here any longer than we have to."

CHAPTER 12

"Oh. Very well. I suppose that's fine."

Del smiled at her. He'd not been clear and she'd misunderstood. "I'm taking you and the boys to my parents' house. You can rest and enjoy sleeping in a bed before we decide on a wedding date." Everyone exhaled at once and he laughed. "Did you think I wouldn't marry you? I already have once. It's no trouble to do it again."

"If you're sure…."

He stood, holding his hand out to help her up. "Let's tell everyone the news, help with breakfast, and get started back home. My parents are waiting. They're not patient people either."

"Should I be worried?" she asked, only half in jest.

"No, flattered. They want to meet you and your brothers." He grabbed the trailing end of the blanket to help her fold. "I've told them everything." Del grinned at her alarmed expression. "Mostly."

"They don't know about Pa, do they?"

He scooped up another blanket. "*Non.* Sam just told me and I'm sorry for your loss."

"The boys have no one but me now."

"Are you needing an argument?" Del took the folded bundle and put it on the tailgate, watching her face as he worked. "Because I can list how many people they have besides you."

She laughed. "Maybe I do need to argue, but I'd rather hear how many people care for us."

Marie stepped from around the wagon with a full water pail. "Are you done with the greetings? I'd like to start the coffee and breakfast."

"Of course, *ma coupin.*"

Ellen shook his arm. "No more coopins for you, Mr. Du Boise. I'm a very jealous wife."

He grinned at the other woman. "Sorry, ma—um, *mon amie.*"

"*Maman,* hmm? So, Sam ruined the surprise?" Marie shook her head while pouring water into the coffee pot. "He promised me to keep quiet for another month just to be sure."

"How wonderful!" Ellen went over and hugged her. "I'm so glad you'll be settled during your increasing."

"So am I. All of this is just so wonderful!"

Del stole a glance at the boys when hearing the sob in both women's voices. Both Winslows were staring at him and he shrugged. Understanding how women think wasn't going to be a skill they'd get from him. He had no idea. "Should I cook breakfast for you?"

"No, no." Marie waved him off. "I can." She wiped her eyes. "Goodness! I'm such a baby." Her eyes filled again. "I'm just so happy."

"Here," said Ellen. "Let me cook while you rest."

Del offered, "Madam can supervise me while I gather Ellen and the boys' things." Both ladies stood at the wagon's back, watching as he climbed in. "Sam mentioned a pushcart?"

"Yes," said Marie. "You'll need it for her trunk."

He found the cart lying on its side. He eased it out and down. Ellen helped him lower it to the ground, their hands touching. He let his fingertips linger, enjoying the surprise contact. Later, he promised his lusty thoughts, when he had her home and in his own bed. She blushed under what had to be a wolfish grin from him.

"Come on, you two. Work now, honeymoon later." Sam peeked around the corner, his men behind him. "Ladies, I smell coffee. Are there biscuits too?"

"There will be." Ellen reached in for the flour, mixing bowl, and wooden spoon. "I'll get started."

"Good. I know what is yours in here. We can help your man get you all packed up."

He exchanged places with Sam. His friend passed the trunk and various blankets to him. Del glanced over at the boys watching him. One could ride with Ellen on Pomme while the other, preferably Buster, rode in the cart while Del pulled. He made sure the trunk was pushed all the way back and used the blankets as a cushion for the rest of it. By the time they finished packing, breakfast smelled ready.

In the times before when Del had sat around a campfire with everyone, he'd been more intent on catching a glimpse of Ellen. Now he was bringing her home. After drinking his last bit of coffee, he stood.

Sam glanced up at him before refilling his cup. "Ready so

soon? What's your hurry?"

"Sam!" Marie tapped her husband on his arm. "Tell me you don't mean that. Let them go already."

"What? I'm not keeping them here." He looked up at his friend. "Am I?"

Del caught Ellen's eye. "Are you ready?"

"Almost." She handed her cup to Lucky and picked up Buster. "Marie, I can stay if you need my help."

"Mercy, no. Go on. I have a crew of young men to do chores for me."

Ellen glanced at him, her cheeks turning pink. "Very well. Boys, let's get ready to go home. Buster, you can bring your biscuit with you. Skeeter, put on your shoes first, then your brother's." She turned to Del. "I think Buster should ride in the push cart. He's lightest and easiest for me to haul."

The idea of her walking to his parents when he had Pomme stunned him. "*Non*, not at all. You and Skeeter can ride my horse while I lead the way with Buster in the cart. No discussion."

She closed her open mouth and grinned. "Boys, you heard the man. Let's get started." Ellen went to Marie first. "Goodbye. I'll miss you so!" They hugged.

Del shook his head and Sam laughed before saying, "You'll see each other tomorrow, next day at the latest. The Du Boise home is on our way."

Both women laughed. Ellen asked, "So my saying goodbye to your wonderful crew is premature?"

"Very. Go, so we can get moving ourselves."

She grinned. "Del, we have our orders." Ellen scooped up Buster and put him in the cart. "Let's go, Skeeter. Pomme's a wonderful horse. You'll love the view from so high."

Del took the handles for the cart and pushed ahead to where Pomme grazed. Ellen got on the animal first, and her brother awkwardly followed. He held on tight.

"Skeet, ease up. I can't breathe."

"Sorry, sis."

He went in front, leading them to his home. He felt the Granville men watching until the wagon hid them from view. As soon as the road smoothed out, Buster fell back asleep. Del glanced at the boy and grinned at how relaxed the little fellow was. He heard the other two Winslows talking behind him. The trunk's contents rattled too much for him to catch any words, just the easygoing tone.

"You'll let us know when we're getting close, won't you?" asked Ellen.

Buster stirred a little when Del slowed down to reply. "Yes. We should get there mid afternoon."

"Oh my! That's not long."

"No." He resumed his prior speed. His arms ached a little, but the pain was worth it. He looked down at the sleeping boy before the road commanded his attention again. None of this, neither bringing home the children or Ellen, had been planned. The suddenness of it overwhelmed him a little. He'd expected to watch the Winslows from afar, waiting until Jack settled in with Lacy Benson. Del grinned when thinking of how surprised his parents would be. His father had only warned of buckshot peppering his hide, not of an instant family.

After topping a slight incline, he could almost see their destination. If not for the sleeping child, he'd be walking at a faster pace. Del wanted them home and comfortable after their long journey. He wanted them to feel settled and secure. Mostly, he wanted them happy and with him. The foothills on either side fell away, leaving the wide-open valley ahead of them.

Buster woke up and sat, rubbing his eyes. "Potty?"

"All right." He supposed they needed a break and possibly a cool drink of water. Del slowed to a stop. "Time for a rest." He set down the cart's legs flush and the boy squirmed out to the ground.

Ellen said, "Skeeter, you get down first and I'll follow. Go with Bust and don't stray far."

The boy slid down and Ellen eased to the ground afterward. Del noticed they both walked oddly and would be sore tomorrow. He tried not to grin at their difficulty.

She took him by the shirt front. "Stop it, mister. No laughing at us greenhorns." Ellen returned his smile and pulled him to her for a kiss.

A moan escaped him as he cradled the back of her neck. He deepened their embrace, certain her brothers weren't watching or she'd not be so forward with him. Del wrapped his other arm around her, pulling his woman closer. He leaned away barely enough to say, "I've missed you."

"You too, my dearest love."

He traced the side of her face with the back of his hand. "I can't believe you're here."

She chuckled. "Only until my brothers return."

"One more before then." Del captured her lips with his own, giving her a kiss that promised more when they had privacy. As he drew back, she reached up and caressed his face. His heart melted. "I love you so much. I call you my heart but you are more. You're my love, my life, and my very soul." Tears filled her eyes and he kissed her forehead. "And I? I am all yours forever."

"Hey, sis?"

Del turned and Ellen looked around him to see Skeeter. She sniffled before replying, "Yes, sweetheart?"

"Buster and I have decided we're hungry. Can we get something to eat?"

"May you?"

"Sis, c'mon! We're hungry!"

She glanced at Del, who nodded and went to his saddlebags. Ellen said, "Yes. You two eat while I go for a short walk."

He retrieved a hard tack cracker and a chunk of beef jerky for each one of them. The three of them worked on their food, first trying to bite and then chew. Ellen came back and he gave her a portion before heading for the creek himself with Pomme. Both horse and man drank before returning to their new family.

Del laughed when he saw all three of them ready to go. Buster sat in the cart, facing forward as if the rolling would start at any moment. Ellen and Skeeter were talking in between chewing hard on their lunch. They looked at him and grinned at his amusement. He picked up the cart handles, ignored the slight ache, and pushed on home.

Various side roads appeared as they went on, and he at last turned down the one leading to his parents. He knew Ellen saw his home when she gasped. He viewed the building through her eyes and smiled. The elder Du Boise had added a second story when Del was a child. The wood siding gleamed with fresh whitewash. A well house and garden were hidden, but the shale-red barn showed up through the trees. He smiled. His mother had insisted every tree remain unless there'd been a solid reason to remove it. Her request frustrated his father, but he did as she wanted.

Ellen pulled the horse to a stop. "Adelard, I don't know about this. Your family is rather wealthy. We don't have anything to offer."

He heard the fear and hesitation in her voice and eased the pushcart to a halt. "You have yourselves and that's more than enough." Uncertainty still showed on her face and he urged, "Let's go and let my parents prove this to you." He resumed his trek to the family home, eager to get there and prove himself right.

A dog began barking and his father stepped out of the front door. Del knew they all must look a sight. *"Allo, papa!"*

"Allo! Qu'es que c'est?" asked the elder Du Boise.

He answered in French, his father only knowing enough English to trade by. "This is my Ellen and her family."

"Mon Dieu! She has children?" Mr. Du Boise held out a hand to help first Skeeter and then her off of Pomme. *"Allo, ma Cherie, comment allez vous?"*

Ellen looked from one man to the other, replying in halting French, *"Je suis tres bonne, et vous?"*

Du Boise grinned from ear to ear, telling Ellen in French, "I'm very fine, young lady. Excellent French you have. Come in and meet Adelard's mother. She'll be so excited. We've heard so much about you."

"Papa?" He didn't know quite how to tell his father, but dove in. "She only understands just what she said. Ellen is still learning."

"Oh? That's too bad, but she has a good start. We'll make a strong Frenchwoman of her yet." He opened the door to find his wife on the other side. "Dear! Adelard is here!"

"I see that!" Mrs. Du Boise looked the family up and down. "Why are they still standing at our door?" She motioned to the Winslows. "Come in, come in. All of you." When they were inside and Mr. Du Boise shut the door, she continued, "Oh, you poor children. Adelard, you didn't tell me they were in such sad condition. I need to feed, wash, and put to bed every one of them." She went over to Ellen. "Such a beautiful girl. No wonder you fell in love at first sight."

Ellen's eyes narrowed. *"Que est coup de fonder?"*

"Oh!" Mrs. Du Boise covered her mouth with a hand. "She speaks French so horribly!" She turned to Del. "You taught her nothing? For shame! The poor thing understands nothing?"

"Del?" Ellen ventured. "Is, um, is this your mother? I assume so."

Her question took him aback. Could Ellen not tell this was his mother? Her native appearance, even in white's clothes, shouted *maman* to him. "I've been negligent, *ma coeur.*" Del saw his father's eyebrows rise. He'd understood enough English to know what his son had said. "This is my father, Jean-Baptiste Du Boise and my mother Mimiteh Du Boise."

"*Non, je suis Mimi.*"

He smiled. "She wants you to call her Mimi." Del turned to the older and paler version of himself. "*Papa, maman, c'est mon familie,* Ellen, Skeeter, *et* Buster." The two older Winslows chuckled while Buster laughed outright at their names said in French. "I know they are a surprise, but their father drowned in the Deschutes. They need us."

"But of course they do! I can smell them from here and they look hungry." She took her husband by the arm. "Jean, you can help me heat water for them while I cook." Mimi smiled at the little group. "They seem terrified. Adelard, explain to them about bathing and eating. Then unpack them into your room. No, you'll be sleeping in the barn until you're married."

"Maman, we are married, remember?"

"*Oui,* but halfway. She needs her people to know she's married."

He sighed, not happy with his mother's decision. Del looked to his father who shrugged. Jean-Baptiste was of no help to him and he scowled. "Fine. We'll marry first thing tomorrow."

"*Mon Dieu,* you are impossible!" She waved him on. "Go and get them settled. We'll argue later."

Leaning over, he gave her a kiss on the cheek. "*Merci, maman.*" Del smiled as she went to the kitchen and he continued in English, "Ellen, boys, I'm to show you where you'll sleep tonight. I'll bring your things inside and then help my parents fill the bath and cook dinner."

"My goodness, Del, that's a lot. I can help too."

"*Allons,* which means come on or let's go, and I'll tell you why you can't." He led them upstairs, grinning when the boys ran their hands reverently over the banister. They'd have to learn how to slide down like he had as a child. "You've worked hard enough and long enough. *Maman,* my mother, insists you're our guests and that you rest." He opened the door to his bedroom, the bed looking a little small for the three of them. "She wants you to stay here for the night and maybe beyond."

"Where will you sleep?" asked Skeeter.

They all looked at him, Ellen biting her lip as if afraid for Del to say anything. "I'll be in the barn with the farmhands."

"In the barn?" protested Ellen. "That's hardly fair for us to put you out."

Del chuckled at her concern. "You've not seen our barn. I'll be fine."

"If you're sure…."

"I am. Excuse me while I bring in your trunk." He left and went to get their belongings. Now in his home, the Winslows' things looked beat up and shabby. So did they, if he was honest. He set down the trunk by the staircase and went to the kitchen. "*Maman,* would it be acceptable to you if I let the boys have my clothes?"

She stirred the stew, preoccupied. "Don't you think they're a little small for your clothes?"

Imagining the small boys in his bigger shirts made him laugh. "Silly *maman,* you know I mean my old clothes."

"*D'accord, mon cher.* Go." She waved a spatula at him. "Let the boys pick whatever they'd like of yours and let me finish here."

His father dumped another bucket of water in the tub at the far end of the room. "We can take them into town later and let them pick out what they like."

"*Oui.*" He left to resume hauling the trunk up to Ellen and the boys. When he walked into the open room, they were all seated on the side of the bed. The three of them looked up at Del and he grinned. "Here, I'll set this here for when you need it." He placed the trunk against the wall and went to his armoire. "My parents want you all to go through these and pick out what you like." He opened the cedar drawer at the bottom. All of his childhood clothes were there and filled the space. They walked over and peered in. The boys sank to their knees and began rifling through everything as if it were Christmas morning. He stepped back, already enjoying their enthusiasm over new shirts and pants.

Ellen peered over the boys' shoulders. "I don't suppose you ever wore dresses?"

He laughed. "No, I'm sorry. Not since my christening gown."

"Really? I'll wager you were a beautiful baby."

"*Maman* would say I was."

"I'm sure." She went to their trunk and opened it. "My other dress is clean. I can wear it for dinner." Ellen took it out, shaking off the dust.

When he saw how worn the material was, his heart broke for how much difficulty she had endured. "Tomorrow morning, would you like to visit the town with me? We can all go and make a day of it."

She paused, holding the dress up, and looked at him. "I'd like to see a real city, but I don't know. It won't be too much trouble?"

"Not at all. We'd planned on this since before I retrieved you." He resisted the urge to cross his fingers behind him at the lie. "With everyone going, we will be sure to get everything we need."

"All right, it sounds wonderful." She smiled. "I hate to be rude, but when will we eat? Whatever is cooking smells so good."

"Soon I hope." His stomach growled as if to agree. "See? Come downstairs and we'll know for sure." The Winslow boys had all the clothes scattered around in piles on the floor. "Have you two picked out what you'll wear after your bath?"

"Yeah," said Skeeter and held up a shirt and pants. Buster saw and mimicked his older brother.

"Good job, both of you." Del motioned for them to follow him. "Let's see how close dinner is to being ready."

The heavenly smell of beef stew grew stronger as they approached. He glanced behind him as he entered the kitchen. The Winslows hung back behind him as if Del protected them. He almost laughed at the idea of anyone needing such a thing from his mother. "How soon until dinner?"

She turned and smiled at their guests. "Tell them soon. First a bath, then food. Your father has the boys' bathtub in the back yard. There's a sunny spot just for them." Mimi went to the hutch. "Your woman will have a bath in here before dinner, if she doesn't mind."

Jean-Baptiste walked in with another pail of water. "*Allo*. The tub out back is ready. The one in here? Another heated bucket and couple of fresh, it'll be done."

"*D'accord*," said Del. He grinned at everyone else. "The boys will get to swim out back. There's a tub just for them. Ellen, you'll be in here when papa is done."

"How will your mother cook if I'm in here? I don't want to disturb anyone."

She was right. They needed a divider. "I could always keep guard."

Ellen laughed. "And do you have coyotes guard your chickens too?"

"Good point. Very well, I'll have *maman* tell us what to do." He went over to the stove. "*Mam*, should Ellen wait until after dinner?"

"*Non! Voici*," she replied and moved the stew over to a cooler area. "This can wait until she's done." Mimi drew the curtains closed for both the window and the inside door. "Now, go keep an eye on the boys. Tell your father this is the last pail. *Allons!*"

He did as she ordered, leaving as she shooed him out. Seeing his father, he said, "Papa, it's the last, mother's orders."

"*Merci!*"

Del turned back to the boys. Both were naked and using the tub like a mini swimming pond. He should have thought to bring soap. Maybe a good soaking would be enough. Taking a seat, he glanced at the house. The boys would be fine here. He'd rather be helping Ellen bathe. But then, what man wouldn't? After a little while, he said to the children, "Try to scrub all the bugs from your hair." Their hollers and then groans amused him, with Skeeter having a queasy expression on his face and Buster a determined one.

His mother came over and sat beside him. "Papa is feeding the animals. I've noticed Ellen needs new clothes."

"I know. I've made the excuse for us to go into town tomorrow. I'd like to get her material for several dresses and one to get married in."

"Good. She's lovely, Adelard. Her brothers seem well mannered too. We'll see if they still are in a week's time."

Del laughed. "You don't think they're perfect angels?"

She gave him a wry glance. "*Non*, no boy is, nor should he be."

He heard the door open and looked behind him. Ellen stepped down, wearing her older dress.

His mother nudged him. "See? She needs new clothes, the poor dear. I'd give her mine, but your wife deserves new things."

Del nodded as Ellen sat beside him. "She deserves everything."

Mimi chuckled and ruffled his hair as she stood. "You're such

a fool, just like your father. Come in when the boys are dressed. I'll
have dinner ready."

Ellen leaned over to him when his mother was in the house.
"Did I hear something about dinner?"

"Yes, that it'll be ready when the boys are dressed."

Both children stopped splashing and Skeeter said, "We can eat
now? C'mon, Bust, let's go." They scrambled out and threw on the
clean clothes. Skeeter was ready first and took Del's hand. Ellen
helped Buster with his buttons and picked him up to carry inside.

Everyone settled in to eat. Mimi had dished up the meal with
a freshly baked batch of rolls. Del pulled one apart, the steam
rising. He was glad she'd fixed father's favorites tonight. Later, he'd
like his new family to try his mother's favorites. Dinner was quiet,
everyone eating or letting guests eat. Before anyone could ask for
seconds, Mrs. Du Boise served another helping. He grinned at
Skeeter. The boy would be either taller than him or rounder than
Randal down at the dry goods store.

Ellen sat back for a moment and then began gathering her
family's dishes. Mimi took them from her in a hurry. "*Non, non, non.*
Guests don't do dishes!"

When Ellen shrunk back, Del leaned over to her. "You are
our guest tonight. Maman wants to spoil you all." He grinned at
her dubious expression. "Don't worry, she'll put you to work soon
enough."

"In that case, if you don't mind, I'm rather tired. I think we're
turning in early tonight."

"I understand," he replied before telling his mother and father
of the Winslows' plans.

"Good night," came the reply, said in English from first his
father, then his mother. Del grinned. They'd learn the language in
spite of themselves, he was sure of it.

He followed the Winslows upstairs and into their room. "I
wanted to say goodnight as well. Don't be afraid to ask for
something if you need it. My parents want to make sure you're
happy. He leaned in and gave Ellen a kiss on the cheek. Skeeter ran
up to him and hugged him. He returned the hug, and when Del
bent down, Buster kissed his cheek. "Thank you, Buster."

Skeeter hurried into the bed, pulling the blankets up to his
chin. "Sis?"

"Yes, Skeeter?" Ellen slipped off her shoes and got in beside him, helping Buster up as well.

"This must be what heaven is like for ma and pa," her younger brother said in a reverent tone.

She looked at Del before replying, "I think you're right, sweetheart."

Instead of kissing her properly in front of her brothers, he left, pulling the door shut behind him. The boys would need their own room soon. He loved them but wanted a real honeymoon too.

Ellen opened her eyes to find herself in a bedroom. The sheets felt too soft to be true, and the pillow cradled her like cotton. The only thing marring her enjoyment was the sound of someone going potty. She glanced over to see Skeeter whispering instructions to Buster. They'd been quiet, but the chamber pot hadn't.

Sausage. Dear God in heaven, she smelled sausage. She could tell when the aroma hit the boys' noses. They turned like prairie dogs hearing a noise. She threw back the covers. "Breakfast! Let's go."

The three hurried out the door and downstairs to find Del and his parents in the kitchen. When he saw them, Del laughed. "I told them you'd be here as soon as food started frying."

Ellen went to the stove and breathed in deep. After months of bacon, the spicy sausage was perfect. A little basket of eggs sat on the shelf and she nodded at them. Mrs. Du Boise nodded with a grin. Ellen turned to her brothers. "Sausage and eggs."

Both children cheered, making all the adults laugh. Everyone except Mimi and Ellen sat down and waited for the meal. When Mrs. Du Boise noticed the young woman hovering, she hollered to her son. He did as requested, grabbing last night's cookpot and saying, "*Allons*," to his love.

She smiled, knowing what he'd said and followed. The boys' tub had been emptied and overturned for drying against a tree. Guilt filled her at someone else doing her work while she'd slept. They stopped at a water pump. Del emptied the pot of its soaking water and put in some fresh for scrubbing.

"Your parents, do they like me?"

"*Que?* I mean, what? Of course they do." He emptied the pot and refilled for rinsing. "You don't understand anything, do you, my dearest?" Del set down the pan and took her hands. "They don't have to tell me in any language. I can see it in their faces that they approve of you and adore your brothers. Who could not? I told them everything about you and your family before retrieving you, and then last night about your father's tragedy."

Her heart beat double time. She didn't want to ask for risk the truth would hurt, but she had to know. "So if you marry me, no one will mind if the boys live with us?"

He paused for a long time. At last he said, "I can see I've been lacking in my duties to you." Del picked up the dish and took her hand, leading her back to the kitchen. Once inside, he said, "Maman, papa, Buster, and Skeeter, attention?"

Everyone paused and his mother moved eggs from the frying pan to a plate. Ellen fidgeted. "I don't know if this is the best thing right now."

Del ignored her, pulling Ellen into the middle of the room and getting down on one knee. He grinned when his mother cheered, and then he glanced over to see his father's wide smile. He looked up at Ellen. "Miss Winslow, I have loved you from the moment we met. My life is nothing without you. I want you and your brothers to be a part of my family. Please ease my heartache and marry me."

Her mind struggled to think amid the love she felt for him. "Yes, I will marry you." The words bubbled out like water over a river's rapids. She couldn't take them back when everyone in the room began cheering.

Mimi spoke first and when she finished Del said, "Breakfast is ready. Maman says congratulations and let's eat before it gets cold."

The boys and Mr. Du Boise were first seated with the rest following. Mrs. Du Boise served everyone before sitting down to eat. Ellen tried to eat slowly and savor every bite. She couldn't remember the last egg she'd had and now sausage too? The biscuits also tasted better than any she'd ever cooked. Was it good cooking or love? She glanced over at Del and smiled. Maybe a healthy dose of both. He returned her smile and Ellen's face grew warm.

Skeeter pushed his plate forward and sat back. "When you get married, sis, will Del be our brother and let us live with you?"

Ellen assumed the children would know they'd always be with her. "Yes on all counts. I'm not sure where we'll live, but it will always be together."

Mimi, Jean-Baptiste, and Del all began talking in rapid fire

French. Ellen heard familiar words, but nothing concrete. Their voices raised as if in argument before they fell silent. At last, Del said, "We'll live here, at my parents' insistence. They want us to have a solid footing before we find a place of our own or for us to even stay here until they pass away."

The idea of Del losing his parents alarmed her. "They're not ill, are they? Tell me they're fine!"

He laughed before repeating in French what she'd said. His father laughed while his mother frowned and gave him a sharp retort. He sobered up in a hurry. "She said I'm not to tease or worry you. They're fine and they just want you to know you have a home with them."

Tears of relief filled her eyes. The Du Boise family was not only healthy, but accepting of the Winslows. Del had proposed with their blessing. This heavenly place really was to be their new home. A sob escaped her and Del pulled her into his arms. She heard him murmur something in French as he patted her back and kissed the top of her head.

"Maman will help the boys change clothes for town while papa saddles the horses. We'll sit here until everyone is ready. All right, sweetheart?"

She nodded against him, feeling bad that Mrs. Du Boise was doing her tasks. A good future daughter in law would push Del away and go help. Ellen kept her eyes closed, knowing she was already off to a horrible start. For now, she just soaked up the warmth of being held by him.

"What is your favorite color, my *coeur?*"

Ellen smiled, pulling away to wipe her tears, and looked up at him. "My favorite? I'm not sure."

"We'll find something you love."

The warmth in his eyes carried through to her soul. She loved the depths of the cinnamon and golden browns in them. "I've already found something I love."

He gave a little moan before kissing her. He'd asked, she'd said yes, and they'd been intimate. With this knowledge, Ellen didn't want to wait another moment. She broke away first. "Adelard, I don't think I can marry you soon enough."

"One kiss is all you need to desire me so?" He nuzzled her ear, whispering, "Just imagine when your brothers have their own bedroom."

She did and broke out in a cold sweat. "Let's go." Ellen stood. "I want to get to town and find a preacher today."

Del paused for a moment, listening to his mother call for them. "*Allons, ma petite.*" He took her hand. "Everyone is waiting."

When downstairs, she saw the knowing smiles on his parents' faces and blushed. The boys already sat on the wide seat. Both of them sat hard over and over to make the springs bounce. Mimi patted Skeeter on the knee. "Halt, *s'il vous plait,*" she said and put a hand over her mouth as if motion sick before snickering.

The boy laughed and Buster joined in. Ellen sat between them before looking into the wagon bed behind them. "How about you boys play in the back while we're going?" Both didn't waste time before climbing over and settling in. Del sat between her and Mimi, holding Ellen's hand. She squeezed him a little, and he returned the affection.

She noticed right away how much smoother the road was now than at any time over the hills from Mount Hood until now. The springs absorbed a lot of the bumps and she looked back to check on the boys. They played a hand clapping game and seemed content, so she faced forward. At times, Del and his parents talked about the farm and its operations. He always gave her a synopsis of their conversation so she didn't feel excluded.

The town they rolled into was more like a city. Ellen stared at all the people, straining to see if she recognized anyone from the travelers they'd passed in months past. She'd seen crowds like this around the various forts. Just not so many buildings. They soon stopped in front of a dry goods store, and Mr. Du Boise said something to Del and Mimi. Ellen vowed to learn French as soon as possible. The language sounded beautiful and she wanted to feel included.

Skeeter and Buster clung to her with her younger brother asking, "Sis, what's going to happen now?"

Del answered for her. "We men are going to the store for supplies. The ladies are going to the dress and fabric store for Ellen."

"What do the boys do?"

"They go with the men." When he translated for his father, Jean-Baptiste laughed and nodded.

"Is he going to say *allons* again?" asked Skeeter?

"Yes, because he's saying let's go and that means all of us."

The men helped the boys and ladies down from the wagon. Alone with Mrs. Du Boise, Ellen suddenly didn't know what to say or do. The older woman's smile reassured her and when Mimi made a follow me motion, Ellen did. They stopped at a store and she stared at the dress in the window. It was the most beautiful garment she'd ever seen. Mimi reached over and lifted Ellen's chin to close her mouth. The younger woman looked at her and saw Del's mother grinning. Ellen blushed at being caught staring. Mimi didn't let her spend too much time embarrassed before opening the door for her.

The bell rang and a lady at the counter looked up. *"Bonjour, Madame Du Boise! Comment allez vous?"*

"Je suis tres bonne, et vous?"

"Comme ce comme ca." The shopkeeper motioned toward Ellen. *"Elle ne parlez?"*

"Non. Anglais."

"I see." The lady greeted Ellen. "Good morning, and how are you?"

"I'm fine, thank you, and you?"

"I'm wonderful, thank you for asking. Now then, what can I do for you both?"

Mimi rattled off a list, it sounded like to Ellen's ears. The woman spoke as fast to the dressmaker as she had her son and husband. Ellen's head swam from all the strange sounds. The other woman looked at her every so often with kind eyes. At last, the shopkeeper turned to her. "Miss, the madam wants you to look at fabrics, preferably in the blue shades. She wants you to pick at least three of whatever you like in the cottons."

She smiled her thanks at Mrs. Du Boise. Ellen went to the wall of fabric bolts, wondering how to choose from the spectrum of blues. She'd glance back every so often to see the two other women talking about the dress in the window, or so it seemed. Shaking her head, she turned back to the fabrics in front of her. Most likely, Mrs. Du Boise wanted the garment for herself. It was certainly lovely enough, and the light yellow fabric would contrast nicely with the woman's black hair and deep brown eyes. Ellen had no idea what the dress was made of, just that it was beautiful and shiny in the light.

Soon, she had a grayish blue, a deep sea blue pattern, and a dark gray paisley. Now the colors seemed dark and drab, but anything else seemed too flashy. Ellen took the three bolts to the counter and set them down. By now, the women had the dress off the form and were examining the seams. Ellen cleared her throat, getting their attention. "I found three."

Mrs. Du Boise exclaimed first. *"Merci!"* She examined each before looking at the owner. *"Meh, trois?"*

"Are these all you want?"

"Goodness, yes. These are more than enough." Ellen tapped the dark gray. "I could put this one back."

The lady translated for Mimi who laughed and shook her head. Then the owner turned to Ellen. "She wants you to get what you love." She set the bolts down on the counter. "Now then. She also wants you fitted for this." The woman held up the beautiful dress from the window.

Ellen shook her head and took a step back. "Oh, no, I couldn't possibly. No."

After a quick translation to her, Mimi held the dress up to Ellen. "Go."

She looked at the shopkeeper who shook her head. "You'd better. Mrs. Du Boise is my best customer and she knows best. Just go in there and change."

She hurried to the door and stepped inside. Maybe a quick fitting and they'd see the dress wouldn't suit her. She fastened as many buttons as she could reach before stepping out. They'd see how loose the garment fit and know it wasn't for her. Ellen picked up the longish skirt and stepped into the larger room.

Del, his father, and her brothers stood there with the two ladies. She caught the younger Du Boise man's eye first. His shock, love, and then pride filled her with joy. She might find a way to afford this dress for special occasions after all if it meant he looked at her like that every time.

"Combien de temps pouvez-vous avoir cette altérée pour elle?"

As soon as Mrs. Du Boise spoke, it broke the spell and everyone rushed to Ellen, talking at once. She picked out English words of pretty, new clothes, and a lot of French she didn't understand, including a flurry of conversation between Del and the shopkeeper. The conversation made Mimi gasp and look at Jean-Baptiste, who shrugged. Ellen looked from one to the other. "What is it?" she asked before remembering they'd not understand.

Answering for his parents, Del said, "I want the dress altered to fit you for this afternoon." He took both of her hands in his. "I'm tired of waiting for you and want to be married by sundown."

"Um, today?" She felt sweat gather on her upper lip and fretted about staining the dress.

"I'd hoped so." He frowned. "Are you not sure?"

"I am." Ellen wanted to be honest without being hurtful. "You'll be getting more than just me. When we married before, the boys weren't part of the bargain."

He scooped up Buster. "Is that all? Your brothers need us and we need them."

She glanced around at everyone in the room. The hopeful expressions on everyone's faces amused her. Ellen shook her head. "All right. This afternoon or evening it is. I assume you know a preacher? Don't even tell me how much this dress will cost, just that you can afford it." He translated her words to his parents and his mother frowned. Ellen went on. "I'll find as many chances to wear it as I can, I promise."

"Let me put in the pins and I'll have it sewn by mid afternoon." The owner pulled Ellen aside and began measuring and marking. "Jessie!" she hollered to the back room. "Come here and measure out fabric for Mrs. Du Boise!" A little mousey gal came out of a door beside the dressing room. When seeing her, the shopkeeper went on. "Here, be sure to ask how much of each." She smiled at Mimi. *"Et pour le garçons?"*

"Oui!" His mother looked at Del, giving him instructions. He led the boys away to find their favorite colors.

"Now then, come along and I'll take this off of you."

Ellen followed her to the dressing room where she gave the woman the marked dress and put on her old one. She smoothed her flyaway hairs back into place and stepped out. Stacks of fabric were on the counter, the three she'd chosen and four from the boys. She knew their favorite colors and looked at the adults. When Mimi saw her, she began a "Tsk tsk," sound and Ellen blushed. No one had to tell her how ragged her dress was.

"Come back in two hours and the dress will be ready." The owner repeated herself in French and the others nodded. Ellen smiled at how Skeeter mouthed the French words. She just knew both boys would soon be bilingual.

The sun shone down hot on her in the cool air. Even though a dusty breeze refreshed, she worried about getting the new dress dirty even before it was done. She bit her lip, not sure she deserved something so fine. Ellen vowed to work hard at the Du Boise home to earn every bit of what the family had done for her and her brothers.

"No, no worries, *ma coeur*." He took her hand, kissing it. "I want today to be our wedding day, not a fretting day."

"Today doesn't give us time to organize anything. Just our families are here. What about Sam, Marie, and the other men?"

"You're right. We should have friends help us celebrate." He let go of her. "Let's go visit the Granvilles." Del spoke to his parents and their expressions brightened.

Ellen let him help her up into the wagon. The boys were secured in the wagon bed, sitting on a couple of feed sacks. Their ability to decide something without argument or anger surprised her somewhat. She smiled at Del when he kissed her cheek and chuckled when hearing Mimi's reproving tone.

"Oh, Nick, look who's here! Your friend Adelard and his parents." Mrs. Granville stepped out. "And look who they brought! That lovely young woman Sam wrote us about and her two scamps of brothers." She bent down and lightly tweaked Skeeter's cheek. "Aren't you just the cutest little boy? Your brother gets all his charm from you, I'll bet." She straightened, examining Ellen. "Hello, young lady." Mrs. Granville motioned Del forward. "This is your new wife?"

"Future. We're getting married later this afternoon."

"Why! You're not married yet? Thank heavens!" She hurried into the house. "Nicholas! Elizabeth! Get Louisa! She has a new little friend to meet."

"Um, Mrs. Granville?" Ellen began before a man and woman followed the older woman back outside. "I'm not sure...."

"What? Yes you are! Look at you! So lovely! I can get you a nice wedding dress, and it'll be no trouble to decorate the house for your wedding!"

She realized the couple must be Sam's brother and sister in law. He'd not mentioned a baby, yet the woman had a child in her arms. Ellen clasped her hands together to stop wringing them. "We'd planned on a quick ceremony in town."

"No! You just can't! Nick and Beth cheated me out of a wedding, and then Sam and Marie did the same thing. You simply can't let me down now, children."

Ellen opened her mouth to argue when a ruckus grabbed everyone's attention. Wagons rolled toward them, the Granville one in front and what she assumed was the Allens behind them. As they drew closer, she realized it was indeed the Allens. Skeeter and Buster both hid behind her until seeing who rode up.

Sam dismounted, leading Scamp while walking with Marie. He waved, "Aren't you all a sight for sore eyes?"

"Darling!" Mrs. Granville ran to Sam and hugged him. Letting go, she looked at Marie briefly before hugging her. "And this must be the cruel woman who took you from me." She stepped back, still holding the woman's arms. "Isn't she lovely? No smart remarks, Sam, because she is." She twirled Marie around before settling her to face her. "My goodness. No wonder he couldn't wait. I forgive you both."

Nick laughed. "You're blessed. It took her a week to accept me and Beth."

When Ellen looked from one Granville to another, and yet another, they all seemed happier than their words implied. Maybe their mother was all bluster instead of truly angry. Ellen had heard so much about Sam's family that she enjoyed seeing all of them in person. Nicholas was just as strong looking as she'd been told, but more attractive than Sam had implied. She chalked that up to sibling rivalry because both men were similar in appearance. Their mother stood almost as tall as her sons, and Ellen wondered about their father's height. An older man walked around the home's corner. She knew exactly who he was without an introduction. Both younger men had their father's eyes, even if in a variant of his brilliant blue.

"Can I guess who everyone is?" asked Mr. Granville.

Mrs. Granville clapped her hands. "Oh, yes, dearest! You'll have to tell us."

"This is almost too easy." He grinned, looking a lot like Sam. "This lovely woman standing so close to my baby boy must be his Marie. Adelard seems rather possessive of the young lady he's standing by, so I'm guessing she's his wife, Ellen?" He peeked around her. "These two rascals must be the Winslow boys."

"Oh, and you were doing so well too! Dearest, Adelard hasn't made an honest woman of her yet. You only got that one fact wrong."

"He'll soon be correct, madam," chimed in Del. "I'm marrying her this afternoon."

Mrs. Granville wagged a finger at both of them. "I insist you two go to town and get married and we'll all be right behind you. Our help can have everything ready by the time we return for a proper reception." Mrs. Granville turned to Marie. "Darling, Beth can take you to your room and help you while I can take care of Louisa. Nick? Would you help Sam, please?"

"Certainly."

"Good. We will be at our church and waiting. Take your time at the dressmaker's. Getting this group to do anything timely is like herding tadpoles." Mrs. Granville repeated everything for Del's parents, surprising Ellen. No wonder Sam was so good at French. He couldn't help it. Ellen turned to see the Du Boises loaded up in their wagon and waiting for her. She hurried over, letting Del help her up and beside him. Ellen decided she liked all the climbing into and out of the wagon. Each time gave her a chance to hold hands with Del. Sitting close enough to touch kept her from thinking about anything else but him. The drive to town was as pleasant as the drive from there had been. Early afternoon shadows kept them out of the sun, and she enjoyed just relaxing as much as the bumpy road would allow.

"There you are, Miss. Come with me."

Ellen did as she was told and followed the woman to the back room. Her new dress covered a dress form. The fabric gleamed in the sunlight, and she was almost afraid to touch it.

"Go on, take and try it on."

She lifted off the garment and hurried to the dressing room. Soon, she stepped out into the main area. If Ellen lived to be a hundred, she'd never tire of the way Del looked at her with such love.

He shook his head. "You are a master at your craft, Mrs. Johnson."

"Thank you for the praise, Mr. Du Boise. I'll still bill you the full amount."

Del laughed. "I'm counting on it." When Ellen turned back to the dressing room, he added, "Dearest, don't change here. Grab your old dress and let's go to the church."

They all piled in the wagon yet again, Ellen sitting up front and feeling like a princess. Mrs. Du Boise spread her dress skirt over hers, trying to shield her from the dust. Del squeezed her hand and she smiled up at him.

"Sis?"

She looked down to see Buster's little face. "Yes?"

"I need to potty."

"Now?"

"Yeah."

"We'll stop in a moment," said Del. He caught his father's attention and said a few things in French.

Ellen assumed he told the other man about her brother because Mr. Du Boise grinned and nodded. He pulled up in front of the church. Mrs. Du Boise got out first and hurried into the building. Ellen glanced up into Del's eyes one last time. "What else besides stopping here will we need to do?"

He laughed. "We don't even need this. We've been married this entire time." Del held out his hand to help her down first and then helped his mother to the ground. His father let out Skeeter first before taking Buster to potty out back.

She shook her head at both her brother relieving himself in near public and her future husband's frivolity. "I hope he doesn't learn to do that just anywhere."

Del shrugged. "I did and turned out *bon*."

"I—" The Granvilles' arrival in a very nice wagon interrupted her. Everyone talked at once as they climbed out, the noise giving Ellen a slight headache. The ladies' dresses amazed her with their color. They reminded her of flowers turned upside down. Each woman carried a basket of ribbons and flowers fresh cut. Ellen recognized some of them from the front of the Granville farm.

And the men? All of them, even the elder Mr. Granville, were handsome in their Sunday clothes. She glanced at the Du Boise father and son, biased in how she found them better looking than the other family.

Still chattering like songbirds, Marie, Beth, and Mrs. Granville hugged her on their way to the front door. Ellen couldn't get a word in edgewise and when she started to follow, Mrs. Granville put a hand on her shoulder. "Not yet, missy. We have serious work to do." The older woman gave her another hug before disappearing into the church.

"Voici pour vous." Mr. Du Boise held up a nosegay of blue flowers.

Ellen took them, amazed at how lovely the wildflowers looked. "When? How?"

"Zuh potty," he replied.

She laughed. *"Merci beaucoup, papa."*

He gave her a swift and crushing hug. When he let go, Jean-Baptist took both Winslow boys' hands, taking them into the church. Ellen followed, as did Adelard, and found Mimi talking with the preacher. The two stopped to grin at her with wide smiles.

The women had placed bows on every pew with flowers tied into the ribbons. The afternoon sun illuminated the pale wood, giving everything a heavenly glow. None of this had been what she'd imagined as a child. Old stone walls, wood nearly black with age, and gilt from golden fixtures that had been hand polished for decades didn't compare to this room's natural beauty. The atmosphere reflected her new life, fresh and lovely. She stepped forward to the altar where Mimi and the preacher were talking. The two stopped to greet her.

The officiate spoke first. "Hello, my dear. Mrs. Du Boise has told me everything. I suppose traveling across the country bonds a couple."

"I think so." Del took her arm, leaning over to kiss her forehead.

The preacher cleared his throat before saying, "Now, now, Adelard, none of that until I give the pronouncement."

Ellen smiled as a blush crept across his face. She tried concentrating on the vows, but the boys playing in the pews behind her kept Ellen distracted. They really needed to settle down as befitting a church. When Louisa began to wail, Beth ushered the boys out with her and the baby. Ellen made a mental note to thank her later.

"Do you accept this man as your lawfully wedded husband?"

The preacher's question pulled her back into the moment. "Yes, I do."

"Do you accept this woman as your lawfully wedded wife?"

"I do."

She glanced at him, so shy at the happiness in his face, she didn't hear the preacher pronounce them man and wife. Her new husband leaned in and surprised her with a kiss. Both boys cried out in anguish over seeing such a thing. Surprised that they'd come back into the church, Ellen squelched a laugh and let their kiss deepen, enjoying the further protesting squalls of the children.

The boys quieted and the smooching stopped when the minister said, "May you always be as loving as you are right now."

Detecting a little bit of a retort in his voice, she hid a smile. Everyone crowded around and hugged each other. Mimi wiped tears from her eyes while saying something to Del.

"Maman would like you to wear your wedding dress to the reception."

While the families all paraded out of the church, Ellen asked him, "Are we're filing our papers now?"

"I've changed my mind, if you'll allow. Let's come back tomorrow and spend the entire day alone." He nuzzled her ear. "We may take a very long time getting there and back."

A tickle of desire went through her. She smiled up at him. "I should probably bring a blanket for comfort's sake."

He laughed. "You should." Del shook his head at his father's puzzled expression. He held his hand out to his new wife and helped her up into the seat.

They took off for the Grandville farm. She glanced at him, letting her gaze caress his strong profile. Did he know what he'd gotten himself into? Before thinking about what he'd answer, she asked, "Will you miss the roaming life? The freedom to go anywhere your heart desires?"

"Yes. I will miss that particular freedom. Just as much as you miss your Missouri home."

She saw the slight tinge of yellow on the trees around them. Sooner than she'd like, winter would be here. The future loomed large in front of her, like a vast empty prairie. Only, not so empty, thanks to her new husband and his family. She'd not have to worry about her brothers' abandonment either. Ellen took his hand, lacing their fingers together in a way that matched their hearts. "I'll miss nothing. You are my home."

Del kissed her, stopping to smile at his mother's throat clearing. "As you are my freedom, my wife."

Laura Stapleton

Other books by Laura Stapleton

The Oregon Trail Series

The Oregon Trail Short Stories
Unavoidable
Undeniable
Unexpected
Undesirable
Unfortunate
Uncivilized
Lucky's Christmas Wish

The Very Manly Series

The Very Best Man
The Very Worst Man
The Very Rich Man

Nova Scotia Murder Mysteries

Imposter
Holidays
Betrayal
Impatience
Pleasure
Surplus
Appearances
Rage
Honeymoon

ABOUT THE AUTHOR

With an overactive imagination and a love for writing, Laura Stapleton decided to type out her daydreams and what-ifs in order to share her lovable characters and their worlds with readers. She currently lives in Kansas City with her husband, daughter, dog, and a few cats. When not at the computer, you'll find her in the park for a jog or at the yarn store's clearance section.

If you enjoyed this story, please consider leaving a review. Find Laura online at https://twitter.com/LauraLStapleton, https://www.facebook.com/LLStapleton#, and at http://lauralstapleton.com. Subscribe to Laura's newsletter and keep up on the latest updates and new releases.

Made in the USA
San Bernardino, CA
14 March 2016